Acclaim for Lori Lansens's

Wife's Tale

"Lansens's clear prose unveils the connection between a body weighed down by flesh and a spirit smothered by loneliness. Mary's odyssey of heartache and hope is not so much about finding her husband as it is about rediscovering herself."

— Lisa Kay Greissinger, *People*

"Lansens's hopeful and gentle third novel (after *The Girls*) opens in the same fictitious Ontario county as its predecessors, but the heroine's journey takes her to a vastly different landscape, both literally and spiritually....When Mary's handsome husband disappears on the eve of their silver wedding anniversary, Mary wonders whether her size or her aversion to adventure chased him off. With few clues, Mary leaves her small town for one of the first times in her life, venturing first to Toronto and then to the suburbs of Los Angeles, where a series of encounters with strangers shakes her out of her lethargy....She's a wonderful character, and Lansens's handling of her eventual transformation into someone capable of compassion and acceptance is handled with a light but assured touch."

— *Publishers Weekly*

"It's the urgency of Mary's quest, along with Lori Lansens's capacity for humor and insight, that makes this book so riveting and compelling."

— Anne Chudobiak, *Calgary Herald*

"Mary wins us over from the start....Lansens limns the world of the chronic overeater with sympathy and grace."

— Cynthia MacDonald, *Globe and Mail*

"Heartbreakingly funny and sad.... Lansens—who lived so memorably inside the heads of conjoined twins Ruby and Rose in *The Girls*—sketches another indelible female character here. Mary Gooch, all 302 pounds of her, stays mostly at home, where she has worn a rut in the silver carpet between the bed and the kitchen, trying to fill the emptiness in her heart with potato chips and candy bars. Though she dreams of a waspish waist, she's also comfortable in her own ample skin, reveling in her nudity—'inhaling the night like a postcoital cigarette' when no one can see her."

—Tina Jordan, *Entertainment Weekly*

"A sensitive but deliciously comic account of Mary's fight against the 'obeast' that has lived inside her since childhood, *The Wife's Tale* offers more than self-improvement: there are loving reflections on marriage and family in small-town Ontario, hilarious travelogues about American obsessions like McMansions and vanity license plates, and a tender documentary of the improbable compassion of strangers for fellow travelers. Of course, there's plenty of self-discovery too. 'Maybe happiness was generally misunderstood,' Mary thinks. 'Maybe happiness was the absence of fear. She felt herself at the launch of her own transformation, and wished she had a Champagne bottle to crack against her knee.'... Lori Lansens has more than a few tales worth telling."

—Casey Cep, *New York Times Book Review*

"Lori Lansens creates a memorable protagonist."

—Cameron Woodhead, *Age* (Australia)

"Lansens's portrait of a woman who hides behind the Kenmore as protection from life's heartache is earthy and primal in its pain. Yet Lansens doesn't resort to an overnight makeover to save Mary. Instead, our heroine uncovers a hidden strength she had all along. Those who loved *The Girls* will be pleased that Lansens is back. Highly recommended."   —Bette-Lee Fox, *Library Journal*

"Lansens writes with acute insight into Mary's bingeing and depression, fully immersing readers in her protagonist's struggle to find a new and better self." —Deborah Donovan, *Booklist*

"Mary is an engaging character."

—Anne Stephenson, *Arizona Republic*

"Sensitively written and thought-provoking."

—Katherine Whitbourn, *Daily Mail*

"Delightful, laced with a breezy, snappy style, good humor, and keen observation.... *The Wife's Tale* is a good read: a page-turner, a life lesson, and a rare romp through the maze of untempered indulgence, rueful remorse, and, in Mary's case, self-discovery, which make up the world of the morbidly obese." —Nancy Schiefer, *Toronto Sun*

"Lansens's rendering of the hell that is compulsive eating somehow transcends these overarching positions, eliciting simultaneously compassion, revulsion, and, for anyone who has ever struggled with emotional eating, undeniable recognition.... Mary Gooch becomes real and unforgettable." —Margaret Wheeler Johnson, *Slate*

The
Wife's Tale

The
Wife's Tale

A Novel by

Lori Lansens

BACK BAY BOOKS
Little, Brown and Company
New York Boston London

Back Bay Books / Little, Brown and Company
Hachette Book Group
237 Park Avenue, New York, NY 10017
www.hachettebookgroup.com

Originally published in Canada by Alfred A. Knopf, August 2009
Originally published in the U.S. in hardcover by
Little, Brown and Company, February 2010
First Back Bay paperback edition, June 2011

Back Bay Books is an imprint of Little, Brown and Company. The Back Bay Books
name and logo are trademarks of Hachette Book Group, Inc.

Library of Congress Cataloging-in-Publication Data
Lansens, Lori.
    The wife's tale : a novel / by Lori Lansens.
        p. cm.
    ISBN 978-0-316-06931-1 (hc) / 978-0-316-06932-8 (pb)
    1. Wives — Fiction.   2. Self-actualization (Psychology) in women — Fiction.
I. Title.
    PR9199.4.L36W54 2010
    813'.6 — dc22   2009022062

                    10 9 8 7 6 5 4 3 2 1

                                RRD-C

                Printed in the United States of America

For Maxim and Natasha

The
Wife's Tale

A Pretty Face

Alone in the evenings, when the light had drained from the slate roof of her small rural home, and when her husband was working late, Mary Gooch would perform a striptease for the stars at the open bedroom window: shifting out of rumpled bottoms, slipping off blousy top, liberating breasts, peeling panties, her creamy flesh spilling forth until she was completely, exquisitely nude. In the darkness, she'd beg her lover the wind to ravish her until she needed to grasp the sill for support. Then, inhaling the night like a post-coital cigarette, Mary would turn to face the mirror, who'd been watching all along.

The mirror held the image Mary Gooch knew as herself, a forty-three-year-old brunette standing five and a half feet tall, so gilded with fat that hardly a bone from her skeleton could insinuate itself in her reflection. No hint of clavicle, no suggestion of scapula, no jag in her jaw, no scallop in her knee, no crest of ilium, no crook of knuckle, not a phalange in the smallest of her fingers. And no cords of muscle, either, as if she were enrobed by a subcutaneous duvet.

Mary remembered, when she was nine years old, stepping off

the scale in Dr. Ruttle's office and hearing him whisper *the word* to her slight mother, Irma. It was an unfamiliar word, but one she understood in the context of the fairy-tale world. *Obeast.* There were witches and warlocks. So must there be ogres and obeasts. Little big Mary wasn't confused by the diagnosis. It made sense to her child's mind that her body had become an outward manifestation of the starving animal in her gut.

Such a pretty face. That was what people always said. When she was a child they made the comment to her mother, with *tsk*ing pity or stern reproach, depending on their individual natures. As she grew, the pitying, reproving people made the comment directly to Mary. *Such* a pretty face. Implied was the disgrace of her voluminous body, the squander of her green eyes and bow lips, her aquiline nose and deep-cleft chin and her soft skin, like risen dough, with no worry lines to speak of, which was remarkable because, when she wasn't eating, that's what Mary Gooch did.

She worried about what she would eat and what she would not eat. When and where she would or wouldn't. She worried because she had too much or not nearly enough. She worried about hypertension, type 2 diabetes, atherosclerosis, heart attack, stroke, osteoarthritis. The contempt of strangers. The mouths of babes. Sudden death. Protracted death. She worried all the more because all the worry made her sleepless, and in her dreamless hours hosted more worries, about her husband, Gooch, and the approach of their silver anniversary, about her menial job at Raymond Russell Drugstore and about her list, which she imagined not as *Things to do* but *Things left undone.*

Weight is only numbers on a scale, she told herself, and her mirror just another point of view. Squinting at her naked reflection when the moon was waxing and the angle just right, Mary Gooch saw beauty in the poetry of her contours, in the expressive, expansive, edible flesh, and understood why an artist sketching nudes might find appealing the mountainous gut, and favor the pocked shore of

sloping thigh, and enjoy the depth and shadow of pendulous breasts and multiple chins. A shape ample and sensuous, like the huge round vase handed down on the Brody side of the family, in which she arranged her ditch lilies in the spring. Or like the dunes of virgin snow on the hills beyond her home outside small-town Leaford.

Mary wished to be a rebel against the tyranny of beauty but was instead a devotee, coveting its currency, devouring images in glossy magazines and broadcast TV, especially the kind that chronicled the lives of the rich and famous. She lingered over the body shots, outlining with her fingertips, like an appreciative lover, the rock-hard abdominals and concrete glutes, sinewy arms and pumped deltoids — so daring on a woman — coltish legs, wasp waist, swan's neck, lion's mane, cat's eyes. She accepted the supremacy of beauty, and could not deny complicity in the waste of her own.

It was often an unbearable burden for Mary Gooch to carry both her significant weight and the responsibility for it, and she naturally sought to blame. The media was her target, just as it was another of her addictions. She would tear through the pages of her magazines, gratified by the celebrity cellulite, horrified by the gorgeous anorexics, noting the fall must-haves, sneering with the critics about fashion disasters, then realize she'd eaten a quart of premium ice cream, coerced by the advertisement beneath the picture of the TV cutie with poor taste in men. Mary knew it was all the media's fault, but finger pointing was too much exercise, and she couldn't sustain the blame for long. Especially since she was so often confronted by the stupid genius of just saying no.

Jimmy Gooch, Mary's husband of nearly twenty-five years, read *Time* and *Newsweek* and *Scientific American* and *The Atlantic* and *National Geographic*. He watched CNN, even when America was not on red alert, and cable talk shows with clever panelists who laughed when nothing was funny. With Gooch working late most evenings, and busy playing golf on the weekends, Mary reckoned they were down to spending only a handful of waking hours a week together and wished to relieve the silence between them, but didn't share Gooch's passion for politics. The couple sometimes found common ground in musing on the vagaries of human nature. "Read the essay at the back," Gooch had said recently, tapping her on the head with the rolled-up magazine—a gesture she charged was aggressive, but he argued, playful.

The article spoke of the ills of North American culture, the mistaking of acquisition for success, gluttony for fulfillment. Gooch clearly meant for Mary to draw a comparison to her gastronomical indulgence, and she did, but the piece was provocative in its own right, posing the question: *Are people generally happier now, with instant access and quick fixes and thousands of channels and brands to choose from, than they were before the Industrial Revolution?* Mary instantly decided *no*. In fact, she wondered if the opposite was true, that in the hardscrabble life of her pioneering ancestors, whose singularity of purpose was clear, there had been no time to ponder happiness. Chop wood. Carry water. It was impossible to imagine that the early Brodys, who'd cleared Leaford from the Burger King to the gas station, had ever endured a sleepless night.

Having read enough magazines, and having spent hours lurking in the self-help section, Mary Gooch knew that she wasn't alone in her morbid obesity or her abstract malaise. Symptoms of despair were everywhere, and formulas for success within her grasp. A person could get a good night's sleep and wake refreshed, shed unwanted pounds without dieting, make dinners for six in twenty minutes or less, rekindle sexual passion, and achieve five personal goals by the end of the month. A person could. But in spite of the step-by-step instructions, Mary could not. The *secret* remained classified. She appeared to be missing some key ingredient, something simple and elusive, like honesty.

Mary had been raised without religion but instinctively drew a separation between her spirit and body. Her spirit had no gravitational pull. Her body weighed three hundred and two of earth's pounds — the two pounds significant because she'd once vowed that she'd kill herself if she got up beyond three hundred. Another promise broken. Further recrimination. The truth of what drove her hunger was as present and mysterious as anyone's God.

Certainly grief fed the beast, and with her encroaching middle age came more and greater opportunities for it. Every passage, but particularly the corporeal kind, further embellished Mary Gooch. Thirty pounds for her mother, accumulated over many months, years ago, although Irma was not actually deceased. The babies, so long ago, had added fifteen and twenty pounds respectively. Then it was the ten when her father died in the spring. And another ten with Mr. Barkley in the summer. She felt vaguely charitable assigning the poundage to her loved ones, in the same way that she was mildly comforted by calculating her load in UK stones, in the British style, rather than North American pounds.

During her painful cycles of grief and gain, Mary thought it would be better to have *any* religion and lose it, than never to have one at all. She relied on dubious knowledge and remedial understanding to cobble together a system of beliefs that she was forever editing and amending, depending on the latest magazine article or persuasive celebrity endorsement. Except for the rule of three — an enduring belief, if unfounded by religious text. Terrible things happen in clusters of three. Death, serious accidents, financial ruin. One. Two. Three. What would end the trilogy after her father and Mr. Barkley, she wondered. Another death? Or just more deceptively endurable misfortune?

Hauling her corpulence the few steps from her truck in the parking lot to the back door of Raymond Russell Drugstore, starved for breath, heart valves flushing and fluppering, Mary would think, *It's me. I will end the trilogy. Here comes my fatal heart attack.* Drowning in regret, she'd see everything clearly, the way reckless adults do, too late. But like all things, the feeling would pass, and she would click on another worry, each one dense and nuanced enough to sustain her interest, with intriguing links to distract her from the larger picture. The ticking of time. The machinations of denial.

Mary Gooch did not so much *pray* to God as *wish* to God, of whom she was sporadically unsure. She wished to God for an end to all wars. And that her manager would catch his scrotum in the cash register at work. She wished for her mother's peaceful death. And that she had something nice to wear to her silver anniversary dinner party. And then there was the wish that pre-empted all other wishes, the one she wished hourly, eternally — that she could *just lose the weight*. This wish Mary would offer to her uncertain God in the smallest and most humble of voices. If I could just lose the weight, Gooch would *love* me again. Or sometimes it was, I could *let* Gooch love me again. The state of her body was inseparable from the state of her marriage, and the universe.

If I could just lose the weight.

For all her uncertainty about God, and in addition to the rule of three, Mary Gooch believed in miracles.

The Night Clock

The night clock never *ticked* for Mary. On this autumn night, the eve of her silver anniversary, the clock *thumped*, a downbeat rhythm in time with her heart, alternative jazz, restless, like a tapping toe or a wandering eye, awaiting the first notes of an uncommon melody.

Adrift, mattress springing leaks in the dark, thoughts scurrying through portals, drawing conclusions, mixing metaphors, Mary felt beads of perspiration mingle in a stream down her temple. Slick and sealish in her faded gray nightgown, a triangle of sweat tickling her crotch, she was dizzy from the dueling sensations of heat and hunger. Heat from the furnace, which she'd tried to shut off earlier, was still blasting through the floor grates in the tiny country bungalow. Hunger, as always, shouted to be heard.

Mary held her breath, listening to the sound of a vehicle in the distance. Her husband Gooch? No. Gooch would be coming from the east. She tossed her undulating flesh and rode the tidal waves until she was breathless on her back, humming a tune to distract the obeast within. She hummed more loudly, hearing faint assurances from a distant chorus that she was not alone. There was hope in the harmony, until hunger snickered from the kitchen.

In the hallway, damp nightgown suctioned to her spread, eating from a foil bag she'd grabbed from the kitchen counter, Mary checked the temperature on the thermostat, licking her salty finger before she slid the lever from Off to On to Off again. The furnace purred, disregarding its directive. Huffing, she set her bag down and threw open the basement door. Scent molecules of must and mildew fled like trapped birds as she flipped on the light, struck by the sight of the rotten bottom stair she'd broken last winter. She hesitated, then closed the door, deciding the heat was to be endured until Gooch got home.

She checked the clock, reminding herself that her husband was often late, and sometimes very late. Mary had kept such nightly vigils over the years, never questioning her husband's whereabouts, never admitting her fear of the dark. She returned to her chip bag, kettle-fried shards piercing her palate, painful but soothing, like the blues. *Enough,* she told herself, then, *Just one more.* And one more. And just the one extra.

Parched, she opened the old Kenmore refrigerator and, while gulping cola from a huge plastic bottle, saw through the window above the sink moon glow filtering through fast-moving clouds. Flipping her tail of chocolate hair, she sailed across the tile floor and pulled open the window, welcoming the breeze, stirred by the fall fragrance of ripened red apples and soft yellow pears, wet earth and decomposing leaves, a savoury decay that would soon fade away when winter came to embitter the car-exhausted air.

The breeze kissed her soft skin and she shivered, thinking of Gooch. A feral cat yowled in the distance and Mary swiveled instinctively to check the silver bowls on the floor near the back door. Mr. Barkley's food and water.

Prick of pain. Gone. No Mr. Barkley. No more worry about Mr. Barkley's food and water. Mr. Barkley's worm infection. Mr. Barkley's tooth decay. Mr. Barkley had been Mary's boy, and no less loved by her than any human child by his mother. A decade ago she had rescued the kitten from a hole into which he'd fallen at the back of the garage, and named him after a basketball player in hopes of getting Gooch to bond. She nursed the mewling wretch from a turkey baster filled with infant formula from the drugstore, cradling him in a hand towel, grooming him with a little wet paintbrush to simulate a tongue. She referred to herself as "Mama" when Gooch wasn't around. Mama creamed turkey for Mr. Barkley. Mama let Mr. Barkley sleep in the scooze of her cleavage. Like any mother, Mama didn't love Mr. Barkley less for his meanness, even though the cat spent the best of his ten years hiding behind the living-room drapes, shedding orange hair on the green chair, and hissing when Mama was late with his dinner.

On a heat-wave summer night in July Mary had skulked into the kitchen for a snack, surprised to find Mr. Barkley collapsed in the center of the cool tile floor. She nudged him with her toe and panicked when he didn't hiss and flee. "Mr. Barkley?"

Unable to kneel down, she pulled a red vinyl kitchen chair to the sprawled cat and, using her feet as cranes, raised him high enough that she could grasp his front paws and drag his limp body up to the shelf of her bosom. Seeing that he was dying, she stroked his ginger head and whispered, "Mama's got the Tuna Treats," so his final thoughts would be hopeful. A brief spasm. Mr. Barkley present. Mr. Barkley past. And no idea why he died, except a guess that he had eaten a poisoned rodent. The vinyl chair mourned as Mary rocked side to side, kissing Mr. Barkley's snout, which she'd never done in life for fear he'd bite her nose.

The lights were on and the air foul when Gooch returned very late that night to find the contents of the fridge weighting the table. Mary was tonguing rhubarb pie from the well of a large silver ladle and didn't care that she'd been caught. When Gooch stared at his wife, not comprehending, she managed to choke out, "Mr. Barkley."

When Gooch still didn't understand, she gestured to the refrigerator. "I didn't want the bugs to get at him."

Thoroughly disturbed by the thought of the dead cat in his refrigerator, Gooch set his large comforting hands on her shoulders and assured her that he would dig a hole first thing in the morning. He kissed her cheek and said, "Near the big trees out back, Mare. We'll plant some bulbs to mark the grave."

"Iris," Mary agreed, chewing and swallowing. "Purple."

With birds rejoicing in the oaks and Gooch towering at her side, Mary sprinkled dirt on Mr. Barkley, whose stiff body she'd wrapped in two hundred feet of plastic food wrap, before Gooch set him down in the dark, moist hole.

Now, gazing into the brooding night past the trees and beyond Mr. Barkley's grave, Mary was sorry to see that there were no lights in the neighbors' houses to either side. It made her feel less lonely when she could observe other people's quietly desperate lives. The fighting Feragamos with their brood of teenage boys lived in the ramshackle Victorian an acre to the west. Penny and Shawn, the young couple with the newborn who screamed at each other whenever the baby cried, were on the other side of the creek. The Merkels' house beyond the breadth of cornfields was much too far to spy on without binoculars, though she doubted there'd be much to see. And the scrubby orange farmhouse where the Darlen twins (famous because the two girls had been born joined at the head) used to live was now the local history museum and kept only summer hours.

The old willow at the end of the drive was suddenly assaulted by a hard-driven wind. Parked beneath the tree, the red Ford pickup truck with its custom-made sunroof gathered teardrop leaves. The sunroof had been jammed open since spring. It had been on Mary's list of things not getting done for months: *Sunroof repair.*

Come home, Gooch. Come home. Why are you so late? Where are you? Mary's worry prompted a craving and she found the beef jerky stick she'd hidden from herself, tucked in the back of the cupboard behind the soup cans. Chewing, she remembered her list. *Sunroof repair. Furnace repaired? Replaced? Checks due at St. John's*

Nursing Home. Work extra shift for Candace. Gooch's suit from the cleaners. She opened the buttons of her nightgown and padded back to her room, farting indignantly, tired of the list, making promises to tomorrow. Tomorrow, self-confidence. Tomorrow, self-control. Balance. Restraint. Grace. Tomorrow.

Whiffing the scent of self-pity as she found her lonesome bed, Mary Gooch thought, as she often did, about a boy she used to know.

Bonds of Distinction

As a girl, Mary Brody had been content spending her summers reading novels in her room or listening to loud music on the radio while her peers gathered in tube tops to smoke their mothers' Peter Jacksons and share their true despair. There were girls down the street, Debbie and Joanne, who, like Mary, read books in their rooms, and with whom she believed she might have struck an alliance, but Mary preferred to be alone, with her hunger.

Even as she wallowed in her feasts, she worried about her mother's keen eye for inventory, and made frequent trips to Klik's corner store to replenish the stock, using money sent by distant Brodys for Christmas and birthdays. Irma had started working full-time as secretary at the tool-and-die shop when Mary was five years old, and had told Mary then that, if there was ever an emergency, she should go get help from Mr. or Mrs. Klik.

The Kliks were a stern couple with six children, one of whom, Christopher, in Mary's grade, had been diagnosed with a rare cancer the year he turned twelve. Mary, the fat girl, and Christopher, the sick boy, had some bond of distinction, though they rarely exchanged more than irritated glances.

Occasionally, as Mary Brody left Klik's dusty store, she'd find the boy parked at the bike rack near the trash bins, perched atop his one-of-a-kind moped, which Chatham Cycle Shop had donated because he was dying. Christopher's photograph had been on the front page of the *Leaford Mirror,* his frail white fingers gripping handlebars, the shop owners, puffed with charity, holding his emaciated body steady on the seat. Mary hoped that Christopher hadn't read the story below his picture, even as she envied the boy his prognosis. He seemed to be better loved for the fact of his imminent demise.

Exiting Klik's store one day when she was in seventh grade, carrying a loaf of bread and a jar of honey and a pound of mixed candy, Mary had cringed to find Christopher hunched beside his moped, holding his legs at his ankles. He looked to be in pain, though he didn't appear to have fallen. She'd stopped without drawing near and asked, "Want me to get your mom?"

The boy shot her a look. "*No.*"

They turned their attention to a large black crow flapping around the trash can. The bird landed on a plastic bag and cocked his head to watch them. "I hate crows," Mary said.

"They hate you too."

"I don't care."

"Like my motorbike?"

She raised a brow, pretending she'd just noticed.

The small boy sat up, finding her pretty eyes. "Wanna ride it?" She thought the question rhetorical. "Nobody but me's ever ridden it."

"I know."

"Everyone wants to."

"I *know.*"

"You can." Christopher glanced down the road to ensure that

there were no approaching cars or strolling people. Then he drew his shirt up over his concave chest. "Do this," he said, pinching the pink nipple on his right breast, "and you can ride it."

Mary had not ridden her own bicycle yet that summer, feeling the effort of peddling and balancing too great for her big, tired body, and she was electrified by the prospect of such vehicular freedom. Had Christopher been a well boy, she might have run to call Irma at work, but he was a sick boy, and Mary didn't consider his request prurient, just odd.

She stepped forward, reaching her stubby fingers toward the boy's translucent skin. When he batted her hand away, she was shocked by his speed and strength. "Not to *me*, dummkopf."

"You just said," Mary said, screwing up her face.

"To *yourself*," Christopher wheezed.

"Oh," she breathed. "Sorry."

"Do it and you can ride my motorbike."

Fair trade. She lifted her ribbed tank top, allowing her pillowy breast to spill forward, and pinched her rose nipple lightly before pulling the fabric back down.

Christopher grinned broadly. "Pervert."

"Can I ride it now, Chris-to-*pher?*"

His regret seemed genuine. "I didn't think you were really *gonna*. My dad'll kill me if I let *anybody*."

She sat down on the curb beside him, scooping slimy jelly beans from her bag, chewing with vigor. Remembering her manners, she offered the bag to Christopher, who said, "I don't like candy."

Mary was incredulous. "But you own the store! You could have all you want!"

Christopher paused for effect. "I could."

They were quiet a moment. The fact of the child's premature death stirred within their mutual sense of injustice.

"No fair," Mary said finally.

Christopher curled his lip and sucked his snot succinctly. For the moment, no distance between them. "You'd be pretty if you weren't so fat," he said plainly.

"Okay." Mary shrugged, flattered. Studying him, she wondered, not for the first time, if he knew he was dying. She was astonished when he answered her thoughts.

"I'm dying from what I got, so."

It was clear to Mary that Christopher Klik was magical, or mystical. "Weeks or months?" Her parents had wondered that at the dinner table.

"What kinda question is that?"

"Sorry."

"Besides, you're dying too. Everyone is."

Struck by the realization that the magical boy was right, Mary watched his tiny whiteness, waiting for further enlightenment.

"Show me that titty again," he demanded.

Meeting his gaze, she lifted her shirt and moved her hand hesitantly toward her breast, plucking at her nipple as he watched open-mouthed.

When she finished, Christopher Klik grinned. "I'm telling *everybody* you did that."

Mary grinned back, because she knew he had no one to tell. She waited to meet his eyes before leaning in to whisper, "I'll be your girlfriend till you die."

The boy didn't pause to consider, but wagged his head back and forth and made a pained move to rise.

Without turning to look, clutching her corner-store bag, Mary hurried off, terrified by the painful burning lump that had suddenly become lodged in her throat, convinced that the dying boy had infected her with his tragic disease. She opened the refrigerator door in her quiet, empty house, hoping that the choking feeling could be relieved by a gulp of juice. Then she thought some honey toast might help, Popsicles, peanut clusters from the freezer, the rest of the mixed candy, some leftover ham.

Christopher did not ride his motorized bike after that day. His funeral was held three weeks later. The Kliks sold the corner store to the Quick Stop franchise, which replaced the candy with cigarettes and batteries. Irma would say, "You just think about poor Christopher Klik when you start feeling sorry for yourself, Mary Brody."

And she did.

Thump went the clock beside Mary's bed. The square bedroom window was open and the breeze had the sage curtains in a tizzy. Dazed and damp and done thinking of Christopher Klik, Mary scrolled through the TV channels, finding only the most profoundly false reality shows, and in between the blather, cruel commercials advertising deep delicious this, sweet 'n' gooey that. No celebrity gossip shows. Shopping channel static. She turned the TV off and tossed the remote control out of reach, wishing to God that Gooch would come home.

The bookshelf near the bedroom window was listing from the tidy stacks of twice- or thrice-read magazines, the glossy images of beauty drooled over, the coveted home decor items already out of style, the celebrity wedding annulled weeks ago. Her hard-core pleasure, the tabloids, she kept hidden between the mattresses.

Gooch and Mary had recently agreed on no more magazines for her, or sports channel for him, until the carpet guy got paid off. The new broadloom had been Gooch's idea, and she knew it was because he could no longer bear to look at the rut she'd worn from her bed to the kitchen. The carpeting was their anniversary gift to each other, and she'd felt some small consolation in its color being silver.

She'd wanted to ask Gooch for a new wedding ring for their milestone anniversary, the original, a modest solitaire, having been unceremoniously cut off by the jeweler years ago when Mary's plump finger had started to turn blue. But there was no money for a ring, and Gooch had pointed out that wedding rings were antiquated symbols anyway. Still, he never took off his own gold band, and she'd felt safe in its presence on his finger.

With no television to watch and no magazine to look at, Mary's eyes rested, as dreamless eyes do, on the smooth, shadowed ceiling above her lumpy bed. She recalled the sense of being transported by a good book, wishing she had one now while she waited for Gooch to come home. She used to enjoy reading romance, mysteries when she was young, and then it was the women's novels with gold book club stickers. Gooch had suggested she take a trip to the Leaford Library, reminding her that it was *free*, and she'd envisioned herself carrying home a pile of books with star reviews, but the effort of the trip and the walking down aisles and the looking at and lifting of books all seemed so great that she'd found excuses not to go. Lately it had been the distraction of planning the humble anniversary party.

The details of the party had burdened Mary's already long list of things to do. Worse, she had only herself to blame, since she'd announced the event months ago, the day she went shopping in nearby Chatham and found the too-tight green silk pantsuit, which a complete stranger had said *makes your eyes pop*. The outfit had been her incentive, but she had bought it before the loss and gain from Mr. Barkley, and the silk ensemble was now two more sizes too small. As usual, Mary had nothing to wear.

The only guests were going to be three other couples — Erika and Dave, Kim and François, Pete and Wendy — whom they'd known, all except Erika, since high school, and the affair was to be a simple one. Dinner at the fish restaurant by the lake, and later a game of poker or bridge in the Gooches' country kitchen. "We have exactly three hundred and twenty-four dollars left in the account, Mare," Gooch had warned, and insisted they serve dessert back at the house.

Mary had begged, "No gifts." But Wendy was making a scrapbook for the Gooches in her crafting class, a photographic tribute to their years together, a thought that made Mary's stomach roil.

Darkness. The toss. The turn. The heat. The hunger. The wish. The worry. For one such as Mary Gooch to find comfort in her bed was not so simple a matter as shifting a body, but an effort of such sweaty magnitude as to move a mountain. Sunroof repair. Checks to the nursing home. Pick up dessert for the anniversary dinner.

Gooch had said, "Around ten or so. But don't wait up." His last delivery for Leaford Furniture and Appliance was in the Windsor area, near the border to Detroit. An hour or so away, but forty minutes the way Gooch drove. His partner was off work with the pink eye, but with his extraordinary size and strength her husband could easily handle the dishwasher on a dolly, and the seven-piece dinette set alone.

There was a current in the air. And that smell. Wet. Sharp. Electric. Hard rain bullets sprayed through the open bedroom window as thunder dropped heavy bass notes in the distance. Mary searched the sky for lightning, remembering how as a child she'd stood in the square patch of grass behind the bungalow on Iroquois Drive holding the metal mop handle above her rain-soaked head. She hadn't wanted to die, like Mr. Pline on the golf course, but to be enlightened, like the woman on TV who'd been struck by a thunderbolt and seen God.

Wiping sweat from her brow with the pillowcase, Mary listened to the rumble of thunder, thinking of Gooch on the rain-slicked roads, trying to ignore a tiny voice warning her that something was wrong. She reached to turn on the light beside her, serrated pain stabbing her sternum. Breathless from the crushing weight of her breasts, heart galloping with the strain of rising in the bed, she shut her eyes. *Breathe,* she told herself. *Breathe.* Rule or no rule, she would not die alone in her bed, dressed in her sour nightgown, on the eve of her silver anniversary.

Sitting up usually brought quick relief, but not tonight. She couldn't shake the sense that there was something in the air beyond the rain, a dark foreboding stirred up by the storm. Gooch's face before he left for work that morning played like a song she couldn't get out of her head.

After breakfast, while a lone crow cawed from the field behind the house, Gooch had stood at the door, furrows slicing his forehead, chapped lips slack at the edges, his round blue eyes searching hers. In his gaze Mary had seen the sum of their life together, and had felt inclined to apologize. What was that look? Pity? Contempt? Tender affection? None of it? All of it? She used to believe she could read his mind.

With the noisy bird crowing in the background, Gooch had cleared his throat before asking, "Have you got something to wear for the thing tomorrow night, Mare?"

Jimmy Gooch was like a vital organ whose function was mysterious but without which, she believed, she would perish. Gooch was her first love. Her mate. Her partner. The only family she had left. Time, for Mary, was measured in "before Gooch" and "after Gooch."

Acknowledging the partisanship of her memory, Mary knew she was making at least some of it up when she recalled the first day she had laid eyes on Jimmy Gooch. She played the scene in her mind the way she imagined modern people made memories, like directors filming their own life stories: wide-angle to convey body language, poignant two-shot profiles, tight close-ups on a long lens, scored with sexy Motown. In slow, heroic motion, wavy hair caught by the wind, Jimmy Gooch pushed through the double doors and into the halls of Leaford Collegiate, where the crowd of students parted like the sea. Sixteen-year-old Jimmy Gooch was a god of sorts. Backlit, star-eyed, straight-A student and distinguished athlete, he was the new starting center for the Cougars, his arrival from Ottawa heralded, already being scouted by American colleges. Long ropy muscles dressing a stunning six-foot-five teenaged skeleton, welts of abdominals and obliques straining his cool rock band T-shirt.

Mary Brody's pretty eyes did not blink as Jimmy Gooch drew near the place where her poundage quivered in roomy stretch pants and over-large school jersey. She felt her uterus contract when he asked,

"You know where Advanced Lit 3 is?" Those were the only words he spoke to her that entire year, despite having their lockers side by side and sharing four classes, but in that virgin moment, when the very tall man-boy looked ever so briefly into Mary Brody's eyes, she glimpsed a kindred spirit, saw a flash of the future and the unlikely entanglement of their fates.

Do all sleepless people play the events of their lives like a television rerun, Mary wondered, heart thudding, saliva gathering at the corners of her mouth, thinking of that morning again.

"Have you got something to wear for the thing tomorrow night, Mare?" Gooch's voice was erotica. He could arouse Mary with the merest stroke of tenor on her hot inner ear. She wondered why she'd never told him so, and felt sorry it no longer mattered.

Frowning, she'd tugged at the waistband of her uniform—the largest of the ladies' plus sizes, so she'd have to go into the large men's sizes now, and Ray Russell Jr., the owner/manager of the drugstore, would have to place the order for her. The thought burned her cheeks, since she'd recently overheard Ray and Candace making unfunny comments about her ass—Candace suggesting they take up a collection for gastric bypass, and Ray remarking that it was so big it should have its own blog. Now she had to clear her throat or cough before entering the staff room.

Mary had assured him, "I'll find something."

"What about the green thing you bought?" Gooch had asked carefully.

"The zipper was broken," she lied.

"Remember what happened the last time you had to improvise? Buy something if you don't have anything, Mare. This is important. Find something *nice*."

Shrunk an inch over the years, standing at the door in his custom-made work shirt and brown corduroy coat and dusty blue jeans from the Big Man's store, ball cap plunked down on his wavy gray head, complexion worn like a catcher's mitt, Gooch looked handsome but weary. She wondered if he seemed more or less tired than any forty-four-year-old man in any small town. She cocked her head, asking, "Are you sorry we're doing this dinner tomorrow, hon?"

He paused, with that look on his face, and said, "Twenty-five years, Mrs. Gooch. That's a hell of a thing. Right?"

"It is," she agreed. "When you gonna be home?"

"Ten or so. But don't wait up." He said the last after the back door banged shut.

It *was* a hell of a thing to have been married for twenty-five years, but no one ever asked Mary her secret to a long marriage. She might have said, "Don't call your husband at work."

Of course, throughout the years, she would have called Gooch's pager or cellphone if there'd been an emergency, but her life was fairly predictable and her tragedies rarely sudden. She'd nearly called Gooch at work when she'd gotten the news about her father's passing, but had decided that, like everything except her raging hunger, it could wait. She started to dial his pager many years ago, when she was seizing with uterine cramps, but had hung up when she realized the ambulance would be there faster. She had left a note on the kitchen table. *Gone to hospital with hemorrhage.* She'd thought of calling him just recently, the night she tipped the scale over three hundred pounds, but had instead collected the pain medications from the bathroom cabinet, remembering her vow to kill herself. Even as she was shaking tablets from vials at the kitchen table, she had confronted her false intentions, and determined that the dosage was not potent enough for her extreme body weight anyway. The door had suddenly opened behind her and Gooch had tramped inside, filling the house with his truck oil scent and strong-man vigor, calling, "Hey. You're still up." Shrugging off his coat, pulling off his boots, he had been preoccupied and hadn't noticed the pills and vials on the table, which Mary swept into a plastic bag and quickly tossed in the trash. At the time, she'd allowed herself to wonder if he had missed her suspicious behavior because he was hiding something too.

The night clock. Palpitations of the heart. *Thud. Thud. Whoosh.* Arteries saturated with globules of worry. She reached for the phone but stopped. A good wife trusted her husband and never checked up on him, or questioned his lateness, or looked through his dresser drawers. The truth she rarely confessed, even to herself, was that she didn't call Gooch because she was afraid she'd discover that he was someplace he shouldn't be, and she didn't want the burden of his confession any more than she thought he wanted hers.

Weight of Grief

Fifteen pounds with her father. Orin Brody died in the spring of a blood clot, a cunning thrombosis that had slithered up from his leg to his lung sometime after Mary closed the door to his apartment overlooking the river in nearby Chatham. "See ya tomorrow, Murray," he'd called out, using Mary's pet name, as he always did. Her mother had called her *dear.*

The blood clot came as a somewhat shocking end, given Orin's history of heart disease and colitis. His post-mortem death weight, a number that had stung Mary and still buzzed her earhole in the dark — ninety-seven pounds. But Orin had lost his appetite completely in his final year, for televised sports, food, life, altogether, all the same. His cadaver was the exact poundage of Mary's squat nine-year-old self when the doctor had whispered the obvious to her slight mother, Irma. Ninety-seven pounds. *Obeast.* Mary unduly expanded. Orin cruelly reduced. The pressing weight of grief made her hungry.

On the morning of her father's funeral, she had risen early after not a wink of sleep, and started for the bathroom to color her hair. She'd found the hair dye box in the bag from the drugstore and opened it before noticing that she'd grabbed the wrong package — not Rich Chestnut but Rich Red. Resigned to her silver roots, she'd stepped out of the bathroom to find Gooch addressing the wakening erection in his large, callused hand. He looked caught, and sat up breathless. "I thought you were going to do your hair."

Not offended by Gooch's habit but aroused, she considered briefly what it might be like to sit beside him on the bed and caress him there, and let him run his hand over the flesh of her back, to heal with strokes and whispers the way they once had. She craved that powerful love but felt too distinctly the message from her body, that it did not want to be touched. "I grabbed the wrong box," she sighed. "It's *red*."

Later, Gooch heard a sound in the bedroom and found her collapsed on the bed. It was not a fatal heart attack or even grief but her stiff black dress, which had been snug at the last funeral, lodged beneath her textured mounds. Seeing her stricken face, Gooch just squeezed his eyes and quietly left the room.

Locked in the bathroom, naked on the toilet though she had no urge to relieve, Mary had scratched her hairless thighs without particular shame or horror. Her hunger was ever-present but her self-loathing came in waves. Clothes didn't necessarily incite abhorrence for her form, but more often for the tight, scratchy, lumpy articles themselves. All garments except her gray nightgown were hateful to her skin. She had been delighted when the uniform policy was handed down at the drugstore — roomy navy pantsuits resembling hospital scrubs, which were supposed to make the front staff look more professional, and in which they all looked like hell.

The women at the drugstore had griped about the uniforms — especially Candace, with her wee waist and cantilevered breasts — but no one had asked Mary her opinion. She had thought one sleepless night, without a ladle of self-pity, that she was, quite literally, the elephant in the room. Her body seemed more illusory for the secrecy surrounding it. Her real weight? Her true size? Only she knew. Hiding food. Eating in private. Feeding the hungry body to which she'd been assigned, abiding with the frantic energy of *want* and *want more*.

Restless on the toilet, having shifted tense in what she supposed was the natural inclination of all people's thoughts — a lobbing back and forth between past remembrances and current anxieties — she wondered what believable emergency might excuse a daughter from her own father's funeral. There was a gentle knock on the door. "Mary . . . ?"

"I'm sorry, Gooch."

"I think this'll work, Mare. Can I come in?" He opened the door.

The image of big Jimmy Gooch in his slender tie and pleated pants lent her the courage to rise. He presented a pair of black slacks borrowed from their short, rotund neighbor, old Leo Feragamo, and a starched white shirt of his own, which she would have to wear open over her only clean white T-shirt. The roots of her hair sparkled like tinsel around her full-moon face. She propped a black wide-brimmed sunhat upon her head and did not look in the mirror again. Gooch flipped a thumb and announced that she looked *funky*, which caused Mary's throat to constrict.

As they drove in silence on the winding river road, Mary wondered if grief was ever a singular event, or if ghosts lurk in any passing. She felt a parade in the death of her father: the erosion of her mother's mind; the splintering of her marriage; the slipping away of the babies she'd named but never known.

The day of the funeral was an unseasonably warm day in spring. Mary felt the embrace of purple lilac on the path to St. John's Nursing Home in Chatham, where her mother had been languishing in dementia for years. She stopped to pick a lilac bouquet for her mother's bedside stand, knowing that Irma wouldn't appreciate or understand the gesture and had no sense of the events of the day, but it cheered Mary to bring her mother flowers. The receptionist huffed, seeing the bouquet, and explained tightly that they'd run out of vases.

Irma was parked in the common room, folded neatly into her wheelchair, silver strands teased to a height, looking more winter shrub than human being, gazing into the distance. Mary imagined Irma turning to smile as the other patients did when their kin came to call. She imagined herself enfolded by her mother's cadaverous arms. The whisper of *Mary. Dear Mary.* She wished to be kissed by that gawping mouth, yearned to touch, to *be* touched, longed for a sliver of connection to the Irma who used to be, the mother who, while gently combing Mary's locks one day, had confided, "My mother used to tear at my tangles. Just *tear* at them. She'd hit me with the brush if I so much as breathed. I still remember that. I would never hit you with the brush." Or the Irma who'd remarked casually, "You have the nicest handwriting, dear."

Orin had loved Mary in the same somewhat grudging way, but she didn't blame her parents for her present state nor fault them for their stingy affection. They weren't rich with it, and gave what they could. "You get what you get and you don't get upset," Orin liked to say when Mary was sulky. When he wanted her to hush up he'd pretend to pass her a tiny key and warn, "Zip it. Lock it. Put it in your pocket."

Pop would have hated it here, she repeated to herself, wheeling her absent mother past her moribund fellows, grateful that St. John's was so conveniently located across the road from Chatham's largest funeral home. As she struggled across the walkway with her wheezy mother and her chafed thighs, she thought of how Irma had passed in fragments, starting in her fifties, little bits of her exiting like players off a field—long-term memory, short-term memory, recognition, reason. At least with Orin, Mary reminded herself, she'd had the chance to say goodbye. *See ya tomorrow, Murray.*

Giant Jimmy Gooch and the hunched old men were gathered outside, sharing a tin flask of some homemade concoction that one of the relations still brewed in his garage. Gooch waved when he spied his wife pushing the remains of her mother up the ramp, and lifted his shoulders, smiling wanly — his way of saying, *Ah, life*. Mary nodded twice and tilted her head, her way of saying, *I know*.

Ah, life. She was moved to think how often they'd exchanged those gestures in their years together, then annoyed that Gooch hadn't rushed to take the chair from her swollen hands. Maybe he was too far away to see that she was drenched and breathless, and had failed to note, in the way the parent is never the first to notice the child's growth spurt, how truly incapable she'd become.

Longing to grieve with her mother, while grateful to be relieved of the burden, Mary'd returned the frail creature to St. John's after the funeral parlor portion, before gathering at the cemetery, where Orin and Irma had joint plots in the vicinity of the other dead Brodys. Mary had spent many sleepless hours, long before the deaths of Orin or Mr. Barkley, wishing that her mother would die, complete a cluster or begin one, but Irma's pulsing body was a wonder of biology, a life but not *alive*. Perhaps she didn't count.

Shortly before he'd passed, Mary'd confided to Orin her sense of feeling stuck and unbound all at once, her failed attempts at optimism, her sense that she could only see the glass half empty, to which he'd responded impatiently, "Forget about the glass, Murray. Get a drink from the hose and push on."

Birdsong scored the graveside service. Hunger pangs tore at Mary's gut as she reflected on the liberation of her father's spirit by a minister who didn't know him from a cherry pit. The man was appealing to God to receive Orin Brody's soul, but Mary knew that old Orin would never venture such a distance, even if he did make the cut. She imagined him a vaporous cloud sparring with oxygen molecules in the airspace above his own headstone, content to be wherever he was, the way he'd clung to Baldoon County all his life. Orin and Irma never saw the point in traveling, and bred a mistrust of wanderlust in their daughter.

As to religion, Orin had been raised Catholic, a faith to which he'd never truly held so hadn't exactly abandoned when he married Irma, who'd been raised Christian but had ideas of her own. Irma had told Mary, when she'd inquired, that they didn't go to her church because it gave her bad dreams, and they didn't go to Catholic church because the priest was a drunk. Mary had once, as a child, watched some Christians scrubbing graffiti from the wall at the Kmart, struck by the dripping red words — *Where is God when you need her?*

No, Mary thought, even Orin Brody's vapor would never leave Leaford, but she threw up a prayer to heaven, just in case. She lifted her eyes when several black crows passed overhead, courting the mourners' revulsion. One of the birds descended, settling atop the gleaming casket, strutting from head to foot and stopping to appraise Mary Gooch. She glared back with reciprocal loathing, and felt she'd won when the bird flew away.

Finding Gooch's eyes wet beneath their fringe of dark lash, Mary yearned to cry along with her husband. She'd felt the same way years ago, watching him reach for a tissue as the Canadian hockey player Wayne Gretzky announced that he was leaving the Edmonton Oilers for the L.A. Kings. And that Sunday afternoon when tears spilled from his eyes as the final scenes of *How Green Was My Valley* played out on the new TV. And the long-ago day his own father passed away, when he'd drunk a whole bottle of Southern Comfort and wept after they'd made love. She'd admired that her husband was man enough to cry, but wondered what that made her.

She flapped her white shirt, the collar damp around her neck, and focused on her breath, or more accurately her odor, *fromage* — oddly pleasant to herself, but she'd need to swab and talc her valleys and crevasses the minute they got home from the cemetery.

The food. Hunger. Details of the wake a blessing. Napkins and plastic glasses on the card table. Casseroles on low in the oven. Pete and Wendy were out of town but Erika and Dave and Kim and

François would be there. The Rowlands, Loyers, Feragamos, Whiffens, Stielers, Nick Todino and his wife, Phil and Judy. Merkels wouldn't come; they barely left the house. No one from the Gooch side.

Gooch's father had died after a car accident in their final year at Leaford Collegiate, and a scant year and a half later his mother, Eden, and her new husband, Jack Asquith—a chain-smoking American whom Gooch referred to as "Jack *Asswipe*," moved to California, where Jack owned a pet supply company in a place called Golden Hills. Eden had promised they'd still see each other, but she'd stopped visiting at Christmas after the first few years. Mary had asked Gooch not to bother trying to contact his tragic older sister, Heather, of no fixed address.

Gooch's voice had grown distant. Not just on the drive home from her father's funeral, but gradually over the days and months and years of their marriage. She thought she heard him say, "Scatter my ashes on the golf course, Mare. Eighteenth hole. That's what I want."

The early trees had just leafed out, and the April rains had greened all that was gray. Impossible not to feel *someone's* god in the pastoral landscape. The resurrection of the black earth fields. Glory in the sun's diving rays. The promise of butter-drenched asparagus and field-warm strawberries. Mary watched the dappled light spray her husband's profile, wondering if he was mourning his own long-departed father and his gone-away mother, his athletic scholarship. He must surely think about the babies, though their names, like curses, went unspoken.

Gooch reached above his head to yank open the testy sunroof, which would never close again. He eased his hand off the wheel to touch her through the wool casing of Mr. Feragamo's slacks. When his enormous fingers found the mulch of her thigh, she stiffened. "Easy on the booze tonight, right, hon? You've got that run to Wawa tomorrow."

"Come with me." He said it so quickly that she made a pretense of not understanding, to give him a chance to retract. But he repeated, "Come to Wawa."

"Tomorrow?"

"It's a beautiful drive, Mare. Take your mind off . . ."

"The lawyer's appointment, though," she countered. "And I can't leave Mum." She tried to catch his eye, adding, "Sorry."

Gooch hadn't really expected her to say yes. He'd asked the same thing a hundred times before. Come with me to Montreal. Come with me to Burlington. *Come* with me. Come *with* me. Come with *me.* He hit the button on the radio, filling the truck with Sly & The Family Stone. "I'm gonna miss old Orin," he said.

Mary closed her eyes and let the music take her higher.

Finger of Blame

Even with the breeze from the open bedroom window blowing against her damp nightgown, Mary felt no respite from the heat. And no release from her hunger. Sweet to follow salty. A biological imperative, surely. A powerful craving driving Gooch's face from her thoughts, and the misery of her parents' passing from her spirit, and the worry over the anniversary dinner from her foremind, and the discomfort of heat from her face. Why hadn't she grabbed that bag of Halloween candy at the checkout? Accursed voice of restraint.

She focused on her list. Details. The silver anniversary dinner. Confirm reservations at the lake. Pick up dessert from the Oakwood Bakery. Gooch? He would be too exhausted and miserable to go ahead with the dinner if he didn't get home soon and get some sleep. He was already anxious about the cost, and worried that their guests would order appetizers and pricey entrees like surf and turf or prime rib. He'd pointed out that Kim and Wendy liked those fancy cocktails, and Pete his foreign beer. Gooch would dread the check. Mary had already spent weeks dreading Wendy's scrapbook, the photographic evidence of who she'd briefly been and what she'd become.

Mary'd dutifully sifted through boxes of old photographs at Wendy's request, tortured by her glossy image, watching herself grow with the years until the only pictures she could find of herself were a turned-away cheek or a running rear. She'd tried to ignore Wendy's impatience when she'd handed over a dozen photographs, none recent and most taken in a single year, the year she was slim. "Fine," Wendy had said. "I'll just have to use what I can find at home."

Rising from the bed, Mary felt the stricture of her heart as she thought of the photographs. She clutched at the wall in the narrow hallway, femur bones at odds with hinges as she made her way to the thermostat and tried once more, unsuccessfully, to shut the furnace off. She worked down the buttons of her nightgown, casting it off her shoulders and draping it over a kitchen chair as she moved toward the breeze from the window.

In searching through her boxes for Wendy, Mary'd found one picture that she'd kept out and slipped into her bedside drawer—a snapshot of Mary Brody and her favorite teacher, Ms. Bolt, arm in arm on the steps of Leaford Collegiate. Mary isn't slender in the photograph, dressed in sloppy sweatpants and a sweater that show-cased her stomach rolls, but seeing the photo again after so many years, she thought her smile was as lovely as it had ever been.

Ms. Bolt, in addition to teaching social studies and homeroom at Leaford Collegiate, had offered an elective course she called Progressive Thought. She was the darkest black woman Mary, with her tender years and limited travel, had ever seen in person. She appeared to float rather than walk, sweeping the floor with her silky caftans, a dozen gold bangles chiming on each wrist, her breasts so enormous they preceded her into the room, while her rump so large seemed tardy.

In the older woman's eyes Mary saw her reflection. Not fat, sulking Mary Brody, but an eager student with a voice of her own and a very pretty face. She felt *known* by Ms. Bolt, who seemed not imprisoned within her abundance but liberated by it, her every breath a celebration. Ms. Bolt was not a rebel against beauty but a particular kind of disciple. Her wildness polished. Her casual studied. As Mary beheld her, the teacher was radiant.

She'd attempted to describe Ms. Bolt to Irma, when prodded at the dinner table about the new teacher. "Her name is *Ms.* Bolt," she'd said, articulating roundly so there was no misunderstanding her heroine's politics. "She's *black.*"

"So I've heard," Irma had said.

"And she's *beautiful.*" She said it like a challenge. "She's big. Ms. Bolt is *big.*"

"Like Mrs. Rousseau?"

"Bigger."

"Bigger than Mrs. Rousseau?"

Mary rolled her eyes — which, apart from overeating, was her single defiant gesture. "She accepts herself. It's part of what she's teaching us. Self-acceptance."

"If Miss Bolt is bigger than Mrs. Rousseau, she's morbidly obese, dear."

"So?" Mary rolled her eyes once more. "Self-acceptance is a good thing, Mum."

"If doctors all over the world call a condition *morbid,* could that be a good thing to accept? Honestly."

Only five students had signed up for the elective class. No girls from the cheerleading squad, but one boy from the basketball team — Jimmy Gooch, having registered for the class on a dare from his teammates. Mary felt the rush of air as Gooch breezed past her toward the back of the room, but she didn't turn to look. She'd learned to avoid people's eyes, convinced that her gaze held some unintended menace.

Ms. Bolt joined her hands together, eyes twinkling, bracelets tinkling, floating down the rows as if the class held fifty, not five. "On your desk you will find a piece of paper and a pair of scissors. Please cut out the shape of a circle." The group did so, Gooch signaling his boredom by sighing loudly from the back corner. "Now," Ms. Bolt continued. "In black ink, on the circle you have cut, write the letters T-O-I-T." She waited. "T-O-I-T." The students finished.

Ms. Bolt's passion was infectious. She was like the preacher who could make you believe. "In your life, my beautiful young friends, you will have limitless choices. You come from a world of privilege and opportunity. You can do *anything*. And it is your duty to take advantage. It is your *raison d'être*. Don't find yourself old and regretful, saying, I wanted to go to college but I never got around to it. I wanted to vote for my leaders but I never got around to it. I wanted to learn Spanish but I never got around to it. I wanted to travel — read the classics — scuba dive — climb Everest — join Greenpeace — but I never got *around to it*. Look at the circles you've just cut. Now you have no excuse."

The students looked at the circles for a long, quiet moment. Finally, it was Mary Brody, speaking in class for the first time, who held up her paper and said, "A *round* TO IT."

Ms. Bolt clapped her hands. "Thank you, Ms. Brody!"

Ms. Bolt was, as everyone at Leaford Collegiate knew, a big *lesbo*, and whether it was her sexual preference or her *too* progressive thinking, or maybe one of her own limitless choices — whatever the cause — she did not return after that single glorious semester. And although Mary had wanted to uncover the roots of feminism and honor her sisters in suffrage, her passion vanished along with Ms. Bolt, the round TO IT crumpled and tossed in the trash. Mary was deeply wounded by the teacher's departure, particularly as Ms. Bolt had told her once that she had a very old soul.

Goodbye, goodbye. A final goodbye. For a short time, a long time, forever. Songs and plays and novels and films written about goodbye. Mary felt it as a theme. Closure — she disliked the modernity of the term describing so ancient a ritual. The acknowledgment of those who had left, those who remained. Gone. A final parting moment.

And for Mary, so many farewells left unsung. She wondered if the accumulation of such abandonments should be held accountable for her hunger. The heavy finger of blame.

There was movement in her periphery, and Mary spun around thinking, *Gooch*. It was a form, beautifully rendered, momentarily unrecognizable in the glass of the window at the door. Mary stood still as the form took shape and saw that it was a woman—a fat, naked woman. *So that is me,* she thought. She clocked the nightgown on the kitchen chair behind her. It had been years since Gooch had seen her naked. She shuddered to think of the last time. Though she loved to remember the first.

Symbiosis

Not a soul in Leaford, particularly Mary Brody herself, could have predicted her weight loss that summer before she entered her senior high school year. Irma guessed she'd become interested in boys. Kim and Wendy from the cheerleading squad, who'd regarded her with alternating doses of pity or contempt since kindergarten, decided that she'd done the grapefruit diet from a magazine. Orin reckoned that his daughter had simply been late in losing her baby cheeks, considering that no one on either side of the family was big. The boys at Leaford Collegiate didn't wonder about her secret, but shared their rock-hard relief that suddenly gorgeous Mary Brody hadn't lost her B-3s, code for *big bouncy breasts*.

The strawberries came early and, as was a Brody family tradition, the three, Orin, Irma and Mary, drove out to Kenny's big "pick your own" farm near the lake beyond Rusholme to fill flats with juicy berries that they'd bake into mouth-watering tarts and pies, or boil with dangerous amounts of sugar to make jam for the winter. Stepping out of the car in the muddy parking lot, Irma took Mary's face in her slender hands and instructed harshly, "Pick. Don't eat."

Orin and Irma were skilled pickers, and set to work—bent at the waist, hands moving furiously, eyes scouring low leaves for ruby treasures. But as Mary could not bend over easily at the waist, she sat on her rear, inching forward like a crab to comb each bountiful plant. She was not expected to keep pace with her parents. And neither would glance back, not even once, to see if she was picking more than eating. Each fragrant berry was a world of senses. Sweet. Sour. Grainy. Musky. Juicy. Gritty. Silky. Silty. Smooth. *That's enough,* she would tell herself—then, *Just one more.*

Some days following, while stirring a pot of volcanic red sluice at the stove (remembering last year, when she'd tested the boiling jam and burnt her lips so badly that she'd had to get a prescription from Dr. Ruttle), Mary'd felt the sudden roiling of her stomach. Perspiring heavily, she'd dropped the ladle and rushed to the toilet, where she liberated an effluence so redolent of strawberries that she would be unable to eat a spoonful of jam that entire year. She had always been fascinated, as she thought all humans must be or should be, with her by-products, and routinely studied her release.

She wondered why it floated, or why it sank like anchors. She marveled at its tenacity. Admired its cohesion. Felt gratified when it did not fracture upon entry, and cheated when expulsive forces shot it beyond her field of vision. While ashamed of her revolting curiosity, she nonetheless appreciated its earthy autumn shades, and found great satisfaction in its variant aromas.

On that day she glimpsed, when she rose to inspect, a thing she'd never seen before—a thing that did not cause her to turn away or scream for Irma, but beckoned her to lean forward, come closer, examine. Wriggling. Waving. Dancing. Greeting. Jubilant. Life. And as Mary Brody discovered the limbless invaders, she realized that, for the first time in memory, she couldn't hear the obeast. In the field of her flora and fauna, a silent battle had been waged and won. Mary Brody was free.

A trip to the Leaford Library confirmed it. Parasites. *Worms.* Not pinworms, though. And not roundworms. Something else. Thicker than thread, the color of fat under chicken skin. She couldn't find a picture of them. Parasites found in animal excrement, viable in dirt, likely contracted by eating unwashed fruits or vegetables — gardening without gloves.

Home from the Leaford Library, after Irma'd announced it was time to get dinner over with, Orin noticed that she only picked at her roast, and slathered butter over her baked potato but didn't eat it. Her mother put a hand to her daughter's forehead, but Mary assured Irma that she felt fine. And she seemed fine. Better than fine. Her secret was a symbiotic, not parasitic, affair.

Having lost her appetite completely, feeling no ill effects save the constant but, Mary would conclude, bearable itching of her anus, Mary only nibbled bits of each meal those first weeks of summer — enough, she hoped, to sustain her occupants. Each trip to the bathroom was agony, as she feared the disappearance of her saviors. She tallied their numbers, keeping mental charts, and by the time sweet corn was ready — noting a marked decrease in population, had panicked that her army might be deploying altogether. Mary surprised her mother by offering to help in the garden. She stopped washing her hands. She began making long, twice-daily treks to the park near the river, where, with a spoon from the cutlery drawer, she shoveled dirt and ate it, hopeful that in one mound hid a nugget that might colonize her anew.

At first Mary didn't notice her melting flesh, and didn't celebrate her reduction the way Irma and Orin did. She accepted their pride in her achievement, though it was not strictly hers, with grunts and tight smiles. "Keep it up, Murray," Orin remarked, watching her decline a coconut cupcake, "and none of the cousins'll recognize you at the reunion this fall." Mary thought that a funny thing to say, for she was certain the Brody cousins had never really looked at her before, and would have no context for comparison.

On that day of the Brody family reunion, wearing her new

Jordache jeans, Mary was several times mistaken for her cousin Quinn's new girlfriend, who they'd all been told in strictest confidence was a stripper from Detroit! They laughed about it, Irma and Orin and Mary, each for personal reasons, but their shared amusement was a major source of the day's remembered pleasures.

Finding her greatest satisfaction in freedom — no longer enslaved, her mind not occupied with the details of food — Mary felt expanded and dared to imagine her future. She pored over magazines that offered courses in fashion and design. She looked in the mirror frequently, obsessively, not admiring herself but struck by the simple truth in her eyes. She was not hungry. Still. Not. Hungry. She took her gift money and walked all the way to the Kmart to buy several coordinating outfits in her new size. She felt the muscles in her stride. The lengthening of her torso. The swing of her shiny dark hair. She continued to eat dirt. She decided to get a part-time job.

Mary's Aunt Peg, recently retired from the pharmacy department at Raymond Russell Drugstore, had heard that Ray Russell Sr. was looking for a girl to work front cash. The staff already knew Mary. In a town so small, with only one pharmacy, the staff knew the whole of Leaford with embarrassing intimacy. Mary had spent more than the average amount of time at the back desk, waiting for her parents' prescriptions, and felt at home amidst the clove oil and Metamucil.

It would have been impossible to consider such a position just months before, since Raymond Russell had the largest assortment of Laura Secord chocolate in Baldoon County; the proverbial kid in a candy store, Mary could not have trusted herself in the presence of such bonbons. But with no yearning for the almond bark and no desire for buttered toffee, she pulled on a sundress, borrowed Irma's mules and arrived ten minutes early for her interview. She would work mornings, the shift no one else wanted, and Saturdays for the rest of the summer, and cut back to just Saturday when school began. Past Mary, present Mary, in-between Mary — like Gooch, the walls of Raymond Russell's had borne witness to most of her life.

Jimmy Gooch hobbled into the drugstore on tall, squeaky crutches one Saturday morning in November of their senior year, having been absent from school for two weeks, during which the Leaford Senior Cougars had lost four straight games. He'd been in a terrible car crash for which his father had been hospitalized, and no one had seen him since the accident. There were rumors at school that his leg was broken in four places. A stitched cut was healing on his forehead, and there was a faint yellow cast to his left cheek, where the worst of the bruising had been. He was wearing a stained sweatshirt and basketball shorts to accommodate the huge plaster cast on his left leg. Seventeen-year-old Gooch searched the store, pinching a square of white paper in his big, trembling fingers, a drowning man, until he spotted Mary Brody sailing toward him.

The sign flickering in his expression read, *I am saved*. Perhaps he saw his own reflection deep within Mary's eyes, and imagined that she already possessed him. Or maybe he recognized her as belonging to his new circle of damaged souls. Their whole lives felt decided in that moment.

Gooch paused, watching her, then lifted his shoulders and smiled wanly as if to say, *Ah, life.* Mary Brody nodded twice and tilted her head as if to respond, *I know.* She gestured for him to follow her to the back, which he did, swinging his long frame on the complaining crutches. She took the prescription and passed it to Ray Russell Sr., quietly asking if he could fill it right away, for her *friend*. She turned to find Gooch waiting, eager, like a pup. She wordlessly showed him to a chair, feeling the heat rise from his body as he lowered his cast to the floor and himself to the seat.

Mary breathed him: leather jacket, unwashed body, dusty scalp. His round blue eyes begged for affection, clarity. As if they had already been married twenty-five years, instead of never having had a conversation before, she frowned reflectively and asked, "What are the doctors saying about your dad?"

Gooch's father, James, a tower like his namesake, had driven the Dodge, in which Gooch was passenger, straight into the hundred-year-old oak tree at the sharpest bend in the river road, on the way home from the strip club at Mitchell's Bay, where Gooch had been sent to retrieve him. James had insisted on driving and Gooch was, tragically, more afraid of his father's drunken rage than he was of his drunken driving. He had buckled into the passenger side, trying to convince himself that his father *did* drive better juiced than sober, just as he professed. Still, he couldn't stop himself from muttering, "Asshole," to which his father responded with a crisp backhand. That was how his cheek got bruised, but no one except Mary would ever know that.

Gooch looked at Mary directly. "Still feels like a dream."

"That could be your medication," she said with authority.

The article in the *Leaford Mirror* didn't mention, under the photograph of the smashed Dodge, that James Gooch had been driving home from the strip club, but it did note his impairment, and describe the paralysis and brain swelling and the unlikelihood that he would wake from his coma. The article also reported that Jimmy Gooch had a leg injury and would not play out the rest of the high school season, further speculating that Gooch's hopes of a basketball scholarship would be delayed, or dashed altogether.

"My dad's having a bad time with his colitis," Mary said, as if to answer some unasked question.

"Want a ride home?" Gooch offered.

"Six-thirty," she responded, "by the time I get done counting my cash."

That evening, when Mary's shift was over, Gooch was waiting for her in the parking lot. She felt curiously calm striding out to the tan Plymouth Duster where he sat smiling shyly. She was intent on the evening air, the curious warmth of the late fall night. She had brushed her teeth in the staff bathroom but hardly glanced at her reflection in the mirror. She hadn't fretted over what she might say. She hadn't worried that she had never been kissed. She knew what was to come as if it were a memory, not a projection.

Gooch and Mary were bound *mystically*, or so it seemed. Even if she would eventually understand that she was the only person in Gooch's life, including himself, who did not hold him responsible for what had happened, or feel somehow betrayed by the consequence of his injury, she'd been right about Jimmy Gooch that first day she looked into his eyes. He was not the cocky star athlete to whom things came easily, but a big, battered boy who needed a safe place to hide.

They drove to the lake in comfortable silence, to a clearing among the trees, a refuge to which Jimmy Gooch had plainly driven before. He knew just where to turn so the branches wouldn't scratch his door. They climbed out of the Duster, Gooch on his crutches, and leaned against the warm grille, a breath apart, watching moonlight stroke the water, lifting their eyes to the stars. Mary tried to recall the constellations from eighth-grade astronomy. The Big Dipper. The Little Dipper. Polaris—the North Star.

Gooch turned to her after a long time and said, "No one but Pete's even come by the house."

"I heard you didn't want to see anyone."

"I don't," he shot, then laughed. "I didn't. At least, I thought I didn't. No one I know."

"You know me. We had our lockers side by side."

"We did?" Gooch asked, cocking his head.

Mary's cheeks burned. "Never mind."

"I'm kidding, Mary," he said. "I remember you."

"I thought, because I look different now . . ."

"Where are you going after this?"

"Home?"

"No, I mean after graduation. Where are you going?"

"I thought I might work for a year and save some money. There's this school of fashion and design in Toronto but that's pretty far. My parents kind of need me right now. My dad's having a hard time."

"Colitis." Gooch nodded, watching the stars.

"I heard you were going to Boston," Mary said.

He gestured to his leg. "Not now. Not to play."

"I'm sorry."

Gooch shrugged. "I'm not. It's a relief." He sighed, loudly enough to scatter wildlife. "It's all a big relief." But he didn't look relieved.

Mary waited as Gooch took another deep breath and, in his exhalation, told her the true story of his life: his alcoholic parents, his father's violent rages, his mother's penchant for scenes, the tragedy of his older sister's drug addiction, his paralyzing fear that he could not measure up. People expected so much from a giant boy.

Mary's eyes never left his handsome face as he spoke, lingering over the asides: describing his passion for writing, his love affair with the U.S.A., his impatience with complainers, his preference for Chinese over Italian, his goal of reading the classics, his embarrassment that his clothes had to be custom-made. He paused, puzzling over her pretty face. She thought he might kiss her, and was unprepared when he said, "Your turn."

Although she might have told Gooch her own life story, confided about her sickly, disappointed parents, her intense loneliness, her hunger. And though she might have confessed her love affair with the parasites, and described her own incapacitating fear of not measuring *down*, Mary Brody did not reveal herself that way. Instead, she moved from the spot beside young Jimmy Gooch, imagining herself a fusion of every brazen starlet she'd ever watched seduce a man.

She reached for the buttons of her blouse, then shifted out of her skirt, then unclasped her bra and pulled down her panties and peeled off her socks, until she was completely, exquisitely nude. She raised her arms, not as a flourish to her striptease but because she was standing naked in the serious moonlight on a warm night in November, and was certain never to do so again.

"I don't want to hurt you," Gooch said, without moving forward.

"You won't," she promised.

Gooch rested his plaster-cast leg on a nearby stump and pulled Mary to him, stroking her hair when she shivered. He helped her up to the warm hood of the Duster and let his lips fall on the swell of cheek beneath her lashes. She held her breath as his mouth sampled the length of her neck, and brushed her soft shoulder, and found her rising breasts. She shivered as his fingers conducted currents from her nipple to her groin. Lips found pelvis. Tongue parted lips. A glimpse of the divine. From her thigh she heard him whisper huskily, "I love your smell."

In the way Mary Brody had been engrossed by food and then obsessed with her parasites, she became, after that night, consumed by Jimmy Gooch.

At Leaford Collegiate's parent night that winter, Mary overheard the guidance counselor, Miss Lafleur, whisper to anxious Irma in her charming French-Canadian accent, "She goes from being Mary to being *Mary*." Sylvie Lafleur was gamine and fair, with strawberry hair in a braid down her elegant back. She cared deeply about her students, and had been encouraging to Mary during the course of her transformation. "She's meeting her new body. Okay she's distracted from her schoolwork. This too shall pass," Miss Lafleur assured.

Mary was struck by the fact that all things *did* pass, and added the phrase to her personal theology, below the rule of three and her enduring belief in miracles.

A distant relative of the famous Canadian hockey player, Miss Lafleur lived alone in a small apartment in a building overlooking the river in Chatham — the same building, in fact just down the hall, where Mary's father had died with his thrombosis. Sylvie had been a godsend, bringing groceries to Orin when Mary couldn't. Stopping by for a chat because she knew he was old and lonely.

The guidance counselor was a woman who knew things, but

Mary mistrusted Gooch's reliance on her advice. During his final year he met with Miss Lafleur weekly, receiving tutoring for the time he'd missed because of the accident, and discussing his academic options. Mary worried that the woman would persuade her boyfriend to choose some faraway university, or counsel Gooch that Mary Brody was clearly not the right girl for him.

Miss Lafleur must have known that it was not Mary's own body she was distracted by, but Jimmy Gooch's. His smooth, tanned complexion, yeasty at his hairline, buttery at his neck. The berry texture of his tongue, the firmness of his cheek, the ripple of his core, the substance of his swell. The talc-soft skin from there to there, and his creamy voice when he asked her to touch it. A sensual rhapsody. More necessary than food. More vital than air. In the months after Gooch's father passed, and when it was clear that he would not play sports competitively again, the two clung to each other, humming with endorphins. Desperate love, dense as gold.

In the early years of their marriage, Gooch and Mary spent Saturday nights (and most weekday mornings) rutting to anthem rock, lost in a guitar riff of scent and motion, pace and pressure, retention and release. *Say something,* she'd beg, while he stroked. Gooch thought she wanted dirty talk, but it was really just the sound of his voice.

By the middle years of their marriage, Saturdays were spent playing cards on a rotating schedule at their friends' modest homes. Pete and Wendy's duplex for euchre. Bridge at Kim and François's backsplit. Poker at Dave and Patti's old manse, before Patti left Dave for Larry Hooper. Gooch liked to gamble and was sullen when he lost, even though the largest pots rarely exceeded twenty dollars, and even if he was reminded a dozen times that it was supposed to be for fun. "I come from a long line of sore losers," he'd joke.

One windswept autumn evening they were at Kim and François's place, over the bridge, on the other side of the river. By then Mary had recovered all of her lost weight, clinging to, as the grief-stricken clutch mementos, the pounds she'd added over the course of her two failed pregnancies. She chose flattering clothes and wore coral lip gloss to complement her green eyes, and dyed her prematurely gray roots rich chestnut every five weeks. She had good taste in footwear. She still had her uterus. As a couple, the Gooches were damaged but hopeful.

The ill wind that night drove branches against the sliding glass door, and Mary moved chairs twice, stalked by the draft. Wendy announced her pregnancy — twins, yay. Kim's middle one had just started kindie, and she'd brought a stack of pictures of the new baby in his adorable doggie jammies. School raffle ticket time again. Mary ate a bowl of dill dip. Gooch won eighteen dollars and drank nine Black Labels.

Heading to the truck at the end of the evening, Gooch squeezed his wife's thick waist, then, remembering how she hated that, leaned down to bite her ear. "You smell like a pickle," he said, which meant she should brush her teeth because he wanted sex.

On the short drive home, as they were discussing the naivety of Dave's young girlfriend, a splendid brown buck leapt from the dense bush into the path of their pickup. But this was no deer caught in headlights. This was a kamikaze bomber slamming the grille, bouncing onto the hood, flipping up to the windshield, then launched back to the pavement when Gooch jammed the brake.

The bright truck lights caught crisp orange leaves stealing from the scene. Furious gusts peeled down tufts at the animal's heaving breast. Gooch peered through the shattered windshield at the buck thrashing on the pavement. Wordlessly he climbed out of the truck, approaching the fallen creature, whose leg was clearly broken. He must have heard Mary shout, "What do we do, Gooch?" But he just stood there, a minor actor in the wings in the thrall of the great star's death scene. Mary waited for her husband to take action. An eternity passed. Howling wind. Horrible tap-shoe hoofs. Gasping clouds of condensed breath. Gooch? *Gooch?*

Mary shifted the gear, pressed her foot on the pedal, and drove at the creature. *Thud.* Stop. Reverse. The only thing to do. Shift. *Thunk.* Stop. Reverse. Shift, swallow hard. Dead. Undeniably. Stop. The wind pushed pebbles of glass onto her lap. She dusted the fragments off absently, heart thumping, watching Gooch climb into the passenger seat, not daring to glance his way. The wind would have blown Mary numb, were she not already so.

After silently appraising the damage to the vehicle — apart from the windshield, a dented front grille and hood — the couple headed for the house. Mary locked herself in the bathroom with a loaf of Sarah Lee, licking the cords of biting-sweet icing from the top of the cardboard package when she'd finished gulping the spongy yellow cake. Afterward she brushed her teeth, even though she was certain Gooch would no longer want sex. She could hear the television on in the living room, where he was watching the nightly news.

The clock thumped on the bedside like a voice commanding, *Do it, do it,* and Mary held her hand over her galloping heart. It was time. As good a time as any to make a long-held confession to Gooch, one she'd resolved to make a thousand times then lost her nerve before she spoke, or had not been availed of the words. Waiting for him to come to bed, she saw that she'd been presented with the perfect opportunity to disclose. The deer in the road. He would understand completely. It was another situation in which no one was at fault.

When finally she heard the bedroom door creak open, and felt Gooch heft his freight into the bed, she reached tentatively for his body and set her heavy hand upon his broad chest. "We need to talk, Gooch."

"No," he replied, and then, more tenderly, "Not tonight, Mare. Okay?"

"I need to tell you something," she insisted. He surprised her then, by kissing her on the mouth. "Gooch," she whispered as he buried his face in her neck. She felt him stiff beneath his briefs. "Gooch?"

He moved against her, gently at first, faster, harder, bouncing, grunting as the headboard flogged the wall, until he'd been seized and arrested, and fell back against the bed. Before passing out he squeezed Mary's arm, but she couldn't tell if the gesture was one of gratitude or apology.

At six a.m., the clock alarmed them both. They rose and began their respective morning routines, Gooch heading out to get the newspaper, Mary cracking eggs. They would never speak of the deer on the road, already firmly entrenched in their habit, which was not to discuss things painful or obvious.

The anchor of Mary's secret floated down to the silty bottom until another storm stirred it up again, but like the food she hid from herself, Mary always knew its precise location.

Her Body Electric

A train rattled by in the distance. The rain tapped against the windowsill. The night clock on the table beside Mary's bed told her it was past three o'clock. The Kenmore sang a love song from the kitchen. Mary eyed the telephone beside the clock, foreboding, like a smell brought in with the wind. She reached for her gray nightgown but remembered she'd left it in the kitchen.

Moving naked through the hall, she felt like a barge sailing toward a cool, distant land. *Just come home already, Gooch. The furnace. The anniversary. I'm worried. And I'm starving.* She looked at the phone but stopped herself from reaching for it.

Squinting from the refrigerator's sharp light, she found a jar of olives. Could he have hit a deer? No. Even the country roads were well enough traveled that an hour wouldn't go by without someone finding him. She leaned against the counter, suddenly aware that she was not alone but one of millions of humans standing on tile floors before their humming refrigerators, hungering for food, cigarettes, booze, sex. Love. She wondered if this was the chorus she sometimes heard above the thumping of her heart. Or was the sound, as she hoped, a beckoning God? Not the vengeful white man from the old movies or the wise black one from the new movies, but a large, round, female God who might enfold Mary in her motherly arms and show her the path to grace? *Ms. Bolt?*

Long ago, it was Irma who planted the idea in Mary's mind, driving past the red graffiti on the side of the Kmart, *Where is God when you need her?* "God could be a woman, I suppose," Irma'd said. "The God I grew up with was so angry. I always liked the look of that smiling Buddha."

"You can think of God any way you want to?" Mary asked, astonished.

"Of course, dear. As long as you don't have religion."

Mary stood watching the night through her kitchen window, as the wind cast the rake from its comfortable lean and set Merkel's dog to barking in the field behind. Suddenly remembering something, Mary hurried to look out the dirty glass of the back-door window. "Snap," she breathed. On the double laundry line near the overgrown vegetable patch, three of Gooch's costly custom-made work shirts flailed like the drowning in the swells of the wind. She was as angry at herself as she was with the storm, because she'd put the shirts on the line a full three days before. Only sloth would explain their loss to Gooch.

Forgetting her nightgown in her haste, Mary pushed open the back door, the wind, her lover, stroking her puckered skin and teasing her hair wild. Not now. Not *now*. Her heart began its ceremonial thud. She fought the driving current as the first shirt was kicked high by an updraft and torn by the stiff maple near Mr. Barkley's grave. Then the wind took hold of the taupe shirt, ripped it from the line and flung it toward Feragamos'. Gone, like Mr. Barkley, before her very eyes.

Mary's cold, bare feet urged her legs to take one step, then another and another, determined to conquer the distance through the wet grass to rescue the remaining shirt. The wind battered her as she stretched to reach the sleeve. A clothespin popped, striking her in the forehead. Startled, she lost her grip on the shirt, and as she stepped back to watch the flying fabric she tripped on the laundry basket and fell hard to the earth.

The wind left Mary Gooch like a hit-and-run victim, sprawled naked in the wet leaves on that stormy October night. Laboring from the weight of herself, chanting the accidental mantra *Gooch Gooch Gooch,* she found a rhythm in her breath and set her thoughts adrift.

Perhaps it was nudity that gave Mary some fresh perspective. Lying there beneath the tempest, sharing her load with the sweet damp earth, she felt together the peculiar sense of utter freedom and deep connection. Freedom from what, she couldn't say. Connection to whom, she didn't know. Or, more important, it didn't matter. Suspecting that oxygen deprivation might be involved in her awakening, she struggled to breathe more deeply, which heightened rather than diminished her awareness that a switch of some kind had been turned on. An electrical current, a hum in every cell that connected sublimely to the pulse of all things, so that she was the earth that cradled her body, and the ant on the twig near her ear. She was the roots of the wind-ravaged willow, and the air that fed her lungs. She was the newborn crying in the distant house, and Mr. Feragamo in his bed. She was each drop of rain; Mrs. Merkel's dog; the compost of her cat. She was all of herself, and nothing but the breeze that coaxed her higher, until she could see her huge babyish figure, peaceful and pretty, undressed by the wind. Her current position too enlightened for regret, she regarded the body she was heir to, and err to, without worry or wish or shame.

The wind blew cold and the rain stung her thighs. A cricket raked its legs together near a branch by her toe. She imagined she heard an orange kitten crying behind the garage. *Mr. Barkley? Is that you?* She had the heart-stopping realization that Gooch could be home any minute; certain that she would rather be dead than seen, she reached for the laundry basket as leverage to crane herself to standing. She started for the back door, her body waves in motion, damning wrathful nature. In answer to her silent hatred, or maybe to teach her a lesson about respect, the wind blasted through the open bedroom window and sent a gust through the house that slammed the back door shut.

The back door locked automatically when it shut but Mary tried the knob anyway, hoping for a miracle. Drawing upon her terror of being discovered naked in her yard in the middle of a storm, she dragged herself toward the garage and heaved open the door, her porcine nudity cruelly splashed by motion-sensor light. *Ha ha,* she wanted to shout to whoever was behind this. *Laugh it up.*

Gooch's tools were laid out neatly at his work table. There were boxes and crates of who knows what, the outdoor broom, the lawn mower, the weed whacker, Gooch's bike. A sound familiar to the sleepless, of a vehicle in the night, set her flesh to quiver. She reached for the shovel and looked out to the road, noting the distant headlights. Each thundering step a testament of will, she waded through the leaves to the locked back door, lifted the shovel's handle and ran it at the glass. She reached in to turn the lock, panicked, as the headlights approached.

The shard met Mary's bare heel the moment she stepped in the door, with a stab of freezing cold followed by a hot shot of pain. She blamed the glass from here to eternity as she hobbled over the kitchen floor to find support at the counter, as the vehicle passed outside.

She craned her neck. She lifted her leg. She bent at the side. It didn't matter from which angle she tried to examine her foot, she could not see past her extensive body. Tossing a dishtowel to the floor to catch the pooling blood, she put her foot down, realizing too late that the shard was still lodged there. She dragged herself to one of the red vinyl chairs, blood spilling off the towel and seeping into the pores of the dirty grout.

Sweating, grunting, Mary attempted to lift her injured foot to her opposite knee so that she could pull out the glass. She tried hoisting with her hands and scooping with her arms, but neither her knee joint nor her hip joint nor the encroachment of fat around the patella would allow the transfer. She strained, barely reaching the slippery, maddening shard, nicking her fingers. There was an alarming amount of blood stemming from the wound. She set her injured heel back on the blood-soaked towel, which released the glass from her foot.

Breathing deeply, calmer than she ought to have been, Mary found her gray nightgown on the chair and pulled it on, not noticing or caring about the bloodstains from her fingers. Regarding her reflection in the window, thinking of that other Mary Gooch she'd met so briefly, hovering in the storm, not defined by this or that but this and that and all of it, she reached for a recipe card on which emergency numbers were written, picked up the telephone and dialed Gooch's cellphone number. The stranger's recorded voice on Gooch's message service apologized, *This subscriber is not available. Please leave your name, the time, and the purpose of your call.*

"This is a message for Jimmy Gooch," she said. "Will you please ask him to call his wife?"

Feeling the wind rush in through the broken window, Mary thought of how Gooch would say, "You're letting out the heat," when she kept the door open, and "You're letting out the cold," when her nose was in the Kenmore. It struck her that there must be some other door left open through which she'd let out Gooch.

A Distant Relation

The green drapes danced as cold stormed the wide-open window. Mary woke as she did every morning, with a start, shocked to have fallen asleep at all. But it was a further shock to see the umber blood on her linens where her nicked hands had bled, and, when she heaved herself up to look, pooled on the bedspread beneath her foot.

Crows mocked from the fields behind the house, insisting she turn to look, but Mary already knew she was alone. She reached for the telephone beside the bed and found the card with emergency numbers. She dialed Gooch's cellphone. When the pre-recorded message answered the call, she managed to sputter, "I'm sorry. It's Mary Gooch again. Jimmy Gooch's wife. If you could have him call me please. It's seven o'clock. In the morning."

Creep of dread. Spiral of fear. Gooch was not home. He was not answering his phone. But then, her phone was also silent. No police calling to say he was in jail. No one banging on the door to say there'd been an accident. It occurred to her that the evening had simply been one of high drama, as happened when people ventured out in the dark. As she had. As Gooch sometimes did. His absence would be explained soon enough, plausibly and with genuine regret for her worry, and then forgotten by them both, or at least never spoken of again. And no real turning point at all, as she'd been so convinced by her brief tryst with the night earth.

Mary turned the alarm off before it sounded, struck by the putridity of her breath, recalling how Gooch liked to pronounce that people had their heads up their asses. She was one of them, of course, though he'd never been so direct with her. Except maybe last year, when she'd won the Caribbean cruise in a raffle and canceled at the last minute, even though they'd gone to the trouble of getting passports. She had insisted that with her motion sickness (and she did have motion sickness) she couldn't endure an ocean voyage. What she could not have endured were the orgies of cruise food she'd heard two women discussing at the hair salon when she went for her biyearly trim. The other problem, and it was always a problem, was that she had nothing to wear.

Gooch had been angry, ranting that there was a whole wide world outside of Leaford, and if she wanted to keep her head up her ass she could but *he* was going on that cruise. They'd given the tickets to Pete and Wendy. Why Gooch hadn't gone alone, she'd never understood. Where was that chorus? That tremolo of hope? Where the hell was Gooch?

Peering out the window, she searched the driveway for the Leaford Furniture and Appliance truck, which Gooch always parked beside the pickup with the jammed-open sunroof. As with the anticipation of her own reflection, she knew before she looked that she wouldn't like what she saw. So severely had her world shifted that she could not find her center of gravity, and had to grasp the sill for support. It occurred to her that she had never *felt* so heavy, a thought chased by the certainty that she'd never *been* so heavy. It had come to this. She'd finally grown so large that she'd displaced her husband altogether. Like water splashing over the sides of the tub.

There was a distant mechanical sound, and Mary lifted her eyes to see Mr. Merkel in his field hunched behind the wheel of his tractor, a big brown dog loping alongside, sprinting off occasionally to chase the plundering crows. Other people's desperate lives. "You can always look around," Irma liked to say, "and find someone else *much* worse off." It was true, and Mary found comfort in the misery of the Merkels, an older couple who had lost their only child, a four-year-old son, during a tornado in the early seventies. The furious wind had stolen little Larry from his own driveway and spirited him to some secret place, never to be seen again. Mary did not set eyes on Mr. or Mrs. Merkel without thinking of Larry, but she hadn't seen much of them lately. No one had.

The sad tale of Larry Merkel was a Leaford legend, like the story of the conjoined twin girls, Rose and Ruby Darlen, who'd been born attached at the head. Mary had rarely spoken to, but had watched the unusual girls from her distant bedroom window at the farm after she and Gooch were wed. She had wondered what they talked about as they huddled on the rickety footbridge over the creek between the fields. Like Larry Merkel's tiny ghost, which Mary imagined she glimpsed darting through the high corn, the Darlen sisters haunted the landscape. Mary's own babies were ghosts too, but silent, watchful types, like Mr. Barkley, who never went outdoors.

Poor Christopher Klik, Mary's first barometer for self-pity, was replaced, after the Darlen twins were born, by Rose and Ruby. "Joined at the *head*. Just imagine that," Irma would say when they chanced to see the pair. But Mary didn't feel especially sorry for them. From what she could see, the girls seemed content in their peculiar shape. Although she would have felt foolish admitting it, and had no one to share such a confession with anyway, she'd envied the girls their inextricable bond.

The girls had written their autobiographies in the months before their deaths, which all of Baldoon County had read, and to which everyone had taken some kind of exception. There were those who protested the geography in parts; others objected to the use of real names; some disagreed with the characterizations; and at least a few refuted the events, some of which must have been fictional, for what Rose Darlen wrote about a glimpsed sexual act between her Uncle Stash and Catherine Merkel could not have been true.

Mary had consumed the book in one sitting, fretting the while that she would find herself on the next page, described in pitiful terms by one girl or the other as the large, childless woman in the house behind, who watched life from the frame of a window. When she was not even mentioned, by either girl, she wondered how such a large woman as herself could be so incidental.

Remembering Rose and Ruby served as an excellent distraction, until replaced by another random force. The furnace began to roar, and after throwing a series of short tantrums, died in a snit. Mary felt vindicated, and hoped it had suffered. Encouraged by the symbolism, she closed the bedroom window and started toward the hall, straining to stay off her wounded heel.

Dawn lit the hallway like a morning-after murder scene, walls smeared with blood from the cuts on her hand, exclamatory stains on the new silver broadloom. It was shocking, but there was precision in the imagery. Something *had* died there in the night.

Finally reaching the kitchen, relieved to see that the wound on her foot didn't appear to be bleeding, or at least not badly, she opened the freezer and snatched a package of corn, cramming a fistful of niblets into her mouth, sucking them to defrost, surrendering to her hunger and the dark disgust that she could even think of eating at a time like this. She wondered if she would be betraying Gooch or rescuing him in making a call to The Greek.

Gooch had been trucking and delivering for Theo Fotopolis, whom everyone called The Greek the way everyone called Jimmy Gooch *Gooch*, for nearly as long as Mary'd worked at Raymond

Russell's. The Greek had hired Gooch to work in the sales office after high school, and then underwritten the cost of his trucking license when his injured leg had healed.

The clock on the wall read seven a.m. The question of whether to call The Greek or not call The Greek depended on which truth Mary was prepared to confront, that Gooch's absence was not accidental, or that it was. There was also the pressing matter of the Laura Secord chocolate order due at the drugstore. Mary had ordered a carton of her favorites, nut clusters and milk chocolate almond bark, minis, assorted soft centers, assorted hard centers, which the supplier gave her on a deep discount. If she was not there to receive the order, Ray would discover her transgression. At best he would be annoyed. At worst he'd find it so hilarious he'd have to tell the whole staff. Besides, there was always a box or two of silky chocolate damaged in transit, or intentionally, to open and share among the staff. Mary took erotic pleasure in the ecstatic mastication of her colleagues, though she demurred when the damaged boxes were passed her way.

Gooch had his own relationship with damaged goods. Their small home in rural Leaford was furnished with pieces from the store that had been broken in transit. A coffee table with a hairline fracture. The burnt umber Kenmore refrigerator whose tone had not precisely matched its stove mate. A sleeper sofa with broken gears. The first of the damaged pieces had been, in that first difficult year of their marriage, the red vinyl chairs with the thick aluminum legs.

Mary had settled into one of their hand-me-down wooden chairs one morning and popped a rickety joint. Gooch didn't fret aloud that his young wife, expanding rapidly in the first trimester of her second pregnancy, might break a chair altogether and fall with some tragic consequence. But he thought it. That evening the four red chairs appeared, one of them with a noticeable tear at the seam, and the old ones sent to the garage. Mary did not ask her young husband if he'd torn the seam on purpose.

Gooch sat in one of the stiff red chairs, lifting Mary's dress so she could straddle his lap. "Did you ask the doctor?" he whispered into her engorged décolletage.

"He says we shouldn't," Mary lied. Halting and ashamed, she'd asked Dr. Ruttle if she and her husband could continue having intercourse during the remaining six months of her pregnancy, and had been quietly shocked by his candid response. "Of course you can. Right up until delivery, if it's still comfortable for you both."

Surely that couldn't be right. Or at least not in her situation, given that she'd lost her first baby (James or Liza), and what with Gooch being Gooch. She decided, leaving Ruttle's office, that the good doctor had forgotten her first miscarriage, and her husband's unusual size. Mary wished she could call Wendy or Patti to solicit their opinions, but she didn't discuss her marital intimacy with anyone. Like eating, it was an intensely private matter.

On a cool October night on the eve of her wedding, the four girlfriends, recent graduates of Leaford Collegiate — Wendy enrolled in the nursing program, Kim off to teachers' college in London, Patti working reception at her mother's realty office and Mary — had gathered for salads and sparkling wine at the Satellite Restaurant in Chatham. Mary's acceptance into their sorority was still fresh; like a foreign exchange student, she found she could observe their customs but, without understanding the nuances of their language, not effectively participate.

She'd opened their wedding shower gifts under the table, sweating beneath her smock, wilting when one girl or another cried, "Hold it up!" A red teddy with matching underwear. A sheer black gown with ruffles at the neck. "You wear it with nothing else," Kim instructed. "So sexy." A blue corset with snaps at the back and cone-shaped breasts. Each of the sets in the size Mary had been briefly, and never would be again.

The girls — all except Mary, who had a low tolerance for alcohol — drank too much wine and talked about sex. Patti put thumb and forefinger together, peering through the tiny space between, and slurred, "Dave's a grow-er. Not a show-er." Kim chimed in about her older sister's *horniness* in the third trimester of her first pregnancy, and how, after the baby was born, she'd let her husband suck her milk. Mary found the image disturbing, and hated the word *horny*, which sounded bestial. Wendy confessed that she didn't really enjoy *screwing* but that she could get Pete to do *anything* (that Supertramp concert?) if she just gave him a quick *youknowhat*. When Kim squealed, "Eeewww," she instructed, "Give him a tissue!" "Or," Wendy screamed, "swallow!"

The topic shifted to Mary's pregnancy. "Aren't you afraid of getting fat again?" Wendy asked bluntly. "I'm *terrified*. And I never *was* fat."

"You're supposed to get fat when you're pregnant. Don't listen to her, Mary. My sister's baby weight just melted off after," Kim assured her. "Especially if you're breast-feeding."

"I'm just saying," Wendy slurred, "I'd rather be dead than fat."

Kim passed the menu. "Should we get one big fries with gravy to share?"

Wendy continued, sucking her wine, "Come *on*, you guys. It's not like Mary didn't know she was fat, right? Right?"

Mary felt Wendy's eyes boring into her. "Yeah."

"Jimmy Gooch didn't *look* at Mary before she lost all that weight and, come on, I'm just saying." Wendy faltered. "I'd just hate the thought of your cheekbones gone and your cute shoes won't fit."

Gorgeous drunken Wendy from the cheerleading squad, who was in love with Jimmy Gooch herself, was just saying what they all thought, Mary most obsessively—that she would grow fat with the pregnancy and be unable to lose the weight (as had been witnessed countless times in everyone's sphere), and that Gooch would leave her to raise their stinky brat alone.

Mary had stopped eating dirt sometime after she and Gooch became official. Gooch alone sustained her. But then, when that first baby was no larger than a thumbnail, her giant gnawing hunger had returned, and like any compulsion, it began again, not at the beginning, but where it had left off. Sneaking from the bed when she knew that fretful Irma and resigned Orin were asleep, she would stand in the kitchen munching from foil bags, slurping cold noodles from the leftovers bowl and grinding rows of chocolate cookies between her big back teeth.

"Is The Greek gonna give you guys a crib set?" Kim inquired, to fill the quiet.

If her fabric had not been woven with lengths of deception and secrecy, Mary might have been able to ask the other girls the many questions she had about her body, about the sexual act, about her husband's libido. Before Gooch, she'd never thought to wonder much about male bodies, too intent on the care and feeding of her own. Her only experiences before Gooch had been revealing her nipple to Christopher Klik at the bike rack, and the time Jerry, the wrinkled driver from the drugstore, had offered to massage her shoulders in the empty staff room. Afraid to appear ungrateful, she'd allowed him to knead her for a full ten minutes while bumping his crooked old-man erection against her firm teenage back. She didn't tell anyone the indecent thing the driver had done. She was naive enough to consider that she'd only imagined his intent. She was also, until Gooch, in the habit of thinking herself too repulsive to be the object of even warped desire.

Gooch and Mary's sexual energy had been powerful, and Gooch's longing for her wasn't dampened after they were married. Just four months after failing with her first pregnancy, they had discovered that they were expecting again, and Mary's confidence had been diminished by the rapid accumulation of pounds.

Straddling her husband on the new red vinyl chair, she had concluded that Dr. Ruttle's counsel was to be ignored. She was much too afraid for the second baby (Thomas or Rachel) to satisfy Gooch in their usual way, and thinking of what Wendy had said on the eve of her wedding, about the spell she could put Pete under, Mary'd pushed her husband's wide shoulders back against the red vinyl chair he'd brought home that day, and whispered into his ear, "Dr. Ruttle said we can't do *that*. But we can do something *else*."

After, as Gooch was zipping and rising from the red chair, she'd sensed, along with some deep appreciation for what she'd just done — particularly as she did *not* pass him a tissue — an undercurrent of suspicion. Reaching for his huge hand so that he could help her from her knees, she had felt compelled to whisper, "I've never done that before." He'd arched a brow but not asked more, and Mary had slept that night with her hand on her rising womb, reasoning that she must have done what she did very well. She was pleased to have gone with her instinct, which was to imagine that his tumescence was edible.

Expressions of Genuine Concern

A gentle morning rain fell over the landscape. A cold breeze blew in through the broken back window as Mary moved to the telephone and dialed her husband's number. It was the machine again, with the unfamiliar voice, which Mary understood must belong to a human receptionist who would pass the message along. "It's Mary Gooch again. Eight forty-five. If Jimmy Gooch could please call his wife at work. Thank you."

Scooping peanut butter with her finger, the sensation of the long, plump digit pleasant in her mouth, Mary tried to recall the last time she'd been touched lovingly by hands not her own.

Outside, the rain made a dreary pattern on the windowpane above the sink. The sunroof! The interior of the truck would be soaked. She'd have to remember to bring towels to sit on, on the way to work. She wondered if she should call in sick, pretend to be asleep when Gooch got home and act feverish and confused upon waking, as if she assumed he'd been there all night.

She focused on her list. Roof repair? Furnace guy? Something to wear to the dinner? The dinner. Cancel the dinner? Laura Secord order.

The craving took her by the throat. Chocolate. Essential. A thing that could not wait. She felt some momentary kinship with Gooch's sister, Heather, who'd spent most of their last visit together rifling through her empty coat pockets. "I'm *jonesing* for a smoke. I gotta hit the 7-Eleven," she'd said.

Before she left, Heather, with her long, bony limbs and sunken blue eyes, had taken hold of Mary's plush upper arms and dug her nails in deeper than she'd intended, saying, "You are so lucky to have my brother."

The way she'd said it, like an ex-girlfriend, or a regretful first wife, had given Mary pause. Heather was an addict, and beautiful, and Mary was naturally suspicious of her motives. It was assumed that Heather had got her cigarettes. She never returned for the roast beef dinner.

Mary searched the cupboard below the microwave as if she didn't already know there was no chocolate hidden there with the recipe books. *Jonesing* for chocolate. Nothing. No sliver. No square. No rogue M&M. Just the wedding binder — not the photographs, but a collection of receipts for every dime Orin and Irma spent on Mary Elizabeth Brody's marriage to James Michael Gooch twenty-five years ago. They'd presented the binder to her in the week before her wedding, detailing each receipt and invoice until they reached the final tally, which Irma had written in thick black ink. "We're not asking you to pay us back, dear," Irma'd said solemnly. "Just, you need to know, there's a cost. To everything."

The night before the wedding, Irma had come to Mary's room, reluctant slippers shuffling toward the bed. Standing, she'd regarded the lump of her daughter under the thick chenille spread, noting that Mary had gained much too much weight for the newness of her pregnancy. She had glanced at the creamy dress hanging on the back of the closet and asked, "Have you tried it on since last week?"

"Today," Mary said, not mentioning that the gown was dangerously snug and that she was afraid for the buttons at her waist.

Irma furrowed her brow and said quietly, "Well, dear, it's too late to talk about relations, which is what you're supposed to talk to your daughter about on the night before her wedding."

A blush crept to Mary's cheek. She winced, but not from her mother's words. Too much bread with the girls at the Satellite Restaurant. She felt hot and strangely ill.

"You're too young to be getting married."

"I know."

"But it's the only thing to do, so."

"Yeah."

Irma cleared her throat. "Your father and I . . ."

"Me too," Mary whispered, when it was clear that her mother would not or could not go on.

"But you've made your bed."

"I know."

"And you've got to lie in it."

The way she said *lie*. "I will."

"And it's going to be up to you, dear. It's not the man who works on the marriage. I can promise you that much."

"Okay."

"You don't let yourself *go*."

"Go where?" Mary asked blankly, then "Oh."

"You put fresh clothes on before he gets home for dinner and you have a *hot* breakfast, not cereal, on the table each morning, no matter if you've been up with the baby all night."

"Okay."

"And a little lipstick never hurt a girl."

"I don't feel well," Mary muttered.

"And they all have a particular habit. A nasty habit."

"A nasty habit?"

"They all do it. All of them. You won't change that. And when you catch him at it, just pretend you didn't see. Don't take it person-ally. That was the best piece of advice my mother gave me."

"I really don't feel well."

Irma settled onto the bed. "That's a good sign. I was sick with you the whole time. I didn't have a second of nausea with my other pregnancies. That's how I knew I wouldn't lose you."

Mary stroked her womb, feeling the rise of bile. "Doesn't feel good, though."

"Lots of things don't feel good, dear."

She drew her legs to her stomach, finding some relief, wishing Irma would stay with her on the bed talking like this for the remain-der of the night. But just as she wished it, like a candle blown out, her mother was rising and, without meaning to sound harsh, saying, "Now get some sleep."

In her childhood bed in the little room in the blue bungalow where she had been raised, Mary watched the moonlight fall on the wedding dress hanging on the back of the closet door. The dress had cost three hundred and seventy-four dollars. And the three separate alterations to let it out, another ninety-two. Shoes, one fifty-nine. So much bread. And most of the fries with gravy that Kim had ordered for the table. And two slices of the cake. Mary would need to spend her entire wedding day inhaling, holding in her pregnant stomach, which she'd planned to do anyway, even though she knew there wasn't a single guest who didn't already know, or hadn't guessed at, her *condition*.

Patti, Kim and Wendy swam around her in a dizzying water ballet. Expressions of genuine concern. Sisterly advice. Sexual frank-ness. The kind of friendship ritual Mary had longed for, but whose genuineness she didn't trust. Frightening bullets of remembered conversation—*I'd rather be dead than fat.*

Some hours after she heard the scraping of kitchen chairs and the settling of Irma and Orin's teacups in the sink, Mary was still wide awake. She was sweating beneath her covers and shivering at the same time. She was hungry. Starving. She crept down the hall toward the kitchen. But she was drawn by the night light in the bathroom, and paused to ponder her pale, pretty face.

The pain was sudden and tore at her gut. Gas. She belched. She caught her breath but couldn't leave her reflection. Mary *Gooch*. Mrs. James *Gooch*. She did not want to change her name, but had not expressed that to anyone. Irma would have rolled her eyes. Gooch's mother would have protested. And Gooch? She'd been afraid to hurt his feelings. How could she become Mary Gooch when she barely knew Mary Brody?

Mary had educated herself, at the back table in the Leaford Library, with a variety of books about pregnancy, one of which showed a weight gain table. She was already off the chart. The same book had explained the issue of incontinence, which sometimes happened during the third trimester or after the birth, with the stretching and slackening of uterine muscles. She knew, though, when she felt the hot trickle between her legs, that she was not peeing. Blood. She sank down to the toilet.

Although she thought it a grave dishonor to the memory of James or Liza to recall with too much detail the demise and disappearance of that blameless soul, the memory often came unbidden to her mind. When she rose for her inspection, she could not connect the flotsam she saw in the toilet water to the chubby dark-haired baby she'd envisioned at her breast. The baby she'd named and was besotted with, with whom she'd already shared a lifetime of wisdom. The little boy they'd joked would be the mini-bar to Gooch's fridge. Or the little girl whose soft hair she would brush the way Irma had hers. Grief would visit later, in the days and weeks ahead, but in that awful moment Mary's instinct was to undo the undone.

She watched the swirl of red, terrified by the swiftness of her action, realizing, too late, that she hadn't even said goodbye. *I'm sorry. Oh God, I'm so sorry.* The plumbing made glugging sounds and then, as if to complete her horror, the water rose slowly back up, spilling over the porcelain, dripping pink acid onto the tiles below. She reached for the towels, falling to her knees to stop the tide from leaking out under the door. It was some small mercy that the plunger was nearby.

Scrubbing blood from the grout on the eve of her wedding, she saw that she could tell no one what had happened without explaining what she'd done. She would convince herself that she had been in shock, that judgment could not be expected from, or imposed upon, a person in shock. Still, the facts remained, as she imagined them presented, that she had unintentionally suffocated her baby with her visceral weight, *manslaughter*, and disposed of the body, for that's what it *must* have been, in a most gruesome fashion, *gross indignity to a corpse.*

The wedding dress on the closet door, the binder of receipts under the lingerie beside her luggage for the honeymoon in Niagara Falls. Bloodstained towels hidden at the bottom of the trash. A cost to everything. Mary shifted under her blankets, enduring her first fully sleepless night. She had no fever and the blood between her legs had slowed to a manageable trickle, but she couldn't stop shaking.

On that morning of her wedding, as on this morning twenty-five years later, she awoke to a world whose essential rotation had shifted. She ravenously ate the blueberry waffles Irma set before her, and agreed with Orin that the bees might be a problem even if it was warm enough to eat outdoors. No matter how much she wanted to confess what had happened, no matter that she understood her loss could not be hidden indefinitely, she could not find the words.

She shivered into her wedding gown. Having lost a good deal of fluid in the dark night hours, the buttons fastened easily at her waist. Irma smoothed her skirt, saying, "Don't be a stranger here, now."

"You and Pop'll come out to our house sometimes too," she returned.

Dressed and done, her dark hair piled elegantly on top of her head, Mary avoided her reflection as she bustled out of the room.

She'd eaten too much. And lost the baby because of it. But how to tell Gooch? A cost. To everything.

When he saw her moving down the short hall, Orin let out a long, low whistle, but she could see he was blinking back tears. He was losing his baby. She had lost hers. It was the saddest day of their lives. The hot metal smell from the bloody pad between her legs rose up from the lace and tulle. Irma clapped her hands and said, "Let's go get this day over with."

As he escorted his plush, blushing daughter up the church aisle, Orin whispered, "You look like a deer caught in the headlights, Murray. *Smile* for Chrissake." She nearly stopped then and ran back out the door, but she walked on instead, entranced by Gooch's smiling face until she found his hand at the altar.

She floated through the hours, a guest at her own wedding, fearful that her lie had stained her gown and that everyone, including Gooch, was pointing at her behind her back. She would not remember the ceremony. The kiss. The pictures. The dinner. The cake. None of it — only the sound of Heather Gooch's tearful voice as she read the insipid love poem she'd written herself, and the look of pain on Gooch's face when he dipped her on the dance floor and she saw that he'd reinjured his leg.

Just before midnight, in the black Lincoln Continental borrowed from The Greek, Mary suggested that Gooch pull over in London, where her hemorrhage was addressed in the emergency room and the doctor informed Gooch, "The baby's been lost." *Lost*. Like a mitten or a set of car keys. The doctor turned to Mary and patted her soft hand and never told the young groom that his bride had miscarried the baby on the night before their wedding.

Gooch entered the drab room limping badly on the morning she was to be released from the hospital. Mary felt responsible for his pain since he'd hurt his leg dancing, even if the dance had been at his mother's insistence and not hers. Gooch was recovering from his third knee surgery in the year since the accident, but Eden had warned that people would get the wrong idea if he didn't take to the floor with his new bride. And she wouldn't have people walking around with the wrong idea. Not anymore.

Eden was a hard woman to ignore, with her sharp blue eyes and short black bob, her manicured nails and high-heeled shoes — a chic beauty, conspicuous in Leaford. In the months after her husband's tragic death she'd found Jack Asquith and Jesus and sobriety, in that order, and even the ounce of dignity her daughter, Heather, had insisted she did not possess.

Gooch could not stomach his mother's affection for the chain-smoking American, and liked to bait Jack over dinner, mocking his interpretations of God's intentions. *God* thinks. *God* thinks. "What does God think about you fornicating with my mother, Jack?"

Forgetting her own pain momentarily, seeing the strain on Gooch's face in the hospital that morning and aware that his knee was killing him, Mary said, "You can have one more pill every four hours, but no more than that. Okay?"

He signaled his relief. "I've got enough till Friday. You'll be back to work by then."

Dr. Ruttle had been alarmed when Gooch finished his first narcotics prescription early, and had refused to write a prescription for any more painkillers. "Sometimes, the best thing to do with pain is endure it," the doctor had said. The vials are under lock and key now, but back then the excess stock was stored on the high shelf over Ray Senior's desk at the receiving door. Mary had stolen the pills with impunity, but a different brand and potency, so that her theft, should it ever be detected, would not be traced to Gooch.

"I'm sorry," she whispered as Gooch approached, smoothing back the sheets on the hospital bed.

"It's not your fault, Mare."

"I know," she lied. She had intended in that moment, as she would intend in moments to come, to tell him the truth about losing the baby, but the aching loss, which she could embrace now that Gooch knew too, and the deep mourning for her very *motherhood*, which Gooch would never understand, stole her impulse back.

He settled beside her on the thin bed, wrapping her in his big arms, his voice sounding for the first time more boy than man. "It's for the best, right?" The affront to her baby in the doctor's suggestion that the fetus had been less than perfect, and so the miscarriage for *the best*, had been great, yet Gooch seemed comforted by it, while Mary felt enraged.

"Okay," she said.

He pulled down the fabric of her hospital gown and laid his cheek on her bosom. She read his mind: *We only got married because of the baby.*

"We only got married because of the baby," she echoed. "We wouldn't have, if I wasn't . . ."

"But we did."

"Gooch . . ."

"Mary," he said. "Drinks are drunk. Music is played. Cash is counted. We're married."

"Your mother'd be relieved if we got annulled," she said, noticing the small diamond solitaire on her ring finger, unable to recall the moment Gooch had slipped it on.

"You know how much that wedding cost your old man?"

"Yes," she answered. To the penny.

They looked out the hospital window at the raw autumn sky. Gooch's voice massaged her shoulders. "When we had our lockers side by side that year . . ."

She sank into his embrace. "When we had our lockers side by side."

"I found one of those notes. The polka-dot ones. I never gave it to you."

Mary stiffened. The polka-dot notes had come sporadically until her transformation in senior year—seven in all, eight counting the one Gooch had intercepted, written in curlicued cursive with hilarious illustrations in the margins, addressing Mary Brody's body odor on account of her not showering after the torture of gym class.

"Why are you telling me this? Now?"

"I thought you were brave, Mare."

"I didn't shower because I was afraid they'd make fun of me, Gooch."

"They made fun of you anyway."

She sighed, looking out the window, wondering if all men had such poor timing.

"You came back to school. That was brave," Gooch said.

"I didn't have a choice."

"There's always a choice."

Mary argued the point to herself.

"You used to sit on that swing in your yard and read novels. We could see you from Pete's window. We spied on you when we were bored. I read *A Clockwork Orange* because of the look on your face."

Mary giggled, then turned serious. "The Droogs."

"I watched you from the window of the car when I was waiting for my old man to get a prescription one time. You were working behind the cosmetic counter helping this little old lady buy some lipstick and you were making her laugh like crazy, and I thought, 'What is she saying to make that old bird laugh like that?'"

"I've always been good with old people," Mary allowed.

"And there was another time, days after we moved here in the summer. I was riding my bike to school to shoot hoops and I saw you walking down your street. I was watching you, the way you walk, and I had this déjà vu. I felt like I knew you. It was something about your walk. I felt like I'd walked with you someplace before."

"Did you make jokes about me? You and Pete? When you were bored?"

"What? No."

"But you thought I was fat."

"I thought you were pretty."

"The way they say *lost*, Gooch. You've *lost* the baby. The baby is *lost*."

"I know."

"Seems like, when you lose something, you should be able to find it again."

They spoke simultaneously, Mary saying, "We should get annulled, Gooch, and you should go to Montreal," and Gooch saying, "We'll work a little while and save some money, and we'll think about college. And another baby."

Gooch kissed his bride's cheek and held her chin, waiting until she lifted her face. "You have the prettiest eyes I've ever seen," he said. "And I thought so the first time I saw you standing by the lockers. You turned to look at me and I thought to myself, 'That girl is so pretty.'"

She bit her lip. "And what a shame?"

"And what an ass." He grinned.

She slapped him playfully. "Gooch . . ."

"Now you're my pretty wife. And this might sound corny but it's true, I just can't think of any place I'd rather be than here with you."

"Are those lyrics?"

"They might be."

"You took that Percodan, didn't you?"

He squeezed her hand. Moments passed with the sound of the clock and the shuffle of feet in the corridor, and the notion of a whisper beyond the cracked ivory door. When no one had said a word for the length of a commercial break, and neither had risen to go, it was understood they would stay together.

They never made it to Niagara Falls.

Steadfast Tomorrow

Assuming that denial is a conscious state, Mary Gooch was aware that she had only herself to fool in rejecting the possibility that Gooch might not come home at all. But choosing this day, their silver anniversary, struck her as much too dramatic a gesture. Gooch avoided drama, having suffered his share in his formative years, with demons of his own. His inebriated mother setting fire to the bed when she found out James was cheating with the secretary. Dumping suitcases full of her husband's clothes into the Rideau Canal when she discovered that he was cheating with the babysitter. Throwing a bottle of Southern Comfort through the plate-glass window when he announced he'd taken a job in small-town Leaford.

His sister, Heather, more chronic than demonic, had been in and out of jail the way Mary was on and off diets. As a teenager she'd been brought home by the police twice, run off with a man twice her age after graduation, returned pregnant and drug-addicted when her father died, banished again after a hair-pulling

fight with her mother and some years later arrested for prostitu-
tion in Toronto. When beautiful tragi-thin Heather wasn't jonesing
for a smoke she was following some other destructive path, which
embittered Mary because, without even trying, Heather had it all.
The last time Gooch spoke to Heather, she was living in Buffalo
with the paramedic who'd resuscitated her after her last accidental
overdose.

The stained silver broadloom. The broken glass. The bloody
dishtowel on the floor. Nothing as it was, nothing as it should be.
Mary denied her fear, scrambling what was left in the egg carton, six
perfect eggs, telling herself that the extra portion was in case Gooch
arrived hungry. At the kitchen table she sat in his chair rather than
her own, so as not to face his empty seat, and so that she could see the
door.

Many years ago, she'd suggested Orin do the same after they'd
placed her mother at St. John's, and he confessed he'd lost his appetite. She understood that the habit of eating together must be as difficult to break as the habit of eating alone. As she shifted the last of
the eggs from the skillet to her plate, worry stung her throat, and she
wondered briefly if she might cry. She swallowed instead, another
habit too difficult to break.

A *good* cry. Appropriate under the circumstances. Tears, snot,
choke, gulp, whimper, whine. But not for Mary. Crying, like traveling, a pointless journey to an uncertain place where she couldn't
speak the language and wouldn't like the food. Even after her hysterectomy and the hysteria suggested therein, Mary had not cried
for the babies that would never be. She'd endured a premature and
instant transit to menopause, aching and paining, flashing with heat,
sweating in bed, but not weeping. Grief stuck like a lump in her
throat.

Digging into the junk drawer, she found the little white box with
the little gold bow that Gooch had given her on her birthday last

March. A cellular phone. She'd been annoyed by the gift, considering he knew she didn't *want* a mobile phone. Instead of thank you she'd said, "You know I won't use this, hon. I won't remember to put it in my purse. Besides, who do I need to call?"

Opening the box now, she was surprised to find a card addressed to her. Inside the card Gooch had written carefully, *Welcome to the new world, Mary Gooch. I have written cellphone instructions for connect-o-phobes along with your own personal telephone number on a card you can keep in your wallet. You have to plug it in to charge it, Mare. And you have to keep it in your purse so you'll have it when you need it. Happy Birthday from your favorite husband.*

Reading Gooch's instructions, she discovered that the phone needed to be plugged into an adaptable charger and the battery energized for the better part of a day. She plugged the phone in, delighted when it proclaimed, *Charging.* Gooch would be proud, she thought, and suddenly felt the weight of his disappointment, which she hadn't noticed at the time. How could she have been so ungrateful? She envied the French singer who regretted nothing. She regretted all.

The willow shivered a greeting as Mary limped out the seldom-used front door, dressed for work in her rumpled uniform, her hair gathered into a pony tangle, a stack of old towels in the crook of her arm for the wet seat in the truck. She started for the truck but her attention was caught by a flag of fabric flapping on a high tree branch. Gooch's shirt. Wearing her old winter boots to accommodate the sanitary napkin she'd taped to her bleeding heel, she turned to scan the distant road.

Inhaling the cold air, Mary wished idly, the way children do, that she could blink and Gooch would be on that road. The wind whipped her face, blowing damp leaves against her legs. She had the sense that she was moving uphill when she was certainly staggering down. She climbed into the pickup truck, a tight, crushing feeling in her chest, blood rushing to her cheeks. She squinted, peering through her vascular tunnels. No lights at the other end. The massive coronary? The timing would be perfect. The triangle could close. Orin. Mr. Barkley. Mary Gooch.

She wondered if Gooch, wherever he had gone, would return for her funeral. Then she realized, with familiar panic, that she did not have a thing to wear. There was nothing to do but laugh out loud, which she did. Nothing to wear but her navy blue scrubs. An image of a large woman in an oversized casket, hands crossed over her Raymond Russell Drugstore uniform, those hideous silver roots. She hit the button on the radio, and cranked up the volume, encouraged by Aretha Franklin demanding R-E-S-P-E-C-T as she urged the truck into gear and rolled out on the rain-slicked gravel.

She had underestimated the dampness of the truck's upholstery, and realized too late that she hadn't brought enough towels. She planned to make some joke about her wet ass in the staff room, before Ray said something behind her thick, hunched back. Acceptance. Denial. Anger. She couldn't remember the order of emotions and so felt them all at once. She wondered if people would be able to tell, just by looking, that her husband had not come home.

In the beginning, Mary'd thought often of the end. She envisioned stepping into the house one evening after work to find a note written in Gooch's scrawl saying he'd never meant to hurt her, reminding her they'd been too young to get married and should have ended it a long time ago. His clothes would be gone from the closet. His tools from the garage. (She always imagined he'd take his tools with him.) He would have given some thought to how they would divide their debt, and mentioned it in the note. She had worried that Gooch would leave after the second miscarriage, then after the hysterectomy. She was certain he would leave after their only vicious quarrel, when he stood firm in his opposition to adoption, arguing that his crazy, drug-addicted sister had given three babies up, as if that were enough said.

She had shouted at him, in the only dramatic gesture she could honestly recall, *But I want to be a mother!* He'd turned on his heel and left, but returned three hours later, catching her with her nose in the Kenmore, tearing the leftover roast beef out of her fingers, kissing her hard on the mouth and guiding her to their bed, where he held her gaze and whispered, before his final thrust, "I love you."

Anniversary after anniversary Gooch stayed. After a while she stopped expecting the note. She assumed that, like Orin, Gooch was content to be where he was. Or maybe—like her with her food, Gooch's father with the booze, Heather with her drugs—the habit of their union had become, over time, an impossible one to break.

The phrase "neither here nor there" came to mind when Mary considered her present state. She wondered if she might find Irma somewhere in this altered universe as she drove the path to work—the one of least resistance, a shortcut back through the county instead of along the serene river road.

The maple trees shook their red and yellow leaves over Main Street Leaford. Hooper's Hardware Store. Sprague's Sporting Goods. The upscale ladies' clothing shop owned by the Lavals. Raymond Russell's Drugstore, whose soda counter had been transformed years ago into a more lucrative cosmetics department. In the parking lot behind the drugstore, watching Ray pull up beside her in his shiny Nissan, Mary remembered a time when no one in Baldoon County drove anything but North American. Ray honked the horn impatiently, rolled down the window and barked, "Not there! Go in your regular spot!"

She cranked down her own window, calling back, "But the Laura Secord's coming in today!"

Ray shouted through the wind, "They changed the schedule. It came in last night. When you were off."

Threatening sky overhead and the wind bearing down on her from the open sunroof, Mary climbed out of the truck. Laughing richly, she turned to present her wide, soggy behind. "My seat was wet," she explained. "From the rain."

Ray, scowling, barely glanced her way. "Good. How's Gooch?"

She paused. "He's got the pink eye."

"And what have *you* got, Mary?" He pulled open the back door and snapped the toggles on the master switch, igniting the fluorescent tubes above their heads.

"Watch yourself," he warned as she followed him inside. Blocking the aisle was a large carton of assorted chocolates on which the supplier had scribbled in thick black marker, *For Mary Gooch*. Mary shuddered from a pain in her gut. "Will you do something with that before somebody kills themselves?" he demanded.

Mary bent to pick up the box but they both knew it was only a pretense. Ray sniffed his contempt and lifted it himself, dropping the cartons into Mary's arms without gallantry.

"Sorry," Mary said, thinking that if she were Candace, Ray would carry the box the full distance to her car, balanced on his squat little erection.

The back door to the pharmacy banged shut from the gusting wind as Mary toted the chocolates out to the parking lot. She lifted it into the passenger seat, wincing from the gas in her gut which she tried to, but could not, release. She turned when she heard a car. A sleek gold Cadillac, Gooch's boss, Theo Fotopolis, at the wheel. She squeezed her buttocks together, afraid to foul the air as he parked in the spot beside her.

Theo Fotopolis removed his swarthy frame from the car and strode toward Mary in her navy scrubs. "I called the house," he said, smiling warmly. "Nobody answered so I drove out."

She nodded dumbly.

"You need to fix that window on the back door. You're letting out the heat."

"Yeah."

"Just put a cardboard for now." The Greek lifted his arms in a gesture of confusion. "So what the hell, Mary?" She caught her breath. "What happened with Gooch?" he asked. "Mr. Chung called me an hour ago to say my truck is blocking his produce guy."

"Mr. Chung?"

"Gooch left it there, my truck, behind the restaurant."

"Left the truck? At Mr. Chung's?" Mary shook her head, not understanding. "When? Why?"

"After they closed. Chung said it must have been after midnight. You tell me why."

"But Gooch had that delivery in Windsor last night."

"He didn't make it. It was still in the truck. Didn't he come home last night?"

Mary paused. "No."

"He didn't call you?"

Another pause. "No."

"It's none of my business but . . . does he do this? Does he not come home?"

"No."

"What the hell, then?"

Mary followed him as he paced a circle. "He just parked the truck and what? Walked somewhere? I don't understand. Did he eat there?"

"No one saw him."

"Had he been drinking?" she asked.

"How should I know? *Has* he been drinking?"

She took a moment to consider. "No more than usual."

The pair stood puzzling as a maelstrom of leaves found their legs. Mary had not considered anything resembling this scenario. The Greek's coat pocket played a ringtone and he reached inside for his cellphone. Mary held her breath. Gooch?

The Greek read the name of the caller. He looked at Mary, shaking his head, and returned the phone to his pocket—the call was not from Gooch. "He's been acting, I don't know, he's different since your father died."

How had Mary not noticed that?

"He's been talking about his family. His old man."

"He hated his father."

The Greek shrugged. "Should we call the police?"

"The police?" she asked, alarmed.

"What if Gooch has been mugged or something?"

"Mugged? Gooch? Who in their right mind would mug Gooch? And for what? Twenty-seven dollars and some Scratch 'n' Wins?"

"You can't . . . Mary, I don't want to pry into your private business, but is there any place . . . any place . . . you can think he might have gone? Does he have a friend?"

What did he mean? Did he know something? Had he known all along?

"Did he take anything, Mary? Is anything missing from the house?"

"No," she answered uncertainly.

"Clothes? Suitcase?" His cellphone rang again, and she braced herself. He looked at the number, telling Mary, "My mother's sick back in Athens. I have to take this." He turned away for a short, anxious dialogue in Greek before closing the phone. "Have you checked the bank account?"

"The bank account? Well, no, of course not. Why would I check the bank account?"

"Never mind. I don't know."

"To see if he's taken money?"

"Maybe."

"Gooch wouldn't do that."

"I just don't understand." The Greek shrugged again, his work, such as it was, done. His cellphone rang again. He took the call, speaking rapidly in his mother tongue. "You tell him to call me,

Mary," he instructed Mary when he'd finished his call. "Tell him to phone me when he gets back. And whatever it is, we'll work it out."

Mary knew she would steal his line when finally she heard from Gooch. *Whatever it is, we'll work it out.* Watching the gold Cadillac disappear, she released, with distinct relief, a symphony of wind.

Ray, standing at the door behind her, hollered, "Nice one, Mary. Class-ee."

The decent thing would have been to pretend he hadn't heard. How long had he been standing there? He held the door open, widening his eyes. "Let's go. Come on! Inventory time!" He clapped out the syllables. "In-ven-tor-y."

Mary found herself paralyzed, keys tingling in her hands, considering the word. *Inventory.* Yes, that's what she needed to do. She needed to take stock. Was she getting this right? Gooch had parked the delivery truck behind Chung's Chinese Restaurant sometime in the night and no one knew where he was? Was this how Irma had felt when life finally stopped making any sense?

"What are you waiting for, Mary? Let's *go!*"

She looked up at the clouds racing past, the sun exposed in fragile, shifting rays.

"I'm not kidding," Ray sneered. "You haven't been pulling your weight around here, Mary. And I'm not the only one who's noticed."

Acceptance, denial — those could wait. Anger.

"Get to work, Mary."

"Go to *hell*, Ray."

In Ray's expression Mary saw that she had indeed said the words out loud. Climbing into her truck, stabbing the key in the ignition, thrusting the gear into reverse, she peeled out of the parking lot without checking her rearview mirror, seized by a burning feeling in her chest as she played back the conversation with The Greek. Gooch gone. Parked the delivery truck. Disappeared. On their silver anniversary.

In all her many years of sleepless nights, Mary had felt the steadfastness of tomorrow implied in the constancy of each broken dawn. Tomorrow, like greeting-card love, was patient and kind. Tomorrow was encouraging, endlessly forgiving. She had not counted on the sudden betrayal of tomorrow, with whom she thought she shared some silent, tacit agreement.

Lightning

Had Gooch been there that morning, he would have plunked down across from Mary as he always did, air rushing out of the cracked red vinyl chair, with his nose in the American newspapers that served the area, stopping to read aloud from the *Free Press* or *News* while she pretended to listen. Gooch loved America, her politics, sports, musicians, authors, her gift of second chances, and Mary felt some pity for him when he mooned over the U.S. of A. He was in love, and the object of his affections didn't even know he existed.

Speeding down the winding river road under a canopy of flapping geese, she felt the burning in her chest ignite and spread. Gooch. Gone. Where? She felt that she was not so much driving as being driven as the black sky rose up in her rearview mirror.

Gooch would have informed her about the weather watch before falling silent with the sports pages. He knew how his wife loved a good storm. Mary didn't have time for the newspapers, too intent on her broken promises, too busy with her failures, too preoccupied by her hunger. Life outside of Leaford was not so much irrelevant to her as it was unconsidered. She didn't view current affairs as essential education—more as a choice, like entertainment. *Crisis in the Middle East* was a dense novel she chose not to read. *Genocide in Africa* was unconscionable, unbelievable, a badly written movie that got terrible reviews. *Global Warming?* Doesn't sound funny. There's a *whole wide world outside of Leaford.* Wasn't that what Gooch had said?

At last Mary parked the truck in the lot behind the apartment that overlooked the river in Chatham. So this was what it felt like to master one's end, she thought. Not a life but a marriage. And not with narcotics but with the truth. She knew what she had to do, but her resolve was not quite firm enough, and like a gunslinger slugging back that final shot of whisky in a western, she sought courage in Laura Secord.

A reprieve in the chocolate. Mary might have described tearing open the cardboard as something like rapture, enveloped as she was by the heavenly scent of cocoa, and lifted by a sense of well-being. Breathing deeply, she peeled the plastic wrapping from one box, and another and another, tossing aside the lids, digging at the confections, shoveling two and three at a time into her unhinged mandible. She didn't care that chocolate squares were spilling onto the seats and floor as she swiped aside the fluted paper cups. Humming, moaning, her pursuit vaguely erotic, *That's enough,* she told herself, and then *Just one more.*

The last time she had been in the corridors of the tall, slender building, which always smelled faintly of mildew, she had said her final goodbye to Orin. At least that's what she told herself. In fact he'd been the one to say goodbye, "See you tomorrow, Murray," to which she'd responded with regrettable harshness, "I picked up a shift, Pop! I'll be late! So don't expect a hot supper!"—which was not goodbye at all.

On that night she had stopped, as she always did, at Sylvie La-fleur's door, not to knock, not to visit, not to thank the older woman for her kindness to Orin, but to listen. To the sound of the television broadcasting *Wheel of Fortune* or some other game show in which regular folk won a fortune in cash and prizes. The sound of the microwave beeping. Dishes clattering in the sink. The balcony door sliding open when Sylvie went out to smoke. Lonely sounds, comforting and familiar, for in them she heard the music of her own life.

The gray carpeting in the building's hallway was soiled with muddy imprints from tramping boots, but apart from that the place seemed unchanged. Mary passed the door of the apartment where her father had lived, and didn't feel inclined to trace the outline of the number on the wall beside the buzzer as she had thought she might. She could hear the sound of loud music — punk? rap? she wasn't sure — coming from within. She'd been told that a single mother had taken the place and was likely to be evicted because of her unruly teenaged son.

She reached Sylvie's door and stopped. She listened. No sound within. She waited. Pressed the buzzer. Nothing. Then she set to banging on the door, but like she wanted out, not in. The sound of the music ceased in Orin's old apartment and the door was flung open by a sullen boy with purple hair and kohl-lined eyes. "What?"

"Sorry," she said. "I was looking for Sylvie Lafleur. Do you know her?"

"Yeah."

"Do you know where she is?"

The boy shrugged and pulled the door shut. Something feline about his expression reminded Mary of her mother — that catlike smile, wary and remote. Irma had fixed that smile on Jimmy Gooch so many Septembers ago, when he'd announced that he and Mary had decided, given her pregnancy, to be married.

Irma'd asked him directly, "You've considered the alternatives?"

"There are no alternatives," Orin had countered, folding his lean arms over his buckled chest.

There had been a vase of glorious pink roses on Dr. Ruttle's desk,

which Irma would have considered too feminine a touch for a man's
office, if she had been waiting with Mary in the examining room the
week before. Mary already suspected that she was pregnant — the
cessation of menses, the swollen breasts, the nausea — but when Dr.
Ruttle confirmed this, she responded with surprise and confusion.
Gooch had, after all, *promised* that she could not get pregnant if he
withdrew before deposit.

Flushed and sweating in the cool September air, munching the
stack of saltines she'd been keeping in her purse to stem her nausea,
Mary had walked from Ruttle's office through the old part of town
to the high school, where Gooch was taking a special class to make
up for the time and grade point average lost to the accident. He was
hoping to start university in January. With the choice of institution
now independent of its athletic record, he'd promised Mary that he
would enroll in Windsor, which was under an hour away. Mary'd
found a nearby night school offering a course in fashion and design,
but she hadn't applied. She was too busy with Gooch and working
at the drugstore and keeping house for her parents, and hadn't got
around to it.

Wading down the high school hallway for the first time since
spring graduation, Mary could not conceive of a way to tell Gooch
about her pregnancy. She glimpsed her huge boyfriend through the
open double doors to the parking lot, leaning against the tan Duster,
shaking his head fatally as though he'd already heard the news. She
was surprised to see cigarette smoke swirling near his ear, and Sylvie
Lafleur beside him, childlike next to the giant teen. Sylvie glanced
up to find Mary watching from the shadow of the hallway, waved,
then ground the cigarette with the toe of her shoe and started in
Mary's direction.

"*You* talk to your boyfriend," she called on her approach. "Tell
him it's a *crime* to throw away his future." She dropped her *h*'s and
th's and said *'im* instead of *him*, and *trow* instead of *throw*. "There are

so many options. So many *choices*." She sounded, briefly, like a tiny white French Ms. Bolt.

The future. Although she tried to see the big picture, Mary found her canvas painted over, scene upon scene, not quite right. A bad angle. A poor perspective. A landscape where there should be a portrait. All the pictures vandalized with graffiti, the same dripping red word, *Gooch*. "Pick one, Murray," Orin would say, holding a bouquet of assorted lollipops. "Pick. *One*."

"She's giving me shit because I don't want to go to McGill," Gooch explained, after Ms. Lafleur disappeared back into the school. "She's already worked it out. Which I did *not* ask her to do."

"Oh."

"I'm not going."

"Okay."

"If I did go, I'd want you to come with me."

"Come with you?"

"Come with me. Or I'd still see you on weekends."

"McGill is in Montreal. That's seven hours away."

"I can't leave my mother anyway. Not now. This thing with Asswipe isn't gonna last. I can't leave her. With Heather."

"You don't even speak French, Gooch."

"The journalism school is outstanding."

Outstanding. Such an American word. "Yeah?"

"She thinks she can help me get assistance. There's the insurance money from my dad, but she thinks I should save that."

"Okay."

"She thinks I'm a gifted writer."

"She does?" Mary didn't mean to sound so surprised. She'd never read anything Gooch had written, even though she knew he'd received the highest grades for his efforts. She crumpled into his arms, as sorry for the banal tone of her announcement as she was to give him the news. "Oh Gooch," she said, "I'm pregnant."

On an evening several days later, gathered around a boozy

campfire at the lake, Mary and Gooch announced their engagement to their friends. The girls squealed their delight and fawned over Mary, envying the way her cup ranneth over, while the boys — young men, really, old enough to drink legally, vote, go to war — responded with short nods and thumps to Gooch's broad back.

No one wondered if the pair was getting married because Mary was pregnant. They already knew that. And it didn't seem a particularly poor decision to any of them. The greatest tragedy, as the young people saw it, was already behind them. Gooch's fate sealed by the accident. He would not go to an American college on a basketball scholarship. They would never see him play on network TV. He had lost his chance, at the sharpest bend in the river, to be extraordinary. Gooch got drunk that night, his tolerance for alcohol out of step with his tolerance for tragedy, and threw Mary the keys when it was time to drive home.

Aware that errant recollections of bygone days never brought comfort or deeper understanding, Mary wondered why she seemed incapable of releasing the past. Her rambling mind seemed to have no more restraint than her wanting mouth. Even struggling out the doors of the apartment building on the river, she thought not of where she was but where she used to be. She missed the sound of her father's voice.

In the white noise of wind Mary heard the ringing of a phone. Pushing down the walkway, she felt the sound like a whip. Punishing. If she had that cellphone in her purse instead of charging on the counter at home, Gooch would be calling. As he was calling her now, she felt sure. He'd likely left a message at the drugstore. And tried her at the house. She imagined him frantic, calling around to find her, as if *she* were the one who hadn't come home.

Reconfigured and Reborn

Outside the apartment building, Mary's attention was caught by the neon lights of the convenience store across the road. Tasting the chocolate and nuts embedded in her molars, she badly needed a drink. And something salty if she had to sit in the truck on surveillance, waiting for Sylvie Lafleur to return. She considered the distance and the darkening sky, and the heaviness of her legs and the cut on her foot, wondering if she should drive. Calculating her distance from the truck, she heaved a sigh and started for the road with slow, percussive steps.

Typically, Mary disliked shopping in convenience stores, with their dearth of fruits and vegetables or boxes of fiber cereal to conceal the cartful of scrumptious junk foods she would actually eat. And she hated the way the foreign clerks watched her drizzling orange cheese on stale nachos or filling gallon cups with soda or lifting snack bags to the counter, thinking their own sniggering cultural versions of *Lady, you need that like a hole in the head.*

Entering the store Mary should have been shocked, but wasn't in the least, to see Sylvie Lafleur at the counter, paying for a carton of king-size cigarettes. This meeting of fat wife and slender mistress in an overbright store on a stormy fall day was simply life in Leaford, a town too small for coincidence. Rain slicker tossed carelessly over pajamas, fine hair curled from the damp air, the French woman looked withered as winter. She smiled seeing Mary Gooch standing before her in her navy scrubs, just as she always did when they chanced to meet. "Mary."

Mary cleared her throat. "Hello, Ms. Lafleur."

"I haven't seen you in so long. Are you well?" Sylvie rasped, though the answer seemed apparent.

Gooch sprang to Mary's mind, the way he would answer a person, when they asked how he was with *Livin' the dream. I'm livin' the dream.* People were charmed by his response, and especially amused when he said it within the context of hauling a sofa bed up two flights of stairs. "Fine. And you?"

Sylvie opened her carton of cigarettes, tearing at the foil with her chipped, stained fingers, laughter resigned. "I spend all day smoking in my pajamas. Retirement suits me, don't you think?"

In her scrutiny of the woman's aging face, Mary could not find a scintilla of guilt. No remorse. No apology. No mea. No culpa. A skinny, amoral *slut*, she decided.

"How's Gooch?" Sylvie inquired innocently. And there it was — a twitch in the eyelid. A blink. A shift. A *tell*. Gooch had taught her about tells, those nervous twitches: a scratch, a pucker, a cough, that tip off the liar's bluff. He could always tell a tell, he'd say proudly, which was why he usually won at cards. Watching Sylvie twitch, Mary felt relieved, like a mysteriously ill person upon finally receiving a diagnosis, to know that it wasn't all in her mind.

Mary admired her own directness, even if it was all she had left. "Gooch didn't come home last night. I thought you might know where he is."

The older woman squeezed her eyes shut, shrinking one vertebra at a time until Mary felt like the big fat bully to Sylvie's scrawny little kid. "Let's go outside. Can we go outside so I can smoke?"

Mary briefly enjoyed the thought that the other woman was *dying* for a cigarette. "Do you know where he is, Ms. Lafleur?"

"I don't, Mary. I don't know where is Gooch."

"He didn't go to your place last night?"

Behind the counter, the Korean man thrust open the hot-dog case. Having served Mary on a number of occasions, he was anxious to get on with the transaction. "Three? Works?"

Mary shook her head without looking at the man. "Did he call you?"

Sylvie glanced briefly at the clerk before launching in a whisper. "You want to do this here? Okay. But you must know I haven't seen Gooch in years. *Years.*"

That wasn't technically true. They'd run into Sylvie just the prior month at the Kinsmen Corn Roast. And they often met, the three of them, in the hallway, when Gooch came along on her visits to Orin. But Mary knew what Sylvie meant, and was inclined to believe her.

"And it was one time. Only. You must *know* this."

Mary was more mystified by this than she'd ever been by the torrid affair she'd always assumed.

"He used to come, it's true, but that was years ago, and only to sleep it off a little on the sofa. We talked. Let's go outside now," she said, soothing her impatient cigarette.

"You talked?"

"Politics. Movies. It's so boring, really." There were tears growing in the older woman's eyes, a babyish crinkle in her chin. It was because she wanted a cigarette that badly, or was genuinely remorseful. "Sometimes I made him cinnamon toast," she confessed.

So there it was. Sylvie Lafleur had cared deeply for her illicit young friend, shared his passion for the planet, a fascination with world politics, an appreciation of old movies. She'd stroked his hair while he slumbered on her sofa, and fed him toast before he drove home to his hapless wife. It was not a lover but a *mother* that Gooch had needed so desperately, and had found in his guidance counselor.

"One time?"

"I promise."

The promise didn't ring as hollow as it should have. "When?"

"It was the last time. It's more than ten years, Mary. I told him he couldn't come any more. That's it. The last time. The only time."

"Why?"

"Why?"

"Yes, why? The one time? Why then?"

Sylvie took a moment before she admitted, "It was after my mother died. I was turning forty-five. I was feeling so *old*. It was already years since any man touched me. I was a little drunk. I thought it might never happen for me again. He pitied me. I felt like such a fool after."

As Sylvie blushed and huffed, fiddling with her cigarette, Mary remembered reading something about French women believing that all women of a certain age must make a choice between their forward faces and lagging behinds. There was some sensible reasoning involved; one needed fat to plump out the wrinkles and make youthful the face, but that same fat weighted the nether cheeks like marbles in a sack. It was obvious in Sylvie Lafleur's sunken eyes and crepe skin, apparent in the road map of vertical wrinkles at her mouth and the horizontal ones at her eyes, that she had chosen to save her ass.

"I'm sorry, Mary. I'm glad to have the chance to say so. I'm so sorry." Sylvie shrugged again, glancing past Mary at the darkening sky. "Can we go out now, so I can smoke? *Please?*"

"No," Mary decided, surprising herself. "And me? Did you talk with my husband about me?"

"Not really. He would say sometimes how he wanted you to be happy."

"But where was he all those nights since? All those other nights?" Mary didn't really expect an answer. She might as well have been asking the Korean clerk.

"It's been so many years. I don't *know* him anymore. I don't know where is Gooch." She paused. "I hope you can forgive me."

Realizing that she was blocking the path to the door, and that there was nothing left to say, Mary stepped aside to let Sylvie by. She had no sense of time, and felt confused when she turned to find that the French woman had disappeared like a puff of smoke from one of her evil cigarettes, gone so quickly that Mary wondered if she'd dreamed the whole conversation. She found the eyes of the Korean watching her, and held up her hand to show three fingers.

Waiting for the hot dogs, Mary leaned against the automated cash machine, remembering her conversation with The Greek — hours ago? Days ago? Years ago? The unseen clock. The spinning hands spiraling out of control. *Did you check the bank account?*

She reached into her purse to find the access card, which she had never used before. Though she'd argued passionately with Gooch, she didn't so much care about the redundancy of human tellers; she was simply too lazy to learn something new. She made several clumsy attempts at inserting the silver card into the slot, and felt smug when it was finally accepted. The machine catered to idiots, just as Gooch had promised. She had no trouble remembering the code — the month and day of their anniversary. Today.

She followed the prompts, asking the machine for twenty dollars and pressing the button *yes* when it politely inquired if she'd like to know her balance. She extracted her card and yanked out the receipt. She read the number. Checked again. She knew the balance in their joint bank account — three hundred and twenty-four dollars. Gooch had warned that's all they had. This number at the bottom of the thin white sheet was incorrect. She jammed the silver card back in the slot as the Korean rang up the sale, asking the machine for another twenty dollars and another receipt. The total balance, incorrect again, less twenty more dollars. Mary puzzled over the paper. Something was wrong. In fact, everything was wrong. Why should the account balance be right?

She slid the plastic card back into the machine, ignoring the Korean and the hot dogs, pushing the buttons without pausing to read, instantly expert, asking the machine not for its typical offer but for more. Would you like another amount? Yes. Not to exceed four hundred dollars. Fine then, four hundred dollars. And a receipt? Yes, please.

She waited as the machine clicked away, anxious that the police might burst through the doors to arrest her. She was asking for more money than she knew they had. Wasn't that the same as writing a fraudulent check? When the machine spat out the four hundred dollars in twenties, she snatched it from the cash cradle and shoved it into the deep pockets of her uniform before the Korean, or God, could see. She looked at the receipt. Minus twenty. Minus twenty. Minus four hundred dollars. But the balance was still wrong.

She left the store, the Korean man, the hot dogs and the soda, clutching the receipt in her hands, assaulted by a fierce driving wind. Mary wondered how sliver-thin Sylvie made it home, and scanned the black sky, expecting to see her wispy form cast about by the currents, like those insipid plastic shopping bags.

Gooch gone. An excess of *twenty-five thousand dollars* in the bank account. *Where is God when you need her,* she thought.

As if to answer the question — as if God had been waiting in the wings and just got the cue — there was sudden thunderous applause and the black day sky was lit by staggered, vengeful lightning. No water effects, just awesome pyrotechnics. Mary made her way across the road, trucking through the still-green grass along the side of the apartment building, the slip of paper pinched between thumb and forefinger the way customers carried their prescriptions at Raymond Russell's. The mystery of the additional funds beckoned, along with her rising fear that Gooch's disappearance was not accidental.

With his dark hood pulled up to hide his purple hair, Mary didn't at first recognize the teenage boy squatting near the back entrance of the building as the boy who was now living in her father's old apartment. He appeared, cloaked in black, like a sullen crow, a giant outcast from the mocking clan dotting the branches of a nearby tree. In the charcoal clouds above there were quick explosive electrical charges, swirling currents and a blinding charge of light across the sky. Not shy sheet lightning but frantic fork lightning, brilliant zagged bolts, protesting shockwaves, rage of thunder, arcing white tentacles dying, reconfigured and reborn. Blazing. Angry. The God Irma grew up with.

It was not Mary's intention to look at the boy with the purple hair or his to look at her, but their eyes met, and at precisely the same time as the boy breathed, "Holy shit!" Mary whispered, "Holy cow!" He drew his hood forward and cast down his eyes once more. The moment over, fleeting as an orgasm and fleeing, like Ms. Bolt. Gooch. The crows shivered and cawed from the barren tree, *Gone, gone, gone.*

Finding the handle on the truck door, Mary climbed inside, assailed by the rich scent of chocolate. She rested her head and closed her eyes, unable to resist the voices of her parents whispering into her ear. *Well, if he wasn't having an affair with Frenchie, he must have been having an affair with someone,* Irma would have said. Orin had been fond of Gooch but would be no less pragmatic about his disappearance: *Well, the only thing to do is find him, I guess. Confront him. If you think you can't let him go. Have you called his mother?*

Called his mother? Why would she call his *mother?* Mary didn't want to alarm Eden if there was nothing to be alarmed about. She was also unprepared to admit to the woman (whom she had telephoned dutifully at noon Pacific Time the last Sunday of each month for the first ten years of their marriage, and who had always sounded equally surprised and disappointed — "Oh Mary, it's *you*") that she'd been right all along. She couldn't call Gooch's mother anyway. The cellular phone was still charging in the socket at home.

She'd told Gooch, when he'd given her the phone, that she would never remember to bring it with her. She also knew she'd never figure out how to use it, since she feared the simplest technology, which, like the automated teller, seemed to offer further opportunity for failure. Every machine, except the cash register at work, was a *gadget* to confound her. For similar reasons, she'd objected when Gooch wanted to get a personal computer "like everyone else in the free world." She'd argued that they couldn't afford it, but she'd also read enough advice columns to worry that the Internet was a passport to porn and would lead to other unsavory addictions. Gooch had called her a Luddite. She didn't know what that meant but she wished she were not one. Then she would have a cellphone, and she could call *someone*.

Legs fast asleep, numb as they often went when she sat too long, she searched through the open sunroof. Still no rain. Slowly, because her fingers were stiff and cold, she inserted the key into the ignition, enjoying the sharp pins pricking her calves as blood streamed to her starving muscles.

Setting the truck in reverse, glancing in the mirror to note the concrete light-stand to her rear, she didn't immediately pull out of her spot. Gooch's face before he left for work flashed before her, and the sound of his silky voice asking about her wardrobe for the anniversary dinner. The genuine way he said it was a hell of a thing to be married for twenty-five years. How he'd urged her to buy something *nice*. Her right foot heavy on the truck's brake, riding the rapids of eternal hope, she didn't notice the approach of the crow. When the bird dove through the sunroof to claim more of the nutty treasures he and his mates had been stealing while she was gone, the thief seemed as shocked by her presence as she was by his intrusion.

Mary screamed. The startled bird cawed, flying not back through the open sunroof but straight into the windshield and then, flapping madly, at Mary, who in batting the bird, released her foot from the brake, inadvertently jamming on the gas, crashing the rear of the truck into the light-stand. Black. Feathers. Black.

Lifting her head off the scalloped steering wheel, Mary expected to see blood. The bird was gone. The chocolate, she noticed now, picked and pecked and shredded on the seat beside her—had the birds done that? Or had she? There was an ache in her forehead but she couldn't find a contusion, not even the smallest of bumps. She shifted her eyes when a shadow appeared in her periphery. The teenage boy. She could tell by the look on his face that he'd witnessed the whole thing.

"Fuck!" he breathed, opening the door and reaching over her gut to set the car in park, and to turn the key on the still humming motor. "Are you okay? That was unbelievable. The bird was like . . ." He gestured wildly with his arms. "And you were like"—he batted at the air in caricature—"fuckin' *unbelievable.*"

"I hit my head."

The boy drew his cellphone like a gun from his pocket. Mary stopped him. "No. I'm okay. How's the truck?"

He stepped back to survey the damaged Ford. "Built tough." He grinned.

Mary took a deep breath, feeling her head again. The space between her eyes. It hurt when she pressed down.

"Sure you don't want me to call an ambulance?"

"I'm sure. I'm sorry."

He noticed for the first time the mess of Laura Secord strewn about the front seat. "Holy shit!" he said.

"I'm okay."

Closing the door reluctantly, he remarked, "You don't *look* okay."

Sweet androgynous boy. He didn't know that she never looked okay. She cranked the window down. "Thank you. Really. Sorry."

The pounding rain, though expected, surprised them both. The boy tugged at his hood and hurried off as Mary turned the key in the ignition, charged by the sound of the motor and the compliance of the shifting gears. She waved, watching the scrawny boy resume his crouch in the shelter of the doorway, hoping that his wait wouldn't be long or, like hers, in vain.

There were no other cars on Leaford's roads. No birds in Leaford's trees. No humans with umbrellas on her sidewalks near the library or the mall. They'd all read the paper. It occurred to Mary, driving through the storm, her windshield wipers droning heavily, righteous rain battering her scalp, that Gooch might have had an accident. He could have slipped in Chung's parking lot on his way to get his Combo Number 5 — it *had* been wet last night. He could have fallen and hit his head and lost his memory, or his reason. She scanned the road for her phantom husband. Like the phantom pain she still felt around the time her period would have come. Like the phantom fat she'd carried around in senior year, even when she was at her most slender.

Competing with the thunder and lightning, the rain pelted Mary's face through the sunroof. Furnace repair. Sunroof. Anniversary dinner. Mother's new meds. Address issue of twenty-five thousand dollars in the account. Gooch's whereabouts? Forget the list — cry. *Let it out.* "It'd be good, Mare," Gooch had often said, "if you could let it out."

She reached for the detritus of Laura Secord beside her, realizing that she'd eaten little more than chocolate the entire day and it was already well past noon. Bringing the square to her mouth, she was overcome by nausea and tossed the chocolate back onto the seat.

The bank was quiet and empty with a lone teller in sight when Mary entered, shaking herself like a wet dog on the rubber mat. A young woman in a beige suit met her at the desk, frowning. "Nasty out there, hmmm?"

Mary assumed that she meant the world in general, and agreed. As she was virtually a stranger to the bank, the teller studied her quietly, waiting. "I just need to know the balance on my account," Mary said.

The woman smiled, taking Mary's bank card and processing it. She raised a brow when the machine answered her query, and handed the slip of paper to Mary. Twenty-five thousand dollars more than they had. Mary was afraid to call attention to the error, in case it wasn't an error. If Gooch had put that money in the bank, those gains could only have been ill gotten and surely had something to do with his disappearance.

Arriving home with no recollection of the drive from the bank to her house, Mary parked the truck and waded through the pouring rain toward the front door, disturbed by the mystery of the money, deciding that Gooch must have lost his mind and robbed a bank. Or The Greek.

She smelled the dead furnace and felt the sting of cold air from the broken glass at the back door as she moved through the small living room, where Gooch liked to watch golf and black-and-white movies, and toward the bloodstained hallway. Her eyes fell upon the kitchen table, where she both feared and hoped to see a note from him.

The refrigerator strummed her pain as she reached for the aspirin in the cupboard above the stove, shaking two, then three tablets into her palm, wondering resentfully why she and Gooch continued to keep medication *out of reach* when they had no children and never would. She swallowed the tablets with her saliva rather than bothering to run the tap, shivering when she realized how drenched she was.

She sloshed toward the telephone, wishing they'd bought that answering machine Gooch had suggested in case he'd been calling all day, in case someone had needed to leave an important message, though the fact that the telephone was not currently ringing off the hook gave her some perverse satisfaction. After testing for a dial tone, she punched Gooch's number from the emergency card. "It's

Mary Gooch. At 3:35 p.m. I'm sorry to be a bother. I'm calling for my husband again. If you could tell Jimmy Gooch I'm home now. And could he please call me there. Thank you. Sorry."

If you think you're not ready to let him go, her imagined Orin had said. She squeezed down the bloodstained hallway. Her unmade bed beckoned. A rest, she thought. To sleep. To dream. Regretting her harsh words with the furnace, she settled her weight down and pulled the bloodstained quilt up to her chin.

Dream Sequence

The ringing telephone drifted inside Mary Gooch's troubled dreamscape and chased her like a stinging wasp over a barren Leaford horizon. She woke frightened, groggy, swatting at the receiver. It was Joyce from St. John's with a reminder that her check was due, that Irma's new meds needed a signature, and that the potluck had been changed to Tuesday night. Mary muttered some polite compliance and hung up the phone, shaking herself awake with dubious recollections — Gooch not home? Sylvie Lafleur not an evil whore? And had the accident in the parking lot actually happened? The surplus in the bank account? The previous hours felt like a dream sequence, and just as confounding in life as it would be in a movie.

The telephone rang again and she drew it to her lap, answering, "Yes Joyce," because Joyce always called back with some forgotten detail. "Yes. I'll do the cake for the raffle."

Where are you, Gooch? And why is there twenty-five thousand dollars in our account? Dialing Gooch's cellphone number, which she had quickly learned by heart, she waited for the familiar stranger's voice. The liquid sky suggested midnight but the clock read seven-fifteen p.m. She'd slept only a few hours. "It's Mary Gooch calling. Again. I'm sorry. If you could tell my husband I'm very worried and would very much appreciate his call. It's seven-fifteen."

On occasion, reading a celebrity questionnaire, Mary would attempt to distill her existence as addressed by questions like *Happiest Moment?* and *Greatest Achievement?* Under *Most Used Phrase?* she would answer unhesitatingly, "I'm sorry." She apologized for the way she ate, with a disturbing lack of discrimination. *Biggest Regret?*—not telling Gooch about the miscarriage on the eve of their wedding. *Greatest Love?*—obvious. *Greatest Extravagance?*—obvious. *Worst Habit?*—obvious. Mary envied drinkers and gamblers, for whom addictions were not necessarily outerwear. *Best Physical Trait?* She'd have to say eyes. On the question *Greatest Adventure?* she had no adventures to describe, great or small. And she had yet to define her life's goals, so also skipped the question *Proudest Achievement?* She shuddered to think how Gooch would answer the questions, if he dared to do so honestly.

The Kenmore sang down the channel of bloodstained hall and, like the doomed sailor, Mary sought to answer the siren call, lifting her feet off the bed and swinging them to the carpet with a thud. The refrigerator hummed more loudly, tone pitched high, but she could not persuade the rest of her freight to couple with her waiting legs. She paused, her wheezy breath drowning the call from the kitchen. The phone rang and she reached for it, answering, "Yes Joyce."

There was silence. Breathing. "Gooch?" she blurted. She felt his ear on the other end of the line, the weight of his sadness, the depth of his love. She thought of the hundreds of things she'd saved up to say, but could not shift one from her brain to her lips. "Please come home, Gooch," she finally managed. "Whatever it is, we'll work it out."

There was a pause, shallow breathing, and then a familiar voice, feminine and sly. "Mary?"

Wendy. Calling from the restaurant at the lake. "Mary?"

It was Mary's turn to pause now. She cleared her throat. "We won't be making it tonight, Wendy. We can't make it."

"Can't *make* it?" Wendy repeated. "It's *your* anniversary, Mary. We're all here for *you*. What's going on with Gooch? Did you two have a fight? Is this serious? I think you owe us an —"

Wendy had a good deal more to say, and was still saying it as Mary hung up. She pictured the six of them gathered at the table she'd reserved months ago, with a view of the wide, choppy lake. After the initial "Oh my Gods" and "Holy shits" and whatever other profanities exclaimed the news, she guessed they would decide to stay at the restaurant and go on with the meal. Wendy would dine on the Gooches misfortune, and bore the others with her bitterness over the time wasted on the anniversary scrapbook. Pete would wonder why Gooch hadn't said anything to him, besides asking idly one day, "Are you *happy*?" to which his oldest friend had responded, "Are you *high*?" By dessert Kim would be glaring at François, who'd inherited a wandering eye. No one would be surprised by the fracture of Jimmy and Mary Gooch. It had only ever been a matter of time.

Mary watched the telephone, wondering if she should call the police. But what would she tell them? Twenty-five thousand dollars had appeared mysteriously in her account and her husband had not come home. The scenario was incriminating. She exercised her sporadic belief in God, appealing for a new pre-emptive miracle. *Just please let Gooch come home,* she begged.

The ringing telephone. An answered prayer. Her heart leapt. Then she heard The Greek's baritone on the other end of the line and braced herself for news. But he hadn't heard from Gooch either, and was, like Mary, increasingly worried and confused. His questions took the tone of interrogation, and Mary felt accused. When The Greek asked again if she'd checked the bank account, she denied that she had, realizing how fully she'd made her bed and lain in it.

In the bedroom, she threw open the closet door. Nothing was

missing. Gooch's lean wardrobe from the tall man's shop in Windsor was on one side and her own mess of plus-sized discount disasters on the other. Mary had never searched for clues of infidelity before, but had read enough advice columns and watched enough prime-time to know what she was looking for. Lipstick stains on his collars. No. The smell of perfume? She couldn't smell anything, nothing at all. Rogue blonde hairs. No. Love notes or telephone numbers folded into squares in the pockets of his jeans. No. She rooted behind the winter coats, where they kept the boxes of cards and photos and VCR tapes, but nothing was amiss. She shut the closet and glanced around the room, spying on the dresser a shoebox labeled *Business Info*. It was open, the lid tossed aside, piled high with crumpled receipts. She looked at the various chits for gas and dining that Gooch submitted for reimbursement from The Greek.

She found a bill for a restaurant with a Toronto address, noting the date, which was the previous month, and the time, early afternoon. Card member James Gooch had lunched on the *dly sp* and *grll chk snd* accompanied by two draft beers at a place on Queen Street. She didn't know Gooch had gone to Toronto.

Catching sight of herself in the mirror as she passed, Mary thought of the hundreds of television shows she'd watched about criminal investigations, the search for evidence, the thrill of justice. She settled down on the bed to examine the receipts more closely. Nothing alarming. No motel slips or invoices from jewelers or lingerie shops. The most shocking chits were for gas. She had had no idea it cost that much to fill the delivery truck's tank. No wonder the planet was in peril! There was a receipt from an auto body shop in Leamington—Gooch had mentioned trouble with the delivery truck. There was an unfilled sleeping pill prescription from Dr. Ruttle, which was surprising, since Gooch slept like a baby. The rest were restaurant bills that confirmed Gooch's habit of healthy eating and his penchant for a cool draft with his midday meal.

Mary was nearly through the box when she found another receipt from a Toronto restaurant. The same restaurant, dated the week before — egg-white omelet and draft beer. And then another dated the week before that — fish special with salad and beer. And another, and another, twice in the same week. And another. Gooch hadn't mentioned that he'd been to Toronto six times the past few months, but then again, she'd never asked. Still, evidence of nothing. He'd driven there numerous times over the years to various manufacturers from whom The Greek ordered specialty items for the store. She had not a scrap to confront him with when he finally made it home. So what if he enjoyed dining at a place called Bistro 555?

The refrigerator hummed, but Mary didn't hear it over the ticking of the clock. *Please. Call. Please. Call.* She looked up at the ceiling, as she'd done a thousand times before, noticing a wide crack stretching directly over the bed. The fissure had been there all the time, grown from thin to thick, short to long, and she'd never noticed it. Or it had appeared mysteriously in the night, the way Gooch had disappeared.

She reached for the phone once more and dialed Gooch's number. When it was her turn to speak she said, "It's Jimmy's wife again." Then, after a pause, "Will you tell him . . . Happy Anniversary."

Focused on the crack, she recalled the moment when she had left her body on the wet leaves. But in the recollection it was not her own body over which her spirit hovered but Gooch's. With that image, Mary left her conscious chaos for the clarity of dreams.

Nothing Nefarious

Trips to the toilet and to drink water from the tap. Aspirin for that pain between her eyes. Experimental dreams. Glimpses of light. Weight of dark. Tap water. Urine. Flush. Gooch's face. Light. Dark. Water. Pee. Flush. Gooch. Mary. The night clock. Screaming at Wendy to please go away. Endlessly ticking, then ticking no more, the batteries dislodged and thrown to the floor. Heat — the furnace hadn't died after all.

In the hallway an amber lamp switched on in a marvel of timed circuitry, stealing into the room like a secret lover. Mary eased her legs as the light adored her dunes, licked her licorice nipples, and sucked her frosted toes. She pulled her lids apart and looked around the room. With the drapes drawn, she was unable to guess between day and night.

Mary rose, her foot aching where she'd been cut, confused by the sequence of her stories and their relation to her dreams. The digital clock on Gooch's side was blinking, which suggested that power had been lost and restored sometime in the night. Her own thumping clock was dead. That hadn't been a dream — she'd taken the batteries out at two o'clock. A.m. or p.m., she couldn't be sure. The dense gray clouds she could see through the slit in the drapes failed to disclose the sun's position. She had the panicky feeling that she was late. Too late. For whatever it was.

As she pulled back the drapes, her eyes were stung by the sharp white snow laid out over the landscape, so that she couldn't find the border of the yard or the site of Mr. Barkley's grave. A thick layer weighting the willow and drifting over the frozen towels in the truck. This much snow in October? Something of a miracle.

Instinctively she looked at the telephone at the bedside, noticing that the receiver had fallen off. She returned it, waited for a dial tone and dialed her husband's number. It was the voice who made the apology this time: "We're sorry. This number is no longer in service."

Mary set the phone back down and bought several deep breaths before she dialed The Greek, who was also listed among the emergency numbers. When Fotopolis didn't answer that line she called the store directly and was surprised to learn that The Greek was gone too, flown off to Athens last week to be with his dying mother. Mary cleared her throat before asking, "Did Mr. Fotopolis speak to my husband before he left?"

The receptionist's answer was polite and professional; she appeared to be following instructions regarding questions about Jimmy Gooch's disappearance. "I really don't know anything about that," she apologized, and then spoiled her discretion by adding, "I have his cellphone here. Mr. Fotopolis found it in the truck. Do you want to pick it up, Mrs. Gooch? Mrs. Gooch?"

Buttoning her bloodstained nightgown, Mary set out through the front door, limping on her swollen heel in her big winter boots, trudging through the snow covering the long, sloped driveway. There was a single set of recent vehicle tracks on the road, and in the gully the snow-frosted newspaper. She bent to retrieve the paper but couldn't. She kicked at the snow with her boot and in doing so revealed another newspaper, and another, and another and another.

She moved between the papers in their thin plastic bags, reading the dates, incredulous. Except for those dreamlike trips to pee or drink, she had left her body to itself, like a quarrelling couple who needed time apart, and had slept a full week.

Noticing that the mailbox was stuffed with correspondence, she gathered the detritus of letters and advertising pamphlets into her arms and moved up toward the house. She passed through the front door and hobbled to the kitchen, caught by the draft from the broken back window. She found the broom near the trash can and brushed the glass into a neat pile in the corner. Then, with what Gooch called crazy tape and a piece of cardboard from her recycling efforts, she attended to the draft.

Energized by the exercise and carrying the broom like a pole vault, she limped outdoors once again, with the tape and cardboard and several large green trash bags, to construct a cover for the truck's jammed-open roof. She brushed the snow from the interior, where it had piled on the seat and drifted to the floor, opened a trash bag and swept the chocolate into it; flinching, she remembered the crow.

As her broom caught the debris from beneath the front seat, a few small, shiny cards fluttered to the ground. She felt her flesh quivering as she worked the broom deeper under the seat, dislodging more of the cards — gold and silver foil strips. Losing instant lottery tickets. Dozens and dozens of them. Along with crumpled wrappers from a hundred mini chocolate bars. The couple's secrets were that pitifully concealed. She climbed inside the truck and began her work on the sunroof.

Tramping wet snow, she returned to the house and found the sink, running the tap and drinking several long glasses of water before moving toward the table, where she collapsed into her red vinyl chair. She looked across the cold tile floor to the silent refrigerator. Not a morsel of food had she ingested in a full week and still hunger's chord was distant, a realization that pleased and alarmed Mary in equal measure.

At the table she sat with the mail—a foreign task, since in their unspoken assignment of chores the mail, which really meant the bills, fell on Gooch, or he'd insisted on being responsible, she couldn't remember. She separated the pamphlets and coupons, setting the bills aside in a neat stack for Gooch to deal with later. She opened an overdue sympathy card from a distant relation and read the sentiments about Orin twice, all the while ignoring the small square envelope she'd spotted right off, addressed to *Mrs. Mary Gooch* in Gooch's scratchy writing. She paused to look at the Kenmore again but, like a spurned lover, it wouldn't meet her eye.

Finally she picked up the envelope. Opening it, she found the note, the one she'd always expected, the one she'd stopped expecting, delivered unexpectedly through the Leaford post. Forgoing the cliché of trembling hand, she read Gooch's scrawl on the square silvery paper:

Dear Mary,

I'm sorry. I wish I knew what else to say. There's money in the account. Twenty-five thousand dollars. It's yours. I won it on the scratch game. Nothing nefarious. Trust me and don't be afraid to spend it. I didn't plan this, Mary. I need some time to think. I hate myself for being such a coward—if that means anything. I promise I'll be in touch.

He had signed the note *Yours*, a term he'd never used before, leaving her with the impression that she'd been mistaken for someone else. She folded the piece of paper and put it back inside the envelope. *Nefarious*. What kind of person used a word like that? And *Yours*. Why would he write *Yours* when the very fact of the note suggested he was decisively not hers?

There was nothing, no thing, in which Mary could confidently believe. It seemed impossible, or at least unlikely, that her husband had won a colossal amount of money in the scratch-and-win lottery and had left her on their twenty-fifth anniversary, to *think*, and would be *in touch*, but there it was, in ballpoint ink on drugstore stationery which he'd likely bought for the purpose. She rose and, stepping on the can to pop the lid, pitched his note into the trash.

She could hear the sound of her husband's words like a movie voice-over as she carried herself to the bathroom — *I didn't plan this, Mary. I need some time to think.* With the shower roaring to drown him out, she slipped off her robe and kicked free of the winter boots. Stripped bare and holding the support rail Gooch had installed for her years ago, she stepped over the tub and found her balance on the rubber bath mat, where her foot leaked bands of blood.

Finding the costly bath products Gooch had given her last Christmas, Mary poured them over herself all at once. Cheeks scrubbed pink, she dried her skin with a clean towel, noticing that there was somewhat less of herself than in previous days. Her bloodstained nightgown too foul to put back on, she stood naked before the bathroom mirror, rifling through a drawer full of hair products, finally finding a large comb. She drew it through her hair, pulling strands from her face until she could see only her gray roots, startled for the first time in her life by her resemblance to her mother. But it was not a curve of bone that Mary recognized, not a similar nose or pattern of aging. It was the look in her eyes, of frozen confusion. The look Irma wore when her existence had become inconceivable.

Gooch had been gone for a week. The letter said he needed time to think. But where had he gone? And how much time was enough? And what if he never came back? Had he really won the lottery? Frozen confusion. But even seeing her mother's expression mirrored in her eyes, Mary didn't worry that she might have Irma's disease. She was convinced that her doom would be more poetic. A massive coronary was what she'd envisioned, and she felt on the verge of it with the absence of Gooch. She reached for the hair dryer, noticing the box of red hair color from that day of Orin's funeral.

Time passed with no tick from the clock. Mary stood before the bathroom mirror, unwrapping a towel from her head. She shook out her mane, more auburn than red, thinking how her mother would have advised against such a brazen look, deciding it was marginally better than those awful gray roots.

In the bedroom she searched her drawers and found a clean pair of navy scrubs, no longer snug at the waistband but loose enough that she had to draw the string. She opened the closet and, after some searching, found her second clean set of navy scrubs, which she folded and placed in a large brown vinyl purse, along with a never-used overnight kit containing dental needs and hair care and her charged cellphone and the cord that had come with it.

In the junk drawer in the kitchen she found a pen and paper, and sat down in one of the red vinyl chairs. She wrote, *Gooch, I'm out looking for* — but didn't finish. For what? In that moment, she wasn't sure.

The Leaving and the Left

There would be no purple lilacs, it being October and the bushes bare on the path to St. John's, but Mary wanted to bring Irma flowers. The flowers spoke of ritual, and this one was important. She eased the red Ford into the snow-carpeted parking lot at the grocery store, pleased to see that her makeshift roof was bearing up under the strain. The climbing sun, appearing briefly from behind the gray clouds, warmed her face as she limped across the lot, wondering why she could barely grasp the scent of fry grease from the burger joint nearby. She entered the grocery store but did not take a cart.

The pretty cashier, whose name tag read *SHARLA*, glanced at the plastic customer card Mary offered and said without looking up, "Hello, Mrs. Gooch." It was a habit of retail that Mary found irksome. She didn't care if it was churlish, she wanted to be anonymous while shopping.

There was hardly any use in pretending, though. The cashier saw her nearly every day. "Hello, Sharla." Mary put the bouquet of sun-flowers on the conveyor.

"That's *it*, Mrs. Gooch? No groceries?"

"Sorry."

Sharla looked up, blurting, "Ohmygod your hair is *red*."

"Yes," Mary said, cheeks burning scarlet to match.

"Nice." Sharla waved the saffron flowers over the scanner. Annoyed, she pressed a button beside her register. "The machine's not scanning. I have to get my manager."

Mary felt the heat of her blame, *If you weren't so fat the flowers would scan.* "I was thinking I should get something smaller anyway," she said.

The girl tapped the microphone on her cash register. "Dick at register three, please. *Dick.*" She turned to Mary, sharing—"That's actually his *name.*"

"I'm sorry."

"It's not *your* fault." Sharla leaned on the button, straining on her toes, flexing her sculpted legs as she searched the aisles. The bass notes of "Proud Mary" suddenly began to blare. Mary let out a shriek, startling Sharla, who helped her find the cellular phone beneath the other travel items in her huge brown purse. The phone was so clearly alien to Mary that Sharla had to take it from her hands and open it and press it to Mary's ear.

"Hello," Mary offered, breathless. It was a message from her service provider, but it took Mary some moments before she understood that it was pre-recorded.

Sharla smiled. "You just close it now. Close it. Just . . . yeah . . . close it."

Mary folded the phone in half.

"You might want to dial down that ringtone," Sharla said, before pressing the buzzer again. "God, I hate my manager."

Mary nodded. "Me too."

"A dick?"

"A *Ray*. But yes."

Pressing the flowers into Mary's arms, Sharla gestured toward the door and told her, "I'll put them on my employee discount and you can pay me back whenever."

"But I have money."

"Just take them, Mrs. Gooch," Sharla insisted, waving her off. "You're in here every day, so."

"I'm sorry."

"Just say thank you."

"Thank you," Mary said, hugging the large bouquet. Leaving the store, she wondered if anyone in Leaford knew that Gooch had parked the truck at Chung's and disappeared. Maybe Sharla knew. Maybe her gesture had been made out of pity. Or solidarity.

She entered the front door at St. John's, wiping her boots on the damp sections of cardboard spread over the carpet as requested by the handwritten sign. The young man at reception, a recent hire, looked annoyed at the size of the bouquet in her arms. She did not apologize when she handed him the flowers, particularly as she was also bringing postdated checks for the next six months of her mother's care. She asked the young man to please take down her new contact number, in case there was an emergency. "My cellphone number," she said blithely, then read it off the card.

She stopped to greet a threesome of elderly women near the door to the common room, proud that she'd had the reputation, at Raymond Russell's, of being "good with the geezers." Nearby, two whittled Williams and a pitted Paul were playing poker for a pot of pennies. She had forgotten about her flaming hair until the eldest of the Williams let out a long, low whistle. "Well, hello Ann-Margret," he cheered.

Old Joe DaSilva, who had been a favorite customer at the drug-store, said, "Hey Red. You like my new robe, Red?"

"You look like Hugh Hefner, Joe," she said, running her hand over the silky fabric of his shoulders, making the old men laugh.

She blushed when the older William patted her breast, which

he'd mistaken for her arm, and said, "Stay for this hand. You can be my Lady Luck."

"Your color looks better," she observed.

"They changed my medication."

"That explains a lot. Stay away from my mother," she joked, leaving the men to their cards.

In the common room Mary found her mother parked alongside the new patient, another frail white woman, Roberta, a stranger from Kitchener who never had visitors. Side by side, snoring in wheelchairs with blankets tucked up to their chins, they reminded Mary of toddlers in strollers at the park, and she understood why mothers said they looked like angels when they were asleep. She found a seat between her mother and Roberta and set her hand on Irma's terminally bony shoulder. "Mum?"

But it was Roberta, afflicted with some mysterious misfortune of aging, who opened her eyes. "Yes?" Mary was too startled to respond. "Yes?" Roberta repeated, catching her gaze so that Mary couldn't turn away. "What is it?"

Mary faltered. "I came to say goodbye."

The old woman shrugged.

Mary clasped Irma's cool fingers, addressing her mother in a whisper, hoping Roberta couldn't hear. "I came to say goodbye."

"You want my forgiveness? Now that I'm dying? Is that why you've come?" Roberta demanded.

Mary paused, seeing the old woman's longing, and answered, "Yes."

Roberta nodded slowly. "I suppose I've waited a long time for that."

"Okay."

"So much time wasted."

"Yes," Mary agreed.

"*Wasted.*"

"Wasted."

"How will you remember me?" the old woman asked, searching Mary's eyes. "What will you think of?"

"The way you brushed my hair," Mary told her, all the while squeezing Irma's hand. "I'll think of the way you brushed my hair."

"What else?"

Mary paused. "And I'll think about . . . how I always admired your strength."

"I've always said what I thought and thought what I said."

"I know you loved me." Mary kissed her mother's parchment temple and joined the two women in gazing at the distance.

Unaware of how long she'd been sitting there—for since the death of the clock, time had ceased to be sequenced, at once here and now and then and before—Mary finally squeezed her mother's bony fingers, the ritual of farewell sadder and more natural than she'd imagined.

On her way out she stopped to say goodbye to the table of men playing cards, and reminded the young man at reception that it was her *cellphone* number they should try if she needed to be reached.

The path tilted before her. She heard a distant cry for nourishment—not a pain in her gut but a cerebral reminder to eat. The Oakwood Bakery was two blocks from St. John's.

The Oakwood was the only independent bakery left in Baldoon County, the Tim Hortons coffee chain having annihilated the competition years ago, but Mary remained a loyal customer, particularly since they had added the drive-through window and she no longer had to expend the energy of leaving her car, or suffer the reproving looks from the other customers, even if she had to concede their point. What *did* a woman her size need with a box of honey crullers?

Opening the door, she remembered her frequent visits to the Oakwood with her mother as a child. Before groceries on Fridays, because Irma never shopped on an empty stomach, it had been their habit to stop at the bakery, where they would find a stool at the large U-shaped counter, and where her mother would remind her, "Don't swivel," a thousand times before she'd have to smack Mary's knee. Irma would order the raisin bran muffin and strong black coffee in those squat white cups, which always came with saucers. "I like the light in here at this time of day," Irma would say. Or "I love how this place never changes."

Mary would have her choice of donut from the dizzying array, a decision that caused more agony than rapture as she often regretted the choice of jam-filled, wishing she'd gone for the custard, the fritter instead of the fancy. Irma would tear off tiny sections of muffin that she popped into her mouth, chewing thoughtfully, and though they rarely breathed a word, Mary felt connected to her in their sensual enjoyment of the place.

On the morning before Christopher Klik's funeral, the Brody family stopped in at the Oakwood for breakfast. Not in the mood to swivel in her snug black skirt and tight white blouse, Mary sat still on the stool between her parents at the counter near the door. The waitress grinned tightly as she dithered between the rainbow sprinkles and the lemon puff, finally deciding on the double chocolate glaze. She asked for a taste of her mother's muffin and a try of her father's cinnamon bun before tucking into the unusually small chocolate donut, which would not remotely satisfy the obeast. She attempted to tear her donut into small pieces as her mother did, but only made a mess of her fingers. "Eat that *properly*, Mary," Irma said.

She saw that her parents had no appetite, and was relieved to think that they wouldn't notice if she ate their breakfast too, lost as they both were in the mortal struggle of the day. She shoved the remainder of her donut into her mouth and turned just as the door opened on the silhouette of stunning Karen Klik, sheathed in black for her younger brother's funeral, long, blonde hair blown bone-straight, lashes coated with waterproof mascara, car keys dangling in her long fingers, no doubt running some errand for the wake. Their eyes locked.

"You have chocolate on your blouse," Karen said.

Panicked, Mary reached up with her hands, smearing more of the chocolate on her starchy cotton shoulder.

"Oh, Mary," Irma cried, diving into action, dunking a napkin into a water glass, yanking at Mary's shirt. "Oh, *Mary.*"

When Mary finally had the courage to look up, Karen Klik was still watching. Mary didn't know the word for what she saw in the grieving sister's eyes. Heightening her humiliation, there had later been a heated discussion among the ladies at the wake about what would best remove the chocolate stain, until Mrs. Klik's sister-in-law pointed out, "She's *bursting* out of it anyway. Send it to the ragbag."

Shaking off the shame of that day, Mary pulled open the door to the Oakwood and stepped inside. The clerk behind the counter looked up, surprised. "Hi, Mrs. Gooch," she said, recognizing her from the drive-through. The conversation across the counter ceased abruptly and all eyes fell upon her. She saw instantly how foolish she'd been to wonder if anyone knew. *Everyone* knew about Jimmy Gooch winning the lottery and leaving his fat wife to go on some middle-aged vision quest.

Casting her eyes down, Mary caught a glimpse of herself in the reflection of a chrome table, struck by the shade of her hair, a deep fire tone that she allowed, for a moment, was not hideous next to her complexion.

Mary hadn't sat at the U-shaped counter since she was a child, and never *this* U-shaped counter, since shortly after her classmate's funeral the structure had largely been destroyed by the second fire in its history, and Irma'd stopped driving there before groceries on Friday. Mary guessed that it was because she could no longer say, *I love how this place never changes.*

To fill the silence, she told the clerk, "I thought I'd have a coffee," and started for the counter. The rest of the customers returned to their cliques—the quartet of farmers, the mother with the brats, the three retired schoolteachers whom Mary recognized from Leaford Collegiate but who seemed not to recognize her. The cashier from the Zellers. The waitress brought her a black coffee. "Excuse me," Mary asked her. "What would be the fastest way to the highway from here?"

One of the farmers answered before the waitress could open her mouth. "Take this road to Number 2. Left on Number 2 takes you straight to the 401. Hope your tires are good. They're calling for more snow."

"Where you headed?" the farmer who was not wearing a ball cap asked.

"Toronto," Mary decided, since the restaurant receipts were her only real lead.

He curled his lip and croaked, "I hate Toronto."

"We put your order in the freezer when you didn't pick it up last week, Mrs. Gooch," the clerk called out from behind the counter. "Do you want them now?"

"I'm sorry?"

"Your cakes, from last week? Isn't that why you're here? Four of them, right? And the pastry assortment."

Mary froze as the room hushed and eyes turned. Flushed, she rose and paid her tab. "Could you deliver the cakes over to St. John's?" she inquired quietly.

"Cost extra for delivery."

Mary tried to stop her hand from trembling as she fumbled for her cash.

Rule of Three

Roaring down the highway in the big Ford truck, listening to the Motown tape Gooch had mixed for her years ago, Mary watched the landscape, the flat farms and soaring silos banked by dense thickets of forest. A few tenacious trees clung to the fall show but most were bare and black from melted snow. She saw a sign for the next service center, reminding herself that she needed to pee and eat something. Even with a break on the road, she hoped to get to the restaurant in Toronto by dinnertime, when more of the staff would be there, to ask questions about Gooch. Gooch was nothing if not memorable. Maybe he'd talked to someone about a trip he wanted to make. A place he wished he lived. Offered some hint of where he might have gone. Mary understood now, though she'd criticized such plots in prime-time drama, that in real life one could do nothing but follow the faintest of clues when the faintest of clues were all one had.

Joints stiff from driving, she caught her breath beside the truck before making her way into the service center, her left foot numb to her ankle. Looking at the sky, she wondered if the snow would really come, or if it needed time to think.

Considering the line at the coffee place and impatient to get back on the highway, she bought a protein bar from the vending machine and chewed it slowly, catching sight of the automated teller nearby. In Gooch's lying note he'd written, *Spend the money.* But she suddenly did not trust—as how *could* she trust Gooch?—that the money would still be there. Joining the long line for the machine, she waited, and when it was finally her turn she flipped her bank card from her wallet and went through the motions, wondering if Gooch had meant *Spend it but on the credit card.* He hated when she used the credit card for the way it unbalanced his books. And how much of the money should she spend? All of it? Half of it? And on what? For a man who liked to be in control, his lack of direction was maddening. She asked the machine for one hundred more dollars, which she added to the thick wad of cash, and waited for it to spit out the receipt. The money was all still there.

Being in the habit of looking down, Mary hadn't noticed the scruffy young man standing in the middle of the instant teller line behind her. Before exiting, she turned to find him watching her, with a *look* on his face. She was familiar with the looks. There were a variety of them, and curiously independent of age, race or gender. The look that said, *That lady is bi-ig.* Or the one that said, *What a waste of skin.* Or *Wonder what she'd have to eat to get that big?* Over the years she had noticed a new expression, one that suggested a comparative study, as in *She's as fat as my cousin, uncle, mother, best friend.* With the North American epidemic of obesity, it appeared increasingly that many loved someone fat as she.

Out in the parking lot, her sluggish steps were no match for the man's wiry sprint, and he was already upon her by the time she heard his running feet. It was the man from the instant teller line. He struck out with a small silver blade he had hidden in the cuff of his shirt. Mary closed her eyes as he thrust his arm. Violent death. The rule of three.

Feeling no sear of metal in her gut, she thanked her poundage for its protection and opened her eyes, confused to find the man holding not a knife but her silver bank card. Silently he urged her to take the card, gesturing back at the building, though it was clear now what had transpired.

"I'm sorry," she said.

The man nodded shortly and turned to go. Mary watched him skip over the slick pavement and into the roadway as a transport truck rounded the curve. The truck driver blasted his horn. The shouting of bystanders did not startle the man, who managed to reach the sidewalk just as the transport bore down. He stopped, not because he heard the truck or noticed the commotion he'd caused, but to wave at Mary, unsmiling, before disappearing back into the building. She watched through the large window as he, having lost his place, joined the end of the automated teller line, and considered all the stranger had risked in his gesture of kindness.

"Thank you!" she called out, though she knew he couldn't hear.

New math complicated the continuum of Mary's drive as she attempted to calculate the date of her husband's return. If he'd won fifty thousand, which was what she supposed, it would eventually run out. A few weeks? Months? Depended on where he was and how he was spending it. What if it was a hundred thousand and he'd gone off on some binge and wasn't remotely the man she thought he was? Or maybe it was a million, in which case, she conceded, she would likely never see him again. Working out the odds of Gooch's coming home on his own was a distraction, she knew, keeping her from reasoning out the odds of finding him at all.

Nearing the big city, the number of lanes increased, along with the speed and need of the other drivers to get wherever the hell they were going. She eased around a bend, awed by the dazzling silver skyline. She'd only ever seen the cityscape in pictures and TV, yet she had the strongest sense of déjà vu. Not as though she'd been here before, but as though she'd felt the same feeling, the exact same feeling, when she had turned the aisle from pain medications to dental needs and seen Jimmy Gooch on his crutches with that look in his eye, more than twenty-five years before.

The traffic on the expressway leading into the downtown core was slow but Mary decided not to mind. She watched the people strolling on the path near the choppy gray lake, bundled up against the autumn cold, the sinking sun basking families in wholesome golden light. She watched teenaged lovers stream over bridges, and in-line skaters trick down sidewalks. So many people. Not one she knew. Not one knew her. She felt pleasantly small.

As the traffic was virtually stalled and the light lost its romantic cast and gray sprayed the cold families and the mean runners and the showy skaters and careless cyclists, she saw what Gooch had been talking about when he had described an editorial from a Toronto newspaper about the continued debate over the lakeside expressways, which were always choked with traffic, and blocked people's access to the water. She remembered being irritated by Gooch's habit of reading articles out loud to her, and wishing he'd just get on with breakfast and leave so she could ravish that leftover peach pie. Enlightened by the encroaching darkness, Mary realized she'd gotten her wish. Gooch was gone and now she could eat peach pie till she bled Crisco.

Finding the restaurant was easy. Queen Street was a stone's throw from the expressway, and she followed the numbers on the narrow shops until she arrived at a small, square storefront with mosaic tile bearing the sign *Bistro 555*. Gooch preferred restaurants that had *grill* somewhere in the name, and Mary, had she been a gambler, would have laid odds that her husband would not choose to eat in this establishment. But she'd have been wrong. And it was not just the one time but six, according to the receipts.

She looked for a place to park and, finding no space on the road, drove on. And on. And on, snaking up narrow streets past skinny Victorian houses with postage-stamp front lawns, and soaring apartment buildings, and ethnic shops and chain stores, only to encounter a confounding maze of one-way streets that led her back to the same one-way streets, and still no parking to be found.

With her sketchy grasp of time, she could only guess that she'd driven in circles for nearly thirty minutes. She had decided, driving through the tight, lively streets, that she could understand why people loved Toronto—and hated it. Finally, several blocks from Queen Street, she saw a sign for public parking. She pulled the Ford into the lot and found an empty spot, startled when a hirsute man appeared beside the truck. "Twenty dollars," he demanded.

She had not seen the sign. "To *park?*" she asked, astonished, and handed him a bill.

"Keys, please," he said, holding out an oil-stained palm.

"My car keys?" she asked, bewildered.

"Please," he said ungraciously.

"I have to leave my *keys?*"

"No keys, no park."

She passed him the keys reluctantly and set off in the direction of the restaurant. On the street, she found that she could not, as was her habit, keep her eyes down, with so many hazards on the sidewalk—joggers and shoppers and pets and skaters and the sprawling legs of ragged beggars. She had never seen so many humans of so many different colors and ethnicities, and bet she couldn't guess half their countries of origin. With her eyes raised, though, she was confronted in every shop and restaurant window by her reflection. She'd forgotten to bring a jacket but she wasn't cold. In fact, there were dark sweat stains spotting her navy scrubs, and a shine of perspiration on her face and neck. Realizing that it was at least *possible* she might find Gooch in Bistro 555, she stopped to catch her breath. She pictured him drinking beer at the bar, and tried not to wonder who might be sitting beside him, running a slender hand up his rigid thigh.

Reaching into her purse, she found a tube of coral lipstick, and swiped it over her lips. Then she found the second set of navy scrubs, and used the smock to blot her glossy face. She started back down the crowded street, watching people scramble past her onto the old-fashioned streetcar with their bags of this and sacks of that. The homeless accosting the hurried. A trio of prostitutes in the shadow of an alley swarming a maroon Grand Marquis.

Finding the mosaic tile above the draped windows. Bistro 555, she steeled herself and reached for the door handle. She pulled but it was locked. She checked the sign in the window. The restaurant didn't open until six. *Six?*

There were easily a dozen people within earshot, but not one of whom she might ask the time. They were moving too fast. Too busy to bother. No one making eye contact. She turned to find a wiry young man with soulful brown eyes, olive skin and a sparse goatee staring at her. She was in his way.

"You have to wait for the streetcar over there," he told her, gesturing at the crowded bus shelter.

"I'm waiting for the restaurant to open," Mary said politely, as she saw the young man had a key to the place and was letting himself in.

"Half an hour," he said, and slipped inside.

Deflated, Mary could hardly imagine walking the remaining paces into the restaurant, let alone wandering the murky, unfamiliar streets for half an hour. She stood at the entrance to Bistro 555 replacing passing strangers' faces with Gooch's, and recapping for herself, the way TV series did at the start of each show, her previous episode and the highlights of what had brought her to this place.

Why would a restaurant not open its doors until six? A big-city pretension, she decided. Among the many pretensions and affectations that folks in Leaford talked about. The big-city people with their big-city ways, looking down on rural communities because they didn't have museums or amusement parks or government buildings or repertory theater.

Open at six. Surely people in the city got hungry before *six*. But then Mary realized that *she* was not hungry. Still not hungry. Her world had been inverted by Gooch's disappearance, and it made some simple sense that her body would cope in this contrary way. She remembered checking every box in a magazine quiz asking, *Are you a stress eater?* She'd envied the stress starvers, like her mother.

Dinner in the Brody house was served at five o'clock sharp when Mary was growing up—at least, until Irma started working only mornings and dinner had been moved up an hour, to four, which was when Orin got home from his afternoon shift. After Orin retired, dinner was on the table when Mary arrived home from high school, and her parents, with their meager appetites, had their dishes cleared and washed before she had tucked into seconds. Irma didn't call it *having dinner*. She called it *getting dinner over with*. In some ways, Mary thought, Irma lived her whole life anxious to get things over with, as if she knew the end of her story all along, and didn't feel the middle pages worth the effort of a read.

Time. No thump, no thud. No ritual, no routine. No trips to the kitchen and back. Time sequenced by nothing. No Raymond Russell. No Gooch. Mary felt surprising relief in her release from time, and didn't wonder how long she'd been standing in front of the restaurant when the door banged open against her rear end and the man with the goatee appeared. "You can wait inside if you want."

She thanked him, wondering if he'd invited her in because of the poor advertising she gave the chic boîte — a huge woman with flaming red hair wearing sweaty navy scrubs and old winter boots. *If you eat here, this could be you.*

Adjusting to the light, she found only tiny bistro chairs available, and took care easing her big, tired body down. She caught her breath, watching the young man tackle chores behind the bar, deciding to be direct. "I'm looking for someone. He's come in here a few times recently, and I thought someone might remember him. Jimmy Gooch?"

"Doesn't ring a bell."

"He's tall. Very tall. Six foot six with wavy hair. Little grey at the temple. Broad. Handsome. People remember him."

The man shrugged. "I've cut way back on my shifts."

"Oh."

"I'm really an actor."

"Oh."

"I look like a young Al Pacino," he said, casting a profile.

"You do," she agreed.

"I get that a lot."

"Is there anyone else I can ask?"

"This guy you're looking for, is he in trouble?" She shook her head. "You could ask Mary." He grinned to himself. "She'll be here any second."

"Mary?" Mary said, feeling cagey.

"Our hostess. Mary Brody. Sounds like a guy Mary would remember."

Just as she heard her own maiden name from the lips of the Al Pacino look-alike, the front door opened to the figure of a woman dressed in a clingy red knit and killer black heels. Her dark blonde hair fell in waves, framing her beautiful face, teasing her bony shoulders. She stepped forward into the light, blue eyes rimmed in thick black mascara, hint of gloss on full pink lips. Dangerous cheekbones. Around her swan's neck she wore a large silver pendant that fell well past her deep cleavage. She looked at Mary and Mary looked at her and together they chimed, "Mary? Heather?"

The actor looked up from behind the bar. "Heather?"

Heather Gooch flashed a grin at him. "Hey, superstar," she flirted. "Where you been?"

"Who's Heather?"

"Nickname." She winked, making a covert face of despair. "Mary and I know each other from the *old days*."

"You're both Marys?"

"Could you give us five? Five? Prep the coffee station for me. *Please*," Heather purred.

Watching her sister-in-law bat her eyes and swivel her hips, Mary thought that Heather was twenty years too old for such coquetry. She was several years older than Mary but looked easily a decade younger, and Mary hadn't seen her in six years, which translated to forty-three pounds. More complicated math.

"You're using my maiden name?" Mary wasn't angry, just surprised.

Heather checked to make sure the swinging door to the kitchen was closed before she bent to take a chair, her huge silver pendant striking the glass on the table as she offered without apology, "It was the first name I thought of when I applied for my last apartment. When did you go red?"

"But why?"

Heather shrugged. "I don't want to be found. By certain old *associates*. Just easier to be somebody else. Why are you here, Mary?"

"Restaurant receipts," Mary answered. "He's been coming to see *you*. Why didn't he tell me?"

This Heather was not the jonesing Heather. Not the tragic Heather. Not the disconnected Heather. This Heather was clear-eyed and present. Mary watched her manicured fingers search the contents of her leather purse and pinch a nicotine gum from foil.

"He came here. He ate lunch. We talked. He's my brother." She reached out, touching Mary's plump wrist. "At least you know he wasn't having an affair."

"Did he give you money?" Mary asked, prepared to feel self-righteous.

"I gave *him* money. I've been paying him back. My boyfriend owns this place. He's loaded."

"When did Gooch loan you money?"

"Ancient debt." Heather shifted in her chair, fiddling with her necklace. "Look, Mary, I'm sorry you came all this way, but whatever's going on between the two of you is between the two of you. You should really go home and work it out."

"He's gone, Heather." Mary bit her lip to keep from sneering. "You *know* that."

Heather looked at her blankly. "Gone *where?*"

Mary waited for the tell, but Heather's lovely eyes shone with such genuine concern that instead of catching her in a lie, Mary found herself the bearer of her own bad news. "He's left. He's left me. He won on the scratch-and-win lottery. A million, for all I know. He didn't say. And he left me."

"He won money?" Heather blinked rapidly.

"He sent a letter in the mail. He said he won on the lottery. He said he needed time to think. He said he'd *be in touch*."

"Wow."

"Yeah."

"I found the restaurant receipts and I thought . . . I didn't know."

"Wow. Have you called my mother?" Heather asked.

"I don't want her to worry."

"You don't want her to *know*," Heather corrected her. "Besides, he wouldn't have gone there. He *hates* Jack."

"So where do I go?"

"Home. Go home."

Mary shook her head. "He talked about a place in Myrtle Beach. This golf resort he always wanted to go to. He wanted to see the White House. The monuments in Washington. Las Vegas? You know how he likes to gamble."

"He wouldn't."

"He could be in Las Vegas blowing it all right now. Or that big casino on the reserve near Montreal."

"He wouldn't."

"Or a Caribbean cruise. He really wanted to go on that cruise I won last year."

"Why didn't you go?"

Out of habit Mary cast her eyes down, but told herself to look up. "If you can think of anything he might have said? A clue about where he might have gone?"

"If he said he needed time, why don't you just give him time?" Heather checked the hands on the wall clock above their heads. "I'm sure it'll work out, Mary. Or if it doesn't, maybe it's for the best."

For the best. The doctors had said the same thing about her babies. She was equally offended by the suggestion that her marriage was better off dead.

"I like the red," Heather said. "Plays up your green eyes."

Mary nodded, looking out the window. A sharply dressed old man, whom she might have described as *toady* had she been of a different nature, let himself into the restaurant, and Heather excused herself to go to him even before he snapped his fingers. She allowed the old man to kiss her neck before she whispered something into his misshapen ear. The old man glanced at Mary dismissively, then headed back through the swinging doors to the kitchen. A cost. To everything.

Heather returned, flushed and guilty, not explaining. She didn't sit down, making it clear they were done. "Well," she said.

Wheezing with the effort of untangling her legs from the cage of bistro chair and table, Mary stood.

"God, Mary! What *happened* to you?" Heather asked, as if whatever had happened had just occurred.

"I cut my foot."

"*Look* at you. You can barely get up off the *chair.*"

"I've put on a few since the last time I saw you."

"My God, Mary. How could you just *let yourself go* like that?"

The first thought that came to Mary's mind was *Don't take any moral high ground with me, Heather Gooch. You're a drug addict.* But she said the second thing, which was "I know."

Heather glanced at the kitchen's swinging door, lowering her volume. She softened, ushering Mary to the door. "If I hear from him, I'll let you know."

Mary stopped her. "Take my cellphone number."

Heather keyed the digits into the tiny phone she kept in her purse as Mary recited the numbers. "Don't worry. He said he'd be in touch, didn't he?"

"What if it's too late?"

"For what?"

For me, Mary thought.

Heather stood silent, watching the massive form of Mary Gooch disappear through the restaurant door. Outside, buffeted by the crowds on the sidewalk, Mary made her way back to the Ford, discomfited by her unnatural state of awareness but sure that if she wanted to find Gooch, she had to look up from now on. She felt she'd been walking for hours, and worried that she'd gone the wrong way.

Heather's shouting was swallowed by the hubbub of the street. The silver pendant bounced on her breasts as she jogged through the crowds. Impeded by her killer heels and her history of smoking, she was completely out of breath when, within earshot, she called, "Mary! Stop!"

Mary did, grateful for the order, and the sisters-in-law stood apart in the crowd, each with lovely long hair and pretty eyes. Heather much taller with her heels, Mary the span of three people. Drug addict. Fat lady. Mary blamed science, brain chemistry, anabolic hormones, ghrelin, leptin, genetic weakness, the media, but stopped when she felt her ancestors, those Baldoon County pioneers whose very survival had depended on personal responsibility, roll in their graves.

"Jimmy went to Golden Hills," Heather breathed. "He wanted to see Mum."

Blotting out the street noise, focusing on Heather's blue eyes, Mary took the information in. "He's in California?"

"I don't know if he's still there but that's where he was going. I haven't heard from him since he hitchhiked up here last week to get his check from the Lotto office."

"He put twenty-five thousand dollars in the account," Mary said. "How much did he win?"

Heather shrugged. "He wouldn't tell me. All he would say was *enough.*"

Enough, Mary repeated to herself.

"He had the ten grand I paid him back, too."

"Gooch loaned you ten thousand dollars?"

"It was a long time ago, Mary. The inheritance money from Dad."

"Have you talked to your mother?"

"You know I don't talk to my mother."

"Should I call her?"

"She'd just lie for him. Like I did."

"I *need* to see him."

"If you want to see Jimmy, then go. Just go."

"Just go to California? Show up on Eden's doorstep? 'I'm here. Where's Gooch?'"

"Unless you've got something better. I heard they moved a few years ago. Have you got the new address?"

Mary nodded. "Twenty-four Willow Drive, Golden Hills. I still send Christmas cards."

"You've got money. Go get on a plane."

"I've never been on an airplane."

"That speaks for itself."

"It does," Mary agreed, unsure what her sister-in-law meant.

Heather glanced around the street, possibly to ensure that she was not being watched by one of her old associates, before she said, "I want to show you something." She lifted the silver pendant, which Mary saw now was a locket, opening it with her long, polished nails, tilting it toward the street light to reveal the picture inside. It was Gooch, at sixteen, Mary guessed—cruelly handsome, that wavy hair, that cocky grin.

"My son," Heather said. "He found me last summer through one of those agencies. His name is James. He's nearly tall as Jimmy. Can you believe that?"

The boy was his uncle's spitting image. "I'm happy for you, Heather. Does Gooch know?"

Heather nodded. "He met him."

Mary felt sparks, some ancient thing resurrected.

"They've shot hoops at the park down the street a few times. He's in medical school. He lives two blocks from me, Mary. What are the odds?"

That stabbing feeling. Not hunger. It was Mary's turn to say, "Wow."

"I've got your number if I hear from him." Heather lingered, appraising Mary's face in the blue street light. "I hope you get what you want, Mary."

"Thanks."

"But if you don't, you know, you have to push on."

Mary felt thirsty, and thought of Orin's pragmatic suggestion: "Get a drink from the hose and push on."

Pressing down the sidewalk, processing the new data, Mary was startled by the ringing of her cellphone in her purse. Proud Mary indeed, she thought, trembling.

"Mrs. Gooch?" the voice on the other end inquired.

"Yes."

"It's Joyce. From St. John's."

Mary glanced around for a bench, sure she should be sitting to hear the rest of the call; finding none, she leaned against an antiques shop window. "My mother?" she asked quietly.

"Mrs. Gooch, I thought you should know that Mrs. Shrewsbury passed away tonight."

"Mrs. Shrewsbury?"

"Roberta Shrewsbury?" The other old woman. "Why are you calling me?"

"Our new receptionist saw you talking with her earlier in the common room, and since we can't reach her next of kin . . . I didn't know you knew Mrs. Shrewsbury."

"I don't."

"But she asked for you."

"For me?"

"She asked for you before she died. Her final words were 'Tell Mary I love her.' I assumed that meant you."

"No."

"There's no Mary listed in her relations."

"Some other Mary." Thinking of Heather's renting of her name, she added, "We're everywhere."

Roberta Shrewsbury was part of someone else's rule of three, like The Greek with his mother in Athens—a distinctly separate triangle of grief—but Mary felt sorrow at her loss.

As the mystery of Gooch's disappearance had been somewhat

unraveled, Mary knew, or at least felt hopeful, that she might find her husband of twenty-five years in California. *Livin' the dream.* It would not be Gooch who completed the trio. She and Irma were running neck and neck.

Forgiveness. The old woman, Mrs. Shrewsbury, had forgiven *her* Mary, whoever she was—daughter or sister, Mary guessed—and had seemed lifted even as she'd mourned the wasted time. Was that all anyone really wanted before they died? To forgive? To be forgiven? She was gratified to think that the stranger at St. John's had had a chance to say goodbye. To someone.

Relieved to see the parking lot in view, she stopped to catch her breath, hoping the hairy man, whom she could see watching her through the window of his tiny shelter, would deliver the keys to her instead of making her walk the remaining steps. Approaching the shelter, she could see him rifling through the huge pegboard on which dozens of car key sets were hung. He turned to face her, pulling open the window.

"You give me your keys?" he asked suspiciously.

"Yes," she answered. "I'm the red Ford pickup." She pointed.

"I don't have. You don't give to me." He threw up his hands, suggesting that the problem was hers.

"You said, 'No keys no park,' and I gave them to you."

"I don't remember," he sniffed. "You look." He turned the pegboard so that she could look, but she did not see her distinctive flashlight key chain among the shiny objects.

"Not there," she said.

"You don't give to me."

"I *did* give to you," she insisted.

He threw up his hands again. Mary heaved a sigh.

"You have more key?" he asked.

"No."

"Someone can bring?"

"No one can bring."

The man smiled sympathetically. "You go home, get keys. I am nice guy. I don't charge parking. Come." Not merely generous but gallant, he took Mary's heavy arm and escorted her like a bride back toward the street, where he whistled for a taxi and helped her ease her load into the cracked back seat.

"Where to?" the driver asked.

God to Soul

Mary Gooch had never in her forty-three years set foot inside an airport, and had no context for the shifting tone of air travel. She knew from television news, which was background noise when Gooch was home, about the tighter security and longer waits, rising jet fuel costs, diminished service. She did not know that purchasing an economy ticket to Los Angeles, California, would deplete the bank account by nearly seven hundred dollars. And she did not know she'd have to take off her boots.

She'd always considered the prospect of air travel, like any travel, with fear and reluctance, but she was too preoccupied by thoughts of Gooch — what she would say to him and how she would say it when, or if, she found him — to focus on anything but their reunion. Looking up as she passed through the security checkpoint, she was vividly aware of people's predictable expressions but felt disconnected from the source, and was not mortified when the scowling officer looked at her passport picture and remarked, "You should get a new photo if you're going to keep the red hair."

As she limped toward the gate to wait for her flight Mary was overcome by dizziness, and stopped at a shop to purchase a granola bar, which she would eat directly, and an apple to save for the plane. There was a wall of magazines—sports mags, home decor, celebrity news, health and fitness—which she glanced at briefly, deciding that she didn't really need to know who had the best or worst beach body, and no longer cared if that beautiful couple adopted another refugee child. She moved toward the book section, basing her choice of three novels on cover art and rhapsodic reviews.

Having already endured a lengthy wait, she did not groan like the other passengers when the announcement over the loudspeaker apologized that the flight would be delayed another hour. What did it matter? An hour. Two hours. A day. Mary wasn't expected. Neither did she have expectations. What was it to journey to an uncertain place if not an adventure? She'd never had an adventure before. It was high time. That was what her sister-in-law had meant.

Mary rolled down the passageway to the plane and squeezed down the aisle toward her seat at the back. She could see what the other travelers were thinking; people were being charged for excess baggage, and she was getting away with something. Worse, they were already hours late leaving and the fat nurse was making them later. *Yes,* she thought, repelling their stares, *I am late. I am fat. There but for the grace of God go you.*

When she reached her row, she found that her seat was in the middle, the space far too small for a woman of her girth. She would be spilling out of it, claiming breathing room from the sullen young man at the window, and the exotic woman with the smooth brown skin and the diamond in her nostril. The young man drew his trim body toward the molded wall when she crammed herself into the spot, and quickly plugged his ears with the white buttons from his music player. There was much ado over the fastening of her seat belt, as she was sitting on one end of it and couldn't see around herself to find the other. The brown woman, who'd risen to allow her passage, shifted the ball of lavender satin she held and found Mary's belt, but it was impossible to buckle, since the previous occupant had not been morbidly obese. Mary panicked, trying to connect the too-short belts.

Careful not to spill the contents of her lap, the brown woman reached over Mary, extending the belt as far as it would go, with just barely enough of the strapping to join over her expanse. When the buckle clicked, the woman flashed a set of blinding white teeth. Mary smiled back and whispered confidentially, "This is my first flight." The woman nodded in a way that made it clear she didn't understand English.

The captain welcomed the passengers aboard the flight, which Mary found charming until they were informed that there would be another delay, whose cause she could not hear over the cusses and groans. The brown woman stared serenely ahead, resting her arms on her lavender pillow. The young man beside her found a small electronic device in his coat pocket — one of those BlackBerrys, Mary guessed, or iPhones — and began working his thumbs furiously over the keys.

Mary reached into her vinyl purse and extracted one of the novels, each of whose covers had promised laughter and tears. She began to read and, finding a masterful storyteller behind its pages, was instantly and gratefully transported to another place. She didn't know how long she'd been sitting there — she'd been somewhere else altogether, with a fictional family on a journey to experience the redemptive power of love — when finally the aircraft started to move.

As the airplane taxied to the runway, Mary found it peculiar that she didn't find it peculiar to be squished into a tiny airplane seat preparing to be transported to a whole separate world that was *not* fictional, and set down her book as the plane found speed, then rose off the ground. She felt her stomach drop as it climbed into the still black yonder, thrilled by the banking loop it took toward the wide glass lake. She'd never ridden a roller coaster, but imagined the gut-churning excitement was not dissimilar to what she felt watching the city fall away, with the itch to scream *No!* and *Yes!* at once. Mary Gooch was leaving, not just leaving Leaford, but her country, for the first time in her life. *Goodbye Canada,* she heard herself think, and was struck numb by a fear that she might never return.

My home and native land. She'd never thought to ask herself what Canada meant to her, the sovereign nation whose proximity to the U.S.A. (at least according to Gooch) infected a portion of the country, like an envious little brother or a disaffected sidekick, with an oft-debated inferiority complex.

Hockey. Gun control. The French. Back bacon. Beer. National health care. A lingering fondness for the British monarchy. She ran over the long list of sports heroes and celebrities who hailed from the Great White North, though many had admittedly found their fame and fortune outside her friendly borders. Gooch would have named a thousand other characteristics that helped define the country, and she realized with some sense of shame that, with her lack of political curiosity, she had as little grasp of the world she was leaving as of the one she was about to enter. She'd taken Canada for granted, like the steadfastness of Tomorrow.

She paused a moment to glance at the faces of the passengers across the aisle. An Asian woman with her teenage son, and a glamorous bone-thin blonde Mary took for an aspiring actress or model bound for Hollywood, all of them staring ahead dreamily with plugs in their ears. Together. Alone. They had already left.

When the craft reached cruising altitude and a silver beverage cart was pushed down the aisle by two comely stewards, the exotic woman tapped Mary on the shoulder and pointed at the restrooms behind them. She gestured to the pillow in her lap, which she appeared to be asking Mary to hold while she was gone. Mary reached out her hands, wondering why the woman didn't just leave her pretty pillow on the seat, then felt the weight of the bundle and the heat of it and saw a tiny brown baby, hardly bigger than a rump roast, sleeping soundly within the satiny folds.

As the woman hurried to the restroom, Mary lifted the infant to the hill of her stomach, trembling. She'd never held a baby — white, brown, squirming, sleeping, wailing or calm. She had demurred, as with the boxes of damaged chocolates at Raymond Russell's, when babies were passed her way, waving them off with a smile. *I couldn't.* Wendy, Patti and Kim had all offered up their drooling progeny, but even Wendy hadn't pressed too hard. They had assumed Mary's pain and had understood her envy. Gooch knew the truth, though — that she was terrified of such fragile creatures. He'd promised, "You won't be afraid when it's your own."

The preponderance of stories in magazines about overweight women who gave birth without ever knowing they were pregnant had once inspired Mary Gooch. After the two early miscarriages, and in spite of the couple's frequent copulation, there'd been no swollen breasts, no morning nausea. Nothing but the trips to Dr. Ruttle's office, and to the specialist in London who couldn't find anything wrong except the problem of her accumulating pounds. Her menstrual cycle was irregular, a fact blamed on her weight, so missed periods were no true indicator, and when in her mid-thirties she first felt the cramping pain in her pelvis and counted that it had been seven months since her last period, she wondered if she was to be one of those fabled fat women just walking down the street or trying on shoes at the Kmart one day, who suddenly collapsed and birthed a perfectly good, if unexpected, baby. She imagined her picture on the front of the *Leaford Mirror*. A dubious distinction, but she wouldn't have cared.

A knotty collection of fibroid tumors, not a fetus, had caused the cramping. They were benign but troublesome, and after some observation it was clear they had to go. Along with her faint hope. *Gone to the hospital with hemorrhage.* The loss of *the works*, as the specialist had explained to Gooch when he thought she was asleep, was as painful as the loss of her children. Mary had been consoled by the Kenmore. And Gooch, because he had no words and was quietly mourning himself, brought éclairs from the Oakwood and chicken from the Colonel and suggested cheeseburgers three nights in a row because he thought it might make her smile.

Pulling back the lavender fabric, Mary found the infant's tiny hand and stroked the soft palm, shivering when the boneless fingers curled around her thumb. Dark matted hair, thick spreading lashes, puffy eyes, squashed nose, blistered lips. She watched the perfect brown baby rise and fall with her labored breath, encircling him, encircled by him. She remembered the photograph Heather had shown her. James.

Under the fabric the baby's lean legs stiffened, and soon he was squirming vigorously. She watched him open his eyes, not in the half-cracked way that waking adults do but suddenly, wide. She stared into the black liquid pupils, unaware that she was smiling until the infant smiled back.

After a lengthy absence during which the child had become fussy, the brown woman returned, sporting wet circular patches on her blouse which she tried to cover with an uncooperative shawl, holding a small bottle for the baby filled with the breast milk she'd pumped in the bathroom. She smiled her thanks and put out her arms to take the child back.

But Mary could no more release that tiny brown baby than she could let go of her husband of twenty-five years, and she gestured to the woman for a few minutes more. The mother seemed relieved and nodded, offering the warm bottle. Mary was unsure how to fit so large a nipple into so tiny a mouth, and laughed when the rubber tip touched his nose and the infant drew his lips open wide as a carp, prompting the mother to say in her uneasy English, "Hunger."

Hunger. Food. Sustenance. Simple and perfect, and perfectly simple to recognize while holding the warm bottle to the infant's gulping lips. Water to flora. Sun to earth. Breath to lungs. Gooch to Mary. God to soul. She imagined Irma holding such a bottle (she knew it had not been a breast) to her own tiny mouth, and wondered when food had lost its divinely simple purpose, for her or for anyone like her, including the blonde anorexic in the row beside. At what point had food ceased to nourish and sought to torture?

The baby closed his eyes, still drinking from the bottle as he rode the wave of Mary's gut. She thought of Wendy's and Kim's and Patti's children, how they'd sit together at birthday parties cramming cake into their faces and shoveling hot dogs down their throats. Their respective parents did not seem ashamed of their glorious gluttony, but rather proud. They boasted about this one or that one being a *good* eater, and despaired of the children who ate just enough. "I swear that boy lives on air," Wendy had said of her youngest.

Living on air, flying through air, watching the baby's tiny eyelids drift together and his sucking mouth surrender, Mary put the bottle aside, prying the lavender satin from his soft, warm skin, and marveled at the body the child was heir to. Perfectly functioning. Eat. Sleep. Love.

She glanced sideways to find the child's mother asleep and the young man at the window with his eyes closed too. Across the aisle the blonde anorexic was flipping through a magazine that Mary'd noticed on the shelf at the airport, whose cover crowed, *Reduce Belly Fat Today.* The woman had no fat, belly or otherwise. She might have stood in for the skeleton at an anatomy class. There the cervical vertebrae. The radius. The ulna. The floating ribs. The woman nibbled her thumbnail. Hungry.

So what of this matter of self-acceptance? The thin wished to be thinner, the old to be young. The plain to be beautiful. Was self-acceptance attainable only by the truly enlightened, like Ms. Bolt, or the purely self-deceptive, like Heather who'd once told her concerned brother, with a shrug, "I need to get high, Jimmy. That's just who I am."

Mary recalled a truncated conversation with Gooch some fifty pounds ago, when he cautiously informed her that The Greek had eaten cabbage soup for ten weeks and lost twenty pounds on his doctor's orders. Gooch wrote out the recipe, which he passed to her, sheepishly suggesting that they both give it a try, and falsely claiming that he'd put on a few himself.

"I'm sick of dieting. I'm done," she announced, defeated, throwing the carefully written recipe into the trash. "I'm a big girl. Maybe it's time I just accepted that."

Gooch took her by the shoulders, embracing her so that she couldn't see his impatience, saying, "I just want you to be . . ."

She pulled away. "Thin?"

"No."

"Healthy? Because people can be fat and fit, Gooch."

"I know that, Mary."

"You just want me to be something I'm not."

"Yes."

"*See?*"

"I want you to be happy." He went on to insist that her weight was restricting her life, and that her condition was therefore something not to accept but to reject. Like the drug addict. The smoker. The gambler.

"But it's who I am," she insisted.

"But you're miserable."

"But that's because of *society*, because of the way *other* people look at me. Because of the way *you* look at me, Gooch."

"You're breathless from a flight of stairs. You're tired all the time. You can never find clothes. Your joints ache."

"I love food," she offered weakly.

"You hate food."

In the pause that followed, Gooch unfolded his newspaper and sat down to read. Mary wondered if he was right. She retrieved the cabbage soup recipe from the trash, dusting off the coffee grounds, venturing, "Gooch?"

Lost in the sports pages, he barely looked up. "Do whatever you want."

"I'm not saying I'm giving up," she said. "Are you giving up? Gooch?"

He nodded and she knew he wasn't listening. Even though she was aware that Gooch wasn't pushing her toward some scrawny notion of perfection — that if she'd been merely fat, chubby, plump, round, not *morbidly obese*, he'd never have pushed at all — she felt abandoned at his silence. He'd stopped pushing, in all ways, after that.

Shortly after their rare and briefly honest conversation, Mary and Gooch had stopped having sexual relations, the days of abstinence accumulating gradually. Unlike his peers, Gooch had not inherited a wandering eye from his father, at least not when he was with his wife, though she knew he looked at other women — slender, naked women with titanic tits and groomed jinnies — in the pages of the magazines he hid on the high shelf under the towels in the bathroom. Early in their marriage, having found the magazines between the mattresses of their bed, she'd said, "I hate those magazines. The way they objectify women."

"Men objectify women. Women objectify men. Women and men objectify *themselves*. There's some natural order in it, Mary. You shouldn't take it personally." Her mother had advised the same about a husband's habit of masturbation.

Mary looked out the window as the plane explored the range of night. She recalled Sylvie Lafleur's admission about her seduction of Gooch, "I was afraid it might never happen for me again." Mary wondered if it ever had happened again for Sylvie. Or if it ever would for her.

To pass the time, she projected forward. In a few hours' time she

would arrive in California. It would be late, too late to show up at
Eden's mansion in Golden Hills, which she knew was in the suburbs
of Los Angeles, beyond the Santa Monica Mountains. And it would
take some time to find transportation to the place, which Eden had
once said was an hour from the airport. She would have to get a
motel, get some sleep and freshen up before arriving at her final destination. Gooch would be there. Or he would not.

She watched the baby breathe in her lap. The beginning of a life.
Days and years stretched out before him, a path to follow or to forge,
concessions to statistics and likelihoods, hope for enduring love. Perhaps this child was extraordinary and would make some mark on
the world. Mary thought of her own path from birth to present. Her
life was not half over, and thus far had been half-lived.

The baby stirred, shuddering and yawning, before resuming his
tender repose. Pondering his unwritten life, Mary realized that the
rest of her own story was no more determined than his. She had
already left her deep, rutty path; this new road had taken her on the
sharpest of turns. She found hope in the miracle of second chances,
and in the heat of the slumbering infant, and in the rhythm of her
heart, which was not thumping or thudding but beating quietly
and purposefully. She could not say whose God it was, so decided it
didn't matter, and felt as sure as she'd ever felt anything that in that
moment she was not alone.

She did not shut her eyes, for fear she'd fall asleep and drop the
baby, so sat still between the two sleeping strangers, considering her
life as a wife, until the wheels bounced on the tarmac on the other
side of the continent. She'd left not only her home and city and country and life but the weight of her old worry, having divined her singular purpose — to find Gooch. Not the husband who'd left but the
man who, she could see now, was lost.

The brown woman woke flustered, grasping at her empty lap,
relieved to find her baby safe in the arms of the fat woman beside
her. Another wait as the pilot announced that there was no gate

available for the late-arriving craft, but the passengers were too tired to groan, and too busy drawing out cellphones and sending messages to loved ones.

Food. Sustenance. Mary ate the apple from her purse, wondering why it had no taste.

California Dreamin'

More than just looking up, Mary found herself looking on the bright side, grateful not to have to wait for luggage like her weary flightmates, and no external baggage to heft as she made her way out of the airport in Los Angeles. She also had hundreds of dollars in her purse, and thousands in her bank account. There was comfort in currency.

Making her way out of the baggage area, she noticed a diminutive bald man, wearing a suit and suffering a badly sunburned scalp, watching her pass with suspicion. When he called out after her, she assumed that he had mistaken her for someone else — or, worse, that he was shouting an insult — and did not turn around. The bald man followed her, startling her with a gentle but firm hand on her shoulder, looking into her eyes and mouthing as though she were deaf, "Miracle?"

"I beg your pardon?"

"Miracle?"

He seemed panicked, holding a sign out for her to read, and she realized it bore a name. "Missus . . . ?"

She could not have pronounced the name. "Me?" Mary said. "No."

His face fell. Without a parting word he shuffled away, extracting a cellphone, mumbling tones of contrition in an unfamiliar tongue.

Mary strode through the arrivals hall, detecting, like a rattle in the dash, a shift in the rhythm of her step, an alteration in the orchestration of her flesh. The earth's pull seemed less, and although she didn't care to guess at the pounds she'd lost in the previous days, for the number seemed irrelevant, she felt herself smaller.

Long ago, when she was being whittled by her parasites, Mary hadn't celebrated her reduction; now, again, she was more focused on the reason for her diminishment. The larger absence. Hunger? She did not hunger for anything but Gooch.

Miracles — yes, she still believed in miracles. What were they but random occurrences that caused wonder instead of random occurrences that brought grief? And the rule of three? Gooch had called it ridiculous, saying, "You can group your tragedies in threes or thirties, Mare. If there are people there is tragedy. It doesn't mean that, just because your gramma and Aunt Peg died, our baby's gonna die too."

Even with the rising sun peering over the parking structure, the air was cooler than she'd expected and she shivered from the chill. As she walked, she found that the pain in her heel had lessened. *It's Tomorrow,* she thought, and she greeted the dawn like an old friend who'd recently waived a large debt.

Outside of the building, Mary followed the signs for ground transportation but decided she must have taken a wrong turn, since she saw no waiting vehicles, no taxi or bus that might take her to Golden Hills and no stray people around to ask for help. As her body was undernourished and she had not slept on the plane, she found a bench upon which to rest while she considered her next course of action. She remembered her cellphone, and decided to dial directory assistance and ask for a number for a taxi. She opened the phone, pressed the three numbers for assistance and held the phone to her ear. Nothing—no dial tone—and anyway she was unsure which buttons to press to connect.

Her passport, which she'd meant to keep in a zippered compartment, was loose in her big vinyl purse, and she took it out to look at the photograph she'd never seen before. Gooch had grabbed the photo before she had a chance to look—the bad lighting, gray roots, full moon face—and laughed good-naturedly. "You look like a convict." His own passport image was typically handsome, but she'd said, "You do too." He had chuckled in agreement. His excitement over the impending Caribbean cruise was not infectious to her, but torturous, for she knew, even as they discussed travel needs and planned day excursions, that they would not be sipping piña coladas on the Lido deck or enjoying a fun-filled day shopping the straw markets of Negril.

When a black stretch limousine pulled up to the curb, Mary naturally wondered, given her location, which of a thousand celebrities sat concealed behind the darkened windows. She waited for the door to open, hoping whoever it was would be a sports star or musician, news to share with Gooch, but the limousine door didn't open and the car sat idling quietly. She suddenly realized that the occupants were not leaving the vehicle because of *her*, because of the way she was staring. The window rolled down and the driver peered at her from beneath his cap. It seemed he was waiting for her to leave, as she was the only human in the vicinity who might interrupt the privacy of the rich and famous within his car, or snap an unflattering picture with a cellphone. She laughed out loud at the thought.

"Hello," the driver called. She decided to object if he asked her to leave. "Hello," he called again, to which she responded in kind. "Where are you going?" he asked.

She thought he'd said, *When are you going?*, and planted her feet. "I'm not going."

"Where?"

"I'm not going anywhere," she shot back. "I'm sitting right here until I figure out how to call a taxi to get me to Golden Hills."

The man climbed out of the limo, approaching Mary on the bench. Seeing the sunburn on his bald head when he tilted his cap, she recognized him as the man with the accent who'd asked about the miracle. He opened the rear door of the car. The deep, leather-upholstered seats were vacant.

"My passenger doesn't make the flight," he explained. "Come. I take you to Golden Hills." When Mary did not immediately rise, he added, "Charge is just for regular car service. Come."

The back seat of the limousine, which faced an identical back seat, was more spacious and luxurious than any couch Mary'd ever played potato to. There were small tables with chilled bottles of water, and a crystal glass full of individually wrapped breath mints, and a mini refrigerator, not a Kenmore, with a glass front showcasing a selection of alcoholic beverages.

As he pulled away from the curb, the driver checked his rearview mirror. "What is your name?"

"Mary," she answered. "Mary Gooch."

"Drink if you like, Mary Gooch. In the basket there is food."

She noticed a wicker basket on the floor filled with a variety of snacks—macadamia nuts, which she'd never tasted, and tidy plastic trays with packaged cheese and crackers, premium chocolate, fresh fruit. She opened one of the chilled waters and drank gratefully, looking out the window, astonished by the sheer volume of traffic on the roadways. It was barely six o'clock in the morning.

"I'm Big Avi," the driver said, grinning.

Avi with the bald sunburned head was not big but small. Half Mary's weight and several inches shorter. He laughed at her confusion. "My son is Little Avi," he explained. "My card is there."

It was, in a tiny silver holder—a business card with the name Big Avi and the company's name. "Miracle Limousine Service," Mary read out loud.

"When my father-in-law started the company the miracle was to get his bank loan. Now, the miracle is to drive in Los Angeles traffic."

Mary nodded, absently slipping the business card into her pocket since her purse was out of reach, thinking of the stalled traffic in Toronto days ago, hours ago. A lifetime ago. "You know how to get to Golden Hills?"

"Of course," he answered. "I'm in the valley also. My shift is done. I'm going home. Now I don't go empty. Good for you. Good for me."

When his cellphone rang he fished it out of his pocket and spoke rapidly in his foreign tongue. When he had finished his conversation he returned to Mary in his rearview mirror. "It's your first time in Los Angeles?" he asked.

She nodded, dizzy from the cars and lack of food. She looked into the basket on the floor. "How much does the banana cost?"

Big Avi waved his hand. "Don't cost. Just eat."

As she peeled the banana, her mouth did not water in anticipation. The aroma of the fruit, freshly eaten, baked into a cream pie, blended into a parfait or boiled into a pudding, had once been bliss to Mary. An ecstasy in whose throes she could not resist a third and fourth slice, or the whole batch, or the whole bunch. But now she realized that the fragrance was only faint, and the taste not a flavor but a notion. She thought of the Oakwood, the apple, the granola bar and reasoned that a sensual deficit of smell and taste, along with the stress of her situation, was behind her lack of appetite.

"Next time you take Pacific Coast. It's more longer but more beautiful. Today we take the freeway," the man explained. She nodded again, watching the scenery blur.

"The airline loses your luggage?"

"No. No. I don't have any luggage. My trip wasn't exactly planned."

He raised a brow, intrigued. "You leave your work and say, 'Okay, now I go to California.'"

"Something like that."

"You are brave. You are, what is this word, *spontaneous?*"

"Spontaneous? Me? No." But brave? Maybe.

Lost in impressions of the world flashing by, Mary found nothing quite as she had imagined it except for the thickets of white oleander and crimson bougainvillea, and the soaring palm trees listing in the wind. Flanking the dozens of lanes of traffic were thick blocks of concrete that seemed to give foundation to the rising hills whose surface was spotted with homes, small and bunched in places, massive and solitary and jutting out from the hillside in others.

"Is beautiful the weather here," Big Avi remarked. "Hot in the valley. It's lucky you miss the fires."

Mary nodded, unsure of what fires he meant. Or where the valley was.

Sensitive to his customer's moods, he offered, "If you like the privacy I can put the glass."

At this he pressed a button and a sliver of dark window began to rise up behind him.

Mary shouted, "No! Please. I don't want privacy."

He grinned. "Most of my passenger want the glass. Mostly I carry the showbizness."

Mary was surprised that she didn't really care whose celebrity ass she could claim to have shared the upholstery with, or what tidbit of gossip he might have overheard. "I never imagined it quite like this. So many cars," she said.

"When first I came here I thought so also and now there is double. Maybe triple. I think Los Angeles is Hollywood. Malibu." He laughed. "It's so many communities make up Los Angeles. Now I know them all. Top ten safe cities in America is Golden Hills. I live in Westlake. Close."

"But the gangs? All the crime and murders you hear about?"

"That place you don't go. It's that way." He pointed. "East. South Central. It's not for tourist."

Mary took a moment to consider that within this vast expanse, one select section of the population was living the safest life in the country while another was engaged in what Gooch had said was a shameful civil war.

"That way is Glendale. That's the Armenians."

"Oh."

"Downtown is the business. And the Asians. Every place has a different character."

"Like a movie," Mary said absently, feeling infinitesimal within the speeding machine among the swarms on the cat's cradle of roads, wondering if from here she might see Grauman's Chinese or the Scientology Center or one of the other dozens of landmarks she knew from movies and TV.

"Good. Is very good traffic this morning." Big Avi exhaled as he eased the sleek automobile toward an exit from that freeway and set their course down another. The road seemed equally clogged to Mary but the driver was gleeful. "Sometimes, back there is a parking lot. Nothing moves. You're lucky today. It's a miracle."

The limousine swam sharklike through the lanes, the concrete still rising in places, the freeway overlooking dense populations in others. Like the main hallway of a big mall, what seemed an endless stretch of road cut through a retail paradise of box stores and chain stores and fast-food restaurants, some with the familiar golden arches but many whose names she didn't recognize. There was the bull's eye for Target, the American department store Wendy and Kim had wanted to take her to for her birthday one year, Kim gently offering, "They've got really cute things in bigger sizes."

"Pollo Loco," Mary read.

"*Poyo*," Avi said, correcting her pronunciation. "It's Spanish. Crazy chicken."

"Crazy chicken?"

"Now we're passing Woodland Hills."

"Calabasas," she read on a road sign.

"Pumpkin is what it means in Spanish," he said. "It's not the spelling right."

"Are you Spanish?"

He checked his rearview, unsure of the joke.

"Armenian?" she tried.

"Israeli. I have been in United States for seven years. Little Avi was born in America the year after I came."

Mary thought of her first unborn child. He or she would be twenty-four. "I'm Canadian," she announced, a statement she had never made before.

The driver's face lit up. "My cousin lives near Toronto. We visit two years ago. I take my Avi to the hockey game. Go Maple Leafs," he added, smiling.

Mary didn't explain that her husband, like most of Leaford, liked the Detroit Red Wings, which sounded unpatriotic out of context.

"Watch, Mary Gooch. It's now the hills."

As promised, the proliferation of buildings receded and before them lay a vista of tawny mountains brushed with scrub and clustered with oaks through which the highway gracefully arced. The shadows cast by the sun gave life to the hills, so that they seemed to rise and fall with slumbering breath, like golden reclining nudes.

"In the spring everything is green, like a banquet, I can't tell you," Big Avi said with a wave of his arm. "And gold with the flowers. It's a weed. But it's beautiful."

Mary'd always felt that way about dandelions. On the roadside she read, "Golden Hills."

"Soon. Few minutes. What address please?"

Gooch. Possibly minutes away. Mary glanced down at herself. Even if the smell was faint, she sensed a sourness leaching from her skin, and thought that at the very least she'd have to shower and change into her other navy uniform before she found Eden's house on Willow Drive. "Oh, well, a motel, I guess," she said.

"Cheap or nice?"

She would have answered, "Nice and cheap," but she remembered the money in her bank account and reasoned that she'd only be paying for one day, given that Eden would most certainly invite her to stay, however long it might be for. "Nice."

"I know *very* nice," he said.

"Just *nice* is fine. Thank you."

"Pleasant Inn," Avi decided. "It's pleasant." As they sped up the ramp at the intersection of Golden Hills and the highway, he pointed left. "This way. Maybe fifteen minutes. Malibu."

"Oh." She would suggest a drive there with Gooch. She imagined them together, rolling up their pants and walking in the surf, reaching out to take his hand, grateful to share her awe. *Whatever it is, we'll work it out.*

He pointed ahead. "You have seen the Pacific Ocean?"

"I've never seen any ocean."

"You must see the ocean. It moves the soul, I can't tell you."

They stopped at a set of lights where three roads and twelve lanes intersected, and where, in a dusty vacant lot, a crowd of small, dark men dressed in faded clothes and baseball caps gathered around a pyramid of thermoses, heads raised off their shoulders, eyes scanning the road like meerkats on patrol.

"Who are they?" Mary asked.

"The Mexicans?"

"What are they doing?"

"They are the day workers. They wait."

"For what?"

"For people to come."

"People just come and pick them up?"

"Maybe someone needs help to make a construction. Or pick the fruit. Anything."

"So they just *wait*?"

"In the morning there are more. Now"—he checked his watch—"a miracle if someone stops. Today these men don't work."

"What do they do?"

"They come back tomorrow. They hope someone stops." He shrugged and set the car in motion, turning into a side road.

"I hope someone stops," Mary said, catching the eye of one of the men, a broad-shouldered man with a trimmed beard who stood apart, in many ways, from the others. The broad man's eyes bore into the window when the limousine passed and Mary shivered, until she realized she could not be seen behind the darkened glass.

"Is terrible to be poor. This I see in my life," Avi sighed, honking at a gleaming SUV whose driver had failed to notice the green traffic signal.

"Do you still have relations in Israel?" Mary asked.

"All are gone. All are dead."

"I'm sorry."

"Only here now," he said, pressing his fist to his heart.

"Mine are too. I only have my husband."

The driver glanced in the rearview. "Your *children?*"

James, Thomas, Liza, Rachel. Mary shook her head, watching the landscape as they drove on. She was unaware that the car had come to a stop at the inn of his suggestion until the driver took his cap off and turned around to face her. "Mary Gooch?" he said softly. But when she looked up she could not see his face, or the building at which they had stopped. Her cheeks felt hot and wet. Big Avi reached over his seat and passed her a tissue which she pressed to her eyes, as though a mere tissue, or a whole box of them, might stem the flood.

After the impatient honking of a horn behind the limo, the driver pulled into a parking place and climbed into the back seat to sit across from her. It took a moment for Mary to realize that he was holding her hand. "I'm sorry," she said, blowing her nose. "I'm not like this. I don't know what got into me."

"Now is out," he said, smiling.

"Are we at the hotel? I should . . ." Mary made a move to reach for her bag, but he stopped her with gentle pressure on her fingers.

"You don't go inside yet. Not like this. Drink some water."

She drank from the proffered bottle, attempting to compose herself.

"You are not spontaneous. You are running away?"

She looked into his red face and answered with the facts. "My husband left me. And I've come to find him. He's here. In Golden Hills. At my mother-in-law's house. At least I think he is."

"I understand."

"I shouldn't have come. I just . . . I didn't know what else to do."

"He has another woman?"

"I don't think so."

Avi paused. "He has a man?"

"No," Mary answered with certainty.

"You can't go to him like this," he said, pursing his lips. He released her hand, climbed out of the back seat and into the front. They pulled away from the hotel.

"Where are we going?" she asked.

"I take you to Frankie."

Uncommon Humanity

T he big black limousine might have been speeding down any street in any town, not through the bleached brown hills of the northern San Fernando Valley. So deeply purged was Mary that she'd left the car, and her body altogether, as she had in the grass under the stormy Leaford sky. She'd been released in the glut of tears, along with a hundred losses, a thousand humiliations, a million hurts. She felt light. And she was enlightened enough to understand that it wasn't just the good cry that had let it all out, but the entire extended episode of "Life After Gooch."

She did not think to ask who Frankie was, or why they were going to see him, or how this man was to help with her situation. The driver seemed so confident that he might as well have said, "I'm taking you to see the sage on the hill. He'll tell you what to do." She had not so much surrendered her will as submitted to the quotidian queerness of life beyond Leaford. Besides, she felt somewhat unprepared to see Gooch, if he was there, and wanted to float awhile longer in the dry, warm air above the limousine, aware that the feeling, like all things, would pass.

As it did when the limousine found its way to a strip mall and Mary was drawn out of the clouds and back into the car, caught by the contrast to any such places she'd ever seen in Leaford or Chatham or even Windsor. The parking lot was vast, adorned with islands of palms and dazzling displays of foliage and impressive water fountains reflected in the gleaming windshields and doors of the vehicles, none of which were old Ford trucks with broken sunroofs. Hummers, which she'd never seen before but which had been so ubiquitous on the highway from the airport that she'd stopped counting, and Escalades and Land Rovers, and Mercedeses and Lexuses and Corvettes and Jaguars. *Gooch would love this,* she thought, aroused by the hot chrome and sexy spoilers, the contour and design and color and symmetry. Perhaps Gooch had bought a new car with the money he'd won in the lottery. She wondered what he was driving.

There were no Dollarama stores with boxes of discount products cluttering the sidewalk here. No submarine sandwich shops or dusty variety stores. Only the sparkling facades of upscale women's clothing shops and jewelry stores and real estate offices. Blowing her nose a final time, Mary drank in the scene, her first glimpse of Californians deployed from their vehicles: sun-kissed children with matching clothes and fresh sneakers, chiseled men in chic suits or embarrassingly snug running shorts. And the women — slender and manicured, with shiny hair and costly jeans and cute shoes with bows and leather handbags with glamorous metallic details.

Big Avi found a place to park in front of a coffee shop outside of which were cedar chairs and huge canvas umbrellas unspoiled by birds or the elements. It had not occurred to Mary that bystanders on the sidewalk or customers sipping lattes would be interested in who was in the limousine, and she was horrified as all eyes turned to watch Avi, in his cap, help her out of the seat. She caught her reflection in the mirrored window of the coffee shop, her long, red hair ablaze in the blinding California sun. She thought she must look like an actor straight from Central Casting—the eccentric nurse with a heart of gold, or the asylum inmate on a day pass.

Big Avi smiled at her and offered his arm, escorting her from the car to the promenade, saying, "After Frankie, you will feel strong. Then I take you to your husband."

A cup of overpriced coffee would not cure Mary's current ill, but it couldn't hurt, she decided. "I'm sorry to trouble you like this," she said, undone by his uncommon humanity. "I suppose I *could* use a coffee."

But Big Avi passed by the umbrellas and directed her toward a large blue door beside the coffee shop, ushering her into a cavernous, butter-colored hive—what Irma called *the beauty shop*. On either side of the room a bevy of women of varying ages sat in swivel seats, being coiffed by a bevy of women of varying ages in white smocks. Leaving Mary at the reception counter before she could ask what this man Frankie had to do with a beauty salon, Big Avi disappeared into a back room through a set of silver swinging doors.

Mary looked around her at the four women waiting on soft leather chairs—two having stopped flipping through their magazines, and the other two having looked up from their hand-held messengers, to assess the newcomer. She ignored her instinct to flee and took a seat beside a teenage girl with long, blonde hair, taking care not to offend anyone with her exhalations. Undecided as to whether she hoped she was dreaming or *feared* she was, she wondered if at any moment she would wake to the crack in the ceiling and the snow out the window and the vacancy of her lumpy bed. An electronic beeping distracted her, and she glanced at the young girl beside her, whence the sound seemed to emanate.

"I think that's you," the girl said, looking up.

"Excuse me?"

"That's you," the girl repeated. "Your phone?"

"My phone?" The beeping did not sound like "Proud Mary."

"You must have a message?"

"Oh. *Oh.*" Mary found the cellphone in her purse. If she did have a message it could be important. It could be *Gooch.* She looked at the phone. The beeping continued. The other women looked up too, watching as she touched several buttons, as embarrassed by the incessant beeping as she was by her ineptitude. She took a breath and said, "I'm sorry. I don't know if I have a message. And if I have one, I don't know how to get it."

Mary held her breath, pressing buttons, until a young woman seated across from her set down her magazine and pointed out, "Could be your battery. Just shut it off." The woman reached out, taking the phone from Mary and opening it, and announced with authority, "It's not a message. You just need to recharge."

"Thank you," Mary said, taking the phone back. She toyed with the idea of asking the woman for a crash course on the cellphone but when she looked up Big Avi was sailing toward her, his sunburned face split by a wide grin, trailed by a voluminous woman with platinum hair piled atop her head and a face so painted that her exotic features seemed to stand out in relief. This woman, years younger than Mary but almost as large, with her black-rimmed almond eyes and enormous berry-stained lips, scrutinized her, unsmiling, like a garage mechanic appraising a wreck.

"This is Mary Gooch?" she asked, with an American accent that seemed to betray foreign roots.

"Mary, I would like you to meet Frankie," Avi said formally. "This is her shop."

Frankie was dressed not in a white smock but in a flowing, long-sleeved, turquoise paisley blouse over a matching skirt that caressed the rolling flesh of her hips and buttocks. She was beautiful. *Big and beautiful.* Here was self-acceptance, Mary thought. Or perhaps Frankie's apparent comfort in her body was just another deception, like those movie stars who celebrated their volume on the covers of magazines, then went on to shill for weight-loss companies.

Mary rose with some effort and offered her hand, which the

woman took but did not shake. "Come with me, honey," she said, pulling her along.

Big Avi patted Mary's shoulder. "Frankie will help," he said, then checked his watch and promised, "I be back. One hour."

Even as she was sitting in the waiting area of the beauty shop, Mary had not guessed that Frankie was a woman, or that the purpose of their stop was a makeover. Feeling far beyond such superficial assistance, she would have protested had she known. She never watched makeover shows on television, too depressed by the quick fixes and confused by the mixed messages. It seemed that people, not just women, were told, on the one hand, to embrace their uniqueness because the superficial was irrelevant, and on the other hand, that an updated hairstyle and a few good accessories could alter the very course of their lives.

She watched through half-closed lids the shivering flesh on Frankie's neck as she massaged a cream rinse into Mary's long hair, and cringed when the woman announced loudly, "My first husband left me too. Six years ago this spring."

"Oh," Mary said, deciding that she was grateful Big Avi had told the woman her story, so she didn't have to.

"Best thing that ever happened to me. Two weeks later I met Bob at Ralph's and I swear to God I have never looked back."

"Oh."

"I'm there at the bakery desk, right, ordering a cake for my nephew's birthday, and Bob's standing there, and we start talking about traffic or whatever. I was a little freaked out, frankly, because in, like, two minutes, he's asking me for a date." Frankie leaned in closer, whispering, "I decided to just put it out there, and I go, 'Are you one of those creeps who likes to fuck fat girls?' And he looks me straight in the eye and he goes, 'If you're one of those fat girls who likes to fuck creeps.' I laughed so freakin' hard. I've been with him ever since."

Mary was shocked by the woman's language and candor, but the story had a certain sweet charm. "That's nice," she said. "Are you Israelite too?"

The stylist shampooing a brunette at the next sink cackled, "She's *Persian*," as if that should have been obvious.

Away from the sinks and with the door in view, Mary once again felt the instinct to flee, but with Big Avi gone and her hair soaking wet she could only sit in the swivel seat Frankie offered and endure the brushing out of her locks. *Irma*, she thought, mildly comforted to know that her mother would be oblivious to her absence, even as it had tormented Mary for so many years that she'd been unaware of her presence. She squeezed her eyes.

"It's hard, honey, I know," Frankie said, reaching for a bottle of milky detangler. "Avi said the airline lost your luggage." Mary was too weary to explain. "Is it another woman?" Frankie asked.

Mary sensed that the women nearby, the customers and stylists, were listening, and she answered quietly, "I don't think so."

Frankie sighed, looking at the strands of damp red hair. "Your ends are *so* damaged, and this length ages you, like, ten years. I'm thinking, take it right up to the shoulders."

When Mary didn't respond, the woman in the next chair spoke up. "You have such a pretty face. Doesn't she have a pretty face?"

Mary smiled at them both in the mirror. "Cut it," she instructed Frankie. "Whatever you think." Frankie grabbed the length of her ponytail and hacked it off like a nasty weed. Mary watched the red tail fall to the floor as if it belonged to someone else.

A customer in the row behind shouted, "You go, girl!"

Blushing scarlet, Mary looked up as Frankie waved her scissors like a wand over the group. "Okay, everybody. This is Mary from Canada," she announced. "Her husband left her."

The women *tsk*ed their sympathy.

"He's at his mother's place over in Golden Hills and she's going to give him a piece of her mind after she leaves here."

All around were murmurs of support, and Mary was struck by the women's unanimous interest. *There but for the grace of God go I.*

"I'm thinking blunt to the shoulders and a little curl around the face," Frankie continued, eliciting opinions.

A stylist behind her called over the din of the blow-dryers, "No bangs. Lana Turner with a side part and some volume at the crown."

Mary felt her heart racing. Her privacy invaded. Her hair cut off. If she'd ever been confused about her identity, she was even more so now. "I shouldn't have come," she whispered to the mirror image of the big woman with wet shoulder-length red hair. "I just feel completely lost."

The woman who'd remarked on her pretty face found her eyes in the mirror. "We've all been there, sweetie. We've all been there."

Another woman, whom Mary hadn't noticed beneath a hair dryer in the corner, looked up from a bizarre wig of aluminum-foil squares and called out, "How long have you been married?"

"Twenty-five years."

"You must have been a baby."

"Eighteen," Mary said.

"I don't care what happened. Twenty-five years is worth fighting for," the woman declared. She stood and shuffled across the room to take the other chair beside Mary. The woman's eyes were held captive by her smooth, rigid face — a sheer serenity that, along with bee-stung lips and collagen-filled nasal labia, had become as standard as any fashion, but which Mary had never seen in person.

Many years ago, in one of Mary's painful Sunday calls to her mother-in-law, Eden had told her in an offhand way that she was having a facelift. Mary had felt a twinge of self-righteousness but stopped herself from begging an answer to *why?* She'd been surprised by Gooch's reaction, when he'd merely shrugged and said, "Whatever floats her boat."

"But what about aging gracefully?" Mary'd asked. "I thought

you'd hate to think your mother was so vain. Don't you think it's wrong?"

"My mother *is* vain. But who are we to judge?" he said pointedly.

"People die from plastic surgery, Gooch. I'm just saying I think it's a stupid risk." Her obesity had swung its trunk in the corner of the room, and they'd said no more of Eden's decision.

Now, surrendering to her beautification, she shut her eyes and accepted the rush of pleasure from the warm air of the dryer. A rare sensual pleasure. She realized that although it had been six and a half years since she and Gooch had had intercourse, the joy of the act had been lost many years and pounds before that.

After their first few years together, when the very thought of his lips had driven blood to her core, she'd begun to make excuses when Gooch reached for her in bed, her desire enslaved by her perception of being undesirable. When Gooch was particularly insistent, never rough or pressuring but with his mouth on her neck or his fingers mining her cleavage, she'd borne the event like Irma with dinner, anxious to have it over with.

When Mary opened her eyes again, she did not recognize the woman with shoulder-length red hair framing her pretty face. She could only say, "Oh."

Frankie smiled — an artist having completed her masterpiece. "You're *gorgeous*," she breathed, followed by a gush of accord from the others. Mary blinked her thanks to them all, searching their faces for tells. She wondered if this display of generosity was what it appeared to be. In discovering her loss and confusion they'd all taken a step in Mary's shoes, or boots, as the case was, and had seen not a fat woman or a thin woman, or old or young or rich or poor, but *themselves*, in a soul who'd been left and felt lost.

The plastic cape that Frankie had draped over her front but failed to clasp around her neck slid off as she prepared to rise.

"She can't wear that," one of the stylists said, pointing out the navy scrubs, and Frankie frowned. Helping Mary from the seat, the big beautiful Persian American woman pulled her through the silver swinging doors and into the privacy of a large, well-appointed bathroom.

"Are you a nurse?" Frankie asked, opening the door to a large armoire.

Mary shook her head, not attempting to explain the navy scrubs, as she looked at the collection of plus-sized clothing with price tags attached. Frankie found a paisley skirt-and-blouse ensemble identical to the one she was wearing but in green, and handed the hanger to Mary. "Put this on. Go ahead. It's my husband's dress business. I'll give it to you at cost. Try it on."

When Mary didn't move, Frankie whispered, "You need privacy. But I'm gonna tell you something, because we're both big girls and I can say this. If you think your husband left you because you're fat, you should thank God you got a second chance."

"Is that why your husband left you?"

"He left me because I was miserable. I was always on a diet. But Bob loves me big. Bob taught me how to own it. If you don't like something about yourself, change it. If you're okay with it, you gotta own it. There's nothing in between."

"Okay."

Before Frankie left, she added, "There's a shoe store at the next plaza over. You can't wear those boots in California."

Stepping through the swinging doors in the attractive clothes, Mary found Big Avi and the entire shop waiting for the big reveal. Feeling like an unwilling contestant on a game show, she twirled, turning scarlet. She stopped in front of the mirror as Frankie fixed her waistband and fiddled with the blouse.

"How much do I owe you?" Mary asked, reaching for her credit card.

Frankie wrote a number on an invoice and handed it to her. The amount was more than three weeks' groceries.

Another stylist hurried out from the back room carrying a plastic bag containing her navy scrubs. She passed it to Mary, whispering, "You can't wear those boots in California."

Smiling to hide his impatience, Big Avi took Mary's arm, escorting her through the doors into the blinding sunshine and back to the leather cocoon of the waiting limousine.

Weeping Willows

Big Avi smiled broadly in the rearview mirror. "You look beautiful. You feel strong? Yes?"

"Yes," Mary agreed, but it wasn't because of the makeover. She was superficially transformed, no doubt, but she did not identify with the red-headed, finely dressed (apart from the boots) woman she'd seen reflected in the mirror of the beauty salon. Her fortification was no product of this transformation, but a strength stirred by those women who had armed her in green paisley and sent her out to battle for love on behalf of them all.

"I just don't know how to thank you," Mary said. "I just don't know a lot of people who would do what you've done for a stranger."

"It's enough," Big Avi said, waving his hands. "I charge you just for regular car service. That's all."

"Thank you."

"So many strangers helped me when first I came to America, I can't tell you. My thanks is to serve. It's enough. You understand? You know this feeling?"

Mary did not know the feeling, as she'd spent most of her life in service to her hunger, and most of her days with her eyes cast down, suffering and frustrated and too weary from her own dissatisfaction to measure the misery of her fellows. She might have said she had served Gooch, but it would have been a lie. She'd found the notion of domestic servitude anti-feminist, and even if Gooch did work longer hours and bring double the money to their joint bank account, she'd resented the chores of sweeping the house and making meals, and had never found glory in a scrubbed-clean oven, or peace in the crease of the shirts she ironed Sunday mornings.

"I know Willow Drive," Big Avi announced. "It's in the suburbs before Oak Hills."

Leaford had no suburbs to speak of. There were huge, beautiful Victorians in the historic old center of the town and wartime bungalows on the periphery, and the rest of the population lived in the country, either farming the land on which they lived, or living in homes on land farmed by others. Mary'd seen the suburbs of Windsor, the ones Gooch described as monotonous for the sameness of the architecture, but those homes were unique in comparison to the landscape she was entering now. These suburban homes were enormous dwellings, monster houses in six repeating models — the single-story, the double, the garage on the left, on the right, the giant bay window, the smaller bow — painted one of three shades of beige, with a cluster of tall palms or a fountain of willow at the center of the landscaping design.

"Welcome to Willow Highlands," Big Avi said.

Set high on the crest of rolling hills, featuring even larger houses, with wide, paved streets and so much free parking that those drivers in Toronto and New York would seethe with envy, Willow Highlands looked to Mary like a movie's painted backdrop, as if a shift in perspective or the touch of a finger might destroy the illusion of paradise. It was mid-afternoon and the suburbanites were presumably at work or school, but she nonetheless felt the souls lingering within their homes, living their American dream.

The few toiling humans she could see as the car rolled past were diminutive brown people. "Are all these people Mexican?" she asked.

Avi checked the mirror again, uncertain of her humor; then, deciding she wasn't joking, he answered, "Everybody has help. The gardener. The housekeeper. The nanny."

"Are they illegal? Even in Canada you hear so much about the illegal Mexicans down here."

He shrugged. "Some. Everybody has opinions on immigration. Me, I do my immigration legal. It was hard. Cost so much money I can't tell you. But I see these people come for a better life. I have sympathy. They want to work."

Mary watched one of the Mexican men wearing an enormous contraption on his back, wielding a fat hose like a submachine gun to blow debris from the white sidewalk. "The leaves fall here too," she remarked.

"Some. Yes. Of course. There is seasons. In winter it's not cold, but at night you bring a sweater."

"In Canada they say we have two seasons — winter and construction," she said, but when he glanced in his mirror she saw that he was confused. "Because summer's the only time the construction crews can work on the roads."

"Ah, a joke." He smiled and turned down another street. "Two more streets is Willow. What number please?"

"Twenty-four." Mary swallowed. Looking out the window, she was surprised to see that the limousine had left the cluster of sprawling homes and found a much less affluent neighborhood at the base of the hills, which she reasoned must be Willow *Lowlands*. Smaller stucco homes with less adorned lawns alternated with rows of two-story townhouses. As her in-laws had significant wealth, she suddenly panicked that she had the wrong address. Or even the wrong town.

"I have to go quickly," Big Avi said, glancing at his watch. "My little Avi has soccer." He pulled to the curb in front of a modest white home with a high arched entrance, outside of which a few neglected plants in clay pots lined a short, cracked walk. "Twenty-four," he announced.

There were two vehicles in the leaf-strewn driveway — a battered red Camry that Mary guessed to be a late-nineties model, and a newer white Prius, the hybrid car Gooch had admired but dismissed as too small for a big man to drive comfortably.

"Someone is there. Yes?" Avi asked, swiping her credit card through his machine.

"I can't imagine that this is the right house," Mary said, hesitating. "My in-laws are quite rich."

"Wealthy is different in California," he cautioned. "This house cost nearly one million dollars."

"No!"

"It's true!" He climbed out of the front seat to help her out of the back. After squeezing her hands and looking into her eyes, he whispered, "Go talk to your husband."

Mary smiled and nodded, waving as the car pulled away. *God,* she prayed, *please help me find the words*. Her heart fluttered, and she cursed herself for not remembering to eat more from the wicker basket. Turning to the little stucco house, she hoped she might sense, the way she did God, the presence of Jimmy Gooch.

But it appeared increasingly likely that she did have the wrong house, considering the no-smoking sign plastered to the glass on the front door. She'd never seen Jack, in person or photographs, without a Marlboro wagging in his yip.

Approaching the door, she strained to listen over the black crows cawing from a nearby tree, but there was no sound within. The wrong house. There must be another 24 Willow Drive in another Golden Hills, California. She remembered that her in-laws' previous dwelling had had a lap pool and tennis courts. Eden had sent a photograph of herself and Jack, in matching designer track suits, leaning against their silver Acura in the driveway of the enormous manse, and Mary recalled Gooch's comment: "Why would they need seven bedrooms?"

The wrong house. What now?

The front door opened and a small woman with pretty black eyes and dark hair twisted into a bun stepped onto the porch, regarding her suspiciously. "*Hola,*" the woman said.

"Mary," Mary corrected her.

"*Hola?*" the woman tried again.

"No, Mary," Mary repeated, pointing to herself. "*Mary.*"

The woman said something in Spanish that Mary did not understand, and called quietly in the direction of a darkened room, "Señora."

"I seem to have the wrong house," Mary apologized. Then she saw through the open door a frail, elderly woman limping down the shadowed hall, and her heart began to race. Although she hadn't seen Eden in nearly twenty years, she recognized her instantly as she shuffled into the light, by her trademark black bob.

If her mother-in-law's face had ever been lifted, the lower half had fallen again. Her rheumy blue eyes slanted catlike toward her bangs, and her cheeks and jowls hung like laundry on the line. Her body was weathered and as fragile as wood left out in the rain. Hands clawed by arthritis punctuated her spindly arms. Eden did not recognize Mary, or couldn't see clearly. "What is it, Chita?" she asked.

"Eden," Mary breathed.

"Yes," the old woman answered, squinting, piqued.

"Eden. It's Mary."

The dawning of familiarity rose in Eden's fallen face. "Mary?"

"I'm sorry to just show up like this."

"I wouldn't have recognized you," Eden said.

Mary touched her swingy red hair, and then realized that Eden was referring to her extreme weight, not her extreme makeover. She stood on the porch, waiting to be invited into the house.

The sound of a beeping microwave drew the Mexican woman back inside as Eden leaned against the door frame, weary from the walk, irritated by the intrusion. "He's not here, Mary."

"But Heather said —"

"Heather?" Eden said, lifting her brow. "Well, he was here, but he's gone."

Mary sniffed the air, hoping to catch his scent, as Eden opened the door and sighed, resigned, "I suppose you'd better come in. But be *quiet*. Jack's asleep."

The fragrance of the house was faint but familiar — a whiff of urine, a hint of decay, like St. John's in Leaford. Christopher Klik's house on the day of the funeral. Led into a small living room crammed with oversized furniture, Mary realized that she was trembling. So close, she thought. She had missed Gooch by hours, days, she told herself, but she knew it was really *years*. She felt faint, and did not so much sit in one of the upholstered chairs as fall into it. "I hate to trouble you, Eden, but I haven't eaten much today. I'm afraid I might faint."

Eden rolled her eyes, calling out in a hush toward the back of the house, "Bring in the prune Danish and some iced tea, Chita!" Taking a place on the sofa across from Mary, she did not disguise her contempt. "You shouldn't have come. And why on earth are you wearing winter boots in California?"

"I had to come."

"He's a wreck. You know that. He's just a wreck."

In twenty-five years Mary had not heard her husband referred to in such sorry terms. It was she who'd always been the wreck, or the wretch, or the mess. Not Gooch. Gooch lived the dream. Gooch triumphed. Gooch accepted his story as it unfolded, while she propped her memoir on her rolling stomach, turning the pages at random, wishing the author had taken it a different way.

"Heather said he won money on the scratch-and-win."

"I know." Eden smiled for the first time, revealing a set of pearl-white teeth longer and squarer than her originals. "The Lord heard my prayer."

"When was he here?" she asked carefully, afraid that Eden might run away like a feral cat, or decide to play dumb like a child.

"Last week. Tuesday or Wednesday. I lose track of time."

Had the circumstances been different, Mary might have offered her own understanding of the loss of time. Instead she said, "I've been so worried."

"He didn't do this to hurt you, Mary."

"We've been going through a rough patch," Mary said quietly, taking the cold glass offered by the Mexican woman, who'd appeared with iced tea and a tray of pastry.

"He blames himself."

"He does?"

"But it takes two to tango, doesn't it?" Eden asked. "And that's what I told him. I said 'Stop blaming yourself, Jimmy. Surely Mary had *something* to do with it.' He didn't say a word against you. Not a word. He didn't tell me how *big* you'd gotten." Eden raised her high brows. "I hardly recognized you. You're twice the size you were when I saw you last."

Mary considered the pastry on the table but could not bring herself to reach for it; the thought of biting into the sweet, doughy bread brought on another wave of nausea, and the forgotten pain between her eyes trumpeted reveille.

"I can only imagine what it's been like for him all these years. That boy had so many gifts. He should have been a writer," Eden said, and Gooch's potential, along with his mother's clear subtext, hung in the dank, pissy air.

It was true, Mary thought. Gooch should have been a writer. He should have been anything other than what he had become.

"Don't you dare spill that tea," Eden warned, as Mary listed in her seat. "That's a two-thousand-dollar Ethan Allen!"

"Oh," Mary said, sipping from the overfilled glass.

"How's your mother?"

"The same."

"I know you've had your share of disappointments, Mary."

"Yes."

"It's no excuse, though."

"Where did he go when he left here? Please tell me if you know, Eden. I'm his wife." Mary pleaded. "I'm his wife."

"He said something about seeing the redwoods. Big Sur. Hiking or some other. He had a guidebook. He said he didn't have firm plans, he just needed some time to think."

Time to think. "He didn't say for how long?"

"He didn't say. And not that he asked for my opinion — not that he's ever asked for my opinion — but I told him he should file for divorce and put an end to it. You both need to get on with your lives. He's still young. He could have thirty good years with somebody else. Look at Jack and me."

Mary cleared her throat. "You really don't know where he went?"

"He was here for all of an hour before he and Jack got into it," Eden sniffed. "That's the price you pay. You put your husband before everything. That's what you do. That's what *you* should have done."

Mary didn't ask her if losing her children had been too great a price to pay, for she could see in the woman's righteous eyes that she felt the loss was theirs.

"I want to *help* Gooch. I want to . . ." The addendum to her want was too complicated and intimate to express aloud.

"I'd ask you to stay, but we've got six coming for prayer circle in half an hour."

If her head had not hurt, Mary might have hammered it with the heel of her palm and exclaimed, *What was I thinking?* How had she ever imagined that she might find Gooch taking his *time to think* in the toxic presence of Jack Asquith? "I'm sorry, Eden. I'm sorry he and Jack got into it. It must have been awful."

Eden softened. "He said he'd come to see me again before he left the state. I told him I'd meet him out at the deli."

"He's coming back?"

"He promised he'd come to say goodbye."

Goodbye. Gooch understood the ritual too. He needed to say goodbye to his mother because he felt her mortality. Or his own. The lottery win had been the force disrupting his inertia. Mary imagined him sitting in his truck behind Chung's, salivating for his Combo Number 3. She could see his face as he scratched that ticket with a quarter from his pocket, and in those three matching numbers found both the impetus and the means to leave his wife, to ponder his existence. *Free.*

"I think I should wait for him," she said.

"Well, not *here*," Eden assured her. "Besides, we don't know when he's coming back."

"Eventually he'll run out of money."

"I suppose."

"And he'll have to go back to work."

"Eventually."

"It's not like he has a million dollars. Did he tell you how much he'd won?"

"Enough. He just said *enough*."

Enough. That word. The suggestion of balance. Just the right amount. A lovely word — until someone yells it at you. *Enough!*

Suspecting that Eden was lying, Mary said, "Well, if he promised he'd come back, he'll come back. And I should be here when he does."

"Suit yourself, Mary, but I can't offer you a room, and even the cheap motels down here are expensive. Besides, what if it's not a day or two days or a week? What if he's gone off for a month? Or more?"

"He wouldn't do that." Drinking the iced tea, Mary calculated the cost of a month's hotel lodging and incidentals.

"And what would you do, Mary? Sit in a hotel room watching television? Ordering in junk food? And if you plan to stay down here at all, you'll need a car the whole time. You can't get anywhere without a car. What are you driving?"

"I got a ride." Adding car rental fees, at which she could only guess, Mary began to fret. Stay in this foreign land to wait for Gooch until her money ran out? Return to Leaford to get on with her life? But what life? Mr. Barkley gone. Orin gone. Her mother a ghost. She didn't even have a job to return to, a fact which she realized she would at some point need to address. "I'm going to stay," she decided aloud.

"Well, I've said my piece," Eden declared, throwing up her hands.

Reaching into her purse, Mary found a pen and scrap of paper. "I'll write down my cellphone number, and you'll call me, won't you? When you hear from him?"

Eden took the piece of paper and set it on the table. "I think it's a mistake. I really do."

The women rose, struggling with their broken bodies as they made their way to the door. Mary had almost reached the porch when she remembered her purse and the plastic bag with her navy uniform. Stepping back into the house, she heard a sound coming from a room at the end of the hallway. Gooch.

So Eden was lying, as Heather had lied, as all people lied for people they loved, or people they owed. He was there, about to step out of the room, believing his wife was gone. "Gooch?" she blurted.

Jack Asquith — bleary and beaten, shrunken and shriveled, an oxygen mask suffocating his cured-leather face — emerged from the room on a small motorized wheelchair. Here was death, hollow-eyed and terrified, approaching Mary at the door. "Jack," she breathed.

"Go get ready for prayer circle, Jack," Eden instructed him. But Jack stayed his course, motoring over the terracotta floor, regarding Mary with squinting mistrust, as if she'd been let backstage for a show without a special pass. He stopped at the toe of her boots, pulled the mask away from his face and croaked, "Who?"

Eden waved him off. "Nobody, dear. Go get ready." Dragging Mary out to the porch and closing the door behind them so he couldn't overhear, she begged, "Please don't get him upset."

"He looks terrible," Mary cried. "Oh my *God*."

"We do not use God to exclaim in this house."

"I'm sorry, I just—"

"Well, you knew he had the emphysema." Mary shook her head, speechless. "He's been going down fast."

"I'm so sorry."

"Imagine *me* having to ask my *son* for money."

"Why?"

"What do you mean, why? Jack's health insurance hasn't covered half the expenses."

"I didn't know."

"Of course you knew."

"It's been a long time since we've talked, Eden."

"You knew we lost the business. You knew we lost the house." Mary shook her head. "I lose track of time. Maybe I didn't tell you," Eden said. "You stopped calling."

It was true. Mary had stopped calling Eden on the last Sunday of every month. So often a message service had answered the line and she had panicked about what to say, then realized that she had nothing to say to Eden nor Eden to her. Finally she had dispensed with the sham of their relationship. As Gooch had done long ago. She wondered if, in his ritual of farewell to his mother, he'd been seeking forgiveness. Or offering it.

"I have money, Eden. I could—"

"Jimmy gave me five thousand. And I've got a bond coming

due next month, and that'll see me for a time. The rest is in his hands."

"Gooch's?"

"God's. Besides, I wouldn't take your share of that lottery money, Mary. You'll need it yourself, to start over."

A *fait accompli* — Mary remembered the phrase from French class at school. A thing finished. Done with. Over. Decided. Dead. That was how Eden saw Mary's marriage, but Mary had enough cash reserves to keep hope alive. Still, she was confused as to just how much money Gooch had won, and how much of it was still in the account. She would need to find a bank, and she hoped the Canadian card would work in American machines.

"There's a Pleasant Inn down near the highway. I'm going to get a room there," she said.

"And . . . ?"

"Wait. I'm going to wait for Gooch."

"For how long?"

"I don't know."

"I can't drive you there."

"I'll walk."

"That's more than a mile," Eden laughed.

"I can walk," Mary assured her. "You'll call me?" she asked, insisting that Eden meet her eyes.

"I'll call you," Eden answered, and with that she closed the door, entombing herself and Jack and the black-eyed Mexican woman inside the fetid house to await God's mercy in their circle of prayer.

Target Clear

The sun inched higher as Mary paused on the sidewalk, waiting in case, like Heather, Eden had been lying and would race out any moment, breathless and regretful, shouting, "You can find him at the such-and-such!" Or "He's staying at a place over in so-and-so!"

When the door didn't open, she realized that she could not walk a full mile to the Pleasant Inn. Neither could she stand still as the sun burned her fair skin and torched her red hair and seared her white scalp. She'd never used sunscreen, having never sunbathed, and rarely allowed her flesh the attention of solar rays. A few more minutes on high and she'd be crisp around the edges.

Laughter and tears, such as were promised by the novels in her heavy purse, fought in Mary's throat as she started down the sidewalk toward Willow Highlands. On the other side of the hill was the main road, where she remembered seeing a shopping plaza. There was a bank there where she could check the balance on her funds before heading for the hotel. One half mile. Over the hill. *Go.*

The hill was less a slope than a vertical ascent and, climbing the white sidewalk, struggling for breath, her feet sweltering in her winter boots, she wondered idly how children ever learned to ride bicycles in Golden Hills. Up ahead, she saw a middle-aged Mexican man hefting a lawn mower from the back of a small red truck near an empty children's play park. She waved to him, ignoring his look of confusion, and called inanely over the clanking, "Hot, eh?"

The spare strength she possessed carried her halfway up the steep hill before she stopped to rest on the edge of a sparkling rock fountain in the shade of a monster garage. Willow Highlands, she thought, catching her breath and looking around. The splendid abundance to which the universe aspired. Ah, beauty. What would Gooch have made of this foreign landscape? Gooch had once repeated to Mary a conversation he'd had with an immigrant from West Africa at a roadside diner on one of his deliveries north of London. The man had told Gooch that it was his dream to raise his children in America, so they could grow up to take things for granted.

Though Gooch coveted Corvettes and longed for Lincolns, he was not by nature—or perhaps it was because of circumstances—a materialist. It was not new things but new experiences that he described craving, in candid moments, in those early years when Mary still played along. "We should take a driving trip to British Columbia," he'd say, or "Someday we should go up the St. Lawrence to see the migrating whales." And "I want to take you skating on the Rideau Canal." He'd never mentioned the redwoods or Big Sur as dream destinations, but they could have been. So could Washington, D.C. Or Yellowknife. Or New York. Or Istanbul. *Come with me, Mary. Come with me.*

Sitting on the fountain's edge with a spray of water at her back, she took long, deep breaths, listening to the white noise of lawn mowers and leaf blowers. There the workers, toiling for the wealthy. Somewhere Gooch, sipping from a canteen, the wide blue ocean rolling out before him, searching for his own truth—or maybe it was God—at the end of all journeys of discovery. What might he talk about with God? World politics. Classic films. Mary hoped God would make Gooch cinnamon toast and let him sleep it off in the sanctity of her wilderness.

It was clear to Mary, when she tried to rise, that she could not continue her ascent. She felt her body's quiet insistence on sustenance. She had not eaten enough and it was retaliating, seizing and stopping and waiting, much the same way it had belched and shat and cramped when she'd eaten too much.

She spotted the Mexican man she'd seen earlier coaxing his tired red truck up the hill, and realized she'd been resting there for the length of time it took to trim the park's lawn. "Wait," she called, waving. "Please." He pulled to a stop at the curb as she wrenched her body from the fountain's edge. She smiled. "Could you give me a ride to the bank, please?"

The man appeared not to understand, and was startled when Mary opened the passenger door and set her big purse on the seat, saying, "I can pay you." Drawing out her wad of cash, she took fifty dollars and pressed it into his green-stained palms. He accepted the money, still not comprehending. "That's Canadian," she said. "But you can change it over at the bank." She hoisted herself into the front seat, gesturing. "You can take me to the bank?"

He shook his head, his eyes expressing regret that he could not understand, or maybe that he had stopped at all.

Recalling that beside the bank there was a fast-food restaurant, she ventured, "The crazy chicken? The Pollo?"

"*Pollo?*" he asked. "El Pollo Loco?" He nodded and put the car into gear. When she could not reach her purse on the floor, Mary shoved her wad of cash into the pocket of her paisley ensemble.

She could not communicate with the driver, so watched the passing homes as they climbed and then descended the hill and the dirty red truck made its way to the main road. Stopped at a light, she noticed writing on the back window of a Chevy Suburban in front of them. She first took it for an advertising slogan, and was surprised to read: *Trent Bishop 1972 to 2002. Always in our hearts.* She'd never seen a memorial emblazoned on a vehicle, and was struck by the poignancy of the indefatigable mourning it represented — the older brunette woman at the wheel reminding the world, with every trip to the grocery store and commute to work, that she had lost a son named Trent but would carry him with her like a picture in a locket, that he would never be forgotten.

Thinking of the big Ford truck with the taped-over sunroof that she'd abandoned in Toronto, she wondered if she might feel compelled to commemorate her marriage in such a way. Paint it on the back window. *James and Mary Gooch 1982–?*

When she stepped out of the vehicle, Mary was glad that the Mexican man did not try to return the money she'd given him. Instead he sped away, afraid she might change her clearly *loco* mind.

The instant cash machine was in view, but there was a drugstore the same distance away and Mary felt its call. A different pitch than the Kenmore's or the fast-food restaurants', more a reminder bell than a luring siren. Food. Heading toward the drugstore, she felt each step like a barefoot walk on hot coals, the sun daring her to stop, her spirit willing her exhausted body forward. She had taken more steps since Gooch's leaving than she had in the entire last year, not treading the same frictionless path but finding each step a new one, uphill, over rock, and bearing the weight of not just herself but her heavy vinyl purse, and the denser weight of her growing enlightenment.

The pharmacy, whose faint scent was as familiar as home, was busy with groups of mothers, and children who must have recently flooded out of schools and into waiting cars, for she'd seen few of them on the short drive over. There were a couple of men in suits with takeout coffees in their hands and telephones in their ears, and elderly women shuffling toward the back counter to pick up their prescriptions. Mary kept her eyes up, aware that she wouldn't find Gooch here — but then again, maybe she would.

Unlike the corn-fed people of Leaford or the mosaic of colors and shapes she'd seen on the streets of Toronto, the population of Golden Hills appeared largely Caucasian, toned and primed for athletics, lifted and enhanced, sucked and implanted. And so *tall*. Even though Mary had lived with one of the biggest men in Baldoon County for twenty-five years, she was still struck by the height of these Golden Hillians, who seemed to aspire to the palms.

Finding the bank of refrigerators, she heaved open a door and took out four large bottles of water. Along with the weight of her purse, they were too much for her torn muscles to handle. She found a shopping cart where she set the water and her purse, and her plastic bag with her navy scrubs, and to which she added a dozen health bars whose packaging boasted energy, nutrients and protein. Feeling the pain between her eyes, she found the pain remedy aisle and a bottle of maximum-strength relief. Passing through the seasonal needs department, she added several large tubes of sunscreen to her cart.

After waiting in line at the cash register, she remembered the dollars in her pocket and peeled out the wad to pay. The cashier shook her head, smiling politely. "We don't take Canadian money," she said. Mary wanted to shout, "But I worked in a drugstore and we always took American money, and paid out the overage when the Yankee dollar was higher." She returned the bills to her pocket and withdrew her credit card from her purse.

The cashier passed the plastic bags to Mary, who heaved them into her shopping cart and started for the door. Her muscles challenged beyond their limits, she was grateful to lean upon the cart and let it carry her parcels the distance across the parking lot to the landscaped borders of the bank. From there she'd have to haul her sacks over the sidewalk, but she was relieved to see a shaded bench that would offer a brief repose to eat and drink before she continued, to solve the mystery of how much money was still in the account. With each step, each exhalation, she felt the *calories out*.

Before the Gooches had suffered the expense of the new silver broadloom, when Mary was still buying armfuls of magazines, she'd read with mounting outrage an article by a nutritional expert (which Gooch had left open on the table on her side of the bed) that outlined, with daring simplicity, the reasons why, even as the Third World was starving, the First World was becoming alarmingly fat. With the equation *calories in* versus *calories out* anchoring the piece, the woman condensed the obvious:

> *We're served too many restaurant meals in double the portions we need.* Calories in. *We let machines do our daily chores.* Calories out. *Restaurants don't always list fat and nutritional information, denying consumers the opportunity to make better choices.* Calories in. *We drive when we could peddle or walk.* Calories out. *We communicate through computers. We watch too much TV. We put off until tomorrow what we could do today.*

There were so many affronts in the article that Mary'd hardly known where to begin when she sat down to write a letter to the editor. The first offense was Gooch's, leaving the article for her — as if she hadn't read a thousand like it, and a million testimonials from women describing their various inspirations for weight loss — but she didn't mention that in her letter.

The second offense, as Mary saw it, lay in the author's simplistic and aggressively unsympathetic approach to the epidemic. In the way unfeeling people said of lung cancer, *Shouldn't have smoked,* and of HIV, *Should have used a condom,* the writer seemed to be admonishing Mary's ilk, *Just eat less and get off your fat ass.* But the implications of morbid obesity, like anorexia (*Eat more and you won't starve to death, dimwit*), were vastly more complicated. Nowhere in the article had the author mentioned heartbreak. At no time had she conceded that food was a panacea for loss. There was not a single mention of the pain of loneliness.

In a color-blocked addendum to the article, beneath the caption *Getting Started*, the woman had suggested that the extremely large might begin exercising in the weightlessness of water, where muscles could gain tone for the challenge of more strenuous earthly pursuits. As if everyone had a swimming pool. As if the extremely overweight were just itching to squeeze into a bathing suit to show their wares in a public place. Mary'd chortled but had turned the page to finish the piece, so she could tell Gooch that she'd read it if he asked what she thought.

And there it was, the final insult—a photograph of the writer, nutritional expert and author of the soon-to-be released *Mama Cocoa—Why Chicks Love Chocolate.* The woman, who appeared to be in her early forties, was a tall, willowy blonde in snug jeans and cowboy boots, pert breasts straining a fresh white T-shirt, and a grin that was not so much winning as boasting that she'd won. Not beautiful the way Heather was but pretty, wife of a cardiologist, mother of two teenagers, living in a converted church in Vermont where she enjoyed baking pies with the fruits of their orchards and whence she dispatched a popular weekly blog. *Livin' the dream.*

Mary scoured the biographical information but there was no mention of the writer's former obesity, no indication that she had ever been more than the skinny bitch staring back at Mary from the white picket fence on which she was perched. The author might *bake* pies, but didn't *eat* them. How dare she?

The letter to the editor began with a reproach to the writer, Mary reminding her that there were varied and complex explanations for weight gain, and many medical reasons that could make weight difficult to lose. But she could not compose the second part, scratching and editing as she wrote, for in each vitriolic line her loathing for the author's form, those languid legs, those sculpted arms, diluted her rationale. It was not so much that she disagreed with the contents of the article, which was hardly original and staggeringly uncontroversial, but that she felt the author, given her lack of personal experience, had not the right to write it at all. The woman had clearly never met the obeast.

Head up, target clear. Plan in place. Check balance at bank. Go to motel. Recharge phone. Wait for call — from Heather, from Eden, from Gooch, from Joyce. Wait, like those Mexican men on the side of the road. Wait. *And sleep.* This she thought with no degree of anxiety or uncertainty, for she knew that, with a plan instead of a list, sleep would come and free her.

Daydreams had been, for her, mostly nightmares — imaginings about her food, visions of her secret stash, fear of getting caught. But she found herself striding the length of the parking lot in the blazing sun, pushing her shopping cart like a stroller, lost in a fantasy of Gooch. She imagined her husband's massive body bent over the instant teller machine, thought of wrapping her arms around his thick torso and whispering into his back, *I'm here, Gooch. I'm right here.* Of him turning and uttering, *Mare. Oh Mare.*

She stopped at the edge of the parking lot, dragging the plastic bags from the cart, and nearly fell backward over a tow-headed preschooler who appeared behind her. The child looked into her startled eyes and howled as if she'd struck him with a backhand.

"Oh," she breathed, looking around for a frantic mother.

The child howled louder and Mary smiled. "No, no, honey. That's okay. We'll find Mommy." She set down her plastic bags and offered a hand, somewhat disturbed that the child took it so readily. She walked out from behind the parked cars and saw the mother, tall and blonde and reed-thin, with two more towheads in hand, steaming forward, shrieking, "Joshua!"

The little boy held onto Mary's plump hand even as his mother and brothers approached, and tighter when the mother stuck out her own arm, threatening, "You don't run away! You do not run away from Mommy!"

Mary felt flustered and guilty, like the time she had left the grocery store with a tray of brownies which she'd hidden from the eyes of other shoppers on the bottom of the cart, then neglected to put on the conveyor belt when she paid for the rest. "I just turned around and he was here," she explained.

The woman did not look at her, so focused was she on the penalty to her offspring. "You just talked yourself out of a Happy Meal, mister," she said through clenched teeth.

The small boy shouted, "You *said!*"

"I *said* if you were *good*," she corrected him, severing his grip on Mary and yanking him along without another word.

Mary returned to the parcels she'd left on the ground and collected them with some effort, realizing that, although she didn't have to bend all the way down to find the plastic handles, she'd lowered herself considerably, and more than she had in recent memory.

She stopped, as she had promised herself she would, on the bench in the shade outside the bank, and found one of the health bars in the bag. She tore at the wrapping and ate the bar slowly, draining half a large bottle of water and resting awhile longer in the gentle breeze as the sun shifted over the landscape, until she felt strong enough to rise again. She hefted her bags and made her way to the instant teller on the other side of the building, but when she reached for the bank card in the wallet, she suddenly realized that she had the plastic shopping bags with her navy scrubs, and the ones with the water and health bars, and the one with the sunscreen and aspirin, but she did not have the purse. The big brown vinyl purse. It was still in the shopping cart, the last thing she'd been about to remove when the child had torn her attention away.

Charged with adrenalin, she made her way back around the building to the parking lot where she'd left the cart. The cart was still there. The purse was not.

Back to the drugstore. Perspiring in paisley, she opened the door with a whoosh, her frantic energy attracting attention even before she called out over the customers, "My purse. I left it in a shopping cart. Has anyone returned it?"

The cashier shook her head and shrugged. A few customers looked at her pityingly, the men because she was pitiful and the women because they knew what it was to lose a purse. *Everything was in that purse.* Travel needs. Unread novels. The bank card. The passport. Identity as defined by identification. Her driver's license, her credit card, her health card. Her *phone.*

Hobbling out the door after the cashier had consulted with a few other shrugging employees, Mary made her way back to the parking lot, to the place she was certain she'd left her purse. There. The cart. There. No purse. And no savior squeezing through the parked cars holding it by the hand, as she had the missing child, looking for its frantic owner.

Lost purse. Vanished husband. Displaced wife. Mary stood motionless in the parking lot, letting the sun beat down on her head.

A Hard Name to Forget

Mary had little experience with banks, as Gooch had been the one to do their personal accounting, and it was only occasionally, when he'd forgotten to withdraw sufficient grocery money, that she would enter the Leaford bank to fill out a withdrawal slip with an amount she unfailingly disclosed to Gooch with a lie. "I got a little extra out today," she would explain, "for Candace's birthday gift," or "for that charity thing Ray's doing." When really it was to pay for the cut of prime rib she'd eaten herself, or the special order of Laura Secord chocolate.

Opening the bank door, she was relieved not only at the sharp, conditioned air but at the sight of the empty teller queues. There were a mere five employees visible in the entire open-design bank — two men on high stools clacking away at their respective computers behind the tellers' desks, and the other three confounded by a computer screen at the manager's desk toward the back. All eyes turned to Mary as she swooned inside. Except for briefly appraising the newcomer and making their respective mental notes — *Large lady walks into bank* — the managers returned to whatever numerical mystery they'd been assigned.

Mary started for the tellers, each of whom looked up from his screen blinking strangely, as if she were an apparition and they were waiting for her to fade.

In the seconds it took to pass the chrome and leather coffee area where no customers lounged, Mary's brain rose to the challenge of deciding which of the tellers to approach, and also noted the striking physical beauty of the two men, for they looked like models or actors or star athletes, groomed above their collars and toned beneath their dark, tailored suits.

The man on the right, whose name tag read *Cooper Ross*, was the lighter version. Sandy hair falling over his tanned forehead, square jaw, white teeth. The man on the left, *Emery Carr*, wore his black hair gelled back, his complexion pleasantly pallid. She saw herself in his eyes and distinctly read his thoughts: *Go to Cooper. Not me! Go to Cooper!*

Her shuddering legs had ideas of their own, or were divinely guided, and drove her directly to the black-haired man, where she set down the plastic bags and began, "I've just lost my purse. Over there," she added, pointing through the window. "My purse. Big brown vinyl. In a shopping cart. Did anyone turn it in here?"

Emery Carr shook his head, distracted when the computer beeped beside him. Cooper Ross, overhearing, offered, "Are you a customer? We can access your account with—"

"I'm Canadian," she said, stopping him. "I'm from Ontario. I'm here alone. Everything was in my purse." She stopped, waiting to see her reflection again in the eyes of Emery Carr, as if to remind herself that she was standing in the bank, and not lost somewhere in the sum of the contents of her big vinyl purse. He looked up at her when she repeated, "Everything."

"We could call your bank in Canada. Are you east coast or west?" Cooper Ross asked, reaching for the phone.

"Ontario," she reminded him, remembering that she was in a different time zone. "Closed. It'll be closed," she said.

"Maybe your purse has been turned in to the sheriff," Cooper Ross suggested.

"Oh." Mary was relieved that someone had said anything remotely encouraging, and struck by how American the word *sheriff* sounded. Cooper Ross found a number and dialed—waited—then, after introducing the situation, handed the phone to Mary, who explained, "Big brown vinyl. My passport. My wallet . . . That's right . . . You can't contact me. I don't have a *phone*."

The tellers returned to their chores, Emery Carr adroitly signing off his computer and standing to organize his work station while Cooper Ross's long fingers tickled the squares of his keyboard.

"Mary Gooch," she began again, after a pause, "Rural Route 5. Leaford, Ontario. Canada." She paused. "I don't know where I'll be staying." She thought briefly of Eden and Jack Asquith. Tears rising in her throat, she reached into her paisley skirt pocket but remembered that it was the pocket of her navy scrubs into which she'd shoved the tissues given her by the limousine driver. It felt like a miracle, albeit a small one, to find the wad of Canadian money, left over from what she'd given the driver of the little red truck, instead. She pulled out the colorful bills and set the pile on the counter as she finished with the voice on the other end of the phone. "The Pleasant Inn," she said. "If my purse turns up, you can reach me there."

Big Avi had said that Golden Hills was one of the top safest cities in America, and as he had relied on the kindness of strangers in his immigration from another world, so did Mary. After she changed her Canadian money to American and found herself with more than five hundred dollars, Cooper Ross said, "Let's get your credit cards canceled, at the very least," and went on to help her with the necessary calls.

That done, Mary gave her thanks and begged one more favor, a call for a taxi, to which Cooper Ross responded graciously, "Emery can give you a ride to the hotel. He's off in five."

Emery Carr smiled brightly and crowed, "Yes. Of course I can give you a ride. It's on my way." But Mary caught the withering look he shot his colleague, and the slight grin beneath the other man's sandy bangs.

Even with a reluctant Samaritan, a ride was a ride. "Thank you. Thank you," she said, as they made their way outside. The falling sun crested artfully over a rocky hill in the distance, and Mary paused to look. Having left nature, like so many things, unconsidered, she felt a sudden rush of pleasure from the rugged beauty of the fading hills, a visual parfait, and was relieved to notice that a slight chill seemed to have crept over the parking lot during the time she'd been in the bank.

Emery Carr, whom Mary guessed to be anywhere between thirty-five and forty-five, drove a Mazda, a tiny, immaculately groomed sports car with stowage instead of a back seat, where he set her collection of plastic bags. Opening the door, she prepared for the chore of setting herself down in the small, squat seat. When she hesitated, he grinned tightly and moved around the vehicle, holding the weight of his disgust with the elbow of her arm. Perhaps he loved no one as fat as she.

Like the elderly, she felt her burden, and her losses rose like ghosts — Irma, Orin, Mr. Barkley, Gooch, brown vinyl purse — to mock her weak knees and quivering chins. Why didn't she just return to Leaford to live out the rest of her days with old Mr. DaSilva and the Pauls and the Williams and her mother in the care of St. John's? She wasn't up to this. She closed her eyes, heart fluppering and fluttering. *Someone will have to deal with my body.*

Emery Carr quietly reminded her that the beeping sound was the car's alert to the passenger not wearing a seat belt. "You need to buckle up, Mrs. Gooch."

"Mary," she said, opening her eyes. "Please call me Mary."

Pulling the seat-belt strap across her body, she once again noted her lessening in the days since Gooch's leaving. *Calories in. Calories out.* The reduction was somewhat appalling to her, though. Having as little control over her loss as she had had over her gains, she felt only the ingloriousness of her decline. She did not mean to say aloud, "I just want to die."

Emery Carr took a deep breath, and though she supposed he was thinking, *Please not in my car, lady,* what he said was, "Somebody will turn your purse in. Don't worry." With that, he roared out of the parking lot. Mary, instantly nauseated from the car's low center of gravity, wondered if, like the passengers in Big Avi's limo, he preferred the glass up.

She glanced sideways, and felt compelled to speak when he caught her staring. "You're nice to drive me to the hotel."

"You're a long way from home."

"Yes."

"Are you down here on vacation?" he inquired absently, inching toward a stoplight in the rush-hour traffic.

"No."

"Work?" She shook her head. "Work or vacation. That's all there is," he laughed.

Or funerals, Mary thought. *Or a mid-life crisis.*

"Someone's gonna turn your purse in. Don't worry. Purses don't get stolen in Golden Hills."

"Have you always lived in Golden Hills?"

"God, no! I don't live here. I'm in West Hollywood." He waited, glancing her way.

"West Hollywood?"

"It's not Golden Hills."

"Is it the crime area?" Mary asked, wide-eyed.

"No."

"The Armenian area?"

"It's the gay area."

"Why do you live in the gay area?" she asked, then answered herself with some surprise. "Oh." He laughed at her lack of guile. "I don't believe I've ever met a gay man before," she said.

"Yes you have." He grinned.

"I'm from a very small town. In *Canada*," she reminded him. "I did have a lesbian teacher once."

"We're everywhere," he said.

"Do you have a boyfriend?" she asked, enjoying her boldness. Intimate conversations with strangers. She'd seen it often in movies and TV, and had been unsure whether she trusted the cliché until she had found herself frightened on the airplane, wishing the brown woman spoke English and might offer her sisterhood.

"Kevin," Emery replied, and she could see that he was not in love. "Six months, which is like twenty years. We're celebrating our anniversary this week. A little wine tasting in Sonoma. Do you?" he added, noticing that she wasn't wearing a wedding ring. "Have a boyfriend?"

Mary touched the scar on her ring finger. "I've been married twenty-five years. Our anniversary just passed."

"But he's not here with you?"

She shook her head. "He's hiking. I have no way to reach him."

They stopped at the light where the three roads met. Scrunched in the seat, Mary turned toward the dusty corner lot to look for the collection of Mexican men, but the pyramid of thermoses was gone. Two men stood like sentries at either end of the lot, scanning the cars, still hoping to squeeze an hour's work out of the day, or maybe they were just waiting for rides home.

As the sun disappeared over the peak of the distant hill, Mary watched one of the men—her height, she guessed, broad in the shoulders, with a thatch of black hair and a trimmed moustache and beard—bend to collect his duffel bag and begin a slow walk to points unknown. Something about him set him apart. It was the man with whom she'd imagined she'd shared a glance from the back of the limousine. He had waited. He had not worked.

His tone officious, Emery Carr instructed her, "You go to the bank tomorrow. I won't be there but Lucy will help you. She'll contact your people and get it sorted out. Someone will return your purse. Stay positive. It's gonna work out."

"Stay positive," Mary said to herself, watching her handsome rescuer stride around the vehicle to open her door. Before he said goodbye, he scratched a name and telephone number on the back of a business card and pressed it into her hand. "This is an old friend who can put you in touch with someone at your embassy if you really get stuck because of the passport."

Emery Carr drew out the plastic bags, hanging them on the hooks of Mary's waiting hands, and checked his watch before asking, "Do you need help getting inside?" Though she did, or thought she did, she could see that he was in a hurry. She shook her head and thanked him again and started toward the hotel doors.

Taking a fresh red apple from the bowl on the reception counter, she checked into the hotel for three nights. The petite receptionist raised a brow when she paid in cash and explained about the lost purse, and the likelihood that someone would try to contact her there. "Mary Gooch," she reminded the woman. "That's a hard name to forget."

Crunching the apple, Mary made her way to the elevator, pausing to notice a bookcase in the lobby filled with novels and magazines. She considered looking for something to read but knew she couldn't manage the extra steps. Once inside her room, she kicked off her big winter boots, wincing from the pain in her heel.

Reading the instructions on the telephone beside the bed, she pressed the single digit to access an outside line and dialed for directory assistance, discouraged to find that Jack and Eden were not listed in the local directory. She had no way to reach her mother-in-law. Eden had no way to reach her. What if Gooch called?

She set the phone down, then picked it up again, dialing another number, waiting as it rang. A young male voice answered, "Hello?" There was laughter in the background. "Hello," she answered. "My name is Mary Gooch. I believe you have my phone. Hello? Hello?"

The call had been cut short on the other end. Mary breathed deeply and dialed her cellphone again, hoping for a miracle. Whoever had her phone might also have her purse. And even if that person had not found it but stolen it, perhaps she could convince him to return the things she thought couldn't be valuable to a thief. Like her passport. Her identification. She dialed again. The young male voice answered, "Hello?" But again the call was cut short. The battery.

She sighed, drawn to the open window and the stunning vista of dark, rolling hills, and reached for the buttons of her pretty paisley blouse. It was not a lover she found in the Golden Hills breeze but a different kind of savior. The mother's touch of cooling air soothing her body, stroking her spirit. And the stars, such as she'd never seen them, so many, so dazzling, so near they might rain down on her head. Mary surrendered her pride and called out to her old friend Tomorrow, begging for one last chance.

Finding the aspirin in one of the plastic drugstore bags, she shook out four, swallowing them with the water, unwrapping one of the health bars to chase the tablets down. She thought how unhealthy it must be to eat only health bars, and reminded herself to eat another apple when she next passed by the bowl. Purse gone. No phone. No contact for Eden. No way for Eden to contact her. No money. No identification.

A plan. She needed to formulate her next plan. As obvious as the calculation of *calories in versus calories out*, and the rule of three, it was clear to her that a person needed a plan. Stripped down to her underclothes, she flopped back on the bed and closed her eyes.

Living the Dream

It was Irma who appeared in Mary's dreamscape, not as she was but as she had been, dressed in a belted cardigan with a smear of plum lipstick over her thin, pursed lips. "Mary," she was saying, from behind the wheel of a stretch limousine, "oh Mary! You've got blood all over yourself!"

Looking down, Mary found fresh stains on the chest of her crisp white blouse. "It'll come out," she said.

"No, dear. Not blood. Nothing gets out blood," Irma argued over her shoulder, not paying attention to the black road. Suddenly Gooch was there, waving his arms madly, struck by the limousine and bouncing up on the hood like the deer in the headlights.

Heart thumping, Mary woke with a start to see not a cracked ceiling above her bed but the emergence of dawn over the hills outside the Pleasant Inn. When she tried to rise she was stopped by a sharp pain between her eyes. The place where she'd hit her head on the steering wheel. Leaford. Sylvie Lafleur. The country house with the cardboard in the window of the back door. Raymond Russell's. Wendy. Kim. Feragamos. The Oakwood. She could neither confirm nor deny the existence of that other life, but remembered that, in her current incarnation, along with her husband, she had also lost her purse.

Massaging her headache, she winched herself out of the bed and, after taking some aspirin and eating a health bar, went to the bathroom sink. There she handwashed her underwear and the pretty paisley ensemble that Frankie had sold to her, with the French milled soap she found beside the faucet. She hung the wrung items in the sun on chair backs near the open window, praying for a quick-dry miracle.

Returning to the bathroom, she set the shower on warm, delighted to find in a small wicker basket all the travel needs the hotel hoped would make her stay more pleasant. These included shampoo and body wash and a shoe polish kit and, to her enormous relief, a travel toothbrush with a tiny tube of paste. She brushed vigorously as the mirror steamed over.

Under the pulsing jets from the shower head she soaped her aching body. After drying her skin and hair with the plush white towels, she was caught by her nude image in the full-length mirror on the back of the door. "I am Mary Gooch," she heard herself say, even as she knew she was someone else altogether. Flaming red hair in a sporty shoulder length with a side part. A very pretty face. She studied her form, which had shifted in dimensions. This was not a body that wore a comfortable rut in the carpet but one that had ridden thousands of miles on an airplane, one that had climbed half a hill.

She found the tubes of sunscreen in the plastic bag and stood before the mirror to apply it. She smoothed the white lotion onto her face where Gooch had kissed her. And her neck, where he'd whispered the unspeakable. And the shoulders he'd once caressed. She imagined Gooch and herself lounging on the sun-filled deck of the Caribbean cruise, passing him the sunscreen with a kiss, purring, "Will you do my back, hon?"

As the lotion disappeared, Mary slathered on more. Beautiful skin, clear, untouched by the damaging rays of the sun. Another mercy by default. She applied the lotion to her chest, smoothing the cream into her cleavage, and, as if her hand belonged to another, watched those restless fingers inch over her enormous, heaving breasts. She shivered reaching the areola, big as a dinner plate, and pinched the rose nipple lightly.

Mary made the bed, even though she realized that a hotel maid would be coming by later for just that purpose, and tidied the mess she'd made around the sink. She could not decide whether she was anxious because Eden had no way to contact her, or because she was suspicious that her mother-in-law had no intention of doing so.

She checked the clock. First a trip to the bank to sort out access to her funds. Then on to Eden's about the lost purse and the unlisted number. She tried not to think beyond the plan, toward the long day and lonely night in the hotel, waiting to hear from Gooch.

In a closet she found an ironing board and iron, and decided that the Pleasant Inn must be a fine chain to offer such amenities. She ironed the billowing paisley on the lowest heat setting, afraid of spoiling the delicate fabric with an iron she didn't trust, and after pressing her underwear she climbed into the still-damp clothes. Even with the weight of her awful winter boots, and although she could feel that her wound was bleeding again, Mary felt lighter in mysterious ways.

Stopping at reception, she took an apple from the bowl and explained her problem to the woman on morning shift. "I'm the one with the lost purse. The sheriff's office knows I'm here. I'm Mary Gooch. Will you call a taxi for me?"

The woman furrowed her brow. "It's gonna be a half an hour to forty-five."

"Oh."

"This isn't New York."

"No," Mary agreed, and shuffled over to the big chairs by the window to wait. Her attention was caught by the bookcase, where she spied, miraculously, the bestseller she had begun to read on the plane and had lost along with the purse. Uncertain as to whether, as in a library, she was required to sign the book out, she approached the counter to ask, "Can I read this?"

"Uh-huh," the woman responded without looking up from her computer screen.

"Do I have to pay? Do I have to sign it out?"

"They're for guests. Most of them are from bookcrossing. This location's a favorite drop-off."

"Bookcrossing?" Mary asked blankly.

The young woman looked up, smiling through her irritation. "People leave books for other people. They do it all around the world. Bookcrossing." She might have added the teenaged refrain—*duh*.

"Why?"

"To share books." Again—*duh*.

As she found a spacious leather chair near the bookcase where she could comfortably read while she waited, Mary enjoyed the idea that a complete stranger had left the book for another complete stranger's edification, and thought of the volumes communicated in the exchange. She quickly found the page where'd she left off reading on the plane and fell back into step with the family drama, fearing for the teenage son, who'd lost his way, angry with the father, who'd taken a young mistress, and cheering for the heroine, who'd been accused of a crime she had not committed. When the taxi arrived a full hour later, she wished for three more minutes to finish the chapter.

The driver of the taxi was surly and silent, a pleasing combination that Mary decided not to take personally. He might be preoccupied by any number of things. Miserable for any number of reasons. He might be lonely. Filled with self-recrimination. Maybe his relatives were dead. Perhaps, like her, he was recently arrived from a far-off land and was no longer certain who he was.

With the morning unfolding in Golden Hills, Mary was glad for the chance to sit quietly in the back seat of the taxi to read her own life story, which had been for so many years meandering and plotless, and which now appeared to be in the throes of rising action. She became excited writing the next chapter, anticipating the moments of her future. A sharp black Escalade, a gas hog (Gooch would have forgiven himself the indulgence when he rented it), parked behind the Prius at Eden's house on Willow Drive. The door opens and he is there, standing taller than she remembers. He's not surprised to see her. He's been waiting. A sloping crease in his forehead begs her forgiveness, a lift of his shoulders and a wan smile say, *Ah, life.*

Stopping at the intersection, she saw the Mexican men, many more than the day before, gathered around the utility pole that anchored their collective. A brown pickup pulled into the lot trailing a cumulus cloud of gold dust. It took a moment, as the dust settled, for her to see the men scrambling over each other, moments ago comrades, instantly contestants for the chance at a day's pay. Once the truck was full, the others shuffled back to the pole, scanning the road for the next employer.

Driving down the main road, she was once again stunned by the volume of cars, but also surprised to see humans dotting the sidewalks or cycling beside them, dressed like the Tour de France athletes Gooch watched on TV, hunched over silver handlebars, lean and grim. The walkers were dressed in workout clothes, ears plugged with music, pumping arms and marching feet. Most but not all of them were slim. One woman, not nearly as large as Mary but of a standardly unacceptable body mass, was chugging down the street with her head held high, eyes focused on a target, ignoring or celebrating the jogging flesh on her bones. *You go, girl,* Mary thought, and wished she could say it as convincingly as other women did.

She paid the driver and tipped generously, although she found it shocking to have to pay seventeen dollars to be carried such a short distance. If she stayed in Golden Hills for any length of time, she'd have to find less costly transportation. There must be a bus. Did all the nannies and maids have cars? *The maids* — she realized she had forgotten to leave money on the bed for them. She'd promised herself long ago that if she ever stayed in a hotel she would tip the maids, prompted by a conversation over cards one night, François accusing Pete of cheapness when, on a Mexican vacation the other couples had taken together, he'd refused to leave money on the bed. Gooch, who stayed in motels when he needed to, had agreed. "You should tip the maids, Pete. Don't be cheap."

"It's not cheap! Jesus, everybody's got their hand out! I hate it! I hate those guys who try to carry your bags! I hate those bathrooms where the guy wants a dollar for handing you a freakin' paper towel!"

"Think of it this way, Pete," Dave had said, "they all wish they were you."

"They all wish they were me wondering when they're getting laid off from the car factory? Fuck them. Be me."

"So you tip a waiter who brings you a bottle of wine but you don't wanna tip the lady who cleans your pubes out of the tub?" Gooch had asked, laughing to defuse the tension.

"He didn't tip the waiters either," Wendy had complained. "It was so embarrassing."

"It's not even my country!" Pete had shouted, over the collective groan.

As the bank doors were not yet open, Mary decided to stroll down the plaza. Crossing the parking lot, she spied a white Prius parked in front of the deli and remembered what Eden had said about arranging to meet Gooch out somewhere, to spare Jack. She strained to look through the window at the customers in the deli's plush booths. Gooch and Eden were not among them.

Scanning the plaza, she hoped to see her prodigal husband and her bob-haired mother-in-law emerging from behind the spraying fountain, or departing the coffee shop where they'd said their loving goodbyes. Her eyes floated over the sea of cars in the parking lot, where it seemed that the few cars that were not sports utility vehicles were shiny white Priuses.

With Gooch nowhere in sight, she found the bench outside the bank and sat to breathe the morning air. Eden had said Golden Hills was close enough to the ocean that it didn't suffer the famous L.A. smog. Mary pretended she could smell it in the distance, salty and sweet. Although she was undernourished, her muscles aching from her uncommon labor, and even with the unfortunate disappearance of both her husband and her purse, she thought she felt better than she had in some time.

A short distance from the bank, the fast-food restaurant had begun grilling its crazy chickens. Mary watched the greasy gray smoke rise above the clay shingles. Behind the restaurant, a gathering of black birds crowed to one another, planning their assault on the trash bins outside the restaurant. Crows. Marys. Gay people. They were everywhere. But these crows, like the rest of the population, seemed genetically enhanced, a fortunate mutation making them bigger, stronger and blacker. They flapped between the enormous steel trash bins, which were sealed with heavy latched lids. One bird hawked at another, "There's no way in!"

She glanced around. There were no overflowing wastebaskets in the vicinity. In this world of plenty slim pickins for crows, with the clear civic agenda of cleanliness, Mary wondered just what the poor birds ate. Carrion? She wished she had some bread crumbs to scatter on the lawn. Her fear of crows, she realized, had been a fear of flying all along.

A fleet of blue vans began to pull out of the parking spots in front of a pool service company near the drugstore. She was watching the vans when a smiling, attractive, middle-aged woman with a name tag that read *Lucille Alvarez* appeared, to open the bank doors at ten a.m. Mary saw it as a sign that, as Emery Carr had promised — as she had promised herself — things would go well.

But the telephone call to her bank, which Mary realized she could have made herself earlier, from the hotel, suggested otherwise. As she had no identification, her identity could not be verified. Worse, she was largely unknown to the Leaford staff. She stopped herself from saying, "I'm the big woman."

When she reminded them that she had been in just over a week ago, and assisted by a new girl, the manager could only offer his apologies that they needed further proof. His tone grew suspicious when she could give only the most obvious and accessible information on the account. On the questions of Gooch's first elementary school, or his mother's maiden name (something Ukrainian), or his access code, she was stumped. When she couldn't recite her bank account number, the manager's tone turned frosty. A conversation with another manager, who was not currently available, was the next step.

The Leaford manager suggested that Mary call back in an hour. She told him she'd call back in two. As frustrated as she was by her fiscal debacle, she was anxious to get to Jack and Eden's in case they'd heard from Gooch. She left the bank, taking two bottles of water from the small cooler in the lounge area to drink on the way to their house.

The hills of the Highlands stretched out before her. Already perspiring, Mary steeled herself for the ascent. Lift leg. Plant boot. Swing arms. Lift leg, plant boot, swing arms. Stop. Rest. Drink water. Climb higher and higher. Drink water. And higher. Swing arms. Beat heart. Higher. *Breathe.*

On the sidewalk in front of one of the monster homes presiding over Willow Lowlands, she stopped to take more aspirin. She blinked to see a familiar face, that accursed mother from the parking lot, trailed by the flight risk, Joshua, and his two squabbling siblings — triplets — climbing out of a shiny black Lincoln Navigator parked beside a huge white Dodge Ram pickup truck, in front of a sprawling two-story home. The trunk door was open, glutted with paper bags full of groceries. The woman, wearing blue jeans and a sleeveless pullover with just the right amount of silver jewelry, carried two sacks in her toned, bare arms. Behind her, trailing like ducklings, the three blonde tykes sang a song and giggled. Mary caught a glimpse of a large shaggy dog lumbering toward the garage.

Watching the woman, with her soft blonde hair and pretty face, Mary felt her cheeks flush with outrage, a craving for vengeance, an urge to scream about the lost purse and all the trouble the woman's neglect had caused. But she hushed her instinct. She wouldn't make a scene in front of the children, and she could see now, with high-density clarity, the utter pointlessness of blame. She stood watching from yards away, invisible to the mother, overhearing her beg the boys, "Help Mommy carry some bags in."

"No," they cried.

"Help me and you can watch TV. Just carry in a few bags and I'll make sundaes."

Wendy and Kim had parented in the same curious way. *Let Mommy visit with Auntie Mary and we'll stop for Dilly Bars on the way home.* But then, she supposed her own busy mother had done the same thing. Leaving packages of store-bought baked goods on the table as after-school snacks for Mary, pretending not to notice when she ate the whole tray. Offering forbidden foods as a reward for her discretion. "Don't tell your father. Let's go to the Oakwood for a honey-glazed." Or "Be quiet while I'm trying on clothes and I'll buy you a Teen Burger."

Permissive Parenting. Children in Charge. Nice Treats for Naughty Tots. She'd judged mothers harshly for their lack of control, but ultimately concluded that she'd probably be just as weak, and just as likely to offer foodstuffs as a reward for the smallest expectation met, or to quiet her own nagging guilt.

Mary thought of her ancestors hand-plowing the clear-cut Leaford soil. What would pioneer mothers and fathers have said when the children complained about having to yank roots and clear rocks, she wondered. *Work hard and we will survive another day.*

The small boy, Joshua, suddenly turned around to face her. His mother swiveled to see what he was looking at, startled to find Mary standing on the sidewalk in her paisley ensemble and heavy winter boots. "Hello," the younger woman called out warily.

"Hello," Mary replied.

"You're the woman from the parking lot."

"Yes."

The mother squinted. "Do you live in the Highlands?"

"I'm here visiting my in-laws. They live down the hill," Mary explained, pointing with one hand, wiping sweat from her brow with the other.

The woman set her groceries down, smiling apologetically as she approached. "I don't think I even thanked you."

"You've got your hands full," Mary allowed, as the boys pulled each other down on the soft green lawn, growling and yelping, a blur of swiping paws and sharp white teeth.

"Joshua, Jeremy, Jacob," the mother said, introducing the scrambled boys. "Where's the dog?"

"He's in the garage," Mary said over the children's shrieks.

"Quit it, boys! Boys!" The mother clapped her hands once, then again when the ruckus continued. "Joshua! Jacob! Jeremy!"

"They're just adorable," Mary said, to soften her sharpness.

"Do I know your in-laws?" the woman asked, surrendering to the din. "I probably do. It's a small town."

"Jack and Eden Asquith?"

"I know Jack," she said, and it was clear in her expression that she also knew Jack's prognosis. "He used to have the pet supply place. He went to college with my dad back east. How's he doing?"

"Not well," Mary said.

"Where are you from?" the woman asked, trying not to notice Mary's winter boots.

"Canada." Mary hoped, on her country's behalf, that she would not be seen as a fashion ambassador.

"You must be enjoying the weather," the mother said, then noticed how Mary was perspiring. "I thought Jack just had daughters. You must be Eden's . . . ?"

"I'm Gooch's wife. Eden's son's wife."

"Are you and your husband staying until Jack . . . ?"

"I'm here by myself." The words felt lonely.

The woman's cellphone rang inside her leather handbag and she excused herself to answer. After a brief and heated exchange she hung up, explaining her tone to Mary. "I've got a Lydia Lee party tonight. Home jewelry sales? You know it?" She flashed a business card from her bag. "And that was the agency calling to say they're sending a new sitter." She turned toward the tangle of triplets in the grass, adding darkly, "The boys don't like new sitters."

"No!" one of them cried to his brother, as if proving the point.

The woman smiled, offering a lovely hand with manicured fingers. "I'm Ronni Reeves."

"Mary Gooch," Mary said, shaking her hand, struck by the contrast of her own plump, chapped hands against the woman's slender fingers.

"Nice to meet you, Mary Gooch. Thanks again for the other day. And give my best to Jack. Come on, boys."

Mary watched them disappear inside their immodest home: Livin' the dream.

Wealth of Food

Farther down the hill, Mary saw the white Prius parked in the driveway of the Asquiths' small home, but no other car. Maybe Gooch had got a ride. She imagined her huge husband perched on the expensive sofa across from his mother, describing the view from the hiking trails, expressing his hopes for reconciliation with his wife. Her feet were hot within her boots, and sticky with blood from her wound.

Finally at the door, she rang the buzzer. When no one answered she became impatient. She hit the button again. After a moment, Eden cracked the door. "Oh Mary. It's *you*."

"Hi Eden, I'm sorry to bother you—"

"You can't come knocking on my door every day until he calls, Mary. We've got much too much going on here."

There was dead silence within the house. No beeping microwave. No motorized vehicle. No draw of breath. "Is Jack . . . ?"

"He's sleeping. Chita called in sick and I've got food to make for prayer circle. Now, I said I'd call and I will."

"I lost my phone."

"You lost your phone?"

"Well, my whole purse actually."

"You lost your purse!"

"I wanted to remind you that I'm staying at the Pleasant Inn if you need to reach me."

"All your identification!"

"I know."

"Your bank card?"

"I'm getting that sorted out."

"Fine, Mary, well, I'll call you at the hotel then, if I hear from Gooch. I really have so much to do."

"But I don't have *your* number. I need your number. It's unlisted."

"It killed me to pay extra for unlisting," Eden complained. "But that phone just rang incessantly. Poor Jack. You're letting in the heat." She opened the door and started down the hall, gesturing for Mary to follow while shushing her with a fingertip. At the back of the house they entered a cluttered kitchen with sliding glass doors leading to a small patio and a neglected green swimming pool.

Eden found a pen and paper and wrote the number with her gnarled fingers, then set about unloading the sacks of groceries on the table. Mary noticed that there were dishes in the sink. Trash and recycle bins full. "I don't want Jack to find you here and start asking questions. It's exhausting for him to have to think these days," she said.

"I can only imagine," Mary said, taking the heavy juice from Eden's crippled hands, pulling groceries from the bags on the counter.

"Chita usually does this. They expect more than iced tea and crackers out here. You're expected to put on a spread."

"Oh."

Suddenly noticing Mary's footwear, Eden clucked her disapproval and disappeared down the hallway, returning in a moment with a pair of flat black loafers that she gave to Mary. "You can't wear those boots in California."

Mary nodded her thanks, kicked off her boots and attempted to stuff her stocking feet into the shoes.

"Without your socks," Eden huffed.

Mary settled upon one of the stools near the counter, straining to reach her socks over the lump of her gut, hoping her mother-in-law wouldn't notice her struggle.

"For heaven's sake, Mary," Eden *tsk*ed. She leaned down, scrunching her face as she helped Mary remove her damp, stained hosiery, disturbed to see the cut on her bloody heel. "That needs to be cleaned."

"I know."

Eden sighed as she searched the drawers and found the little first aid kit she was looking for. "I hope I've got a big enough bandage." It was clear that Mary couldn't dress her own wound, so Eden pulled a chair up beside her stool and gathered her daughter-in-law's plump foot onto her bony lap. "Have you never had a pedicure?" she asked.

Mary knew the question was rhetorical. She watched Eden's stern face as the old woman roughly cleaned the cut. "Eden?"

"Yes?"

"You will call me when Gooch calls, right?"

"I said I would."

Mary paused. "Heather said you'd lie for him."

"Heather said *I'd* lie!" Eden laughed.

"She looked really good, Eden. Heather looked good."

Eden was careful not to glance up. "So Jimmy said," she conceded.

"She quit smoking."

Eden snorted but kept to her work of drying the cut and applying a healing salve, and did not ask questions about her wayward daughter. Mary wondered if Gooch had told his mother about Heather's found son, and was about to deliver the news when she noticed her mother-in-law's frustration in trying to open the bandage with her clumsy hands. "Here, let me."

Before passing the bandage back, she found Eden's eyes. "Thank you."

"It wasn't as bad as it looked."

Mary shoved her feet inside the still-snug black loafers. "I guess I haven't exactly been thinking about shopping. What with my purse and all."

"I hope you're not going to ask me for money."

"No." Mary watched Eden open the refrigerator, astonished to see a wealth of food, as it appeared that the frail woman and her dying husband dined on little more than hope.

"Because I've been writing checks all week, and even if I wanted to—"

"No, Eden. No. I don't need money. I'm sure the bank in Leaford is going to sort it all out. Or my purse will be returned. The sheriff's office could have it right now."

"I've got to get going on the food." Eden reached for a knife, her twisted fingers losing their grip, silver clattering on the counter.

Mary stopped her. "I'll do it."

"They expect a spread," Eden reminded her, watching Mary root through her cupboards for a cutting board, too grateful to object.

"What's your maiden name, Eden?" Mary asked, remembering that it had been one of the questions from the manager at the bank.

"Why?"

"The bank asked me. To verify access to my account. Gooch's first elementary school. His mother's maiden name. I'm going back to the bank after I leave here."

"St. Pius Catholic School. I was estranged from my family." Eden's people were from Western Canada, her father a farmer, her mother a seamstress. An only child, she'd left home at fifteen, married at seventeen and been a widow at twenty when she met James Gooch

Senior at a restaurant in Ottawa. Her ancestry was Ukrainian. "My father was Gus Lenhoff."

Mary felt the weight expressed by her response—whatever had happened between Eden and her family, she could still, a lifetime later, not claim the name as her own. Mary wanted to pursue the details of their estrangement, but saw that the older woman was too fragile for such a remembrance.

In the refrigerator Mary found strawberries and fresh melon and sharp expensive cheeses, boiled eggs, cured meats and olives. She would have eaten the things whole a few weeks ago, gobbled handfuls of the berries, devoured the cheese in chunks and gulps, washed it down with the big baguette, belched, wanted more. Now she gazed upon it like a color palette, deciding how she would mix and compose it. Halved berries as garnish for goat cheese on crostini. Cured ham wrapped around crescents of melon.

"Chita usually gets the groceries. I had to go this morning and leave Jack by himself," Eden said. "I'd never be able to live with myself if that man had to die alone."

Mary'd often imagined a lonely death. A heart attack in her bed while Gooch was working late. In a dark ditch on a country road. Seated on the toilet.

"Why don't you go lie down. I'll finish this up and you can rest before your company comes."

Eden didn't need persuasion. She disappeared down the hall, leaving Mary to prepare the feast. As Mary pitted and husked and rolled and spread, she recalled a thousand recipe suggestions from the pages of her magazines that she'd promised Tomorrow she would make, but her eager mouth had always been too impatient. Eating from bags or sacks or tins. Her choices were more of the "empty contents into pot and stir over medium heat" or "microwave on high for eleven minutes" variety than the cutting, chopping, caramelizing kind. Perhaps she was more like Irma than she knew.

Maybe Gooch had been right, and all these years she hadn't loved food at all.

Hours later, after she'd prepared the food and washed the dishes, Eden appeared, casting a critical eye over the kitchen. "We use the blue plates," she said. "But that's fine."

The sound of Jack's hacking from behind the closed door of his bedroom made Mary shiver. Eden winced and said, "It's better if he doesn't see you, Mary. You have the number now. You really should call first."

"Yes. I'll call."

"We could be right in the middle of something."

"Of course."

"And the mornings are the worst. A terrible time for company. Terrible."

The telephone rang, shattering the silence. Eden picked up the phone. "Hello? Yes? Hello? I can't hear you. Hello?" She hung up, explaining to Mary, "Lost call."

"Lost call?"

"It happens all the time."

Mary left the house thinking of the lost caller. It could have been Gooch. She checked her watch, realizing that she had only an hour before the Canadian banks closed for the day. She begged her feet to walk faster, grateful for the mercy of the snug black loafers.

A Disconnected State

Mary started back up the hill, playing with suspicion, unable to shake the feeling that her hunch had been right about Eden protecting Gooch. Why had she told Mary not to come because they could be in the middle of something when Eden and her dying husband were so clearly at the end of it all? And why would she say the mornings were the worst when it appeared from her face that all times were awful? Mary suddenly felt sure that the telephone call was from Gooch, and had not been lost at all.

Reaching the fountain halfway up the hill, she paused but did not sit down on its rocky ledge. There were no cyclists on the roads. No people marching on the sidewalks. It was mid-afternoon, and much too hot for such bodily endeavors. That was why the people here were all out jogging and cycling and marching in the mornings. They had active times, like animals in a zoo. She could hear the whir of leaf blowers and lawn mowers in the distance — the workers. Not too hot for them? She inched farther up the hill and thanked gravity for helping her down, and when she reached the bottom she could only cede to her body, which swore it could not walk one more step.

She found a tall palm to lean against, glad to share her weight with the scratchy trunk. But the tree offered no relief from the sun's boring rays, and she felt dizzy from the heat. Perhaps this was another dream—a nightmare of an uninhabited dystopia. If there had been any cars around, she might have thrown herself in front of one. *A coma,* she thought hopefully, a short coma from which she might awake to the crack in her ceiling and Gooch beside her. "Someone else do it," she heard herself say. "I can't. I can't go on."

Glancing up at the perpetual blue, Mary cued God. *This is where you send the reluctant savior. The answer to my prayer.* But there was no miracle. No little Big Avi in his black limousine. No Mexican man in a dusty red truck. No Gooch shouting out from behind her, "I've been calling all over for you!"

So where was God when you needed her? Last rites in the Third World? Attending the Asquiths' prayer circle? Celebrating the divine victory of some sports team? Mary pushed herself away from the palm and started back down the road toward the bank. She had to. So she did. And there was God—not in the wings but in the act. Or it was heatstroke. She massaged the spot between her eyes.

Nearing the shopping plaza, she realized that she'd walked the remainder of the distance in a disconnected state. She was nothing but the exhalation of her breath and the momentum of her muscles, a ruminant meditation. Only now did she feel the blisters from the too-tight loafers.

Reaching the bank, she pulled the doors open and surrendered herself to the care of handsome, sandy-haired Cooper Ross, who helped her to the chrome and leather sofa and plugged the phone into the jack beside her and even dialed the number of her bank in Leaford.

As the manager on the other end of the line had not been briefed on her situation, she was required to repeat the sad tale, including the tedious details of name and address and contact number. Her brain suffering from lack of nutrition, she could not remember Gooch's first elementary school. Saint Something. And husband's mother's maiden name "Gustoff" was incorrect, though she was positive that was what Eden had said. The manager insisted that he could not release funds to her, or divulge any details of her account, until she had proper identification and could fax those documents to his attention. She thought of the number Emery Carr had written down for her, someone at the Canadian embassy.

She begged one more favor before rising from the sofa, the call of a taxi back to the hotel. "It could take up to an hour," Lucy said. "This isn't New York."

She couldn't wait an hour. As much as she dreaded the evening alone in the hotel, she knew she could not sit on the black leather sofa in the sterile bank a moment longer. She thanked the bank employees and started for the door.

Outside the bank, her feet aching in the too-tight loafers, Mary could barely heft her legs down the ramp toward the parking lot. The laser sun assaulted her eyes. The parking lot. The purse. Surely it was here. Must be here. Hidden before by some parked car. It *must* be here. Done with tears for the time being, she wanted to laugh when she realized that she was jonesing for her purse.

Nearby a cellphone rang, reminding her that someone might be calling the hotel with information about her lost identification. Heather. What if Heather had heard from Gooch? Heather had no way to contact her either. She'd have to remember to call the bistro in Toronto. And Gooch? What if the lost call had not been Gooch? Maybe he didn't even have a phone. What if he'd had an accident while hiking? What if he was lost and had no way to call for help? She felt the familiar force of centrifugal fear. A memory of skating on the Thames River. Crack the whip—it's Mary's turn to be at the end. Divot in the ice—gash on the forehead—Irma appearing in rubber boots. An embarrassment of blood. Scar still there.

She might have stood in the parking lot reminiscing with despair, but for the sun's glare on her shiny pink cheeks and the certainty that she had sweated off her layers of sun protection. It was not possible to stand still, she saw, and remembered that she needed a plan. Go back to hotel. Call man who knows Emery Carr. Call Heather. Wait. Rest. A ride to the hotel.

Other than inquiring of customers at the drugstore whether they needed help to locate a product, Mary was not in the habit of approaching strangers, of which there were precious few in small-town Leaford anyway. Seeing a pleasant-looking young woman opening the door to her Subaru, Mary cleared her throat. "Excuse me? I need to get to the Pleasant Inn, down near the highway, and I wonder if I could trouble you for a ride?"

The woman, younger than Mary had first thought, answered, "Like, this is, like, my dad's car, right? Like, I'm not, like, allowed to have, like, passengers. Especially not, like, strangers."

Of course, Mary thought. She was a stranger and caution was appropriate. Then again, this was Golden Hills, one of America's safest cities, where purses did not get stolen and strangers gave strangers rides.

An older woman dressed in a pressed black track suit, loading groceries into her trunk, felt Mary's approach but didn't turn. "Excuse me?" Mary called to her. "I'm sorry to trouble you. I need to get to the Pleasant Inn and—"

The woman turned, unsmiling. "The drugstore has a phone if you need to call a taxi."

"The taxis around here take a long time," Mary explained. "This isn't New York."

"Well, I can't give you a ride. I've got frozens," the woman said, offering her groceries as proof. "I think there's a bus somewhere. Over there somewhere. I've seen the Mexicans waiting."

A pregnant woman pushing a stroller approached but Mary did not try to catch her eye. She'd long ago learned to avoid pregnant women, who smiled at her round stomach in that conspiratorial way and pleasantly asked about her due date. Two sharp arrows in a single sisterly gesture.

Another woman, middle-aged with a bleached blonde ponytail and a stern expression, was striding toward a beat-up hatchback whose trunk was loaded with cleaning supplies, dust mops, a compact vacuum. Mary approached her. "Excuse me?" The woman turned, smiling, as she launched her request for a ride.

"I can take you," the woman said, in a thick accent of whose origin Mary was uncertain. Before she could express her gratitude, three more women, all fair of hair and hard of face, appeared beside the old car. The first woman explained to the others in her native tongue — Russian? They appraised Mary briefly, shrugging their acceptance as they crammed themselves into the compact back seat.

In traffic on the main road, Mary had a sense of déjà vu. The kindness of strangers. The women spoke loudly in their native language, laughed and slapped each other's thighs. Armenian? She wished she understood what they were saying, and longed to be part of their glorious sisterhood. The trip toward the highway was faster than the one she'd taken with Emery Carr. She could see by the sun listing over the distant hills that it was earlier, before rush hour.

When the woman driving pulled up at the curbside near the intersection where the three roads met, Mary didn't understand at first that she was meant to walk the rest of the way. The woman smiled apologetically. "It's okay you walk? If I go this way, is only one-way street. I have to come back and wait again at the light."

"Oh."

"I don't want to miss the traffic."

"Of course. Thank you. Thank you so much."

Mary waved to the women as the little car pulled away, and pressed the pedestrian button at the roadside. She stepped out when the walk light turned green. Measuring the wide expanse of roadway, she worried that she could not get across before the red hand began to flash. *Faster,* she told herself, wiping her brow. So focused was she on the changing of the light that she didn't hear the running footsteps behind her. She was startled when a small, dark man blew past her into the intersection.

What happened next was quick as rifle fire—snapshot images. An angle of the man in front of her, red plaid shirt, belt cinching the waist of too-large blue jeans, workboots scuffed and soiled. A wider shot of a white van making a reckless right turn on a red light. The moment of impact—the van's grille hitting the man's torso. His body launched into the air. Falling with a thud. The brown man sprawled, inert and bleeding from the mouth, on the green carpet of a roadside oasis.

Mary was the first to reach the man. He was older than he'd appeared from behind. She fell to her knees, touching his shoulder gently. "Sir? Sir?"

He opened his eyes, confused, grabbing her hand as he strove to focus on her face. "Angelica," he sputtered, splattering blood on her arm.

"Mary," she whispered. "I'm Mary."

The suspension of time. Freeze-frame seconds that held like minutes as she gazed into the man's frightened eyes. "It's okay," she said. "You'll be just fine." She wondered if it was possible that no one else had seen what had happened, as the traffic roared on behind her. All was as it had been, but for the man on the grass and his grip on her hand.

In her periphery, Mary saw a millipede of faded blue jeans advancing in a cloud of dust. A pair of legs broke free from the pack and dropped to the ground beside her to look into the broken man's face. The voice was bass and weighty. "Ernesto. *Ernesto?*" Responding as if to a command, the injured man lifted himself by the elbows, expectorating blood over Mary's paisley ensemble.

She looked up to see that the white van had pulled to the side of

the road and the driver was climbing out. He was in his early six-
ties, she guessed, tufts of gray hair crowning a plump red face, slender appendages, a tight, round belly that she wanted to thump like
a melon. He was wearing a work shirt, and as he drew nearer she
made out the name embroidered on the front pocket. *Guy.*

Guy stood over them, wringing his hands. "We gotta get him to
the hospital," he said, eyes scanning the busy road.

Mary gently shifted the man's scraped cheek and showed the
deep gash in the side of his tongue. "It's his tongue," she said. "He's
bitten his tongue." She gathered the fabric of her skirt and held it to
his mouth.

"Angelica," he said again, smiling into her green eyes.

Impatient, the driver tapped the shoulder of the other man. "We
should get him to the hospital. *Now.* Get him in the back of my van.
It'll be faster than calling an ambulance. *Come on.*"

His urgent tone made Mary shudder. "We shouldn't move him,"
she cautioned, when the fallen man winced and held his gut.

But the other man stood quickly, lifting his injured friend to his
feet. "Come on," he said, offering his free hand to help Mary rise
when it was clear that Ernesto would not release his grip. As she
struggled to lift herself, Mary looked into the stranger's molten
brown eyes. It was the man she'd seen before, at the dusty lot. The
broad shoulders. The trimmed moustache and beard. He returned
Mary's stare curiously, with something like recognition.

Guy strode ahead, yanking open the back doors and disappearing into the front seat of his van, whose bumper sticker read, *Gun
control means using BOTH hands.* Ernesto held fast to Mary, implor-
ing in Spanish as he dragged her toward the waiting vehicle. His
friend translated: "He wants you to come."

"Why?"

"He thinks you're an angel," the man answered, with the barest
hint of ridicule, and no trace of an accent.

"He hit his head," she said in his defense, as she climbed into the back of the van and settled down on a rear-facing back seat, still clutched by the car-struck stranger. She was set to protest her participation when she heard a prayer whispered by the frightened man, and saw herself the answer in his wide black eyes. Apparition or not, she was ensnared by his need. A mother to an infant. A bride to a groom.

The white van tore over the gravel and eased onto the road. Mary watched the men in blue jeans return to the dusty corner lot. Four minutes could not have passed since she started across the crosswalk, and now she was in the back seat of a stranger's van holding the hand of a bleeding Mexican. This was what happened when people left their comfortable ruts.

The driver called out from the front, "How's he doing?"

Ernesto gestured at his corrugated ribcage, speaking rapidly in Spanish to his friend. Mary turned to see the driver's worried expression in the rearview mirror. "He might have a broken rib," she said.

The driver watched the road, wiping perspiration from his brow, smoothing the tuft of gray hair from his forehead. "Either of you boys speak English? Anglaysay?"

"No Anglaysay," Ernesto said.

"No Anglaysay," the other man repeated, his eyes piercing Mary.

"They're gonna ask a lot of questions at the hospital," the driver cautioned.

"Wouldn't there be someone who could translate?" Mary asked.

"Not those kinda questions."

She swiveled in her seat to watch the road signs. There was the familiar symbol for "Hospital"—next exit. The man drove past. Perhaps he knew a faster way. "I'm afraid he might have internal injuries," she called to him.

"If we go to the hospital, they're gonna involve the police," he said. "*Policio,* Julio. *Policio,* Juan." They did not respond. Mary did not remember either of them telling the driver their names.

"You're my witness, lady. He was crossing against a red light."

"But it was still *green*. I was crossing too. You made that right turn without even looking," Mary said, thinking, *and if I could have moved faster, I would have been the one you hit*. There but for the grace of God.

He blinked, calculating his risks. "Can he move his neck? How's his breathing?"

Ernesto looked up at his friend but said nothing. Mary answered hesitantly, "He's breathing better. His eyes are clear. I really think he's got a broken rib, though."

The friend called to the driver, in a thick Spanish accent, "No 'ospital."

"But he should see a doctor," Mary argued.

"No 'ospital," he repeated, silencing her with his look.

"No 'ospital," Ernesto agreed.

"*No policio. No hospitalay*," the driver said, relieved. "Wise decision, boys."

"He should have X-rays," Mary pointed out.

The driver laughed heartily. "You have health insurance, Miguel?"

The two men appeared not to understand, and did not answer.

"Near Avenida de los Árboles. Hundred Oaks," the friend said, in that same thick accent. "Home. *Por favor*."

The driver nodded. "Hundred Oaks. We're headed right that way."

They were silent as they pulled off the highway and crawled through traffic to the main thoroughfare of a town whose backdrop of mountains was more rugged, whose shriveled medians paid the price of civic neglect. After journeying down a wide road flanked by box stores, they arrived at a neighborhood of tiny clapboard houses where bicycles chained to fences stood in for landscaped fronds, and plastic toys for rose gardens. The narrow streets held no canopy of the boasted hundred oaks. A few maples were all Mary could see, some tall conifers, the odd sycamore. As the van moved slowly down the street, mastiff creatures snarled from behind rusted iron gates.

Ernesto's friend pointed at a small, square house on the corner of the street where a collection of children were jumping though a waving sprinkler on a patch of stiff brown grass. Mary saw a throng of bodies moving inside, behind the open windows, and a group of men gathered around a smoking charcoal barbecue, through the slats of the backyard fence.

When the van pulled into the driveway, the children vanished and the group of men Mary'd seen in the yard streamed into the house. Movement stilled behind the windows as the driver went around to the back of the van to open the door. Ernesto finally surrendered his grip on Mary's hand. She climbed out of the vehicle, watching the strong younger man drag his injured friend into the house. He stopped before opening the door, casting a backward glance at Mary, a wan smile that she returned before turning to confront the driver. "He should go to the hospital."

"He should go back to Tijuana," the driver snorted. "Now, since Pancho and Raul have turned me into a taxi service, just where is it *you* need to go? And don't say Reseda because I'm not driving back into that traffic."

"You can't just leave him like this. You didn't even give your information," Mary reminded him.

"Look, lady." The way he said *lady*. "If they'da picked him off at the border like they shoulda I wouldn't be here talking to you right now. Look at that." He gestured at the tiny house, the dozen bicycles chained to the gate. "I bet they got twenty of 'em in there."

"Twenty of 'em?"

"Those sons-a-bitches aren't gonna be giving me trouble." He planted his feet, intimidating. "Are *you*?"

"You should give him money," she blurted. "In case he has to see a doctor after all."

"I should call Immigration."

"You should give *me* money, then," she said, trembling as her voice rose. "I have your license plate number, *Guy*."

He looked at her for a long beat, the acrid odor of righteousness leaking from his pores. He tore a wallet from his pocket and peeled off a wad of dollars. "I got two hundred dollars here. And we're done. This never happened."

With that, he marched to the front of the van, climbed into the driver's seat and, before speeding away, concluded, "*You* are a fat fucking hog."

The insult struck her like a grain of sand. She was fat. True. But she was neither fucking nor a hog. She was Mary Gooch, who, on her way home to an uncommon existence, found herself under surveillance by a group of Mexican children behind an open window in a town called Hundred Oaks. Counting the money, she walked the short steps to the house and rang the doorbell. She rang the bell again but no one came to answer. The children were silent behind the drapes. She knocked hard on the door, impatient with her predicament. She'd still have an hour to wait for a taxi and could only guess at the expense of such a long ride.

She took a breath, knocking again, the length of her body tingling with tiny convulsive cramps from her blistered toes to her torched red scalp. Finally, the strong man with the beard cracked the door. She didn't wait for him to speak but thrust the money at him, saying, "He left that for you. In case your friend needs something."

He took the money, glancing beyond her, seeing that the man had abandoned her. "I need a taxi to take me back to Golden Hills."

"I'll take you when my cousin gets back with the truck." He looked around before opening the door. "Come on. Come in."

The first thing Mary noticed were the shoes arranged neatly on the linoleum square in the front entrance: a row of workboots, another of sneakers, a pile of sandals, in all shapes and sizes. A hundred pairs, it seemed. The rooms, of which there were too many for such a small abode, were painted in vibrant shades, pomegranate, saffron, azure, aubergine. When the man called out something in Spanish that must have meant the coast was clear, adults and children poured out of a small back room, scrutinizing the strange woman in their midst, speaking over each other in rich, rolling vowels that hung in the air like subtext. They were talking about the accident, no doubt, wondering what part she had played, given the bloodstains on her clothes, and why the man, to whom they showed clear deference, had let her inside.

Following him into the tidy kitchen at the back of the house, Mary found old Ernesto sprawled on a chair, shirtless, the extent of his injuries clearer. A bruised torso where a rib or two were likely fractured. Layers of skin peeled from his bony shoulder. Cheek shredded by the blades of grass. Tongue still oozing. A wizened woman with a kerchief tied around her head tended to his abrasions while a tiny girl with a solemn face held a washcloth to his whiskered chin.

Ernesto's eyes widened at seeing Mary. And sparked when he saw the dollars in the other man's hands. "*Gracias,*" he said. "*Gracias, María.*"

"How do you say, *you're welcome?*" Mary asked the other man.

"*De nada,*" he answered, amused. "Means *it's nothing.*"

And it was nothing, she thought. No need for thanks. She'd done what people do. Gone to the aid of someone in need. It had not been a decision. There had been no choice. She had merely offered comfort to a frightened man, held his hand. "*De nada,*" she repeated shyly.

She blushed when she glanced up to see the other man studying her. He reached out—not to shake her hand, but to take it and lift it and hold it in a firm and gentle manner as he introduced himself. "I'm Jesús García."

"Hay-su?" Mary repeated, pushing the unfamiliar name off her tongue.

"It's spelled like *Jesus.*"

"Oh." She giggled, and wondered if she might faint from the heat in the tiny, damp room. "I'm Mary. Mary Gooch."

He was her age, she guessed. Perhaps a little older or a little younger. His brown face was etched with deep lines. His cheeks above his trimmed beard were tight and round, almost cherubic. It was his physique that suggested relative youth—strong, straight back, the pigeon-toed gait of an athlete. Held by his gaze, she felt dizzy.

Reading her thoughts—or perhaps it was obvious in the way Mary swayed—Jesús García pulled out a chair and helped her sit down beside Ernesto. "You remind me of someone I used to know," he commented. "Her name was Mary too."

Mary had never been told such a thing before, and could not envision a world in which a man like Jesús García might have known a woman like her.

He caught the attention of one of the children. *"Agua por la señora."* The child shook her head, gesturing that the tap at the sink was not working. Jesús closed his eyes briefly, then reached into the refrigerator and drew out a bottle of beer. Popping the cap, he passed it to Mary. She translated for herself—*agua*—water.

The sharp amber fluid stung her throat but she drank deeply, embarrassed by the burp when she pulled the bottle from her lips.

"Your dress is ruined," Jesús García said, gesturing at the bloodstains on her skirt. "Nothing gets out blood."

She nodded, drinking the beer, stealing a glance at his broad back when he turned to look out the window. The enormous shoulders and arms—a weightlifter, no doubt—sculpted cheeks over thick, muscled thighs. He turned to find her staring. His face held no opinion.

The others in the house, having been informed by Jesús of the details of the accident and Mary's marginally heroic deed, returned to their respective appointments—the men back at the barbecue, the women hanging wet laundry in the grill smoke—all but the children, who did not go back to the sprinkler but remained in the kitchen, the oldest wielding sharp knives to cut potatoes for the evening meal while the others shucked corn from a sack near the waterless sink.

A cellphone rang. Jesús García reached into his pocket, checking the number, waving his hand over the crowd, which instantly fell silent. He answered the call, speaking rapidly in Spanish as he made his way out to a private spot in the backyard.

The sound of a rasping rake made Mary homesick for Leaford, where the sun did not shine every day but where she was familiar with the customs and understood the language. Tiny, rural Leaford, where there were only a handful of recent immigrants, most of whom spoke English well enough. She thought of the color of Baldoon County. Mostly white. Some black. There was Rusholme nearby, populated by the descendants of slaves escaped from the southern United States — the Joneses and the Bishops and the Shadds, who'd cleared half of Baldoon County alongside the Brodys and Zimmers and Flooks — but their immigration was more than a century old, and their struggles knit into the county's fabric with the first original stitches. More recently there was Mr. Chung, who owned the restaurant. The four Korean families who ruled the kingdom of Quick Stop. And one Indian family who managed both of Leaford's Tim Hortons coffee shops.

Orin and Irma had not held opinions about the recent immigrants so much as *emotions*. Toward the business owners they felt contempt and envy. "I guess if I had a store and could charge four dollars for stale bread I'd be rich too," Irma'd remarked of the Koreans. "I saw the Chinese fella's putting in a pool," Orin'd said. "He must think he's died and gone to — wherever it is they go." And one day, after a visit to one of the Tim Hortons franchises for coffee, Orin complained, "That Vikram fella drives a *Lincoln*."

For less fortunate immigrants — like the single mother down the street who came from the West Indies, whose teenaged son had gone astray, who shopped with food vouchers and collected unemployment when her modest business venture failed — for her they had scorn. "Sucking on the government tit," Orin would say. To which Irma would respond, "That's a disgusting image, really, Orin."

Behind Mary, a child ferried out a basket of corn that had been oiled and seasoned for the barbecue, just as a platter of slick grilled meat was paraded into the kitchen. The children grinned as the platter was presented like a birthday cake, the smaller ones straining on tiptoe to catch a glimpse. Mary counted the children in the kitchen, the old woman, Ernesto, the men through the window out back, the women criss-crossing the rooms down the hall. The van's driver had been correct—about twenty of them. The quantity of meat on the plate, although substantial, could not satisfy so many people. Nor the flat rounds of bread, nor the dozen ears of corn, not even with the small diced potatoes roasting in the tired old oven.

With some panic, Mary feared she would be asked to dinner. She could no more conceive of chewing and swallowing food with this collection of strangers than she could dream of depleting their meager rations. She prayed that Jesús would stop talking on his cellphone, and that the cousin with the truck would arrive quickly. She focused her attention on a display of photographs held by magnets to the door of the old Frigidaire. Most of them were photographs of a family—Jesús García's family. A plump, pretty wife with almond eyes and dark wavy hair. Two young sons with identical thatches of spiky black hair, the same molten brown eyes as their father. Mary had secretly been happy to be an only child. Her sister, she was sure, would have been the skinny one.

The front door opened and an elderly man limped into the kitchen dangling a set of keys. He was older than Ernesto, desiccated by the sun. He locked eyes with Mary, his expression shouting the obvious: *She should not be here.* His frown deepened when he turned to find injured Ernesto flinching at a lash of antiseptic from the cloth in the old woman's hand. He put the keys on a hook near the door, croaking to the men turning corn on the barbecue. Even though he spoke in Spanish, Mary could translate: *What happened to Ernesto? Who's the big white woman?*

As the dinner was set on the table, one of the women offered Mary a plate, encouraging her with a smile. *"Buen provecho,"* she said. *"Métele mano."*

"Bwen provayko," Mary repeated.

One of the boys standing nearby translated for her. "Eat the food. She's telling you to eat the food. Enjoy."

At the risk of appearing rude, Mary could only shake her head, explaining futilely, "I'm still too shaken up from the accident." The crowd descended eagerly upon the kitchen, but without disorder. The children helped themselves first, taking smaller pieces of beef that had been cast to one side of the platter, halved ears of corn, three olives from a bowl. The adults following, filling their plates according to rank and appetite. So much chatter. Standing or leaning to eat. Plates held under chins. Moist, hungry mouths opening and closing around forks. Teeth uprooting niblets of yellow corn, mashing cubes of potato. Mary could not smell the food, but felt its pain. She felt with mounting certainty that any more exposure to the meal was going to make her *huck*.

"Come on," Jesús said, taking the keys from the hook. "I'll take you home."

Shooting Stars

Ensconced in the grimy truck amidst the other vehicles streaming toward the expressway, Mary imagined Wendy e-mailing the rest, *Mary Gooch got into the car with some creepy Mexican in California and got her throat slashed. Idiot, I know, eh?*

She stole a glance at the stranger's profile. She'd seen the way the rest of the people in the house regarded him; he was not tall but he towered above them with his imperious jaw and impervious gaze. His pathos and gravitas. She had not seen the plump woman from the photographs on the fridge among the others in the room. His wife. She had no idea which of the children belonged to him.

Night had fallen swiftly, the rising mountains snatching the sun. Stars pricked holes in the velvet night, reminding her of the childish rhyme Irma had taught her — *Star light, star bright, First star I see tonight, I wish I may, I wish I might, Have the wish I wish tonight.*

Jesús García cleared his throat. "Thank you."

"I didn't do anything."

"Ernesto asked you to come. You came. He is grateful."

"He thought I was an angel."

Jesús was silent, focused on the road. He didn't curse, as Gooch would have, when a blue BMW cut him off. And didn't speed up to glare at the driver, as Orin had on many occasions. She followed his gaze to the stars.

She could feel his heat the way she had felt Gooch beside her, in the truck, on the sofa, beside her in bed — radiant and unwavering. Suddenly, a fire in the night sky, an explosive cosmic tail streaking across the black horizon. Brilliant. A shooting star. Brief, like lightning. Like a person's life. Divine sleight of hand — *How'd she do that?*

"Did you see that?" Mary asked, pointing, hoping it was a sign.

Jesús nodded, unimpressed.

"I've never seen a shooting star before," she breathed.

"Never?"

"Don't I make a wish? Don't you make a wish when you see a shooting star?"

Jesús García glanced at her sideways, squinting one eye as if he was pained to inform her, "They're not really stars."

"They're not?"

"They're fragments of meteor burning up from the pressure of the earth's atmosphere. Nothing very magical."

"Seems magical, though."

"Some of the stars we're looking at now died a long time ago."

"That's magical. I think I knew that. I'm still going to make a wish." She squeezed her eyes shut, wishing for Gooch's swift return. Opening her eyes again, she wondered at the heavens. "The stars don't look like this back home. Even on the clearest nights."

"Where's back home?"

Although she was reluctant to share the details of her situation with the stranger, she did not want to appear mistrustful. Hoping for some bond of distinction in their displacement, she said, "I'm Canadian."

"Canada," he repeated, nodding approvingly.

"Just different borders."

He glanced at her, confused.

"Mexico. Canada," she explained.

"I'm American," he bristled.

"Oh." She felt she should apologize but was unsure of the slight.

"Born and raised in Detroit."

"Detroit! That's just an hour from Leaford. Just across the border. That's where I'm from!"

"My family had a restaurant in Mexican Village," he said hopefully. "Casa García?"

Mary shook her head. "I never went to Detroit." He looked surprised. Or disappointed. "My husband used to go to the auto show," she added.

My husband. *My* husband. *My husband.* How often had Mary Gooch said those words in the last twenty-five years? "My husband is doing great." "My husband likes his beef rare." "My husband and I have a checking account." She also began a great many sentences with "Gooch says" or "Gooch thinks." To whom would she refer if Gooch, her husband, was no more?

Jesús García signaled to change lanes. "Is your husband waiting at the hotel?"

"I'm actually not currently here with my husband right at the moment," Mary said, realizing that she sounded insane. She sighed. "Wishing on a meteor fragment doesn't sound the same, does it? Is the sky always this clear at night?"

He pointed at the horizon. "You know the constellations? That band of light there? That's the Milky Way. You see the Big Dipper?"

"I know that one." She watched his thick fingers trace the ladle in the sky.

"Draco, the dragon — that pattern there, between Ursa Minor and Ursa Major."

She did not see the dragon, but nodded. "You should just drive, Hay-Su."

He laughed, then resumed a more thoughtful tone. "The best place to see the stars is at the ocean."

"I haven't seen the ocean."

"You have to see the ocean."

"People always say that."

He turned to flash a brilliant smile, the first she'd seen.

"I must have learned the constellations in science class," she said. "I must have known that shooting stars aren't stars. I think I retain information on a need-to-know basis. And I never need to know. Do you remember all that about the stars from science class?"

"Library. I spent a lot of time there after . . . when I was unemployed."

"Studying the constellations?"

"Walking down the rows. Picking random books."

"I suppose that's what young people do now when they go Googling, or whatever that's called."

"I'm not much of a computer guy."

"You're a random-book guy."

"It wasn't just the books. I liked the place. The library. The dust. The quiet."

Offering proof of his proclivity, the man fell silent once again. Mary watched the night sky, hoping to see another meteor fragment alight in the atmosphere. "I'm right off the highway. The Pleasant Inn," she noted.

Emboldened by the shooting star, or maybe it was the buzz from the bottle of beer she'd consumed, she demanded, "Why did you pretend you couldn't speak English?"

He shrugged. "Sometimes it's easier."

Heather Gooch had said that too. *It's easier to be someone else.*

When they stopped at the intersection, Mary's eyes fell upon the dusty lot, the scene of the crime, where she'd first seen Jesús García scanning the road. When he followed her gaze to the utility pole, she felt caught. Managing to sound both pitying and patronizing, she added, "It must be awful to be a day worker."

"I work at the plaza down the road," he said. "My uncle, the old man with the bad hip? He picks me and Ernesto up here on his way out of the valley, when he can."

"And when he can't?"

"We take the bus."

It was obvious from his apparel that he did not work at the bank. As he did not expand on the nature of his employment, Mary felt disinclined to ask. She was curious, though. The drugstore. The travel store. She'd seen a sign for a shoe shop. The chain restaurant.

Helping Mary out of the truck and seeing her into the hotel lobby, Jesús García took her hand. "Thank you, Mary. *Gracias.*"

"You're welcome, Hay-su." A smile played under his moustache, and she hoped he might flash that brilliant grin once more. "Do I say it wrong? *Hay-su?*"

"You say it fine."

Mary watched him pass through the hotel's double doors and out to his waiting truck. The receptionist at the counter, whom Mary recognized as the girl from the previous night, called out, "Mrs. Gooch?"

"Yes?"

The receptionist saw the stains on her outfit. "Is that blood?"

"There was an accident," she explained. "It's been a long day."

The girl smiled. "I have your purse."

Nothing Gets Out Blood

Mary's joyous reunion with her brown vinyl purse soured quickly when the receptionist repeated what the police had told her. The purse had been found by a sniffing dog in the bushes near the corner lot at the intersection. The woman's raised brow implicated the Mexican day workers, which Mary thought unfair. There were some personal items left in the purse, but no wallet. No phone. No passport. The sheriff held little hope that her identification would be returned. "My manager says we're gonna need a credit card imprint if you're staying past tomorrow night."

Back at her room, Mary noticed that she'd unintentionally left the *Do Not Disturb* sign hanging on the door handle. Inside, she found everything as it had been. The made bed. The health bars on the table. The water. The sunscreen. She kicked off her tight shoes and settled down upon the bedspread to open her purse, bitter that it had shown up without her wallet.

She caught her reflection in the mirror over the dresser. Unmoored, unidentified, unidentifiable. If only there were twenty people just like her crammed into the room, from the same world, in the same predicament, equally unsure what to do next. Not company for her misery but a band of brothers and sisters, like the Mexican immigrants. A tribe. She could see that she needed a tribe, and saw her folly in making Gooch her whole existence.

Jesús García had a tribe. He was the king of the tribe in that house splashed with color and guarded by the hundred shoes at the door. She remembered the photographs of his family on the fridge, the pretty wife with the almond eyes and the handsome, dark-haired boys. Perhaps he didn't wish on stars because he already had all he'd ever wanted. She thought of his face as he pointed out the Milky Way. He said there was nothing magical about the stars, but he seemed under their spell nonetheless.

After retrieving the number for directory assistance and being passed on to a Canadian operator, Mary asked for the number for Bistro 555. A plan. A dubious plan, but all she had. She would explain her predicament to Heather and ask her to wire a humble sum, which she would pay back immediately when her situation improved.

Mary waited, breathless, recognizing the voice on the other end of the phone. "Hello," she said, "I'm calling for He—Mary Brody. May I speak with Mary Brody?"

"Who's calling, please?"

"It's her sis—friend. Old friend. I was in earlier this week. You're the actor, right?"

"Yeah. I remember you." The fat woman looking for a tall man. "Hold on."

The phone clacked against the brushed nickel counter three thousand miles away. The background noise was deafening. As she waited, Mary checked her toiletry bag, which appeared to be unopened. She was pleased to find her hairbrush, since the hotel had only offered a comb. Who would steal her spare set of navy scrubs? Finally the actor/bartender returned to the line. "Someone said she went out of town."

Mary thanked him for his help and gave Eden's number, which Mary Brody should call immediately upon her return.

Where was that business card on which Emery Carr had written that telephone number? She glanced around the room. The maids had not come to clean, so the card couldn't have been thrown out. She rose, scouring the tabletops. Checking the wastebaskets. She imagined herself standing beside Emery Carr's sporty Mazda. He'd handed her the card and . . . and she'd put it in the pocket of the paisley ensemble! Yes!

Which she'd washed the previous night. Heart sinking, she reached into the pocket of the voluminous skirt and felt the flaccid rectangle. The black writing was smeared. Impossible to read. And Emery Carr was tasting wine with his boyfriend in Sonoma.

She could call Wendy, she thought, realizing that she was desperate. Or Pete. She could call Pete at work. Ask him to wire money. Or Joyce. She'd left postdated checks at St. John's — maybe there was a way to access her money through them.

The time was eight-thirty, but with the three-hour time difference it was past business hours and too late to call the gang of old friends, whom she'd never really counted as hers but Gooch's anyway. She leaned against the sturdy table unwrapping a health bar. Before she could take a bite, she caught sight of the dried blood on her arm, and bent her weary head to take full account of the splattered, rusty stains already set in the flimsy fabric.

She unbuttoned the blouse and stepped out of the skirt, rolled the lovely clothes into a ball and pitched them into the trash. *Nothing gets out blood.* Once again she had nothing to wear. Then she remembered the other navy scrubs that had been in the plastic bag from the beauty salon.

As cool water thundered into the shallow sink, Mary checked the deep slash pockets and was gratified to find another card. *Big Avi. Miracle Limousine.* More than ever, she believed in miracles. She reached into the other pocket and her hand met a small, slender book that she knew was her passport, which she now remembered stuffing into her pocket when the limousine driver pulled up to the curb at the Los Angeles airport. *Her passport.*

That awful mug shot. Mary Gooch. Citizen of Canada. Born March 1, 1964. Staring at her photograph, her proof of identity, she paused to distill the day, the common and uncommon dramas and the mercies small and large. Joy — she added it to her repertoire of recent emotions and thought, *I am cured.* She was no longer a victim of abstract malaise. None of her feelings were abstract. She could have named each glorious sensation — hope, excitement, panic, grief, fear — and drawn a map to its derivatives. This was also what happened when people veered from their carpeted ruts, she thought. They found themselves on roller coasters and got addicted to the ride.

It was hardly nine o'clock in California. Those late-eating people in Toronto were just finishing dinner. Food! Once again she had forgotten to eat. Or neglected to eat. Or been too nauseated to eat. She glanced around for the health bar but became distracted by the chore of washing her navy scrubs. *The passport!* She had no one with whom to share the news, so she thanked God, providence, fate and Big Avi.

After scrubbing her clothes vigorously, she wrung them out and pressed them with the hotel iron on high heat before hanging the damp items on chair backs near the window. Returning to the bathroom, she climbed under the pulsing warm water in the shower. Up. Down. Lean in to take the curve. She felt alive.

The passport. Lost and found. Like Heather's son. A miracle. All that had happened because she had lost it. She wouldn't have gone back to the bank. She wouldn't have asked the cleaning women for a ride. Would the white van have hit Ernesto? Who would have held his hand? And there were all the things that could happen now she'd found it. She could determine her balance. Access her funds. She could continue at the hotel and wait for Gooch to return. It could only be a matter of days. A week, maybe. Two at the most.

Toweled off and hair blown dry, Mary climbed into bed but could not sleep. Her hand shot for the television remote control but paused. That novel. She had hidden it on the top shelf before the taxi had ferried her off for the day. But she had no dry clothes to wear down to the lobby. She reached for the telephone and called the front desk. "I'm sorry to trouble you," she began, "but I was reading a book in the lobby. I left it, well, I hid it, actually, behind the travel books on the top shelf. Is there anyone who could bring that book up to me?"

"Right away, Mrs. Gooch," the woman responded, though Mary had not mentioned her name.

Right away, Mrs. Gooch. So it was true. Ask and you shall receive. Mary'd never asked for much before, particularly of herself.

In minutes there was a timid knocking, and she accepted the book through the slender crack she made in the door. "Wait just a sec," she called, afraid to sound like a big shot. She found the roll of dollars and peeled off an American five for the squat brown boy at her door. "*Gracias,*" he enthused.

"*De nada,*" she answered, realizing she had overtipped.

Mary tore open the book the way she once had torn open the takeout from Chung's, salivating for the story. She settled down to read the family saga, a fictional roller coaster but no less thrilling; the next chapters revealed that the accused main character was found innocent, and the teenaged son, after nearly dying tragically, found redemption in the assisted suicide of his terminal aunt, and the cheating father, as the author sought final vindication, was diagnosed with impotence. She slowed her pace as the pages dwindled. She did not want the book to end.

The stars were framed in the large window beyond the bed. She set the book aside and settled on a height of pillows, staring into the cosmos, thinking of Jesús García's expression when he'd first seen her face, a tender reminiscence, and recalling his comment, which had explained his stare: *You remind me of someone I used to know. Her name was Mary too.* For the first time in memory, her final thoughts before sleep were not of Jimmy Gooch.

A Fait Accompli

In the morning Mary could not remember her dreams. She did recall that she'd been awakened in the night by a mournful sound and had staggered through the dark to the window, thinking of Mr. Barkley the cat. She couldn't see the blackened hillside but realized that the sound was coyotes howling in the dense chaparral. Eden had talked about coyotes on the phone in a conversation long ago, after a neighbor, while soaking in his spa, had his head confused with some furry prey and was surprised by a coyote clamping its jaws around his skull. But surely that couldn't be true. It occurred to Mary that she couldn't really trust anything Eden said. Especially in regard to Gooch. Any mother would lie to protect her son.

Cramming her blistered feet into Eden's loafers, she remembered the hundred shoes at Jesús García's doorway. The plaid shirt. The accident. The bitten tongue, and the bruises on the old man's sepia skin. The meat on the platter. The woman's kind smile as she urged, "*Buen provecho.*" She touched her right palm absently, thinking of Jesús García's grip on her hand.

She was anxious to get to the bank, but it wouldn't open for a while. Mary knew Eden would be up, though, if she ever slept at all. She glanced around the tidy hotel room, remembering the previous day, when she'd despaired of a long, lonely night there. Instead she'd been led down a different path, driven by an enigmatic stranger.

Dressed in her pressed navy scrubs, and after leaving a five-dollar bill on the bed for the maids, she set out for the lobby. There, she requested of the male receptionist, whom she'd never seen before, the favor of a call to the taxi company. Before he could respond, she said, "I know it'll take a while. I'll be over there reading."

"The taxi guy is in there," the young man said, pointing at the hotel restaurant down the hall. "He's a big fat guy with a toupee." He was suddenly red-faced, realizing his gaffe.

In the restaurant, she spied the rotund taxi driver lost in a newspaper at a table near the window. "Excuse me," she began, pointing at a car in the parking lot. "Is that your taxi?"

The man set down his newspaper, smiling warmly. "Where do you need to go?"

With an urge to adjust his hair, Mary answered, "Willow Drive." Unlike the taxi driver she'd ridden with the previous day, this man was friendly and chatty as they climbed into the car. "Lucky you found me before I ordered," he said. "They put up a good breakfast here. And you would love their lunch buffet."

From a distance she counted nearly a dozen day workers waiting at the utility pole. She strained to look as the taxi drew closer but could not find the face of Ernesto. Jesús García had said he worked at the plaza, but Mary was still disappointed not to see him among the hungry men in the dusty lot.

Between the men's faded blue legs, her eye caught a flash of color—a flourish of pink garden roses in a soda bottle vase. And another bouquet of flowers scattered on the ground nearby. She imagined that one of the day workers had brought the flowers to beautify their surroundings. Or maybe teenaged lovers had rendez-voused there the previous night. "Mexicans," the driver muttered under his breath as they passed.

As the taxi joined the throngs on the main road heading in the direction of the Willow Highlands, the driver claimed knowledge of every alley and side street from Camarillo to Pasadena, freely shar-ing his classified secrets about the best routes to take to places she'd never go at various times of the day and on certain days of the week. "But if you're heading into L.A. you gotta be on the road before six or you're dead at the 405."

"Twenty-four," Mary said, pointing.

"You're thinking 23, which takes you up to Simi Valley."

"Twenty-four," she repeated. "Right there. The house. Please." She noticed the Prius in the driveway, but no other vehicle. Gooch was not there. Yet.

As she crept up the cracked walkway of the small white house, she could not reconcile the chill she felt with the full glare of the sun. A scent. Familiar. Electricity, but not a storm — the storm was past. Something burnt. Hair on Irma's curling iron. Popcorn in the microwave. A *fait accompli.*

She knocked once, sensing a presence. Eden opened the door, her half-raised face fallen completely, her eyes wide and startled. That deer-in-the-headlights dementia she'd seen in Irma's eyes. Frozen confusion — she knew it well. There was that chill.

"I made tea," Eden said, and started back toward the kitchen. Mary followed, closing the door behind her, entombed. Jack. Where was Jack? She saw it clearly now. Jack was dead, and Eden was stunned. That was the look. Even expected death, even merciful death, was shocking. Here today, gone tomorrow. Jack present, Jack picked. No more jumping candlesticks.

"You found your purse," Eden remarked when they reached the kitchen.

Mary nodded, glancing past her into the room where the sick man slept. The bed was empty. She pushed forward to look for the motorized chair. It was not in the room. "Eden? Where's Jack?"

"He wasn't here. Thank the Lord."

"Where is he?"

"It's Tuesday. Or is it Thursday?" Mary didn't know for certain, but thought it was Wednesday. "The church group takes a few of them out to the park for an hour every other day. I can never remember which day is the other one." Eden leaned against the counter. "I made tea."

"Tea sounds good."

"They all drink iced tea down here. I never have got used to that. I like my tea hot. Two cubes. Do you want a cube?"

Mary typically took four sugar cubes, and cream rather than milk. "Just black."

"I suppose the money and all was gone."

"The wallet was gone," Mary said, sipping, "but I found my passport."

Eden nodded but hadn't heard. "You haven't heard from Jimmy, have you?" Her mother-in-law's tone implied that she wasn't keeping secrets about Gooch after all.

"He has no way to contact me, Eden. He doesn't know where I am, remember?"

Something caught Eden's attention, and in an instant she was out the sliding patio doors, sidestepping the murky pool with a broom in her hand to beat the devil out of a cowering green bush. "Get out!" she screamed. "Get out!"

This was the mother Gooch had described to Mary on that first night under the serious moonlight. The one who made scenes. The one who'd thrown her husband's clothes into the Rideau Canal. She wondered briefly if Eden had started drinking again.

Following her outside, Mary saw no creature scamper from the bush as her mother-in-law slashed wildly, cracking branches, scattering leaves. "Eden? Eden?" Avoiding the swinging broom, Mary drew closer, calling, "It's gone. It ran out that way."

Eden set down the broom. "Was it a rat?"

"No! My God, do you have *rats?*"

"Of course we have rats. Everyone has rats. And we do not use God to exclaim. Jack would be so upset if he heard that."

"Thank the Lord Jack wasn't here for what?" Mary asked.

"The call," Eden sighed, scouring the yard for the rodent.

"The call?"

"They found Heather."

Mary pitied the poor woman her confusion, then panicked. "You don't mean they found Gooch? Eden? Who called?"

"The police called." Mary's heart beat wildly. "They found Heather. In a motel room in Niagara Falls."

"Heather?"

"They said it was an accidental overdose."

"Heather?"

"I wanted to laugh when they said they didn't suspect foul play. It's all foul. Her whole wasted life."

"Overdose?" Mary repeated, sure Eden must be mistaken. She'd just seen Heather, with her beautiful face and her big silver locket and her nicotine chewing gum and her new-found son. "When? When did this happen?"

"Yesterday."

"But I just saw her. I just saw her in Toronto. She was different, Eden. She'd changed. I told you."

"I've been expecting that call since she was a teenager, Mary. People don't change."

But people did change. Whole countries changed. They were all just the sum of their habits. "She *had* changed."

"They said she was using an alias," Eden said dryly. "Mary Brody."

Mary struggled to breathe. Heather Gooch dead at forty-nine. In a motel room in Niagara Falls. Accidental overdose? No, Mary thought, calculated risk. Dead of calculated risk. The death part had been an accident, but she'd known the risk she was taking. Might have told herself, *Just this one last time,* as she took that foul journey, led astray by certain old associates, the siren's lure of the altered state. Having been seduced by the Kenmore for most of her life, Mary understood only too well.

Foul play. A wasted life. How? Seated on the toilet? Alone? Or had someone been there to hold her hand? Hear her beg forgiveness? Whisper goodbye? Heather. Ah, beauty. A *fait accompli.* The rule of three. The triangle complete. But Jack soon to begin another, to replenish the fear of the second and the worry over the third. *You can group your tragedies in threes or thirties, Mare.* Maybe Gooch had been right about that too.

"Will there be a funeral?"

Eden shook her head. "She had a will, if you can believe someone as reckless and irresponsible as Heather would go to the trouble of making a will. She wanted to be cremated. No funeral. She left everything to Jimmy. Not that she had anything but debt, I'm sure. Jimmy'll have to figure out what to do with her ashes when he gets back. I wouldn't have a clue."

"Gooch'll know what to do," Mary agreed, moved by Eden's certainty that he would in fact return.

"Lord have mercy on her soul," Eden whispered, casting her eyes heavenward.

"Amen," Mary said, surprising herself.

Eden took another deep breath, casting her eyes over the green pool. "We had a lap pool at our last house. I swam a hundred laps a day."

"A hundred laps?" A hundred oaks. A hundred shoes. A hundred Heathers.

"I was very fit for my age." Eden had no more to say on the subject of her daughter's untimely death. No confessions of remorse or regret. No mournful lamentations. No hot tears filling her eyes.

Returning to the house, noticing the disarray, Mary asked, "Did your helper call in sick again?"

"It's her son this time. She has four children and one of them's always sick. She's the third girl since we moved."

"What time is prayer circle?" Mary asked.

"Two-thirty."

"Do you want to lie down?"

"Yes, Mary. I do," Eden answered, shuffling toward the door. She stopped, sighing deeply, and whispered to the hallway, "I wish Jimmy were here."

It was no use telling dry-eyed Eden to let it all out. It would let itself out when it was damn good and ready, Mary knew. "Me too," she said.

A short time later, as Mary was stretching plastic wrap over the culinary offerings, the front door opened with the sound of clanking metal and quiet voices. She peered down the hallway to see Jack in his motorized wheelchair being assisted into the house by two pleasant-looking men. She waited until the men had settled him into his bedroom before sliding out the back door. As eager as she was to get to the bank to sort out her account, she felt bound to stay until Eden woke, as she believed in saying goodbye.

She stopped in the backyard to enjoy the warm breeze, sweeping aside the broken branches on the ground, and found a chair to rest in at the green pool's edge. Looking up into the blue sky, she thought of the shooting star and felt a wash of shame remembering the gratitude in the bleeding man's eyes. She had done so little for Ernesto. And *nada* for Heather. She hadn't done as much for her broken sister-in-law in the past twenty-five years as a half-dozen strangers had done for her in recent days. She imagined Heather's obituary in the *Leaford Mirror*. Survived by her mother, Eden Asquith of Golden

Hills, California, a brother, James, and sister-in-law, Mary Gooch, of Leaford, Ontario. Son James, a medical student in Toronto.

She thought of her own left-behinds. A mother, a husband, the bones of a cat. Heather Gooch had left a son who might one day cure cancer. Or save multiple lives. Or just be a contributing member of society. Mary allowed herself a soupçon of bitterness. She would leave no one without a mother, and had made no mark on society. She didn't even vote.

She heard a rhythmic ticking, not the clock but a woodpecker in a tall eucalyptus near the fence. She thought of the night clock on the bedside table of her small rural home. The ticking of time. The machinations of denial. But her appetite for denial had been left, along with her appetite for food, in the fluted brown cups of Laura Secord chocolates.

Watching her wide, rippling reflection in the greasy green pool, she wondered how such a large woman had made so little impact on her little world. Of course, there would be people who missed her, who missed her now. The old folks at St. John's Nursing Home. A few of the customers at Raymond Russell's would have asked about her. But what was she really *leaving*? Like a tribe and a plan, a person needed a legacy. She could see that now, too.

At two o'clock Mary couldn't wait any longer, and padded to the back bedroom, rousing Eden with a gentle shake to her shoulders. "I put plastic on everything."

Eden nodded, rising from the bed, propelled into the hall by a retching sound from Jack's room. Mary stood still, unsure what to do as the hacking and gagging continued. In a moment Eden appeared, holding a towel animated by shivering bloody mucus. Mary looked away.

"Please don't go in there," Eden said, by way of goodbye.

Anxious to leave, Mary made her way to the door.

"Mary?" Eden called. Mary turned, waiting. "Will you come back tomorrow?" Her voice was small. "I just can't count on Chita."

Mary nodded, hiding her surprise. "I could come back tonight," she offered hopefully.

"Come in the morning. He's awake for a few hours then. Sometimes he cries."

Poor Eden, Mary thought. A lost daughter. A departing husband. Mary had never considered that she might one day have so much in common with her mother-in-law.

Damaged Art

Walking out the front door, Mary could not shake thoughts of Heather Gooch. So lost was she in her contemplation of her sister-in-law's life and death that she didn't see the black vehicle pull up in her periphery, and didn't recognize the voice of Ronni Reeves calling from the driver's window, "Do you need a ride somewhere?"

The young mother looked different. No lipstick. Stringy blonde locks leaking from a floral scarf on her head. Blemishes on her forehead that Mary hadn't noticed before. She decided not to count the woman's appearance as a miracle. Not even a wild coincidence — this town was as small as Leaford, and she lived on the same street, after all. "Thanks," she said, opening the car door. "I'm just going down to the bank at the plaza."

"That's easy," Ronni Reeves said, brushing Cheerios from the leather upholstery.

Looking into the back seat, Mary found the triplets dressed in white karate robes, two of the boys asleep with their heads joined ear to crown. Joshua, the runaway imp, clutched an enormous bag of Cheetos, his lips and fingers and white uniform stained orange as the setting sun. He studied her from his car seat, his face twisting into a grimace.

"Did your car break down? It was Mary, right?" Ronni Reeves asked, when Mary was arranged in the seat.

"Mary Gooch. I don't have a car."

"You don't have a *car*?"

"No."

"Are you a nurse?"

"No," Mary said, glancing down at her damp navy scrubs.

Throwing a glance at the back seat, Ronni said, "You remember the nice lady, Joshua. The one who found you in the parking lot before? Say, 'Hi Mrs. Gooch.'"

The little boy squinted at Mary. "You stink," he said, hurling an orange Cheeto at her head.

"*Joshua!*" his mother shouted, twisting to yank the bag of Cheetos from the boy's hands. "Say you're sorry and I'll give them back," she told him.

Mary thought of the English nanny show she had watched on television. And the movie she'd seen with that wonderful British actress whom Mary admired for her graciousness, and always thought looked just right in award-show photographs. Those nannies with the British accents would not return the Cheetos to the naughty boy, even if he did apologize. Mary thought they must raise lovely children on the other side of the ocean.

"How's Jack?" Mary shook her head fatally, stung by a tug at the back of her scalp. "*Joshua!*" Ronni bellowed. "Get your filthy fingers away from her head." Mary untangled the orange fingers from her hair.

"My husband left us six weeks ago." Ronni paused to find her breath, as if the shock of it was upon her again. "The boys have really been acting out."

"How was the new babysitter?" Mary asked, when she couldn't think what else to say.

Ronni Reeves, the wife left with triplets, shook her head darkly as she raced down the street toward the stop sign, relieved that her son had become distracted by painting the car window with his licked-orange fingers, until he began kicking the back of Mary's seat. "Stop that," she hissed. She glanced at Mary, saying, "He should be napping right now. But I had to shift their karate class. Jacob had an eye appointment. And I still have to meet with the lawyer. We were supposed to look at preschools."

The list. Mary could see Ronni's list of things not getting done, and caught the whiff of her abstract malaise. Even her bounty was a burden.

The young mother's purse rang. Mary watched the pretty woman drive with one hand, catching the gist of the conversation as she spoke. Ronni was being asked to cover another Lydia Lee home jewelry party tonight, and had to decline because she could not get a babysitter on such short notice.

"I could babysit for you," Mary interrupted, uncertain of her impulse.

"No. I couldn't ask you to."

"You didn't ask. I'm offering."

"Are you good with kids?"

"I'm good with old people."

"I hardly know you, though."

"You know Jack," Mary said, realizing how profoundly she was dreading the long night in the hotel room.

"That's true. You're practically a family friend. And I don't exactly *know* the women the agency sends," she reminded herself. "It would only be for a few hours. Are you sure?"

Stopped by the curb at the bank, the women exchanged telephone numbers and arranged a time for Mary to be at the house. Six o'clock. Ronni thanked her profusely but Mary just waved her off, watching the big SUV with its license plate promising *RoNTom* pull out of sight.

She headed into the bank with her brown vinyl purse under her arm, the passport safely zipped inside. With the proof of the passport and the help of Cooper and Lucille and the Golden Hills bank manager, the Canadian bank sorted out her situation and promised to send a new access card in care of the Golden Hills bank.

She made a withdrawal of a few hundred dollars, to see her through until the card arrived, and waited breathlessly to see the bank balance on the receipt that Cooper Ross handed her. It was unchanged from the last time she had checked. So that was that. Whatever that was. Gooch had not taken money from the account. But what if he did? He could, she realized. He could take it all.

Mary thought of the suspense novels she'd read in her youth, the thrillers she'd enjoyed on television. She wondered if her own mystery would be solved with small puzzle pieces or revealed in a tragic surprise ending. Like Heather's death.

After thanking the bank staff and stuffing the bills into the zippered compartment of her purse, she set off across the parking lot toward the shoe store. There was a sale rack outside but nothing to fit her extra-wide feet. Inside the store she found a pair of sneakers in her size, a package of six white socks and, on a display of handbags by the window, a sporty blue canvas tote bag with silver detail. She paid for the items, wearing the sneakers out of the store, and transferred the other things from the old purse to the new one, taking care to remember her passport, before ceremoniously tossing the brown vinyl purse into the trash.

Mary's attention was caught by a reflection in the glass of the pool company's window. A creature inching toward her, frail and stooped, balancing a spun nest of golden hair on her half-cocked head. She reminded Mary of an elderly customer she'd had at Raymond Russell's, the one who'd cried over the discontinuance of her Elizabeth Arden lipstick. The woman had such severe bone loss that her spine had curled inward to form her body into a lower-case *r*. This woman had a similar curvature, though not so dramatic. But more striking than her posture and the shuffling gait it imposed was the woman's face: the skin so stretched that she risked a fissure if she tried to blink or close her mouth; the eyes so wide that she appeared on the threshold of terror. She was wearing snug blue jeans that pinched the loose skin around her waist, and a tight, long-sleeved T-shirt that gave the impression of tattoos. Mary was unaware that she was staring, and didn't realize she was blocking the path until the woman was upon her, saying, "Excuse me."

Stepping back to allow her to pass, Mary saw from the back the old woman's flat rear end in the snug blue jeans, and a bulge that she recognized as adult wetness protection. When the woman turned and caught her staring she felt ashamed, but she could not stop herself from marveling at the woman's body, like a piece of damaged art, wondering what it had once been and what journey had transformed it.

Turning, she caught sight of a sign in a window that read, *Pool's Gold Cleaning Service. Great Deals for New Customers.* Following an impulse, she went inside the shop to make arrangements for the company to attend to her mother-in-law's neglected swimming pool. Even if Eden could no longer swim a hundred laps, she might be able to swim one or two, she thought, aspiring to lessen the woman's misery.

When she emerged from the pool place a short time later, she noticed a man looking at the discount shoe rack outside the shoe store a few doors down. There was something familiar about him, but with the sun in her eyes, she couldn't tell right off who it was standing there, holding a pair of yellow ladies' sandals in his big brown hands. Her sight adjusted and she saw that it was Jesús García. She was set to call out his name when he suddenly shoved the yellow sandals under his coat jacket and loped away.

Mary flashed on a memory of Klik's Variety Store. She'd purchased so much candy from the couple that they'd never guessed she was stealing it too. Snatching, scoffing, lifting, hiding candy bars deep within her pockets when they were ringing up another sale, trying to appear innocent, awaiting her engorgement.

Stunned by the swift and strange nature of the theft, she watched Jesús García recede down the mall's promenade. Eager to know the fate of Ernesto, she started to follow but stopped, worried that he would guess she'd witnessed his crime. She feared that she might embarrass him or, worse, anger him. She would never have taken him for a thief, but there it was. All people had secrets.

No one was who they appeared to be.

Cuatro Chicas

Walking had become easier in the days since Gooch's departure, and Mary found further redemption in her new white sneakers. She hardly noticed the distance she'd covered before pressing the traffic button at the intersection. She scanned the dusty lot on the corner, surprised to see diminutive brown-skinned women gathered around the utility pole, and a dozen more wildflower bouquets scattered on the ground. Had the women brought the flowers? She'd never seen women at the lot before.

She crossed the street, drawn to the flowers, convincing herself that the tribute could not be for Ernesto, since surely Jesús García would not be out stealing shoes if his dear friend had just died. Still, she was curious about the roadside memorial and the women standing beneath it. Not caring about the fine dust on her new sneakers, she walked toward them.

There was a sign pinned to the pole, decorated with a single wreath of faded plastic flowers. Spanish writing. "What is this for?" she asked.

They spoke at once, rapidly, in Spanish.

"Not Ernesto?" she asked, suddenly unsure.

The women, most of whom appeared to be around her age, did not understand. She pointed to the sign. "Is this about a man called Ernesto?"

But the women's attention was caught by a silver van turning into the dusty lot. The driver, a slender man with cropped hair and pock-marked cheeks, pulled to a stop. His eyes fell briefly on Mary as he rolled down the window and called out to the heaviest of the Mexican women, who was also the oldest and the grayest and the weariest, "We gotta move, Rosa. We got one hour."

The sullen man climbed out of the vehicle and came around to release the side door. The women piled in. He paused to look at Mary.

"I'm not with them," she explained.

When he laughed Mary turned to walk away, vaguely insulted, but all at once she felt pain like a bullet, a burning sensation in the spot between her eyes, that launched to her chest to cue the hammering of her heart. She grasped for the utility pole.

The man stopped laughing. "Are you okay? Should I call an ambulance?"

"No," Mary said. "I just need to catch my breath."

He smiled and shrugged as if to say, *I tried*, and was set to close the door when he counted the women within the van. "I said meet me here with *four* girls, Rosa. *Cuatro chicas.*"

"*Sí*," the weary woman said from the back seat. "*Cuatro chicas.*" She counted the women in the van as proof. "*Cuatro.*"

"Four *counting* you. Not four *plus* you. My boss said four. I can't bring five."

"It's okay," she promised. "We share the money."

"I can't bring five. I can't bring five when he said four. One of you has to get out."

The women were silent at the indignity. Mary squinted through her pain, watching them as they turned to Rosa within the van and began a quiet conference of wide eyes and shifting brows and pursed lips until the matter was decided. Eight brown eyes turned on the smallest woman, who was also the youngest and, Mary saw as she stepped down from the vehicle, in the later stages of pregnancy.

Coughing from the dust of the departing van, the young woman took a cellphone from her bag and attempted unsuccessfully to make a call. Cursing in her mother tongue, she turned to Mary, her smile towing the deep scar on her right upper lip. She looked too pregnant to be working as a house cleaner. And too young to be pregnant. "You have the cellphone?" she asked.

"I don't have a cellphone," Mary apologized.

The pregnant girl counted the bags in her hands, then looked up, ashen, to find the van disappearing down the road. She cursed in Spanish.

Mary knew that look too well. "Did you lose something? Did you forget something?"

"My lunch," the girl said in careful English, before cursing in Spanish again. She rubbed her cumbersome belly and looked toward the street. "There is a bus?" she asked.

Mary swiveled to look for the transit shelter and felt once again the calamitous pain in her head.

"You are sick?" the young woman asked, recoiling slightly.

"No," Mary said, swaying. She closed her eyes and could almost hear the night clock in the roar of the traffic. She waited but the feeling did not pass, as she stood at the wreath-bedecked memorial on the dusty lot in Golden Hills, California, and saw that this was the end. She had never imagined such a death scene, and felt some strange thrill in the unexpected. So her final view would be of the blue sky and healing sun. Her last sound, horns on the 101 freeway. And the last person she would lay eyes upon would be a petite, pregnant Mexican girl with a scar on her upper lip. Maybe this girl was God. And had the power to forgive.

Mary pried open her eyes, hoping to catch a glimpse of the divine.

The girl was gone. No sign of her on the road. Perhaps she'd never been there at all. Counting heartbeats, Mary waited for the final sting, but the tightness eased in her chest and she breathed deeply, drawing the golden dust into her lungs. The pain in her head grew quiet too. Not now. Not here. Not yet. In the stillness, she prayed.

If any of the passing drivers found the sight of a large white woman propping up the utility pole at the Mexicans' dusty corner lot a surprising one, no one stopped to investigate. Grasping the pole, Mary had a sense of déjà vu, remembering her brave young self holding a metal mop handle during an electrical storm, attempting then, as now, to do the extraordinary.

Pushing off from the pole, she started toward the hotel, tentative steps at first, then longer strides. *Not me. Not here. Not now.* She wished she were a writer like Gooch, that she might make a poem of her gratitude for the gift of second chances.

Breathless, glistening with the sheen of victory, she entered the hotel lobby, remembering her promise to babysit. She wondered if the warmth washing over her was endorphins from her labor or if the feeling was anticipation of the night ahead, as she recognized that the little boys might be something like the tribe she had longed for. She glanced toward the window of the hotel restaurant as she passed, and was surprised to see the pregnant Mexican girl from the corner lot nursing an iced tea in one of the back booths.

She studied the girl, whose eyes darted from the watch on her wrist to the parking lot beyond the windows to the breakfast platter sitting untouched in front of an elderly man at the next table. Though she typically stayed out of restaurants, and never approached buffets, Mary entered, following a mysterious impulse. As all eyes in the crowded place, some more discreetly than others, clocked her movement toward the smorgasbord, she began to perspire. She shouted at herself silently — *What the hell are you doing?*

Standing before the bounty on display — thick slices of juicy roast beef and lemon-pepper chicken, creamy macaroni, salty diced potatoes, hot buttered rice—she suddenly understood why she'd come in. She collected a tray and plate and addressed the meats. Undecided between the beef and chicken, she put both on her plate, then a scoop of macaroni, the rice, a cob of steaming corn and several rolls with butter. She could feel the eyes of the other diners boring through the tissue of her back as she added a parfait glass of pudding and a slice of cherry pie to her tray. Two cartons of milk. A bottle of iced tea. The cashier did not meet her eye as she paid for the food.

Gliding past the other diners, she found the girl with the scar on her lip and set the mountain of food down before her. The girl looked up. Pretty almond eyes, like in the picture of Jesús García's wife. Young enough to be his daughter. Or Mary's. "*Buen provecho*," she said. "Eat."

The girl's gratitude was implied in her acceptance as she tore into the beef. Mary stood at the table, moved by her mastication, living her hunger, but not for food. Giddy in her gluttony, the pregnant girl did not see Mary leave the restaurant, as the other diners had, swallowing a lump in her throat.

Back in her hotel room, Mary settled down to read but could not focus. There were still two hours before she was expected at Ronni Reeves's for her babysitting job. Ample time to accommodate the hour-long wait for the taxi. The small print blurred as the pain between her eyes sharpened and Heather's face invaded her vision.

She closed the book, pushing aside thoughts of Heather to fantasize about Gooch's return. She'd have to find something to wear. Something green to play up her eyes. She decided she'd like to have their reunion at Eden's instead of the hotel, in the backyard, under the shimmering eucalyptus. She thought of Gooch's face upon seeing her, how he would lift his shoulders and smile that wan smile—his way of saying, *Ah, life*—and how Mary would nod twice and tilt her head, her way of saying, *I know*.

No matter what conclusions he might have arrived at, no matter what clarity he'd found in conversations with God, he would be devastated by his sister's death. Mary hoped Eden would be spared the burden of telling him. In her mind's eye she saw herself with Gooch, folded into too-small airplane seats on their way back to Canada, wondering what to do with Heather's remains. "She liked the water," Gooch might whisper. "She was such a fish when she was young." Or he'd have gone with dark humor and suggested sprinkling her ashes over a field of poppies, or maybe hemp.

Mary called the front desk for a taxi, and sat quietly in the back seat when it arrived. Passing the growing memorial at the corner, she scanned the faces in the thin crowd of men, wondering if Jesús García was among them, waiting for his uncle with the bad hip, the stolen yellow sandals hidden in the duffel bag he brought to work.

Imagining the yellow sandals among the carpet of shoes at the front door of the teeming house, she remembered that Jesús had said he worked at the plaza, which made his offense seem even bolder. She guessed that the sandals were a present for his plump, pretty wife. But wouldn't she find that odd? Or had he stolen before, different styles and sizes, to add to the impressive collection by the door?

Annoyed at her curiosity about Jesús García, Mary turned her thoughts back to Gooch, the mystery of one man enough for now. She wondered if Gooch would like her red hair.

Till Death Us Do Part

The black Lincoln Navigator was parked beside the big Ram in the driveway of abandoned wife Ronni Reeves when Mary arrived by taxi at 5:45. As she approached, she heard a symphony leaking out the windows and doors—the shouting percussive mother, the trilling trio of children, the bass barking dog. The thought of a night alone in the hotel was suddenly appealing, but Mary could not stop her feet from carrying her up the walkway, or her finger from pressing the buzzer.

The sound of screaming was instantly replaced by the natter of a television cranked too loud. After a long moment the door opened. Ronni Reeves, red-faced and puffy-eyed, was attempting to smile. "Hi Mary. Come in."

"I heard . . . from the street . . . it sounded—"

"Everything's fine," Ronni said, surprised to see that Mary was still dressed in the navy scrubs she had had on earlier. "They're just a little wound up tonight."

Mary smoothed her smock over her round stomach, as if that could excuse her poor choice of fashion. "I suppose you get used to the noise."

A commotion beyond the door. A shriek of pain. Children screaming. Ronni inhaled sharply. "Boys!" she shouted, clapping her hands. The dog barked from a distant room as the boys bawled over each other.

"Oh dear," Mary said.

"My husband left us six weeks ago," Ronni said. "None of us are coping well."

"You said that before."

"I told you? I already told you that? God, the neighbors don't even know yet."

The noise of breaking glass. The women shared a look before busting down the hallway, finding the three boys standing in the back room amidst the shattered remains of a large TV. The triplets had been shocked dumb by the accident, and stayed put when Mary instructed them, "Don't move." She plucked each boy to safety, lifting them over the shore of glass pebbles to the arms of their broken mother.

"I just want to scream," Ronni said quietly.

Mary understood, and led her toward the front door. "Go. Just go."

"Are you sure?"

"We'll be fine. I've got your number. Go."

"Thank you, Mary. Thank you." Ronni reached for her handbag, kissed each boy on the head and said, "You boys be good for Mrs. Gooch." She did not so much leave as flee. Mary watched her pull out of the driveway and turned to find the children at her heel.

"I wanna watch TV!" Joshua shouted.

The other boys agreed loudly. Mary studied them a moment. "Okay then . . ."

She led them to the back room but stopped, pretending to be surprised. "Oh dear, boys. The television is broken."

"We wanna watch it!" Joshua yelled.

"But it's broken."

"No fair!" he screamed.

"TV, TV, TV," the other two chanted.

"I am so sorry, boys, but I *broke* your TV," Mary explained.

Joshua stopped wailing. "*You* didn't break it."

"I didn't?"

"*We* broke it," he insisted, outraged.

"Well then, you have only yourselves to blame," Mary said, shrugging.

The triplets studied the strange woman heading into their kitchen. "What are we gonna do?"

"I used to like crayons. I can show you how to draw a puppy."

They shrugged and found seats at the kitchen table. "The craft box is there," Joshua said, pointing to a basket half-filled with torn coloring books and broken crayons. Mary found a few blank pages and sat down with the boys. "I have a few tricks to draw a puppy. Even a two-year-old could do it."

"We're three," they said at once.

"Oh, three, well then you'll have no trouble. If you're three I can show you the tricks for a kitten and a horse too."

Once the children were involved in their artistic pursuits, stubby fingers leading crayons, pink tongues lolling on lips, Mary stopped to glance around the beautiful open-concept home. She wondered at the pleasure Ronni Reeves must have had in decorating it, even if her choices had been ill advised. The furniture, too elegant for a home with three boys, was nicked and torn, badly stained and dented. What did that say of the poor woman's marriage? It was unthinkable that the three beautiful boys could have ruined the union the way they had the decor, but Mary could see the trajectory — the new mother harried and overwrought, the husband underappreciated and neglected. She too tired and resentful for love, searching for it elsewhere. The miracle, Mary thought, was that any marriage survived.

Till death us do part. Did brides and grooms still say that to each other? Wouldn't that be the height of hypocrisy, when each entered the union knowing the odds were fifty-fifty they'd endure? Mary wondered if the encroachment of obesity on North America's population had risen in tandem with divorce statistics. The mistaking of gluttony for fulfillment. So often a spouse spoke of wanting more. Needing more. Not having enough. Her own marriage was less enduring than endured, at least by Gooch, as evidenced by his departure. So what had kept them together all these years? Beyond inertia?

There must have been some force exchanged by their bodies, even after they'd stopped connecting in the physical sense. Love, or the potent memory of it, mysterious and complex. She remembered that it had been just the past Labor Day that she'd laughingly told Gooch about overhearing Ray's comments about her ass. Gooch had risen, seething, from the red vinyl chair in the kitchen and started for the door. She'd stopped him from driving to Raymond Russell's to confront her boss, but had secretly adored his rage. Loyalty. Not bound by a gold band around a designated finger, but kept in the core like a vital organ.

She was pausing, purple crayon over fresh white paper, her mind frozen on a picture from her wedding day, when she was poked by a tiny, bitten finger. "You're fat," Joshua said, his hand disappearing into the fold at her navel.

Tickled by the intrusion, and charmed by the twisted mouth of the tow-headed boy, Mary found his hand. "You don't want to tell someone they're fat," she said gently.

"Why?" he asked, blinking.

"Because they already know." Mary winked.

"You're fatter'n Uncle Harley," Jacob decided.

She laughed. The boys appeared to have no negative connotation for the word, as if it was just another shape in their primary hearts. Circle. Square. Fat.

After coloring for a time, Mary made paper airplanes for Jacob and Jeremy. When they started dropping crayon bombs on each other, she found a bookcase filled with children's books and gathered the little boys on the sofa in the formal living room. The three squirming shapes soon molded themselves against her big, warm body as she read aloud the books they pressed into her hand, one resting sticky fingers on her arm, another absently twisting her red hair, the third climbing aboard her thigh, captivated by the simplest of narratives. Mary sighed, touched lovingly by hands not her own.

After reading eleven books, three of them twice, she was parched but nonetheless disappointed to hear a car in the driveway. She lifted herself from the sofa and moved to the window, her heart skipping a beat when she saw that it was not the black Navigator but a silver Mercedes. She told the boys to stay on the sofa as she went to answer the front door. "Hello," she said, to the wiry, dark-haired man on the porch.

"Who are *you?*" the man shot back, trying to look past her into the house.

"I'm the babysitter."

His expression was critical of both her size and her attire. "Are you from the service?"

"Family friend," Mary said confidently.

"Where's Ronni?" He tried to push past her but she blocked the door. "Boys!" he shouted into the house. "Joshua! Jacob! Jeremy!"

The boys stormed the hallway, barreling into the wiry man's arms, shrieking, "Daddy!" The big shaggy dog, who'd been sleeping near the sofa, began to bark and howl, nipping at the father's heels.

"I'm taking them for ice cream," the man shouted over the dog, carting the delighted boys to his still-running car.

"No!" Mary objected. "You can't *take* them! You can't take them *anywhere!*"

He hustled the boys into his car as Mary continued shouting and the big dog protested with angry barks of his own. She danced around the car as he shut the children inside. "You haven't even buckled them in!" she cried. But he climbed into the driver's seat and jammed the car into reverse. Panicked, Mary raced around to the back of the vehicle and stopped the silver trunk with her hands. The dog joined her there, no longer barking at the man but at her.

The boys' father rolled down his window, laughing at the absurdity of the large redhead standing behind his car under siege by a barking dog. "You've got to be kidding me," he called. The dog ran around to his side of the car, jumping at him through the window. Mary folded her arms, leaning her rear against the trunk. He called her bluff, releasing his foot from the brake. She stood firm, the heat from the exhaust burning her leg.

From the corner of her eye Mary saw Ronni Reeves tearing up in her Navigator, blocking the Mercedes. The mother climbed out of her vehicle, shouting obscenities at her glaring husband. Mary opened the door to the Mercedes and lifted the boys out, the shaggy dog herding them all back into the house, to shield them from an obscene vocabulary lesson as their warring parents drew blood in the driveway.

When she stepped through the front door a few minutes later, Ronni looked battered. "I'm so sorry that happened, Mary."

"Now the neighbors know," Mary said.

Ronni winced. "He is such an *asshole*."

"The boys might hear you," Mary cautioned, but the children had already fled to the kitchen to tease the still-barking dog.

"You'll never sit for me again, will you?" Ronni asked, biting her lip. "You have no idea how hard this all is."

Mary paused. "My husband left me too."

Ronni reached out with her beautiful hand to touch Mary's meaty arm. "Younger woman?"

"He needed time to think."

"Tom said that too. He didn't say he needed time to think about his dick in his girlfriend's mouth, but that's what I concluded." Mary was as startled by Ronni Reeves's language as she was fascinated by her rage. "Sorry," Ronni added. "But I'm sure you know the feeling. I was going to ask you again for tomorrow night."

"Tomorrow night? Oh, I don't know," Mary floundered.

"I have a chance at another jewelry party. I really need the money." She reached for her wallet and pressed some bills into Mary's hand.

Pushing the bills back, Mary said, "No, please."

"I usually pay my sitters."

"Consider it a favor. I'm a family friend, remember?"

"Will my family friend come tomorrow?"

"I suppose I could come tomorrow." Mary wondered how many books she could read aloud without losing her voice.

"Maybe we could even make it a regular thing? For as long as you're in town. A few hours in the afternoons, and on the nights when I do Lydia Lee?" Ronni asked hopefully.

"I really don't know how long I'm going to be here."

"Of course. You're just waiting until Jack . . ."

"I'm waiting for Gooch. My husband."

"You just said he left you."

"He did, but not permanently."

"Oh. When's he coming back?"

"When he's had his time to think. He's hiking somewhere and then he's coming back to see his mother again," Mary explained. "And I want to be here when he does."

"So you can convince him to go back home with you?"

"There's so much I need to tell him."

Ronni Reeves squeezed Mary's arm. "No matter what you say, no matter how you say it, take it from me—he's already made up his mind."

Meteor Showers

The song of the long, sleepless night, once so familiar to Mary, had morphed from the turgid requiem she heard in Leaford to a blasting rock opera in Golden Hills, the strum of the Kenmore replaced by howling coyotes, the tick of the clock by night birds repeating the refrain—*He's already made up his mind.* Flashing scenes of strangers in a strange land, accompanied by stings on electric guitar. Ronni, the bitter wife. Tom, the betraying husband. Even her in-laws were strange relations. The blonde cleaning women. Ernesto, who thought she was an angel. Jesús García and his stolen yellow sandals.

As dawn broke over the hillside, Mary thought of the pregnant Mexican girl with the dark almond eyes, remembering the ravenous way she'd eaten her food. Mary could not remember her own last full meal. She told herself she should be hungry, and replied that she was not.

She focused on the day's agenda. Go to the bank for new access card, which was set to arrive today. She was eager to check the balance, worried that the money might disappear suddenly, just as it had come. She had no confidence in the constancy of objects. After the bank, she would go to Eden's to make food for her prayer circle and do whatever else needed to be done, if Eden's housekeeper had not shown up. A rest with a good book at the hotel in the afternoon. Sitting with the Reeves boys in the evening.

The sun had risen when she made her way out to the road, and she decided to walk to the bank for the exercise. She squinted from the glare of the wide concrete road. The space between her eyes began to throb again, and she worried that she'd sustained a greater injury than she'd thought when she'd banged her head against the steering wheel in the parking lot in Chatham. The aspirin weren't working. She needed something stronger for her pain.

Up ahead she saw a crowd of men, no women, waiting at the corner lot. Dozens of bouquets decorating the memorial now, and below it a large jar beside the wilted flowers in the soda bottle, collecting coins and dollar bills. A photograph was pinned beneath the sign on the utility pole. She drew closer. The photograph was black-and-white, dated. A young man, steel-eyed beneath a fedora hat. Clearly not Ernesto. She smiled at a few of the workers, who regarded her suspiciously. "Does anyone speak English?" she inquired shyly.

"You need workers?" one man answered eagerly.

"No. Oh no. I don't even have a car. I wanted to ask about Ernesto. He had an accident here a couple of days ago. I know that's not him," she said, gesturing to the picture, "but does anyone know him? Does anyone know how he's doing?"

The man who'd hoped for work shook his head. "That's not Ernesto."

"Yes, I know."

"That's Guillermo."

"Guillermo?"

"He died in the field. From the heat," he said, accusing the sun.

"Oh. That's awful. That's just awful."

"Yes."

"Is that for his family?" she asked, indicating the jar of money.

He shook his head. "That's for his funeral."

The other men watched from under their ball caps as Mary moved toward the utility pole. After studying the photograph for a moment, she reached into her new blue tote bag with the silver detail, extracted a wad of bills and bent to fill the jar with all the cash she had.

Along with the joggers and walkers and cyclists, Mary made her way down the landscaped sidewalks toward the bank, wondering if Gooch, cosmically sensing the tragedy of Heather, would be drawn back to his mother through this day's circle of prayer.

Her new bank card had arrived as promised, and she was eager to try it in the machine on the outside of the building. She withdrew the maximum amount and looked at the balance on the receipt. An additional amount of money had been withdrawn from the account. An additional four hundred dollars. Gooch — it could only be Gooch. The withdrawal was the closest communication they'd had since he'd looked at her with that expression the night before their anniversary and said, "Don't wait up."

Crossing the parking lot, she felt her heart flutter with hope. The withdrawal proved that he wasn't dead. He hadn't fallen from some ridge. He was not lost in the woods. He could be, this very moment, racing down the highway, having found the answers he'd been seeking. He might have made the bank withdrawal to see him through the final leg back to Eden's. She strode the aisles of the drugstore, her sense of optimism slowly strangled by that pain between her eyes. She approached the pharmacist at the back counter, asking about the strongest pain reliever. Realizing that she couldn't manage the distance to Eden's house on foot, she asked the pharmacist for the favor of a taxi call. "I'll be waiting in the shade over by the restaurant," she said.

"It'll take—"

"I know." She smiled.

Inhaling the air outside, Mary judged not a scent but a moisture content. The limousine driver had said the ocean was the opposite way down the road from Golden Hills. A brief quarter-hour drive from where she stood. She longed to go there, to stand in the surf with her pants rolled up, to feel the salty spray on her pretty face and to pray to the sea god for her husband's return.

The road was obscured from her seat on the bench, hidden by a row of slender cypress trees. Big band dance music blared through a speaker hidden inside a faux garden rock at her feet. She closed her eyes, enfolded by a pair of strong, thick arms, swaying slightly to the music. She could count on her hands the number of times she'd danced with her husband, each occasion being at some wedding over the years. Gooch would insist on the last dance, pull her to her feet and lean down to kiss her ear, because he wanted to have sex.

The rest of the evening she'd spend in her chair, sucking a stash of Jordan almonds from pouches of white gauze. Wedding after wedding, Mary had congratulated herself for her independence. She didn't need Gooch to sit with her all night just because she didn't like to dance, or didn't know how to dance, or couldn't conceive of shaking her bountiful booty among strangers. And she wasn't just independent, she was confident and secure, encouraging Gooch to take to the dance floor with other women. *Take Wendy for a whirl. Go boogie with Kim and Patti.*

All the women wanted to dance with Gooch. To feel tiny in those big strong arms and possessed by that huge hand at the small of their backs, to feign innocence in the brush of thigh to hip as soft hairs teased blushing cheeks. Flagrant fouls forgiven or forgotten by tomorrow's hangover. Gyrating groins. Shaking titties. Humping asses. A flurry of holding penalties.

Gooch liked to joke that Mary "pimped him out" at weddings. "Go dance with Dave's aunt. Her husband died five years ago," she'd say. Or "I told Joyce I'd put you on her dance card. Her husband's got the gout."

They'd been strangers at the last wedding they'd attended, the marriage of Theo Fotopolis's eldest daughter to a boy from Athens. The table of ten at which they were placed was the most distant one from the bride and groom, denoting the Gooches' rank and stature as guests. The position suited Mary, who had nothing decent to wear and was dressed in a too-casual blouse and skirt ensemble amid a sea of sparkle and shimmer. Introducing herself to their tablemates, she saw that this was the island of odds and outcasts: the morose widower, the chatty spinster aunt, the unmarried photographer, the priest and his mother.

One seat, the chair beside Mary, sat vacant throughout the long, delicious Greek dinner, which was to Mary's mouth as sex had once been to her core. Instantly addictive. She wanted it all and more, and although she hated eating in public, she cleaned her plate of each rich course until dessert. That was when the final guest arrived to fill the seat beside her.

Mary was in her mid-thirties then. The woman was around the same age but younger looking, much taller and slender, with stylishly short brunette hair and a simple blue dress that hugged her high bust and curving hips. She took her seat, whispering to Mary in a sisterly way, "The singles table, huh? I hate weddings." Setting eyes on Gooch in his dark suit, she grinned and added, "Maybe not."

A spontaneous toast to the bride had stopped Mary from introducing Gooch as her husband. Feeling the fullness of wind in her gut and realizing that she'd eaten too much too fast, she left the honey-infused pastry on the plate and excused herself to find the restroom.

As she was returning, the band struck up the first chord and the new arrival was pulling Gooch to the dance floor as the big band played a slow song. Gooch spotted Mary in the crowd. He raised his shoulders as if to say, *What do I do?* Mary turned in the other direction and headed for the truck in the parking lot, leaning against the grille, listening to the music on the breeze, wondering how many songs it would take for Gooch to see she was gone.

He was there in an instant, scanning the parking lot from the big oak doors of the banquet hall. His long legs drove him forward. He was angry. "You're not allowed to just run away like that."

"Let's go home."

"We're not going home," he said, standing his ground.

"I'm going home."

"I'm staying, Mary," he said, calling her bluff, and he spun on his heel and left.

No matter how much expertise she had in denial, Mary could not leave her husband alone at the wedding. Back inside the hall, she saw the pretty woman find Gooch in the crowd at the bar. She observed their body language as he spoke to the woman over the din. She looked Mary's way, then returned her attention to Gooch, grinning. Gooch said something else. The woman looked at Mary again, stunned, then contrite, apologetic, embarrassed. Mary forgave her, though, for like the association exercises given to preschoolers, who would ever draw a pencil line between Mary and Gooch?

The last dance of the night—the last dance they had ever danced—Gooch approached with that cocky grin, his hand outstretched. "Last dance, Mare."

She smiled, lifted her hand to his and let him pull her to the floor. His hand at her back, of which no part was small, he drew her close and guided her in a slow circle through the few remaining dancers and leaned down to kiss her ear, whispering, "I love you."

They moved about, Gooch singing into her ear, breath hot, voice rock-star raspy. Mary settled against his body, closing her eyes, opening them when she felt the bump of another rump on the dance floor. The pretty woman in the blue dress — she was dancing with the twelve-year-old nephew of the groom, the boy's cheeks scarlet with bliss, his mouth a terminal grin. Died and gone to heaven. Mary felt sick.

In the course of dancing, every view Mary lost of the beautiful woman was one gained by Gooch. She imagined that he was no longer turning at all, his eyes fixed on the boy's pretty prize. When she felt his fingers squeeze the fat of her back, she flinched. When she felt the growing lump of his erection she pushed him away, saying, "Let's go, Gooch."

Gooch misunderstood the gesture, and was confused when the grasping of her breast in the car was met with a slap. "Not when I'm driving," she scolded. She cleared her throat and tried not to sound accusatory. "I know what you're thinking about, Gooch."

"I thought you were thinking the same thing," he laughed, reaching for her thigh.

"I know what you're thinking about, Gooch," she said again, picturing the woman in the blue dress.

His arousal at odds with his comprehension, and seeing things would not go well, he shook his head. "I'm thinking that it's been a long time, Mare. I'm thinking I want to make love to my wife," he said.

Mary was shivering from the memory of that last dance with Gooch when the taxi pulled up, much sooner than expected, driven by the friendly man with the traffic advisories.

Reaching Eden's, she saw the Prius but no other car parked in the driveway, and reckoned that Chita had again not shown up for work, just as Eden had feared. She rang the buzzer, wondering if her mother-in-law was out beating rats from the bushes when she didn't answer the door. Finally Eden appeared, flushed and breathless. "He's at the hospital. He had a seizure when the nurse was here last night. I've been up with him all night. I've just gotten back."

"Oh Eden," Mary said, stepping inside the dank house, noticing the disarray as she followed the older woman down the hall to Jack's room.

"Chita quit," Eden said. "She called yesterday."

The drapes were drawn in Jack's room, but Mary could see in the dim light the dent in the mattress where he had lain, medications spread out over the bedside tables, a pile of soiled linens on the floor. For the first time, she was glad for her diminished sense of smell. Eden pushed back the curtain on the floor-to-ceiling window but a clip was stuck on the rod. She yanked at the fabric again and again, startled when she pulled the rod clear of its hooks and the curtain fell to the floor. With the sickroom suddenly bathed in bright sunlight, she moved from the window to open the closet door. "I have to decide which of Jack's suits should go to the cleaners."

Mary noticed a collection of photographs on Jack's dresser and thought of the lovely scrapbook Wendy could make of them, evidence of the couple's enduring love. Pictures from the exotic vacations they had gone on. Photos of the two holding hands on a sailboat Jack had owned, in front of the mansion with the lap pool. "Jack had a boat?"

"He loved the sea. It was awful for him when he couldn't sail any more. He missed it more than driving. Will you help me decide between the blue and the gray?"

Mary understood that they were choosing Jack's burial clothes, and paused to consider before she answered. "Blue." Scanning the photographs again, she realized. "Doesn't Jack have daughters?"

"Three. Eldest is in Redding. The other girls are up in the Bay Area."

"Are they here?"

"No."

"Are they coming?"

Eden shrugged.

"Do they know?"

Eden didn't respond.

"Shouldn't they know, Eden?"

"They never had the time to say hello. Why would they need to say goodbye?"

"They're his children."

"They never called. They never visited. They demonized that poor man. They believed everything his ex-wife said. Jack didn't even get to meet his grandchildren. He prayed every night those girls would see the light. They just broke his heart."

The ringing of the telephone on the bedside stand startled them both.

"Hello," Eden said into the receiver. "Hello? Hello?" After a moment she hung up, saying, "Lost call."

"What if it was Gooch? What if it was about Jack?"

"They'll call back if it was anything important."

The two women stared at the phone. "Our silver anniversary is in January," Eden said, twisting the diamond cluster wedding ring on her crooked left finger.

Mary admired the way the stones scattered the light. "Ours was a couple of weeks ago."

Eden turned, dawning with memory. "October. Yes. I remember." She noticed Mary's ring finger. "Your wedding ring."

"I had to have it cut off years ago. My finger got too fat."

"Jimmy was still wearing his," Eden told her. "When he was here. I noticed he was wearing his gold wedding band, if that means anything."

Mary smiled.

"Well," Eden said, casting a glance at the phone, "I guess it was nothing important. I need to lay down for a bit." She took a breath but said no more as she rose, shuffled across the hallway, twisted the knob on the door with her cruelly bent digits and slipped inside her room.

Mary looked down at her own hands, grateful for their marvelous mechanics, thanking all ten fingers for their years of support. Turning to go, she caught sight of something in the mirror on Jack's dresser. A flash of silver at her scalp. She was already growing roots.

Drawn by the sun, she let her feet urge her out the back door to the patio near the pool, wondering if the pool company had come by to clean but been shooed away by Eden, or had found no one at home. She saw her soul's reflection staring back from the murky green water, but different from the last time she'd glimpsed it. Her changing perception of time had altered the sum of her reflections. To the past she was no longer servant, and to the mirror comrade, not conspirator. That elusive happiness she'd so often pondered? Maybe happiness was generally misunderstood, she thought. Maybe happiness was the absence of fear. She felt herself at the launch of her own transformation, and wished she had a champagne bottle to crack against her knee. She watched her form in the rippling water and felt a peculiar urge to shout, "Fat Girl Revolution!"

Was that what this all amounted to? This leaving of Leaford? This parting with her appetite? This relinquishing of her fear? A revolution — not *against* herself but in support of herself? She had Gooch to thank, in many ways. But she could see how even a revolutionary could lose perspective. And patience.

A short time later, she heard noises in the kitchen and went to find Eden.

"I'm going back to the hospital."

"Do you want me to come with you?"

"No. You could stay though, if you like."

"Do you want me to stay? Until you get back?"

"I just thought it might be nicer for you than sitting in a hotel."

When Eden was gone, Mary stripped the sheets from Jack's

bed and opened the windows to sweep out the stale air. She vacuumed dead skin from the waves of worn broadloom, and dusted the framed photographs on his dresser. After a thorough cleaning of his room, she washed the dishes and put on the laundry and swept the terracotta floor in the hallway. She hummed while she worked, pondering her satisfaction. "You know this feeling to serve?" Big Avi had asked her.

The Son's Wife

With Eden still not home, Mary plumped the pillows on the Ethan Allen and sat down to rest. The drapes were partially drawn and the room in shadow as she scanned the bookcase, where there were dozens of old books, including some titles she recognized, and a large leather-bound Bible. She opened the Bible, extracted some of the cash from her purse and tucked it neatly inside before returning it to the shelf, jangled by the ringing phone beside her. She was unsure if she should pick up, and then panicked that it might be Gooch.

"Hello?" she answered tentatively.

The receiver went dead on the other end. Or nobody had ever been there at all. Another lost call. Eden said it happened all the time — like the incidence of left wives, Mary supposed.

As she set the phone back down, she caught sight of a turquoise Chevy pulling up in the driveway. A vintage beauty, which Gooch would have loved, but she saw that the driver was not Gooch, nor was he among the people climbing out of the car. She had decided not to answer the door, and was hiding in the hallway out of sight, when she heard a knock. A voice called, "Hello?"

Mary turned to see the face of a young man with blue eyes peering in through the tiny window beside the entrance. Opening the door, she found four people watching her from the porch. The young blue-eyed man. An elderly woman with gray eyes. A bony old man with a sable beard and black eyes. A middle-aged man dressed in spandex, who looked as though he belonged on a running truck or in the pages of a fitness magazine, had green eyes.

"I'm Berton," the bony old man said. "This is Michael." The runner. "Donna." The old woman. "Shawn." The blue-eyed man. They smiled as the bony, bearded man continued, "You must be Mary."

"Yes," she said, confused as to who the quartet might be and why they knew her name.

"We're here for prayer circle," the man said, looking beyond her into the house.

"Oh dear," Mary said. "Eden didn't call you? Jack was taken to the hospital."

Given the nature of his illness, the group seemed unreasonably surprised.

"I guess prayer circle is canceled," she added, holding the door.

The young man jolted. "We don't cancel prayer circle."

"We never cancel prayer circle," Berton agreed, gesturing into the house.

Mary shifted to allow the four inside. She had envisioned a less diverse group. And hadn't Eden said there were six? "I haven't made food," she remembered, and was relieved when the old woman — Donna — smiled and patted her arm.

"Will you join us, Mary?" Berton asked, making his way to the living room.

Not wanting to join them, but without reason to decline, she nodded and followed, squinting when Shawn pulled back the drapes to let in the sun. Berton and Michael took the chairs by the window. Mary found a place on the sofa between the other two.

"Gil and Terri won't be joining us," Berton announced, before reaching out to join hands with the runner on one side and the blue-eyed man on the other. Mary gave her hands to the young man, and the old woman, who also joined hands with the runner.

They considered each other, Mary following their lead, gazing into the blue eyes, the gray, the black and the green. She was surprised to see that no one in the prayer circle had a Bible, and wondered if they'd borrow Eden's and find the money she'd hidden between the pages. It was Shawn who finally spoke, his smooth young voice liberating vibrations from his throat that trickled down his arm and flowed from his hand to Mary's. "We are your humble servants. Shawn, Donna, Berton, Michael and Mary," he said, casting her a glance. "We're gathered today to pray for Jack. Lord, have mercy on our brother Jack."

Together the group murmured, "Let us pray."

"And we're here to pray for Mary," he added, as all eyes turned toward her.

She yanked her hands back from the strangers. "You don't have to pray for me."

Shawn tilted his head. "Eden told us why you're here."

The son's wife. Of course, Eden had told her prayer group about the fat daughter-in-law who had come to California to look for her wayward husband. She could see by their expressions that they had prayed for her already. For Gooch too, no doubt. Mary wondered if Eden had told these people about Heather. The blue-eyed man said nothing about praying for the lost daughter's soul.

"Please, Mary."

Wedged between the old woman and the young man, certain of her obligation to Eden and with nothing more to lose, Mary took his hand and joined with Donna once more. In the glare of the hot sun, she shivered when Shawn said, "Lord, help Mary Gooch find what she's looking for." The group murmured their assent. "Let us pray."

Mary lowered her gaze along with the others, waiting for the prayer circle to begin. She guessed that they would take turns reading Scripture before offering their special prayers for Jack's soul. And their meditations on her own search. She hoped they would pray for Heather. Someone had to pray for Heather.

The clock ticked but no one opened their eyes. With the sun on her face and the bodies pressed against her and the heat of the strangers' hands in her own, Mary watched the foursome of bent heads. Were they really talking to God? Could such communion be read on a face?

She thought of Jack, sorry for his end, even if he was little more than a stranger. And sorry for Eden, who would be left, like her, alone. God help Eden, she thought, and wondered if it counted as prayer. How many times in how many nights had she prayed to God? Wished to God? Given hollow thanks. Made shallow requests. Uncertain as to the exact nature of the him or her or it she was trying to reach. She considered her altered relationship with her own spirit; here she was, thousands of miles away, different. People did change. The path of a life could take a sudden left and deliver a very different future.

Focused on her breath, thinking of Heather's half-lived life, Mary was determined that her own end would not be one of calculated risk. She saw her path rise up, not a trench in the mud but a cobbled road under a canopy of trees. As she waited for the prayer circle to begin, she realized that it already had.

When it was over, she felt cheated by the brevity of their silent joined prayer, and was shocked to see by the clock that a full hour had passed. The quartet left as quietly as they had come, no clap of thunder, no shouting rhetoric, no platitudes, no proselytizing. No words at all.

When the Prius pulled up a short time later, Mary was enjoying a respite of calm on the Ethan Allen.

"I forgot to bring some pictures for him," Eden said, bursting into the hall.

"Did they say how long he'd be in?" Mary asked. "I cleaned out his room. The sheets are in the dryer."

"He won't be coming home, Mary," Eden said stiffly.

"Why don't you sit down a minute?" Eden took a spot beside her on the sofa. "Why don't I make you some tea?"

"I don't want tea," Eden said. "I want Jimmy. I want Heather. Oh Mary, what have I done?"

Mary gathered Eden's fingers.

"The last time I saw her, she had vomit on her sweater," Eden said. "I can't stop thinking about that."

"The last time I saw her," Mary said, remembering Heather with the locket, "she was smiling."

After a time, feeling Eden's quiet breath beside her, Mary realized that the old woman was asleep. Like a weary mother with a sick child, she closed her eyes too. When she opened them again she was alone, Eden clanking dishes in the kitchen down the hall. She followed the sound, stopping at the doorway as Eden announced, "We should eat something."

"Yes," she agreed, though neither moved toward the fridge.

"I have to get on the phone with the agency before I go back up to the hospital," Eden reminded herself.

"You don't need to hire a replacement for Chita. I could help, Eden. I'll help."

Eden paused. "Would you stay with me?"

"You want me to stay with you?"

"You could sleep in Jack's room."

Mary checked the clock, remembering her babysitting job. "I can't be back here until nine, though."

"Why not?"

"I'm babysitting for a woman up the street."

"Babysitting?"

"It's for someone I met. She knows you and Jack. Ronni Reeves. I sat for her last night."

"Well, I suppose you always were the type to make friends easily."

Nothing was further from the truth, Mary thought, but said, "Yeah."

"I'll be at the hospital until late anyway. I just can't bear the thought of sleeping in an empty house."

Having forced some toast and strawberries on both herself and her mother-in-law, Mary set off to check out of the hotel. She could not imagine, climbing the hill to the Highlands, where her strength was coming from, and wondered what sway the prayer circle had with their maker.

The roller coaster again. Oscillating, vacillating, careening between hope and despair. As the traffic droned by, she saw Gooch behind the wheel of each passing car. Gooch should be here. His mother needed him. His wife needed him. She closed her eyes and sent a plea on the wind. *Jack is dying, Gooch. Please, come here.*

Thinking of her shrunken father-in-law in his wheelchair, she remembered that Gooch had seen Jack too, and must have known how close the man was to the end. Gooch hadn't even left a number to call him in case Jack died. *Damn you, Gooch,* she thought suddenly. Damn you all to hell. She remembered a word he'd written in the letter he sent to her. Coward. *Yes.*

Walking the street in the precocious dust, she remembered that she'd meant to stop at the plaza to call a taxi. Now it was too late. Too tired to go forward. Too far to go back. The streets were clogged with traffic but there were few people on the sidewalks. When she heard footsteps behind her, she clutched her sporty blue tote bag to her chest. The footsteps drew closer. She wished she had a can of Mace like the ones she'd seen on television, in case the only mugger in Golden Hills was coming after her.

A teenage boy ran past her in a blur of testosterone, meeting a teenage girl stepping out from the shelter of the trees. They embraced — roaming hands, hungry mouths — under each other's spell. She thought of herself with Gooch in those early days. They had been such wanton lovers.

Mary hadn't noticed that the girl was wearing earphones until she tugged out one of the pods and stuffed it into the boy's ear. He wrapped his arms around her waist and swayed, pressing his pelvis to hers, staring into her eyes. Even in her fury at his cowardice, Mary might have given her life in that moment to have one more dance with Gooch.

Afraid of the Dark

In spite of being frazzled, Ronni Reeves looked chic in her red knit dress and high-heeled leather boots and clinking silver jewelry when she answered the front door. "Tom went out of town today so you won't have to worry about another scene tonight, Mary. How's Jack?"

"He's in the hospital," Mary said. "He won't be coming home again. I'm going to be staying with Eden."

"I'm sorry."

Mary nodded, and gestured at Ronni Reeves's dress attempting to lighten the mood: "That color looks nice on you." Ronni thanked her, trying not to notice her navy scrubs. "I haven't had much time for shopping," Mary explained, shifting her smock. "I forgot to ask you last night about the boys' bedtime."

Ronni scrunched her nose. "They don't really have a bedtime."

When their mother was gone, Mary found the boys waiting for her on the living-room sofa beside a stack of books. She settled in beside them as they jostled to pass her their favorite. "Read this one, Mrs. Goochie," Joshua begged.

"Goochie!" the other boys shrieked.

"How about you boys call me Mary?" she said, laughing.

After she'd read a dozen books, she saw that the lads were getting sleepy and said, "Let's go find pajamas."

With no TV to beg for, they quietly followed her up the plush stairs and into the huge bedroom they shared. There the sleepy boys were revived, and began to chase one another over the trio of tiny beds. Mary tried to stop them, shouting, "This is not what we do before bed!"

Jeremy laughed. "This is what *we* do before bed."

"Boys!" she said, clapping her hands as their mother had done, the gesture just as ineffective for her. Jacob threw a pillow at her head. She reached for the light switch, flipped it off and closed the door so they were in blackness.

Jeremy shouted, "No!"

Jacob screamed, "Turn it on!"

She turned the light back on. They regarded her strangely before resuming their play, throwing pillows and jumping on the beds. She flipped the switch off. "Turn it on! Turn it back!" She flipped it back on. And so it went, until the triplets, whose labor of stopping and starting play was more intense than hers, finally gave up.

After tucking the tykes into their beds, Mary kissed them each on the forehead. "Leave the hall light on, Mrs. Mary," Jeremy pleaded. She wished she could tell them that it wasn't the dark they needed to be afraid of.

When Ronni returned, she was confused by the quiet, surprised to find Mary sitting on the sofa with a book. "Where are they?"

"They're asleep."

"No fussing? No tantrums?"

"None."

"You're not Mary Gooch — you're Mary Poppins." Ronni counted some bills from her handbag and passed them to Mary, insisting, "I don't feel right not paying you. And I did really well tonight. Thank you."

Pushing the bills back, Mary said, "I can't take the money. I can't work here. Remember? I'm Canadian. And I really don't need it." She reached for the door and stepped onto the porch to breathe the air.

"Everyone needs money," Ronni said, joining her on the porch, pressing the bills back into her hand.

"I don't. Really. My husband won the lottery."

"Right."

"He really did. He won on the scratch-and-win. He put twenty-five thousand dollars in my account."

"He won the lottery and put twenty-five thousand dollars in the account before he left you," Ronni said drolly.

"Yes."

Ronni saw that she was serious. "How much did he win? As his wife you're entitled to half."

"Gooch would know that. My guess is he won fifty."

"But you're not sure?"

"I know Gooch. He'd do the right thing."

"He left you. He won money and left you. But you *know* he'd do the right thing?"

Her tone made Mary shiver. She started down the walkway, saying, "I should get back, in case my mother-in-law . . ."

"Why don't you rent yourself a car?"

"My purse was stolen and I don't have a replacement driver's license yet."

Ronni Reeves smiled with a thought and stepped back into the house, appearing after a moment with a key dangling from her lovely hands. "Take the Ram." She pointed at the big white pickup in the driveway.

"Excuse me?"

"You don't have a car. Take the Ram. For your babysitting services. For however long you're here. That's how I'll repay you."

"Take the Ram?"

"It's Tom's. For his warrior weekends. He said he'd be out of town for a while. Have you ever driven a truck?" She pressed the keys into Mary's palm.

Plowing down the hill toward Eden's house in the Dodge Ram, Mary felt giddy thinking of the freedom offered by the wheels, reminded of how badly she'd wanted to ride Christopher Klik's motorized bike that day so long ago. She parked in the driveway, surprised to see the Prius since Eden had planned to stay at the hospital into the evening.

She crept into the house in case Eden was asleep and found her mother-in-law on the Ethan Allen with the telephone in her lap. She was staring straight ahead, disconnected, startled when Mary spoke. "I borrowed a vehicle. A truck. Is it fine that I parked it in the driveway?"

"You borrowed a truck from whom?"

"From Ronni Reeves. My friend up the street. The one I babysat for."

"Your *friend?*"

Mary was reminded of Irma in her middle age, the beginning of her frozen confusion. "I met her a few days ago, Eden. I told you about her earlier. Her father went to college with Jack. Ronni Reeves?"

Eden shook her head. "Jack knew so many people. We couldn't go to dinner without seeing someone. It got tedious. Anyway, that's nice you have a vehicle. You did mention something about babysitting."

"I was thinking I might drive to the ocean."

"It's late, Mary."

"But it's not far, right? And I'm not tired. Will you come with me?"

"I'm going back up to the hospital for a few more hours. I just came home to make some calls." She paused before announcing, "The two from the Bay Area are driving down in the morning."

"Jack's daughters?"

"The other's going to call when she's booked a flight." Eden rose, her black bob swinging over her sunken cheeks. "I dug out a few of Jack's old polo shirts. He was big for a while. You'd never guess that to see him now. One of them might fit you, Mary." She grabbed a sweater from a hook at the door. "That hospital is so cold."

After waving goodbye to Eden, Mary found several pastel polo shirts laid out on the bed and chose the largest, a mint green color. After relieving herself of her navy smock, she pulled on the cotton shirt, pleased to see that it fit over the lump of her gut.

Hoisting her body into the Ram, charged with anticipation, Mary thought of how she had never dreamed of seeing any ocean until Big Avi had pointed the way, but now it felt like a quest. The road to the coast was another roller coaster, but this one in the dark. Twists and turns and climbing up and racing down, past unseen landscape she could barely imagine. A turn in the road and she caught the distant glass of the Pacific in the thrall of a starry black night. She drove on, past the lit-up mansions nestled in the hills toward the coastline, opening the truck's windows, letting the wind lash her face.

She reached the coast and found a place to park on the side of the road. The beach was empty and dark but she couldn't hear her fear over the call of the surf. She climbed out of the truck, judging the distance to the black water, then slipped off her sneakers and made her way through the cool sand.

Her breath came in gasps as she soldiered on toward the surf, and she felt her soul shift within her body, as though straining for a better point of view. With only the ambient glow from the highway to light her way. She stopped at the shoreline, holding her hand to her heart, not because she felt that familiar pain but because she was stung by the night's beauty, the black water rising before her, the nearness of the heavens and the feeling of being so small as to be a grain of sand beneath her feet, and so light that she might be swept up by the evening's breeze. She paused to worship at the ocean's feet, to concede the tininess and brevity of life, to pray for humanity in distant lands across the water and to give thanks because the world was a marvel.

"*Agua*," she said aloud.

She lifted her pants and dipped her plump pink feet, shocked by the icy cold, picturing Gooch standing in the surf of the same ocean. What would he be thinking? Surely by now he'd have come to some conclusions about his life, his marriage. *He's already made up his mind.*

Finding a cool, dry place in the sand, she settled down. Checking to ensure that she was alone, she stretched out on the white grains, arms at her sides, like a child making a snow angel, reminded once again of the night in Leaford she'd lain naked beneath the storm. She found the Big Dipper, the Little Dipper, the band of light Hay-su had pointed out as the Milky Way, and let her eyes roam, hoping to see another shooting star so she could make a wish. No matter that Jesús García claimed there was no magic in the cosmos; she understood, lying beneath the dazzling canopy, why people put their dead in the heavens. Why they imagined God in the sky. After a time she closed her eyes, searching her lids for clarity, hoping that God would throw in her two cents.

Orin had told her to get a drink from the hose and push on. Heather had said the same thing. But if pushing on meant returning to Canada without seeing Gooch, she could not. Each time she imagined leaving, a nagging voice warned that if she left she would be missing something vital. She decided that, at the very least, her waiting was not for naught. She felt valued by Eden. And by Ronni Reeves and her boys. She had a vehicle, and money in the bank. This pondering of her predicament did not feel familiar. No spiral of despair. Just a quiet consideration of her existence. That internal revolution.

Without drawing conclusions or mixing metaphors, Mary left the wondering about her husband and turned to the curiosity of her lost appetite. She could name each morsel she'd ingested in the previous few weeks, less food than she'd eaten most days in her other incarnation. That demon hunger, her constant companion, had morphed into gatekeeper.

But a thing lost could be found. Like her purse. Her husband. Or maybe it was gone forever, like her babies. Heather. Gooch? She never again wanted to hear the roar of the obeast, but knew she couldn't sustain herself indefinitely with a vague nausea around the subject of food.

She rose, pushed through the sand, fished for her truck key in the pants pocket of her damp navy scrubs, strangely comforted to be wearing Jack's old polo shirt — as if she'd brought his essence along with it, to bid farewell to the sea.

Driving back into Golden Hills, Mary stopped at the light where the twelve lanes met and cast her eyes toward the dark vacant lot where the memorial to the fallen man stood. The pain between her eyes, which she'd been managing with the tablets from the pharmacist, flared unexpectedly and she wondered if she might have to pull over. But it passed.

Like all things. All things.

Third Eye Blind

Waking the next morning, Mary expected to see dawn greeting the blanched hills behind the motel, and realized how quickly the unfamiliar had become the expected. Leaford had been her only home until a few days ago, and although she'd never wanted or intended to leave, she had quickly grown accustomed to the view from her Golden Hills window, and to the landscaped medians of the little town, and the brilliant blue sky, and the fiery, healing sun. She wondered how long it would take for Eden to become accustomed to Jack's absence. Or her to Gooch's. Who was missing Heather? Had her son been told?

Jack's room. Beyond the floor-to-ceiling windows where the curtain rod had fallen, the towering eucalyptus and murky rectangular pool in the backyard. Jack's presence lingered like an odor in the room, his residual energy crackling and popping throughout the night, and Mary'd slept fitfully in the too-soft bed. Sometime in the night, overheated, she'd torn off the navy scrubs she was wearing as pajamas, and tossed them onto the table with the photographs of

Jack and Eden. She noticed that the strap on her worn gray bra was hanging by a thread.

Watching the breeze tease the pearl-leafed bushes outside, she hugged her nearly naked body beneath the crisp white sheet, not considering her proportions one way or another but enjoying her vessel's most recent accomplishments. The climbing of hills. The walking of miles. The lifting and twisting and hefting and shifting. Kissing little blonde heads. Standing at the ocean's shore. She stroked her shrinking stomach like a sleeping cat.

She was startled by the shadowy figure of a man darting behind the trees in the backyard. She sat up, squinting, heart racing. Gooch? Not tall enough. The man was wearing blue coveralls and a ball cap with long fabric flaps that protected his neck and face from the sun. He slipped into a shed near the rear of the green pool. Mary waited, heart thudding. When the shed door opened again, she saw that the man had relieved himself of the top half of his coveralls, tying the empty arms around his waist and exposing a broad, deeply tanned, toned torso. He carried a pool skimmer, and whistled while he worked.

Straining to the left, she could see in the mirror the reflection of the company's blue van in the driveway — he was from the pool cleaning service. Having no experience with pools, she could only guess that the legend of the sexy pool man was drawn from real life.

With no curtains on the window of Jack's bedroom, she was fully exposed to the backyard. She pulled the white sheets up over her worn gray brassiere, praying to be invisible. She could not reach her navy scrubs on the dresser without rising from the bed, and couldn't risk being seen. Seeing the pool man draw nearer, she shut her eyes lest he catch her looking.

After a moment, bearing the suspense no longer, she peeked to judge his location, and could not tear her gaze from his body.

She watched as he scooped leaves, the knotty muscles of his wide shoulders and back coiling with his efforts, thick ripples hardening beneath the curling hairs of his torso, nipples growing rigid within the brown areolae. Gooch had said there was natural order in the objectification of the body. Mary noted the dimples hovering above the man's carved buttocks, and was startled by what she recognized as the blush of arousal.

He set to work, scrubbing the sides of the pool and dousing the green water with tablets he handled with yellow gloves. Mary heard the woodpecker in the eucalyptus and once again felt the ticking of the clock, not thumping or thudding but speeding forward at face-bending velocity. It seemed no sooner had the man begun than he disappeared from the backyard and was standing on the front porch, ringing the buzzer.

She hurried out of bed, pulling on the navy scrub bottoms and the old green polo shirt of Jack's, remembering that she'd agreed to pay the pool company in cash and hoping to reach the door before Eden. But the white Prius was already gone from the driveway. Opening the door, she busied herself counting the cash in her hands. She could not bring herself to meet the pool man's eyes, even though he'd tugged his overalls back on.

He was involved in writing her invoice, and didn't look up as he explained, "We've cleaned it and shocked the water. You'll be swimming by the end of the week."

She knew his voice instantly. That weighty baritone. Behind the cap with flaps, the face of Jesús García. "Hay-su!"

"*Mary?*"

"Oh my God!" she said, laughing, handing him the money. "You work for the pool company?"

"You were at the hotel."

"This is my mother-in-law's house. I'm staying with her now." Mary and Eden sharing the space of a small house, waiting for their men, one to leave, one to return. "Your friend Ernesto?" she remembered.

Jesús García nodded. "Broken ribs. He won't be back to work for a while."

"I'm so sorry to hear that. And you, Hay-Su? You're well?"

"Thank you. Yes."

"And your wife and sons? They must be getting excited about Christmas."

He cleared his throat but did not respond. He found that Mary had miscounted the money, and passed back twenty dollars.

"Keep it," she insisted. "A tip."

"No tips. Company policy."

"Oh."

"We're allowed to take water," he said, arching a brow.

Mary opened the door and drew Jesús García back to the kitchen, where she gave him a cold bottle of water from the fridge. Squinting from her headache, she found her pain tablets and, shaking too many into her palm, said, "I've had this pain. Right here between my eyes. It just doesn't want to go away."

"Your third eye," he said.

"My third eye?"

"In some Eastern religions, they believe we have a third eye in the middle of our seeing eyes where we can find higher consciousness. See the future."

"You really did spend a lot of time at the library." He shrugged, looking away. She smiled. "Maybe my third eye has gone blind." But reconsidering, she wondered if her third eye was not losing sight but birthing it, and if the pain she felt there was something like labor.

"You could try boiling willow bark. You wouldn't have to take the pills."

"Willow bark?"

"It has salex, like salicylic acid in aspirin."

"Random book at the library?"

"My mother. We didn't have Blue Cross. We had *Back Yard*. Yellow foxglove for my dad's high blood pressure. Willow bark for pain and swelling. Yerba buena for nearly everything else. You have some growing back there." He pointed in the direction of the innocent shrub that Eden had blamed with her broom.

She walked with him toward the front door and was struck by an urge as she passed her blue tote bag on a hook nearby. "Wait." She opened her blue purse and grabbed a thick wad of bills. Pressing the money into his hand, she said, "Maybe you could buy the children a few extra things for Christmas."

Curling his fist against the cash, avoiding her eyes, he set his jaw. "No. Please."

She stuffed the bills into the pocket of her polo shirt, instantly regretting the gesture, which had clearly been misunderstood.

"I should go," he said.

"I didn't mean it as charity, Hay-su," she said quickly, seeing she'd hurt his pride. "And the money, it's not really *mine* anyway. Not exactly. My husband won it in the lottery."

He returned the flapped cap to his head. "I should go," he repeated, and he was gone, swiftly, the way he'd stolen the shoes. Watching the blue van pull out of the driveway, she rested her eyes on the big white Dodge Ram. She grabbed the keys and started for the truck.

Ronni Reeves seemed surprised to see Mary standing on the porch. "Hi, Mary. Did you leave something last night?" The boys ran to the door, tumbling at her feet, singing her name. She felt her cheeks flush with confusion, then saw that their affection was genuine, their trust so quickly earned. She almost forgot why she'd come.

"I came to return the car," she said, when the boys had disappeared down the hall.

"You can't be here without a vehicle."

"But it's your husband's. It's not right."

"I told you, Tom is out of town and won't be back for a while. Besides, it gives me some satisfaction to think that his Ram is being used for good, not evil. Please. For me. It really is fair trade for watching the boys."

"All right," Mary said reluctantly.

"What's the light-switch game?"

"I'm sorry?"

"The boys have been asking me to play the light-switch game."

"We had fun." Mary took a breath, realizing that she hadn't just come about the car. "I think I offended the pool man."

"Excuse me?"

"The pool man. I tried to give him extra money for the . . . his family. He wouldn't take it."

"I wouldn't worry too much about the pool man's feelings," Ronni said, sensing that Mary had more to say. "Maybe he doesn't know English."

Mary paused. "Last night, I didn't want you to have the wrong idea about my husband."

"The one who won the lottery and left you?"

"See, that's what I mean."

"Don't mind me, Mary," the woman said, softening. "I'm going through my angry phase. You're still in denial."

"You don't know Gooch."

"You want to come in for a coffee?"

Mary suddenly knew that this was why she'd really come — for a coffee klatch between two left wives. Following Ronni to the kitchen, she tingled with nervous excitement, the feeling unfamiliar, as she'd never before reached out to make a friend.

Over coffee at the kitchen table, while the boys played about their legs, the women shared their stories. Ronni told Mary about growing up with her family back east, her delirious courtship with Tom when they were both young law students, her joy at the birth of the triplets and the misery that her marriage became. Mary told Ronni about Orin's colitis and Irma's Alzheimer's, and her own sordid affair with inertia.

"I don't think your husband deserves you," Ronni said.

"It's not like that."

"I hope you don't think you didn't deserve him. I hate when women underestimate themselves."

"There were . . . misunderstandings."

Ronni nodded. "Their brains are in their balls."

"We didn't communicate very well."

"Mars and Venus."

"We weren't honest."

"*He* wasn't honest. *He* was the one who wouldn't talk. Right?"

"Gooch talked and talked. We just never seemed to talk about the right things. We spent so much of our lives together." Mary closed her eyes. "Hungry."

The women talked until Mary noticed how late it was. She waved at Ronni from the window of the big Dodge Ram, promising to come again. The sun had begun to set over that distant mountain range, and the roadways at once snarled with rush hour traffic. Mary did not surprise herself by turning right, in the direction of the highway, instead of left toward Eden's house. She drove without self-deception, straight to the dusty corner, looking for Jesús García. In spite of what Ronni Reeves had said, she *was* worried about the pool man's feelings. She didn't know exactly what she'd say when she found him. He might need charity but he didn't *want* it, and she felt inclined to further apology.

At the stoplights where the dozen lanes met she saw him, just as she'd prayed she might, standing in a group of three other men with thermoses. His appearance felt like a miracle. She pulled into the lot slowly, so as not to shower the workers with dust. The men, all but Jesús, hurried toward the Ram and scurried into the back of the pickup truck before Mary could stop them. She rolled down the window, calling, "Hay-su?"

Startled to see her, he set off toward the truck carrying his duffel bag. "You need workers?" he asked, confused.

She shook her head. "I came to see you."

"Me?"

"I wanted to apologize. I didn't mean to—"

He interrupted, calling out in Spanish to the men who'd invaded the pickup. They groaned and jumped out of the truck.

"Weren't they going home?" she asked. "It's nearly dark."

"If you have work, they'll work."

"I wish I did. Anyway, I came to apologize."

"You didn't do anything wrong."

"I offended you, giving you money like that."

"It's okay."

She bit her lip, unconvinced. "You're waiting for your cousin?"

"He's late."

"I'll drive you home." When he shook his head, she insisted. "Please." He jogged around to the passenger door as the other men shouted protests in Spanish.

Mary found her way to the highway. "You'll have to remind me of the exit. I know it's somewhere in Hundred Oaks."

He took a breath. "You don't want to go around just giving people money. Even if your husband did win millions on the lottery."

"Not millions."

"It's none of my business. Just, you shouldn't be so trusting."

"Twenty-five thousand. That's what he put in my account."

"You shouldn't tell people that."

"I've spent my whole life not telling anyone anything, Hay-su. My husband, Gooch, won the scratch lottery, and then he left me. That's why I came to California. He needed some time to think. That's why I'm here. I don't think it'll be much longer now. I expect to hear from him any minute, really. He won the money. So you see what I mean? The money? I feel like it's not really mine."

He shifted uncomfortably.

She turned, addressing his profile. "You must think I'm such a fool."

"I don't think you're a fool."

"Pathetic, then. You must think I'm pathetic. A pathetic wife come all the way to California to wait for the husband who left her."

He shrugged, watching the horizon.

"I won't wait forever."

"No."

"But for now."

"Sure." Jesús tried to change the subject. "It's almost Thanksgiving. You have that in Canada too, right? Back home in Detroit, wouldn't be long before we'd have our sleds out for the early snow. We used to ski, too. The only Mexicans at Pine Knob."

"I never skied."

"But you skated? Everybody skates."

"A little. On the Thames River. Doesn't freeze over any more."

"Global warming," he said, nodding.

"Have your children ever seen the snow?"

He shook his head.

"You should take them one day. Sledding and skating and whatnot."

"Yes."

"Have they played hockey? That's our national sport. But being from Detroit, you must have played hockey. I suppose you wouldn't have a lot of arenas down here. Do they play? Your boys?"

"They were killed three years ago. My wife. My sons."

The news was so shocking that Mary wondered if she'd heard him right. She was mystified by his matter-of-factness.

"They were walking home from school. Drunk driver jumped the curb. The guy had a suspended license. Prior convictions."

Mary swallowed, without words, as the ghosts of his family stole the air from the truck. A *fait accompli*. Get a drink from the hose and push on. But how did one push on from such an unimaginable loss? How did one wake each morning, dress, eat, walk, *breathe* under the weight of such grief?

"I was working at Amgen. We were saving up for a second car. Two more paychecks. But after, I didn't leave the house except to go to the library. Then my mother-in-law came from Mexico. Then my brother-in-law. Then . . . well . . . you saw them."

A hundred shoes. A hundred sorrows. "I don't have any children," she said, which he did not seem to find inappropriate.

"I shouldn't have told you. Please don't cry."

Mary wrestled for self-control. It was the least she could do for the strong, broken man. They drove the rest of the way in silence, Jesús pointing out the way, until they arrived at the tiny house with the square of patchy brown grass. He lingered. "You're a nice lady, Mary. I hope your husband comes back soon."

She nodded, watching him, waving as he disappeared inside the house.

Rolling down the road, back toward the highway, passing the box stores and chain stores, she wondered how her foot pressed the gas or her hands turned the wheel when she was so utterly numb. She could not say what possessed her to obey a red and yellow sign that beckoned, *Enter*. She pulled in, stopped at the menu board, trembling as she called into the speaker, "Three double cheeseburgers. Extra-crispy chicken combo. Strawberry shake. Fish sandwich." She took the grease-soaked bags at the next window, nodding when the cashier asked if she was all right.

Pulling into a parking spot, barely remembering to put the truck in park, Mary tore open the bags, grabbing at the burning fries,

gobbling the burger, stuffing her mouth with the salty fried chicken. Her body fought the assault. She could not swallow. She opened the door and released the mess, heaving with dry convulsions. Taking the bags to the nearby trash can and hurling them inside, she looked up toward the heavens at the long-departed stars.

Mercy

Jack rallied and failed and rallied and lingered, not for days but weeks, and even Eden had to question God's mercy. Time sped forward as she watched daily the murky pool grow clearer, and shift from green to blue, but it was not Jesús García who came when it was Pool's Gold day to clean. He'd been replaced by a taller man who did not take off the top of his overalls or handle the tablets with yellow gloves. Mary was sure his disappearance had something to do with his tragic confession, and was sorry to think she might never see him again.

The prayer group moved their meeting location to the chapel at the hospital but Mary declined Eden's invitation to join, believing that Jack needed focus from the members, not the meandering mind of a searcher.

The sun rose and fell over the passing days as she danced to the rhythm of her new life. She awoke at daybreak to collect the *Los Angeles Times* bundle waiting at the end of Eden's sun-bleached driveway. While Eden slept, or while she prepared for her visits to the hospital, Mary read the small print, addicted to news of the world the way she once had been to celebrity gossip.

As a freshman student of the morning papers, she realized that political nuance was still lost to her, or perhaps she just didn't understand the country in which she was guest. She read with interest an article questioning voters' response to the religious affiliation of various political hopefuls, with speculation over whose God would be more or less damaging in the polls. She wished that Gooch were sitting beside her to help her fill in the blanks, and she wished that God would tell them all to keep her the hell out of politics.

Finished with the newspapers, she would set to work cleaning the house, preparing meals that went uneaten, after which she would drive to spend afternoons with the triplets, bringing a craft box filled with pipe cleaners and clay and glue and glitter. She was delighted to find such willing artists in the triplets, and was reminded what it felt like to create. And she was grateful for the companionship of their mother, a friend in need.

There was the daily phone call to St. John's to check on Irma. A long walk through the Highlands in the evening if she was not babysitting. Every other day she made a trip to the bank, and had several more times found additional funds withdrawn from the account. Four hundred dollars. Four hundred dollars. The last trip had shown a withdrawal of five *thousand* dollars, which had briefly sent her into a spiral, for she couldn't guess what it meant. An airline ticket to a distant destination? Payment for a gambling debt?

Driving around the pretty town in her borrowed truck, Mary'd noticed more memorials to the beloved dead painted on the back windows of cars and trucks. And there were so many personalized license plates. And bumper stickers—everyone had bumper stickers. She liked the one that read, *Sometimes you have to believe to see.* She'd noticed a few stickers shouting, *America. Love it or leave it*, and decided that the challenge was distinctly unpatriotic. She mused on the different personalities of Canada and America, wondering what conclusions Gooch was drawing as he fraternized with the Yanks, wherever he was. She imagined him engaged in hot political debates in some country saloon. But then, Ronni Reeves had told her that Americans didn't much talk about politics unless they were on the same side.

Gooch had found friends, she was certain, and she wondered if within his circle he'd also found a lover. Terrified as she was by the prospect of losing him forever, she could not hate him for any imagined infidelities. She understood loneliness. Had a fleeting memory of desire. Perhaps she still did possess a remnant of denial, though, for she imagined that he was too preoccupied by his thoughts to have fallen in love.

Daily, Mary drove past the place where the intersections met, telling herself it was because she preferred the gas station near the dusty corner lot, or needed to stop at the convenience store for something Eden might need, not because she hoped to see Jesús García. She walked the length of plaza in front of Pool's Gold, telling herself it was for the exercise, not because she hoped she might run into him coming out of work, or scoping the shoe store where he had stolen the yellow sandals.

When she knew Eden would be at the hospital for a long stretch in the evenings, she'd drive down to the ocean to study the stars. On mornings when she'd risen especially early, she'd go there to watch the sun rise over the cliffs, moved by splendid nature. Mary continued to shrink, and proceeded to grow.

While the rest of Golden Hills was enjoying roast turkey and sweet potato pie on Thanksgiving, Jack breathed his last, with Eden and his three daughters surrounding his chronic-care bed. Eden felt that his death falling on the Thanksgiving holiday was auspicious. There was much to be thankful for, she said. A twenty-five-year marriage to the man she loved. A final mercy in seeing Jack's forgiveness of his misguided daughters. Or was it the other way around?

On the morning of Jack's funeral, Eden, dressed in black, emerged from her bedroom looking tiny and afraid. Mary drew her to the table in the backyard for a cup of hot tea. They didn't even pretend they'd eat breakfast. "I had a dream about Jimmy last night," Eden said.

Mary still dreamed of him every night.

"I dreamed that we were standing around Jack's grave throwing dirt on the casket, and when I looked up, there was Jimmy. I forgot how handsome he was. People say when someone dies, you forget what they looked like. They say you lose the details of their features. They say that after a while you can't remember their faces."

"You won't forget Jack's face."

"When I woke up, I had this feeling like I was late for the hospital. I suppose it'll take some time to adjust." Mary nodded, sure that it would. "One of the ladies was saying she could get me into that retirement village in Westlake. They offer subsidies for people like me. I'll have to think about that at some point."

"Yes." She admired Eden's survival instinct.

"I always thought I'd die with Jack. But I'm still here."

"You're still here."

"God has other plans for me. I just have to trust in that." Eden sighed deeply, watching a big black crow land in the eucalyptus tree beyond the glimmering pool. "Jack just loves birds. He used to feed them out here but it made such a mess. We're going to release white doves after the burial. The prayer group arranged it as a tribute."

Mary prepared food for the wake, grateful for the excuse to miss the funeral since she'd arranged to be at Ronni Reeves's to sit for the boys. Eden didn't protest, and Mary wondered if it was because she hadn't told everyone about her lost son and waiting daughter-in-law, and was just as happy not to have to explain. Or maybe she realized that Mary had nothing to wear to a funeral, and would stand out in her navy pants and Jack's polo shirt like the sorest of thumbs.

The triplets were excited to see Mary at their door, clamoring, "What are we gonna make today?"

Ronni did not always leave immediately when Mary arrived to babysit. On the day of Jack's funeral, Mary covered the boys with smocks and suggested finger painting outside. As the children splashed color onto their canvases, Ronni Reeves lingered at the door. "Have you checked the bank today?"

Mary nodded. "He made another withdrawal."

"And you asked if you could find out where the money's being taken out?"

"They won't give out that information over the phone."

"Bastards."

"I'm sure he had some good reason."

"What if he's just dropped out, Mary?"

Mary had considered that scenario, of course—Gooch missing but *not* presumed dead. People did surprising things.

"Have you thought about what you're going to do?" Ronni asked.

After Ronni left, Mary cleaned up the paint-splattered boys and hung their creations on the corkboard in the kitchen. She opened the refrigerator, put off by the smell of the leftover Thanksgiving dinner. When she suggested a snack of turkey sandwiches the boys screwed up their faces. "Turkey smells like farts," Jeremy announced.

She prepared peanut butter on apple slices, imagining the doves flapping over the cemetery.

"I like donuts," Joshua complained.

"Me too." Mary smiled, thinking of the Oakwood. "But they don't like me."

"Do you give donuts to your kids?" Jeremy asked.

"I don't have any kids."

"Why?" Joshua asked, licking the peanut butter.

"I just don't," she said, finding the lump in her throat.

"If you had kids, would you give 'em donuts?" Jacob asked.

"Well, sometimes, I guess. But they're not good for your body. They're made of fat and sugar."

"I like fatten sugar."

"*You* might. But your body doesn't want that stuff."

"Yes it do," Joshua corrected. "If you get some kids, are you gonna give 'em donuts?"

Mary smiled and rose from the table to avoid further conversation about children and donuts. She caught sight of her reflection in the gleaming steel of the Sub-Zero refrigerator; the oversized polo shirt, the uniform pants, which felt larger by the day, the flicker of silver roots at her scalp. She checked the calendar on the corkboard and counted the days since her silver anniversary. Five weeks.

Ronni Reeves arrived home later, hefting a shopping bag, wearing a grin. She drew Mary into the living room and pulled clothes out of the bag—a pair of drawstring denims, several pretty blouses, a long black skirt. "Those are never going to fit you," Mary said.

Ronni laughed. "They're for you!"

"For me?"

"I was in the mall at Hundred Oaks and I thought, being from out of town, you might not know where to shop."

Mary took the bundle of clothes, looking at the tags, noting that they were three sizes smaller than her regular size. "Oh, these will never fit me either."

"Try them on. If they don't fit I'll take them back."

"How much do I owe you?"

"You owe me nothing. I owe *you*, Mary. It's selfish, I know, but I hope you never go back to Canada."

Mary laughed and took the clothes to the privacy of the bathroom. Standing in front of the full-length mirror, she pulled off her navy bottoms and polo shirt. That awful gray bra puckering at the breast and sagging beneath her arms. Her underwear, shapeless from daily washing. She studied her reflection. Feathers lost from a pillow, air from a balloon, her aging, collagen-depleted epidermis hung in pouches over her pubis and in folds around her torso. She wondered where it might end.

The clothes fit. They were even a tad too large. She imagined walking into St. John's in the elastic-waist blue jeans and fresh crisp blouse to find her mother in her chair at the window. If Irma could have recognized her, she wouldn't have. Ronni was delighted when Mary stepped back into the living room. "You look ten years younger," she announced, "except you're going to have to do something about those gray roots."

It was dark when Mary returned to Eden's, and she was surprised to find the house empty and already tidied up. Everything as it had been. Nothing as it was. She moved through the house, checking the rooms, and found Eden in the backyard staring up at the eucalyptus, just as she had done that morning.

Eden saw Mary out of the corner of her eye and raised her finger to shush her, then pointed to the tree. It took a moment for Mary's eyes to find, amid the leaves, a squat, shadowed owl perched on a high gray branch.

"That's a screech owl," Eden whispered. "But they don't really screech at all. They sound like babies." The owl flapped away, insulted. "They're the reason you don't see stray cats around here. Them and the coyotes. You wouldn't leave a small dog out overnight, either."

Mary moved to the pool, kicking off her shoe, setting her toe in the cool, clean water.

"You look better," Eden said, gesturing at her new clothes. "You always did have such a pretty face. I remember thinking that on your wedding day. You were such a beautiful bride."

"I lost the baby," Mary said, shaking the water from her foot.

Eden paused. "I know."

Mary looked up. "I lost the baby the night before. I had a miscarriage the night before. Before the wedding."

"I know."

Mary was struck dumb.

"When Jack and I drove up to London to see you in the hospital, I asked the doctor, and he told me point-blank."

"He told you?"

"He thought I was *your* mother. He asked me if you'd had any cramping in the night and he said you likely lost . . . well . . . he said you might not have been aware it was happening, but it was likely that you'd lost the baby the night before."

"I did."

"Even then, I knew you knew."

"Did you tell Gooch?"

"Of course." Reeling at Eden's confession, Mary hid her face in the sky. "He said it didn't matter."

"He did?"

"He said he loved you. He said no one knew you the way he did."

Her secret had been no secret at all. *Gooch had known all along.*

"When you lost the second baby I thought it was a blessing, Mary. I really did. I never expected the two of you to last. I thought it would be harder if you had children. Maybe I was wrong about that."

Mary nodded, turning away.

"One of the ladies from the church has invited me up to a retreat in Santa Barbara."

"That's good."

"I'm leaving in a few days. I'll be gone for a couple of weeks. I hope you'll stay, Mary. I just can't imagine coming back to an empty house. And you want to be here when Jimmy calls. You still . . . you haven't changed your mind about that, have you? You haven't been thinking about going back to Canada?"

Mary shook her head. She had forgotten Leaford's face.

Eden gestured at the pool sparkling under the stars. "You've had a service come to clean the pool."

"Don't worry about the cost."

"I saw someone out back this morning. If I had a suit, I'd get in right now."

"It's cold."

"I like a cold pool. It's bracing."

"Let's go in," Mary said suddenly.

"I just said I don't have a suit."

"I don't either." Mary gestured at the trees and the high cedar fence. "No one can see."

"Swim *nude?* I haven't done that in forty years." Eden glanced around.

The women stood apart, doffing their clothes, careful not to glance at each other as they escorted their fragile bodies to the pool's edge. Eden gasped when she felt the cold water on her crooked toes, and waded in slowly, squealing. Mary eased her naked body down the ladder and fell into the deep end with a splash. She shrieked when she came up for air, and they laughed like girls.

"Freezing!" Mary said.

"Feels good, though." Eden stroked the water.

"It does."

Weightless and fluid, their bodies were not forms of flesh and blood but charges, impulses, releasing bolts of fear and grief. They swam silently, as grateful for each other's company as they were for the magic of the stars, and the bracing cold water, and for each inhalation of breath that reminded, *Ah, life.*

Lost Calls

Swimming in the mornings and walking in the evenings, Mary took note of her rapidly changing body, nodding to the muscles that peered shyly from behind deflated pillows of adipose tissue. Her weight loss, she knew, was merely representative of other losses, and gains. Her appetite, like Gooch, stayed away.

Gooch was making continued withdrawals from the bank. Another four hundred. Another four hundred. Standing at the instant teller in the hot sun one morning, Mary had wondered suddenly if it was possible that the withdrawals were strategic. Could he be back in Leaford, taking money from the account to draw her home as if *she* were the one in hiding? Not likely. And just as unlikely that he had left the state without at least telephoning Eden.

Mary read novels until her vision blurred, and throughout the days forced tiny bites of apple and toast down her gullet. She offered further support to Ronni Reeves, making trips to the grocery store to stock the Sub-Zero with fruits and vegetables, weaning the boys from their diet of fast and processed foods, including cooking parties with her crafting sessions so they could concoct their own dips for carrot and celery sticks, and make muffins with mashed bananas and applesauce.

My boys, she took to calling the triplets, who barreled into her arms when she arrived and clung to her legs when she left. Their father had not been seen since the day he'd come to steal them away for ice cream, but had informed Ronni that he was moving to Florida with his new girlfriend. Ronni had sobbed on Mary's shoulder, because she'd hoped to reconcile and now saw they never would. Mary had stroked her friend's back and stopped herself from saying that it was for the best.

Cued by the passing of Thanksgiving, Christmas lights had gone up all around the neighborhood, and the Willow Highlands shone as bright as the pictures of Las Vegas Mary'd seen on TV. Twinkling pixie lights creeping up thick palm tree trunks. Multicolored cone lights netting the towering evergreens. Dripping icicle lights hanging from leafless eavestroughs and fences. Massive, electronically generated, air-filled Santa Clauses and reindeer obliterating bay windows. Sparkling angels watching from rooftops. Enormous synthetic snowmen staked in fresh-cut green lawns. Christmas was still a few weeks away.

"He can't stay away forever," Eden had said, zipping her suitcase on the morning she left for Santa Barbara. "He's sure to make it back for Christmas. You know how Jimmy loves Christmas."

Mary had nodded and waved goodbye from the porch, thinking, *Yes, Eden, he could stay away forever,* and realizing how precious little her mother-in-law knew about her only son. Gooch hated Christmas.

On that point she and Gooch had found common ground. He saw the Christian holiday primarily as a commercial venture, and Mary'd been disturbed by all the tempting food and forced gaiety. Over the years they'd spent Christmas afternoons at Pete and Wendy's or Kim and François's, watching their badly behaved children guzzle soda pop and baked goods, obnoxious as drunks. For dinner they'd gone to St. John's to keep company with Orin and Irma, partaking of the tragic turkey and gluey potatoes prepared in advance by the cook. At home alone in the evening, they'd opened the gifts they'd chosen for themselves and instructed the other to buy. For Gooch it had always been hardcover best-sellers from the bookshop in Ridgetown. For Mary it had been perfume and hand lotion because she couldn't think of anything else.

Mary woke, alone for the second week in Eden's little house, suffering that familiar pain between her eyes. She thought of the pain pills in her blue purse but did not rise from the bed to retrieve them. She was startled by movement in the backyard and remembered it was Pool's Gold's day to clean. She waited, watching the figure of a man straining to skim leaves from the water. Jesús García.

Ignoring her impulse to run out into the backyard, she snatched her new jeans and blouse from beside the bed and dove into the hallway and out of sight so she could dress. She had combed her hair and brushed her teeth by the time the buzzer sounded. "Hay-su," she said, when she opened the door.

He seemed surprised to see her. "Hi Mary," he said, passing her an invoice.

"Come in and I'll get my purse."

Jesús García stepped inside the house, waiting as she went to the living room. "Do you want some water?" she asked.

"No thank you," he said.

"Are you hungry? The freezer is stuffed with leftovers from the funeral."

"The funeral?"

"My father-in-law passed away. He'd been sick a long time."

"I'm sorry."

"I thought you'd left your job," she said, laughing to hide her embarrassment that she'd noticed his absence.

"They changed my route. They've changed it back."

"I could defrost a muffin? Some cake?" Her stomach turned at the thought, as she'd hardly ingested a bite of solid food since the fast food in the parking lot.

"No thank you, Mary," he said pleasantly, preparing to leave.

"Please don't be sorry you told me," she said. "About what happened to your family."

He cleared his throat. "I don't talk about it."

"I know. But don't be sorry you told me." He nodded shortly. "I thought maybe, when you didn't come to clean the pool . . ."

"I thought you'd be back in Canada by now."

"I haven't heard from my husband yet."

He glanced away.

"You were right about the ocean, Hay-su."

"You went to the ocean?"

"It is the best place to see the stars."

"I haven't been in years."

"I saw you steal the shoes," she blurted suddenly. He looked at her blankly. "From the plaza. The yellow sandals."

He shifted in his workboots. "Ernesto used to garden for the owner."

"Oh."

"He cheated him out of a month's pay."

"Oh."

"One more pair and we're even."

Mary considered the way people stole from each other. Rationally. With impunity. "How is Ernesto?"

"Good. But still not back to work. What about you, Mary? Don't you have a job you have to get back to?"

She shook her head. "I've got the money Gooch left me. Listen to me, I'm saying that like he's dead." They were interrupted by the appearance of the vintage blue Chevy in the driveway, and the bony old man climbing out with a plate wrapped in tinfoil. All Mary needed was more food.

"Hello, Berton," she said, taking the plate.

The old man eyed Jesús García, noticing the pool cleaning uniform, deciding he was not a threat.

Jesús smiled at Mary. "See you next week."

She watched him stride out to his van, and barely heard Berton ask, "I know Eden's gone to Santa Barbara, but will you join us at Shawn's house this afternoon, Mary?"

She was assaulted by that pain between her eyes when she shook her head *no,* explaining that she had a babysitting job. Once the van and the Chevy were gone, she took off her clothes and went out to the clean pool to swim in the nude.

Later that afternoon, after reading to the Reeves boys and after playing duck duck goose and after cleaning up spills and receiving the tenderest of kisses from Jeremy, who was typically the most reserved, Mary declined Ronni's offer of iced tea on the patio. The spot between her eyes ached and, although she'd planned a drive to the ocean at sunset, she headed back to Eden's, dizzy from lack of food.

The telephone was ringing when she entered the house. She picked up the receiver to find the crackle of static. "Hello?" There was no response. Another lost call. She didn't wonder any more if the lost calls were Gooch.

She found her way to the kitchen but could not bring herself to open the refrigerator, none of whose bounty would appeal, she knew, and most of which would repulse. She sat at the table, promising the cupboards, *I'll eat something in the morning.* But she realized she was still deceiving her old friend Tomorrow. Tomorrow, to whom she'd promised balance. Tomorrow, where she would struggle to find grace. Were she not so tired, she would have stayed awake till sunrise, to beg for one last chance.

A Certain Kind of Freedom

The following morning Mary busied herself with housework until she was expected at the Reeveses' to babysit. At the doorway she bent to embrace the boys, and laughed good-naturedly when Ronni chided her about "those awful gray roots." Ronni suggested a trip to the hairdresser for some new color but Mary was disinclined. Even if the red had become brassy from the chemicals in the pool, she would not give up swimming for the sake of her hair. She did submit to her friend's insistence on a cosmetic makeover, though.

In the huge master bathroom, the boys watched her transformation slack-jawed and silent. When their mother was finished rouging Mary's cheeks and darkening her lashes and shadowing her lids and staining her lips, Jeremy pronounced her beautiful. Joshua said she looked like a clown. And Jacob said simply, "I don't like them colors on your face." Mary didn't like the colors either.

As Ronni was fishing through a bathroom drawer, Mary spotted a pair of barber scissors. "Cut my hair, Ronni," she said impulsively.

"No!"

"Yes. Please. Just cut it off. I want to cut it right back to the silver roots."

"Yes!" Joshua said. "Silver's pretty."

"Oh Mare," Ronni protested. "It'll make you look, you know . . ."

"What?"

"*Dykey.*"

"I don't mind. Dykey is fine with me." She thought of Ms. Bolt. "I'm sick of the roots. I'm tired of the red." She closed her eyes. "Cut it. *Please.*"

The boys clapped their hands, watching in the mirror as their reluctant mother held the blades poised at the nape of Mary's neck.

"All the way," Mary reminded her, not peeking.

Ronni inhaled, closing the scissors at Mary's scalp and snipping a hank of her pool-damaged hair. It was too late to ask if Mary was sure.

The triplets collected the strands as they fell, Mary suggesting that they keep the hair to put in the craft box. She'd never felt beauty in her hair. The consistency of its length had just been more inertia, and the loss of it felt like a certain kind of freedom. Finally, feeling the air on her scalp and the weight of the final few locks shorn from her head, she opened her eyes.

"Okay," Ronni inhaled.

In the mirror, Mary saw a large woman with a shallow cap of thick, soft, silvery hair hugging a nicely shaped skull and framing a pretty face with expressive green eyes, full pink lips, a deep cleft chin. "Well," she said, thinking, *That is me.*

Even Ronni had to admit that the severe cut suited her. "It's chic."

"It really is," Mary agreed.

Ronni found a pair of large silver hoops and a choker-style necklace from her Lydia Lee supply box to complete the look. The boys unanimously decided, because they did not know what *chic* or *dykey* meant, that Mary looked like a man wearing jewelry, which made both women cackle. The mouths of babes. When Mary announced that she wanted to take them all out for dinner as payment for hairdressing services, Ronni shook her head. "You've done enough. I'm cooking dinner for *you*."

Watching Mary pick at her salad and nibble her grilled chicken, she frowned. "You don't like it?"

"I do," Mary said. "Remember I told you before? I've completely lost my appetite."

"I thought you were just saying that because you like to eat alone. Look at me. I've gained nine and a half pounds since Tom left," Ronni confessed. "Potato chips, ice cream and really bad sitcoms."

Mary nodded, remembering her old friends. "Gooch took out another four hundred."

Ronni shook her head. "How much is left?"

"Fifteen and some."

"You could sue him."

"I could never sue Gooch."

"You check with all his friends back home again?"

"They said they'd call."

"You believe them?" Mary shrugged. "But you still think he's coming back?"

"I don't know any more."

"I'll bet he's in Vegas. I bet he's been in Vegas this whole time."

"I'm done guessing."

"Take it all out!" Ronni said suddenly. "Take it all out and leave him with nothing."

"What if he needs it?"

"*Fuck him*," Ronni mouthed, so the children couldn't hear.

"I couldn't leave Gooch stranded like that."

"Like he left you?" Ronni asked pointedly.

Later, after the two women had taken turns reading stories to the sleepy boys, Mary kissed the triplets good night and accepted Ronni's invitation to a glass of wine on the patio. As she had been a cheap drunk at her highest weight, she felt the warmth of the alcohol after only a few sips. She sighed deeply, looking into the starry sky, and mused, "Two months ago I was working at a drugstore in Leaford, Ontario, thinking about new winter boots."

"Tom and I were planning a vacation to Aruba. He never had any intention of going on that trip."

Mary thought of the Caribbean cruise she'd denied Gooch. "You're so . . . so beautiful, Ronni. You'll meet somebody else."

Ronni laughed and poured herself more wine. "I have three three-year-old boys, Mary. Down here that's called *baggage*. For all the trouble, I'd rather date my vibrator."

Feeling loose from the alcohol, Mary offered with a giggle, "Gooch . . . ?"

"Yeah?"

"Has a large penis."

Ronni threw back her head. "Mary Gooch!"

"A *very* large penis."

"You said he was your only lover! How could you possibly know?"

"I looked around," Mary assured her. "Plus, we got cable TV a while back."

"You naughty little thing!"

Mary'd never been called naughty or little. She drank a gulp of wine. "I haven't had sex in six years."

Ronni stopped laughing. "Why?"

Mary grew somber. "My body . . . I . . ."

"I can't imagine living without sex *forever*. Really. I mean, not for a relationship, but just for the exercise."

"I never thought of sex as exercise."

"Could you see yourself with someone else?"

"No," Mary said. "There's only Gooch. There's only ever been Gooch."

Treading Water

The balance in Mary's account, which she was still checking daily, was her sole connection to Gooch. Just to keep in touch, she'd continued to withdraw money in increments of one hundred dollars. One afternoon when Ronni had taken the boys to meet their father, who'd blown into town for an urgent business appointment, Mary'd driven herself to the big mall in Hundred Oaks to shop for toys to put under the triplets' tree. She and Ronni had agreed not to exchange gifts. Their friendship was enough.

At the toy store she'd chosen preschool board games and art sets and storybooks, avoiding a display of foam-dart semi-automatics that she knew the boys would love. Boys and their guns. Pete and Wendy had had a strict "no weapons" policy when they were raising their two boys, but brooms had become rifles in their grimy little fists, and fly swatters swords, and when the oldest boy consistently bit his sandwiches into the shape of a pistol, they'd finally surrendered. Americans had an infamous relationship with guns, Mary knew, but the right to bear arms was a foreign concept to her, and she did not understand the legacy. Ronni had admitted to keeping a weapon in a shoebox in her closet, but Mary understood from her reading that her friend was statistically more likely to use it on her cheating husband than on any home invader.

Lugging the shopping bag through the mall's corridors, she was drawn to a shop window displaying curvaceous plus-sized mannequins. She needed some new clothes, since even the elastic-waist pants that Ronni had bought for her were now too large. With the current retail slump, the sales staff were delighted to see Mary Gooch appear in their midst.

In the roomy dressing room with its slenderizing three-way mirror, she felt annoyed with herself, wondering what had compelled her into the store, and why she hadn't objected when the woman showed her a selection of holiday gowns. She tried on a few sets of casual slacks and tops, then reluctantly slid into the flowing black stretch jersey dress the girl had insisted she try. She watched her reflection in the mirror, unblinking. The shorn silver hair. The Lydia Lee jewelry. Her ample proportions adored by the slinky midnight fabric.

One of the salesgirls announced, "You could model."

Another enthused, "That dress was *made* for you."

Mary protested, "I really just needed some new bras and panties."

Another girl flew to the lingerie section and returned with a stunning selection of lacy bras and underpants. Mary tried on the lingerie, disbelieving her reflection until she finally could not deny that she looked, and felt, *sexy*.

Blushing, she dumped the clothes and lingerie onto the counter. "I'll take it all." Wading out into the mall with her heavy bags, she fought her guilt, trying to reconcile her delight in the pretty clothes with her suspicion that she did not deserve them. Her third eye ached. She stopped, setting down her bags near a gushing water fountain, and sat on a bench feeling dizzy. *You need to eat something*, she told herself, but the thought of chewing made her nauseated, and she couldn't swallow for the lump in her throat.

She'd found a blender in Eden's cupboard and tried blending fruit and yogurt, but had had trouble keeping the thick beverage down. Lately she'd been managing only sips of orange juice several times a day, and even Ronni had noticed that her energy was flagging.

In the big Dodge Ram on the way home, traveling the road she'd traveled with Jesús, she let her eyes drift toward the stars. She wondered about the essence of Jesús García's strength and magnetism. "See you next week," he'd said. She hoped he would have time to linger again, to drink a glass of water, tell her more about her third eye. Then she reminded herself that longing for one man was enough — uncertain, now, whether that man was Jimmy Gooch or Jesús García.

Later, swimming nude in the pool, Mary stopped in the shallow end, feeling the familiar fluppering of her heart. Not now, she begged. Not yet. Not when she felt so close. So close to what, she couldn't say, but she felt another change on the wind, smelled it like an approaching storm. Maybe it was Gooch. She promised herself to attempt to drink another fruit smoothie. If Gooch was coming back, she was going to need her strength.

It was the drink that spurred the memory of the events of one evening a decade into their marriage. Mary'd been bedridden for a week, crippled by a flu virus she'd picked up at the drugstore. Gooch had taken time off work to care for her when he saw that she was so weak she couldn't make it to the toilet by herself. He'd worried over her like a mother, bringing steaming soup on a tray and blending clumpy fruit smoothies with a potato masher and whisk. At the end of her convalescence, she found her appetite and heard the Kenmore's call. Thinking Gooch was out, since the house was so still and quiet, she was shocked to find him glassy-eyed at the kitchen table, scribbling in a notebook. He looked up, guilty. Caught. "You're up!" he shouted inanely.

"What's that? What are you writing?"

"Nothing." He closed the notebook.

"Gooch."

"Nothing."

"What is it?"

"It's *nothing*."

"If it's nothing, then let me see."

"It's private, Mare."

"Private?"

"It's nothing. It's a story."

"A *story?*"

"I'm writing a short story," he said wearily. "It's stupid. I . . . the *Leaford Mirror's* having a short story contest and I . . . it's stupid."

She attempted to hide her surprise. "Let me read it."

She expected him to decline, and had never seen his eyes so vulnerable as when he handed her the book. "It's just a first draft. It's not very good."

Taking the notebook back to her bed along with a tin of peanuts, Mary settled down, feeling hot fear mingling with her low-grade fever. She wasn't afraid that the story would be awful and she'd have to lie. She was afraid the story would be good and she'd have to admit to Gooch, and to herself, that he'd missed his calling and that it was all her fault. Or worse, that it would be so good that he would submit it and win the contest and realize that he'd never meant to be what he'd become, and leave her for a charmed life as a famous author.

Mary sank with the first line. The story was about a furniture delivery man who fell in love with a young widow while his own wife lay dying from a disease that sounded suspiciously like abstract malaise. The main character had delivered a faulty oven to the other woman and found excuses to return daily to check on its performance, eating tray after tray of burned baking while his wife languished in her bed. The prose was sturdy and spare, poignant and humorous. In the end the man did not consummate the relationship, but returned to his wife out of a sense of obligation and duty. Mary finished the last line, hot with outrage, but did not call for Gooch to come to their room.

An hour passed. She heard the television snap on in the living room. She waited, seething, sure the story was autobiographical, certain he was about to confess. Finally, it was her hunger that drove her from her bed. Gooch shut the television off when he heard her plod down the hallway. He stood at the doorway watching her root through the fridge for cheese and salami. "Well?" he said.

Mary chewed thoughtfully and sighed. "I didn't understand it," she announced, plopping down at the kitchen table.

"It's just a first draft," he reminded her.

"But his wife is dying," she said, throwing up her hands.

"That's the *point*."

"That *is* the point," she huffed. "How could he do that when his wife is *dying?*"

"It's not about you, Mare," he said tightly.

"I know." She paused. "But you're a furniture delivery man. People will think it's about *you*."

"It's a world I know. That's all. It's not about you. It's not about us."

"Well, he's not very sympathetic," she said. In spite of herself, Mary *had* felt sympathy for the yearning husband and the lonely widow. "He could be a different kind of delivery man."

"I guess."

"He doesn't have to be married."

"But that's the conflict."

"Okay."

"What about the *writing?*" he asked.

She shook her head. "Some of the words are a little . . ." She rolled her eyes.

He took the notebook from her greasy hands. "It's okay. It doesn't matter."

"Gooch," she protested, "I'm just saying that if you use words people have to look up in the dictionary, it makes them feel dumb."

He nodded and returned to the living room to sit in the quiet. She finished her snack and made her way back down the hall. She pretended to be asleep when Gooch shifted his weight into the bed, wondering how even the greatest of writers could have rendered the accuracy of such longing without direct and intimate knowledge.

Mary assumed that Gooch had not submitted his story to the contest. She was certain he would have won.

She climbed out of the swimming pool, nude, and rested a moment under the thick shroud of night. The door buzzer rang. She slipped into an old robe of Jack's she'd taken from the closet and moved through the house to answer, for once not dreaming that it was her wayward husband. Even if her third eye had conjured the picture, she would still have been mistrustful of her future sight, and too weary for hope.

There were Christmas carolers at the door — ten children dressed in Dickensian costumes, led by a woman from a church group who explained that they were raising money to support a beleaguered school in east Los Angeles. Mary stood at the door, damp and shivering in her robe. She heard not the children's voices but the collective hum in the night air. When they finished, she took several hundred dollars from her purse and gave them to the stunned and grateful woman.

The Ethan Allen called her to come and have a rest but the refrigerator chimed in, reminding her that she needed to eat something. She pushed herself toward the kitchen, opening the fridge and finding a fresh, cold apple. She sat at the counter drawing the apple to her mouth. A voice begged, *You have to eat something.* She was for a moment transported into the body of a dying anorexic she'd watched in a documentary several years earlier, and she set the apple back down on the table.

Peeling off her robe, Mary returned to the backyard and the cold water of the pool, kicking slowly toward the deep end before she realized she was too tired to swim laps. Arms outstretched, legs kicking, weightless but heavy, she fought the metaphor—all this time waiting for Gooch, was she really just treading water?

Later, she woke to the ringing of the telephone and reached for the receiver beside the bed. "Joyce?" she asked, groggy.

"Mary? Mary? Are you okay?"

"Is it my mother?"

"Mary? It's Ronni. What's going on? I've been worried. I was just about to put the boys in the car to drive down there."

Mary sat up, surprised to find the room filled with sunlight. She looked at the clock. It was past noon. "I slept. I overslept. I'm sorry. I'll be right there."

"No, Mary. It's okay. I'm taking the boys to the mall. We have to do some shopping. I've decided to go back east for Christmas. We're leaving next week."

Mary could not respond. Leaving?

"Are you there?" Ronni called through the line.

"I'm here."

"The boys and I want to celebrate Christmas with you early. Okay?"

"Okay."

"Mary?"

"I'm here."

"Your mother-in-law will be back, right? I mean, you're not going to be alone?"

"She'll be back," Mary lied. Eden had telephoned her the day before to say she'd decided to spend the holiday in Santa Barbara. She was keeping company with an old friend of Jack's, and Mary had sensed a burgeoning relationship in her tone. Her mother-in-law had started to see Jack only weeks after James had died from the car crash, so Mary wasn't surprised, but she wondered what granted Eden such strength and resilience.

Dragging herself out of bed, she dressed in one of her new outfits and walked to the end of the driveway to collect the newspaper. She settled down to read but couldn't focus. She went to the kitchen, glancing at the refrigerator apologetically. She decided to drive to the bank.

Outside the bank, she checked her balance record. Gooch had withdrawn more money. She fumbled with her access card, shoving it back into the machine, demanding the maximum amount. *I will take it all out, Gooch,* she heard herself think. *That money is rightfully mine.* She thought of Ronni Reeves's rage, which had dimmed over the passage of days, and felt the rise of her own. *Left me without a word. Coward. Taking money that belongs to me. Bastard.*

She was stuffing twenty-dollar bills into her wallet when she nearly collided with a man exiting the bank. "Emery Carr," she said. With her shorn silver hair and substantial loss of poundage, he did not recognize her. "Mary Gooch. You gave me a ride when I couldn't find my purse."

"Wow," Emery Carr said, remembering and recognizing her. "You look different."

"Yes."

"I thought you'd be back in Canada by now. Lucy told me you got everything sorted out. This is a long vacation."

"It's not really a vacation," she said, walking alongside him.

"You look like a completely different person. Were you down here for one of those makeover shows? I love *What Not to Wear*."

Mary laughed. "Sort of."

"Well, I love what they did."

She blushed, realizing that they'd walked toward the nearby deli and he was holding the door for her to enter. "I'm going for a late lunch too. Will you join me?"

Inside the restaurant Mary fought her nausea, ordering coffee and scrambled eggs and toast. Emery Carr squinted when he saw that she was not eating. "You want to send it back?"

"I just can't eat," she confessed.

"Well, you have to eat," he insisted. "I can see you're on a diet, but..."

"I'm not on a diet. I just... can't. I can't seem to swallow."

Emery patted her hand. "You've lost an awful lot of weight. I mean, from the time I first met you."

"I know."

"Good for you. It's just... you have to eat *something*."

She nodded, pretending to nibble at her toast. The black coffee gave her some false energy but it was his company that revived her. They talked about the political climate. "It's like there are two Americas," he said. "We think differently. We interpret the Constitution differently. We're divided straight down party lines. Is it like that in Canada?"

"I don't know. I don't think so. My husband said *liberal* and *conservative* mean different things there. Plus we have more parties. We have the NDP and the Greens." She was proud of herself for remembering, but could not have explained any of the parties' platforms. She wondered if she should buy a computer so she could look such questions up.

"You Canadians are more progressive."

"Because we have national health care?"

"Socialism is scary."

"Because of our gun control laws?"

"Don't get me started."

"Gay marriage?"

"Gay marriage. I don't believe in marriage anyway—straight, gay. It's unnatural. But not to allow it? That's discrimination."

"My husband said people don't want to see gay marriages because they're afraid you're going to start recruiting."

"What about your husband?" Emery Carr asked. "Has he seen the new you?"

Mary looked up from her coffee cup, took a deep breath and, in her exhalation, told the handsome teller the story of her life as a wife.

Outside the restaurant, he surprised Mary by giving her a gentle hug. "You looked like you needed that."

"I did."

"You're not gonna die, you know. You're gonna pick yourself up and dust yourself off. You are woman. Hear you roar."

She laughed and nodded.

Later that night, she sat on the edge of Jack's bed, staring at her reflection in the mirror above the dresser. *You're not gonna die*, Emery Carr had said.

Existence

In the advertising pages of the newspapers Mary'd been confronted by invitations to dozens of local New Year's Eve events. She hated New Year's Eve the way she hated Christmas. So many sleepless nights she'd tossed in her bed making promises to Tomorrow, and those promises to the New Year, the *resolutions,* seemed even more contractual. *Next year will be different. Next year, self-control. Next year I will talk to Gooch. Listen to Gooch. Go with Gooch when he asks.* She had been aware of the statistics on holiday depression long before she started reading the newspapers. The spiral was familiar.

Where, in the previous weeks, she hadn't considered that Gooch might not have returned by Christmas, she felt certain now that he would not be back by New Year's and perhaps not by her birthday in March. As she had dropped out of her old life, so had Gooch, and he had less reason to return than she did. She'd even stopped thinking of the dwindling balance in the bank account as a barometer for his homecoming. Gooch was resourceful. Whatever money he had, wherever he was, he would survive.

Swimming in the morning, she thought of Eden, and Jesús

García—left, bereft, they sailed forth. She felt her chest constrict when she rose from the water, remembering the little house in Leaford with the broken glass in the door and the bloodstains on the walls. She thought of Irma with her gawping mouth and sunken, distant eyes. The wide Thames River, where she'd skated as a child. She had forgotten Leaford's face but heard her call, wintry and severe.

Arriving at the Reeves house for her Christmas celebration with the boys, Mary forged a smile. When they gathered around the huge faux evergreen in the formal living room, she accepted the triplets' hugs and kisses and was choked to receive their gifts — photographs of the boys in frames decorated by each with glitter and heart shapes. She led them in singing Christmas songs, and choked down a few bites of the lumpy potatoes the boys had mashed and the salad they'd helped make especially for her. Ronni was as drained as Mary by the end of dinner, and still had to pack for her trip back east.

Embracing her friend, Ronni promised that the week would go quickly. "At least you only have one relative to deal with, Mary. I've got twenty-four, and every one of them will have something to say about Tom and me. I'm sick just thinking of it."

"It'll be good for the boys to be with family."

"I hate to think of you alone with your mother-in-law."

Back in the truck, Mary started toward the house but made an impulsive U-turn in the road, deciding to head to the ocean to look at the stars. At the intersection she glanced at the lot, and was shocked to see Jesús García standing alone at the utility pole. She pulled in when the light changed. He grinned broadly when he recognized the Dodge Ram, shouting out with surprise and confusion, "Mary!" He strode toward the vehicle, pausing when he saw her shorn silver hair.

Her hand flew to her scalp. "It's awful, isn't it?"

"It suits you."

"I was just heading down to the ocean. Let me drive you home first."

"You got nothing better to do?"

"No." She laughed.

He climbed into the truck. "I'll come with you, then."

"To the ocean?"

He paused, uncertain. "If you don't mind the company."

Blood rushed to her cheeks as she pulled out of the dusty corner lot and set course down the long, hilly road.

"Maybe you'll see another shooting star," he said, flashing that blinding smile.

As they drove, Mary glanced sideways at her passenger. "You said it's been years since you saw the ocean. Why?"

"Time. Circumstances. I have other obligations."

"But you used to take your family to the ocean?"

"I used to take my family to the ocean. We never swam, though. I was fifteen when we moved down from Michigan. A boy drowned that summer. My mother wouldn't let me go in past my knees. She was afraid I'd be carried out by the riptides."

"Sounds like my mother. In the winter she was afraid I'd fall through the ice."

"My mother had a dream. A vision of me drowned in the sea."

"That's awful. What an awful thing to be told."

"I don't swim. To this day I've never been in past my knees."

"But you're so strong."

"I wouldn't let my boys go in past their knees either."

"Did your wife think you were crazy?"

"She believed in visions too. Miracles."

Mary did not have to ask if Jesús believed in those things. "Wishing on shooting stars."

"Of course."

"I never swam much," she said.

"Afraid?"

"Not of the water."

They drove the rest of the way in silence, soothed by the rising hills.

Once parked at the roadside, they agreed to a short walk in the surf. Night had fallen but Mary felt safe in his company, stealing his strength to make her way through the sand. "It's so dark," she said.

"That's why it's the best place to see the stars."

"How do you say *stars* in Spanish, Hay-su?"

"*Estrellas.*"

"Es-tray-as," she repeated. Lifting her eyes, Mary beheld the sky, and was suddenly stricken by sadness for the collective of souls to which she'd once belonged, standing on their cold tile floors with their noses in refrigerators, needles in their arms, cigarettes in their mouths. She inhaled the salty air, fixed on making a memory — the water, the breeze on her shorn silver scalp, the dazzling *estrellas* before her.

At the water's edge they took off their shoes and rolled up their pant legs. Mary was glad for the cover of night when she asked, "Who do I remind you of, Hay-Su? That day, you said I reminded you of someone."

"My fifth-grade teacher. Miss Maynard. Mary Maynard."

"I remind you of your teacher?"

"I broke my leg that November I turned ten, and for the whole winter I had to stay in with Miss Maynard at recess and lunch. She gave me licorice whips and extra worksheets. Told me how smart I was. Once she kissed my forehead. I never wanted spring to come."

"She looked like me?"

"She said my name just how you say it, *Hay-Su.*"

"Was she big? Like me?"

"Yes," he answered plainly. "She smelled like cookies. Pretty green eyes. I had such a crush on her."

The rolling ocean scored their journey through the sand. "Let's walk up that way," Jesús suggested.

"Hay-su?" she called into the night. "I can't see you."

He stepped back, finding her at the water's edge. "Take my hand."

She reached out, feeling for his fingers, the pleasant shock of joining palms. They walked on, leaving footprints in the sand that were instantly stolen by the pulsing water. She could not remember the last time she had held Gooch's hand. Had she known what was to come, she would never have let go.

"Can you see that crest there?" Jesús asked, gesturing at a faint shadow in the distance. "That's the best place to see the whales. They come so close."

"I'd like to see that."

"They migrate in the spring."

Mary stopped, realizing. "I won't be here in the spring."

"Your husband will be back before that."

Mary joined him in gazing at the sky. "My husband isn't coming back."

"You've heard from him?"

She wagged her head in the blackness. "No. I just wanted to say it out loud. See what it felt like."

"What did it feel like?"

"Pretty much what I imagined."

"You're done waiting?"

She fell silent.

Jesús set his hands on Mary's shoulders, turning her to look up at the sky. "Fall is a good time of the year to see the Andromeda constellation." She followed his pointing hand. "Perseus. And there, below, see the V-shape? — Andromeda. And below that the square — Pegasus." He searched the sky a while longer. "Pisces. The fish. Can you make it out?"

"Pisces. That's me. I'm supposed to be artistic and sensitive."

"Are you?"

In the darkness she turned toward him, taking his face in her hands, pressing her mouth to his, an impulse as shocking to the kisser as it was to the kissed. She stopped, feeling his lips cold and rigid. "I'm so sorry."

"Don't."

"I don't know why I did that."

"It's forgotten," he said crisply. "Come on. Let's walk."

She was hot with humiliation. "I didn't imagine . . . I don't imagine . . ."

"Please, Mary."

"I do know why I did that," she said. "I'm afraid. I'm afraid I might never be kissed again. My husband is not coming back." *My husband is not coming back*. The ocean breeze swept up the words and tossed them to the fates to make destiny.

"Come on, let's walk," he said. He was moving swiftly, pulling her by the hand. She stumbled.

"Can we stop? Please?" she asked.

He stopped.

"I've been Gooch's wife for twenty-five years."

"That's a long time."

"If I'm not Gooch's wife, I don't know who I am."

"You have to make it up as you go."

"What'll I do, Hay-su?"

"You'll do what you do."

"I don't do anything."

"Then do something, Mary."

"I wish it were that easy."

"Who said it was easy?" he asked. "Keep telling yourself the worst part is over."

"I didn't get to say goodbye. I think that's the worst part," she said. Then she remembered the cruel denial of farewell this man had suffered. "Oh Hay-su, I'm so sorry."

He pulled his hand free, his voice tight. "Don't feel sorry for me. Please. Don't pity me."

She was startled by his swift transformation. "I didn't mean to—"

"Don't look to me for answers, Mary. I don't talk about it. I don't think about it. I have no survival strategies. I rely on clichés just like everybody else—one step at a time, one day at a time. I didn't mean for you to get the wrong idea." She opened her mouth. "Don't say you're sorry. Don't apologize. Please. Just don't say anything."

The energy between them had shifted. The connection was lost. They said no more as they trudged back through the sand toward the road where they'd parked the truck. They drove back to Hundred Oaks in thick silence, like lovers after a spat, uncertain who'd thrown the first punch, or what exactly hurt, or why.

At the curb in front of Jesús García's house, Mary waited as he paused with his hand on the door handle. Together they said, "Good night."

He started for the walkway, then suddenly raced back. She rolled down the window, massaging her breast bone where her heart had cracked in half.

"Christmas," he said, wincing.

"Yes."

"It's in two days."

"It is? Yes, it is."

"Will your mother-in-law be back?"

Mary nodded. "Yes."

"You're lying."

"She's staying in Santa Barbara."

"You'll be alone."

"I don't mind."

"You can't be alone on Christmas."

"I don't mind."

"You'll come here."

"No. I couldn't, Hay-su. I'd make your family uncomfortable."

"They won't notice." He flashed that brilliant grin. "I'll pick you up in the truck when they've gone to church in the morning. I won't take no for an answer."

Mary hesitated before answering. "Thank you."

The kindness of strangers. She reckoned that someone had been similarly kind to Jesús in the days after his devastating loss, and he was returning the cosmic favor. She cleared her throat. "I know you don't think . . . I know you could never think . . ."

"It's nice to be with someone who didn't know you before," he said.

"Yes. Yes it is."

"I'll pick you up at ten."

She nodded, cringing as the pain traveled from her heart to the spot between her eyes.

"You okay?"

"Yes," she lied.

"You sure?"

She nodded.

Jesús García glanced back twice as he made his way up the short walk and lifted his arm in a wave before disappearing into the house.

Driving the road to the Willow Lowlands, Mary attempted to draw deep calming breaths, which left her gasping for air. The pain between her eyes was not to be borne.

In the kitchen she reached for the pain pills from her tote bag. Her heart thumped in rhythm with the cricket outside the sliding glass doors.

Hear me roar, she thought.

The Night Clock

The following day Mary couldn't focus on the morning papers, her thoughts drifting to Jesús García, replaying the scene at the ocean, fretfully anticipating Christmas at his home. She was sure the man regretted making the invitation as much as she did her acceptance. She would ruin Christmas for the family with the shoes at the door, and if he couldn't take her pity, she didn't want his either. She considered driving to the Pool's Gold office to leave him a note but worried that the gesture might be misunderstood by his employer. In the kitchen, feeling lonely for Eden, she boiled water for tea.

Ignoring the call of the fridge and the shouts from the cupboards, she climbed into the big truck and headed for the bank. Emery Carr did not raise a brow when she asked for help in withdrawing three thousand dollars in cash. His expression said, *You go, girl.* Still, he could not help from worrying. "You shouldn't be walking around with so much cash, Mary."

Feeling the load of money in her blue purse, Mary didn't wonder if the depleted bank account would drive Gooch back to her. And had not factored him into her decision to withdraw it, except to excuse herself from feeling guilty. The lottery money had been both liberation and bondage. Had financed an escape and funded a journey. Its presence felt bound to Gooch, and she had an urge to dispense with it the way she had with the vigil for her wayward husband. Of course, she knew she would need money for the future, but she was tired, too tired, for all but the most immediate of plans.

She considered driving to the mall in Hundred Oaks to shop for gifts for the children at Jesús García's house but could not begin to guess at the number of children, or their ages. At the drugstore she saw a box of *Feliz Navidad* cards and decided to stuff them with the hundred-dollar bills Emery Carr had counted out at the bank, for the children and adults alike. She hoped Jesús would not take offense, but decided she didn't care if he did. Standing at the counter, weak from malnutrition, she took a health bar from the display, replacing it at once when she felt queasy at the thought of the mush in her mouth.

Mid-morning already, and only a few men were left at the corner lot when she swung the big Ram into the dust. She moved toward the men at the utility pole, handing each a hundred-dollar bill from the wad in her purse, saying, *Feliz Navidad*, as they accepted her largesse. She avoided their eyes. She didn't want gratitude for relieving herself of her burden.

She didn't expect to see Jesús García among the men, but was disappointed nonetheless.

An unusually warm day for late December, even in southern California. Mary thought of Leaford. Seasons marking time. The autumn days spent driving to the lake to see the leaves change. Irma bringing the salt shaker to tap over the sour green apples they bought at the roadside stand. Hail. Crunching boots on the iced snow. Thunderstorms. Sullen skies. Merkel's dogs barking in the distance.

The sun stung Mary as she made her way to the swimming pool. She had much to consider and thought the cold water might help revive her. She swam across the pool and stopped to tread water until her muscles ached. With barely enough strength to climb the ladder, she found a chaise at the pool's edge where she stretched out on her front to dry her naked body in the sun. The woodpecker hammered at the eucalyptus above her head, ticking like the night clock, reminding her of her old life, but as if it had happened to someone else. She focused on her beating heart.

Mary had, in the days since leaving Leaford, dreamed a number of erotic dreams. Most of the dreams featured Gooch, and some, unsurprisingly, Jesús García. One dream of a sexual encounter with the darkly handsome man was so vivid that she was awakened by her body's shuddering climax. So when she felt a finger prod her foot and heard a smooth voice whisper, "Mary," she assumed it was another dream. But she opened her eyes and saw that the sun had shifted in the sky, and that Jesús was standing above her in his blue coveralls holding the pool skimmer, looking at her big white body burned scarlet by the sun.

"Oh my God," she breathed.

"You're burned."

She attempted to rise but was reluctant to further expose herself. "In the house. Through the patio door. There's a robe."

Jesús returned after a moment, wincing at the sight of her pink thighs and back. "You'll have to put something on that."

"I will. I'm sure Eden's got something in the house," she said, slipping into the robe.

"You're so pale. You think it's a good idea to be out here sunbathing in the nude?"

"The pool guys usually come tomorrow," she said. "I fell asleep."

"Lucky for you I came today."

"I'm so embarrassed."

He shrugged. "Seen one pink Canadian, seen 'em all."

"Why did you come today?"

"I switched the schedule. The other night you seemed . . ." He helped her into the house when it was clear she could not walk on her own.

"I'll just find some lotion." Mary started down the hall, groaning softly from the pain.

He stopped her. "Go lie down. I'll look in the bathroom."

She found Jack's bed and stretched out prostrate, arms at her sides, stung from her neck to her ankles, the flesh of her red buttocks tortured by the weight of the thin robe.

After a moment, Jesús appeared carrying a large potted plant he'd found in the living room. "Aloe vera," he said, breaking open one of the thick, spiky leaves, spilling cool, clear gel onto her burnt calves. "This'll help. It will take the heat out."

"Thank you," she managed to say. "It's so awful. I'm so sorry. You really don't have to."

"It's fine. I don't mind."

"Really, Hay-su."

"You can't just leave it."

His fingers pushed the gel up the backs of her thighs, stopping at the ridge of the bathrobe. "You're . . . can you reach back here?"

Mary shrugged off the bathrobe, forgetting her nudity, desiring only the salvation of the cool gel on her flaming skin. "Please," she whispered. With her eyes closed, she could not see him break another leaf from the plant, and could not imagine the expression on his face as he squeezed the gel onto her shoulders and dribbled it onto her lower back, and the mounds of her dimpled scarlet buttocks. He stroked the gel over her hills, his touch professional, like that of a doctor or a parent.

She tried not to moan. "Thank you."

"You're lucky it's December and not July. It probably looks worse than it is."

"I wish that were true about everything. *It looks worse than it is.*"

He broke another leaf and another, her skin drinking in the

healing fluid. She imagined that his hand was lingering on her thigh. She imagined that she felt a shift in his intentions. The telephone rang, startling them both. Mary reached for the receiver beside the bed.

"Hello?" She expected to hear Eden's voice. Or Ronni's. The calls had dwindled in the days after Jack's death. It was an automated sales call, which she cut off abruptly.

Jesús stood. "I should go."

"Wait. Are you hungry?" she asked, sitting up.

He ate the bread she cut, and helped himself to the vegetable lasagna she'd warmed in the microwave. Their comfort felt oddly post-coital, Mary naked under Jack's old robe, Jesús wearing the blue coveralls stripped to his waist, white undershirt straining against his pectorals, biceps like hills with trails of blue veins. She could smell him, damp earth, chlorine.

"You're not eating," he said.

She shrugged.

"For a long time I couldn't eat," he said.

"I don't want to make you talk about it."

"I couldn't swallow. I had this big lump in my throat."

"My whole life I've tried to stop myself from eating too much. Now I can't eat at all."

"You can," he urged, pressing the fork into her hand.

"I can't." A *fait accompli*. "I can't."

"You can't live without food, Mary."

"I'll have to hope for a miracle."

"You eat because you have to. You taste because you can. Sometimes you enjoy, because you're alive."

"Did you read that somewhere?"

"I live it." He took her fork, scooped some of the food from her plate and lifted it toward her mouth. She shook her head slowly. "Open," he whispered.

She put her hand over his. "What if I can't stop? Once I start eating again. What if I can't stop?"

"You can do anything," he said. "There's your miracle."

She allowed her lips to part, overcome by the scent of tomato, red pepper, zucchini. She pulled the food into her mouth.

"Chew."

She did, recognizing the sweetness of the creamy cheese, the bitter tinge of oregano and the bite of basil. Taste. Scent. He lifted another bite of food to her lips as she savored his expression, like a small boy who'd just lured a feral cat. She wanted him to go on feeding her, but he handed her the fork and instructed, "A few more bites."

She anticipated nausea but it did not come. He waited until she'd eaten a little more before taking the plates to the dishwasher. She watched his broad back, calculated the thickness of his limbs. "You could go in past your knees," she said. "You could, Hay-Su. In the ocean, go in past your knees."

He smiled and opened his mouth to say something, but his cell-phone rang and he excused himself and spoke rapidly in Spanish as Mary watched, hypnotized by his lips moving beneath the crisp moustache. He finished his call, apologizing. "I have to go, Mary. I'll see you in the morning."

"I'll be ready."

He leaned in and brushed her cheek with a kiss so soft that she could not say with certainty it had been a kiss at all. *"Feliz Navidad,"* he said.

"Feliz Navidad."

The night clock did not tick or hum or make any sound at all, but her skin ached and itched from the sunburn and Mary could not find a comfortable position in bed. She tore the last meaty leaf from the aloe vera plant and squeezed the clear gel over the backs of her legs and shoulders.

She was not caught by her reflection but sought it out in the closet mirror door, dropping her robe from her shoulders as she approached. She remembered that girl, Mary Brody, lonely and uncertain. The young bride with her secret. The wife she'd become.

A lifetime consumed by hunger. She was no longer that woman. She saw beauty in her form, its subtle animations, its mysterious intentions and universal conclusions. Like the brown hills undulating on the horizon. The cresting ocean waves. Her head did not ache. Her heart did not flutter. She felt she might be electrocuted by the light she felt within.

In the darkness she found her way out to the swimming pool and eased her legs into the cool water. Floating beneath the stars, she thought of the day she'd quit her job at Raymond Russell's. Stocktaking day. *You've come a long way, baby,* she told herself, then realized that the slogan came from an advertisement for cigarettes and was deceptive in its congratulations to the liberated woman.

Remembering the magazine questionnaires that condensed celebrated lives, Mary decided that she would edit most of her responses. To the question *Greatest Adventure?* she now had an answer: Mary Gooch had climbed to the top of Golden Hills. Battled her beast. Searched for God. Found acceptance. *Biggest Regret?* She was through with regrets. And to the question *Greatest Love?* She would keep Gooch with her in a locket around her neck. A graphic on a T-shirt. His name emblazoned on the back window of a car.

Her potential cheered from the trees shivering beyond the pool as she considered her future. She could climb Everest, join Greenpeace. Go to college, learn Spanish, read the classics. Vote. She recalled Ms. Bolt's admonitions as she saw the path before her rising and falling, making sharp turns over ragged cliffs. No worn broadloom. No comfortable rut. A dazzling existence beckoning with uncertainty. Proof that there are miracles.

Tomorrow came, and Mary rose like the phoenix in the timid light of dawn. She wrapped Jack's old robe around her body and moved into the kitchen and toward the refrigerator. She was hungry. Not starving. Not craving. Not jonesing. Just hungry. The way people get hungry. She opened the cupboard and found a can of tuna. She cut slices of tomato and avocado and took some grainy bread from the freezer. She sat down at the table and ate the food slowly, chewing and swallowing carefully, considering the nuance of tastes and textures, satisfied by the modest amount. There was no beast in her gut, gatekeeper or otherwise.

There was just Mary Gooch, eating enough.

Acknowledgments

I wish to thank those women in my professional life who've guided me over the years as together we've published three novels. I'm especially grateful for the critical eye of my longtime agent, Denise Bukowski, for her frankness in discussion, her wise counsel, and her friendship beyond work. I'm also thankful to the talented editors that helped shape *Rush Home Road* and *The Girls*, and whose insights were critical to the final draft of *The Wife's Tale:* Judy Clain from Little, Brown and Company; Diane Martin from Knopf Canada; Lennie Goodings and Ursula Doyle from Virago UK.

Thanks also to Michael Pietsch of Little, Brown and Company; Louise Dennys of Knopf Canada; and Richard Beswick of Virago. Sharon Klein, Marion Garner, Deirdre Molina, Carolyn O'Keefe, Heather Fain, David Whiteside, Nathan Rostron, Jericho Buenida and Gena Gorrell, my thanks to you, too.

On a more personal note, I want to express gratitude to my children, whose love is divine, and to my husband of twenty-five years, who inspires me still. As my research for this book consisted mostly of conversation and observation, I thank my parents, Judy and Phil;

my brothers, Todd and Curt; Kelley (my sister-friend); Sherry and Joyce, my two oldest and dearest; and Allegra. Thanks as well to my husband's family and to the many friends, not all of them wives, or even women, with whom I've shared confidences over the years, and who contributed to the story of *The Wife's Tale* in ways they couldn't know.

Once again, I owe a debt to southwestern Ontario, in whose memory I find Baldoon County. Finally, I wish to thank my tribe in southern California, the folks in my adopted home beyond the Santa Monica mountains, and most especially the group of mothers from a Topanga school who welcomed this transplanted Canadian into their fold as I wrote the story of an outsider searching for her place.

About the Author

LORI LANSENS was born and raised in Chatham, Ontario, a small Canadian town with a remarkable history and a collection of eccentric characters, which became the setting for her first two bestselling novels. Living with her family in southern California now, she could not resist the pull of her fictitious Baldoon County when she set out to write *The Wife's Tale*. She took the journey, along with her main character, from Canada to the Pacific Coast of America, where she enjoys the sunshine, and has learned a thing or two about transformation.

For more information, visit www.lorilansens.com.

Reading Group Guide

The

Wife's Tale

A Novel by

Lori Lansens

Coming of Age

*Lori Lansens writes about her inspiration for Mary Gooch
and reader reactions to her books*

I have been writing about this overweight female character in some form or other since I began to write in my early twenties. It was only a matter of time before Mary Gooch stepped out from behind the curtain to insist that her story be told. Sometime during the completion of *The Girls* I started to hear Mary's voice. I could see her in my fictional town of Leaford waving from the window of her rural farmhouse. She revealed herself nearly formed, which is to say morbidly obese and living a marginal existence. She was exactly my age, which is to say "middle." It's a time of life when one is standing at a precipice looking back over the first act, imagining the second, hopeful that it's not too late. I was excited to take this journey with Mary, to slowly peel back the layers and find the core of her character. I loved when one early reader called *The Wife's Tale* "a coming-of-age story."

Typically when we read about weight the emphasis is on losing it, and I wanted to avoid that cliché in *The Wife's Tale*. I felt that whatever weight loss Mary Gooch experienced should be incidental, and I wanted the focus of the narrative to be on her sense of enlightenment as she gets to know herself for the first time as someone other than Mrs. Jimmy Gooch. The character that I plugged into did not hate her body and "could see the beauty in the poetry of her contours." What Mary hated was the thing that restricted her life and stopped her from living it to the fullest — the "obeast" that she had surrendered to. That was something I understood. That was something that I felt could be understood universally.

Hearing from readers has been enormously gratifying. I've enjoyed hearing from readers who've described their surprise that they could so easily and intimately relate to a morbidly obese character, and I've been moved by the many readers who have shared their own struggles with weight and identity. One woman wrote to tell me that she would be getting on a plane for the first time in twenty years because, "I figure, if Mary can do it, so can I!" A number of readers have insisted, "I *am* Mary Gooch," or "I *know* Mary Gooch and gave her this book." Many readers have asked for the sequel (my author-self and I are in discussions about that) and some readers have even suggested story lines revolving around Mary's new life and love. It seems that few readers care about seeing Mary thin, or slender, or even average weight. They just want her to continue on the path of self-discovery and her search for peace and balance.

I've heard from a great many readers about the cover designs for *Rush Home Road, The Girls,* and now *The Wife's Tale.* The conversations intrigue me. Some readers feel that the cover designs have misrepresented my books by suggesting a lightness in tone (read: "chick lit") when the stories tend to be more literary and unflinching in subject and language. I've also heard from readers that they love the cover designs and bought the books based solely on the artwork. No consensus at all. In the photos section of my website I've included a number of foreign jacket designs for all three novels. It's interesting to see how countries outside of North America interpret the book for their market.

I have not loved all of the covers of my books — some I dislike — but I understand that the publishers are seeking to appeal to their respective markets by finding a single image that they feel best represents the book. Tough job. And, really, how could I say to my Turkish publisher, "I know just the image that will excite your readers"? I haven't a clue. If I found a particular design offensive I would object, and I have resisted a few, but ultimately I defer to the publishers, trusting their knowledge of their markets.

The Girls is a story about conjoined twins — but it's also about sisterhood and identity and love. Almost all of the publishers around the world chose to represent the connection of the sisters with images of feet or shoes. (So many people wrote to me taking issue with the feet, because clearly they could not belong to Rose and Ruby!) The feet were merely an artistic suggestion of the contents of the book. Same with *The Wife's Tale.* Some readers have written saying they loved the image on the U.S. hardcover: the woman's legs — poised and balanced — ready to leap. Others have been disappointed that the woman's legs do not belong to Mary Gooch. (Interestingly, England, New Zealand, Australia, and Poland all went with images of a woman of size — see my website, www.lorilansens.com.) I find the U.S. cover appealing because it speaks to the spirit of the book. I know that in discussion with my publishers the one thing we didn't want to do was have the book misunderstood. The bottom line is that it's difficult to distill a book to a single image that will appeal to everyone.

All of my characters stay with me like cherished friends (or relatives I can't shake), and Mary Gooch still frequently crosses my mind. I hope to meet up with her again someday, but for now I imagine her in that other universe, active in book clubs and social networks, cooking and enjoying delicious food, walking uphill and coasting down, living fully with rich friendships and a sense of purpose.

Three Questions for Lori Lansens

Joshilyn Jackson talks with the author of The Wife's Tale

Your main character seems to be nothing like you. How do you inhabit shoes different from your own?

The protagonist of my first novel, *Rush Home Road,* is an elderly black woman. In my second novel, *The Girls,* the characters are conjoined twin sisters. Mary Gooch is the morbidly obese heroine of my latest, *The Wife's Tale.* On the surface, the only thing I have in common with any of them is that I am, like Mary, in my forties, but these disparate characters have given voice to my interests and preoccupations and defined different stages in my life. All three books are set in fictional Baldoon County, inspired by the landscape where I was born and raised in southwestern Ontario, near the border of Detroit, Michigan.

In the first book I drew on the rich history of the place — a hunting and fishing ground for the neutral Indians, a terminus on the Underground Railroad, a hot spot for bootlegging during Prohibition — to tell the story of Addy Shadd, a descendant of fugitive slaves who helped settle the area. With *The Girls* I explored the nature of identity, inspired by the birth of my two children, with whom I felt an inextricable physical and emotional bond. In *The Wife's Tale* I wanted to examine the struggle of a morbidly obese woman approaching middle age, not because I'm morbidly obese but because I understand hunger and the feeling of being out of control.

The overweight female character has been with me since I began to write decades ago. I'm not overweight but I feel keenly the struggle of my fellows. It's impossible to ignore the epidemic of obesity, and where twenty or even ten years ago a woman weighing three hundred pounds (as Mary Gooch does) would have been rare, we see her now with increasing frequency. We work with her. She's our aunt, our cousin.

I joke that I'm a method writer, meaning that I inhabit the characters that I write about. Or do they inhabit me? It's a way to describe empathy. When I was writing *Rush Home Road* I had the sense that old Addy Shadd had taken over the keyboard and was writing the story down like it was a memory instead of a creation. With the conjoined twin sisters I had to leave one's fictional reality in order to find the voice of the other. Mary Gooch and I had some junk-food binges together. I lost my appetite when she did and suffered heart palpitations (did hers come first or did mine?) for the duration of the writing process.

How important is the setting in your novels?

Baldoon County serves as a character in *Rush Home Road*. Addy Shadd's response to her journey, which included a perilous boat trip to America, then back to Canada, was dependent on the setting. I'd been writing that book in my head for many years before I wrote the first sentence, and so much of it was inspired by history and the memories of my youth.

In *The Girls* I stayed in Baldoon County, a small town called Leaford, because I wanted to find the humanity in the conjoined sisters' situation and didn't want to present them as freaks, or for them to perceive themselves that way. In Leaford, where they live and work, they're just "the girls." Had they lived in a large city they would have seen themselves mirrored in the eyes of strangers every day, and I believe they would have grown up very differently. The rural setting was important because the twins, for all their restrictions, find freedom and peace and beauty in the fields surrounding their run-down farmhouse and rely on nature for their spirituality.

I resisted the lure of Baldoon County when I set out to write *The Wife's Tale,* but it kept pulling me back. I was most interested in writing an extreme character — so overweight, and so sheltered, her life so small while she is so large, that the small-town setting was all that felt right. I considered creating a neighboring town but the fact was that I first saw Mary in my fragmented writer's imagination, waving from a window in a farmhouse near where "the girls" used to sit together on a bridge over a creek. Leaford was the place where Mary and I both felt most comfortable, which heightened the drama of eventually having to leave.

Describe your journey as a writer.

I started writing in my early twenties and published my first short story — a love story about an obese young woman and an elderly man — in the *Wascana Review*. The eleven dollars I received as payment for the story bought my young husband and me a six-pack of beer and the sweetest victory either of us can remember. I received only an impressive stack of rejection letters for the next six stories I sent out and decided to shift my focus to writing for the stage. I wrote some terrible plays, veered off into acting for a year or so, returned to my typewriter, and wrote my first screenplay, *South of Wawa,* which was made into a film by a Canadian company.

More screenplays followed, dozens in fact, most of which were never made into films. For a few years my husband and I made films together, but I found writing screenplays unsatisfying and craved a more direct connection with the audience. I tried my hand at being a film auteur and, together with my husband, attempted to produce a movie based on my original screenplay, which I would also direct.

Years of frustration followed — a number of false starts, deals that went sour. When finally it was time to let the film go, my husband suggested I sit down and write the novel I'd been talking about for years. That novel was my first, *Rush Home Road.*

I worked on the story for a year and a half, most of that time while I was pregnant with my first child and without telling a soul what I was writing. I didn't know what to do with it when I finished the 500-page tome. I had no connections in the book world and learned from a reference book at the library that I should first look for an agent. I didn't read the part about most unsolicited manuscripts being sent back and only learned what a slush pile was when a prominent agent called me to say that she had retrieved my manuscript from the top of hers and invited me in to meet. That begins the charmed part of my journey as a writer, although I don't discount the years of struggle and uncertainty. The book was sold at auction in Canada and the U.S. and made foreign sales before there was an edited manuscript. My second novel, *The Girls,* was chosen by the Richard and Judy Book Club in the UK, Britain's version of Oprah's Book Club. I've been tremendously fortunate.

The thing that I struggle with most as a writer is the thing that challenges all working mothers — balance. It's important to me to be the one who takes my children to and from school and the one who ferries them to sporting events, but all of that cuts into an already short writing day. I've missed field trips for deadlines and deadlines for field trips, and I frequently worry that I've shortchanged either my children or my work. I know I've shortchanged my husband and friends. The focus and obsession that it takes to commit to a character and story for a year, or years, cause deficits in other areas. I know one writer who finds it difficult to be in public during the novel-writing phase. She says she walks around with a blank stare she calls "writer's face" and can't hear people talk for all the white noise of her characters shuffling around in her brain. I think I have writer's face too. I know I have writer's hair. Still, how lucky I am to have the opportunity to sit alone in a room all day making up stories to share, even if I do have to set my alarm so that my children aren't left at school.

Joshilyn Jackson is the author of the bestselling novels *Gods in Alabama*; *Between, Georgia*; and *The Girl Who Stopped Swimming*. Her conversation with Lori Lansens was originally published on Jackson's blog, *Faster Than Kudzu* (joshilynjackson .com/ftk). Reprinted with permission.

Questions and topics for discussion

1. Mary Gooch is described as being a "devotee" of the tyranny of beauty. What role does beauty play in *The Wife's Tale*? How do Mary's attitudes toward beauty evolve?

2. Jimmy Gooch, unlike his wife at the beginning of the novel, takes an active interest in the outside world. How would you explain Mary's indifference in the face of Jimmy's enthusiasm?

3. To what extent is Mary ruled by fear? What keeps her afraid?

4. There are many different types of hunger in *The Wife's Tale*. How would you define them? Do they interact with each other? What do you think drives Mary's hunger?

5. Mary believes in miracles and is superstitious, often to her disadvantage. What role do you think religion plays in her life? Does *The Wife's Tale* have a spiritual message? If so, what do you think it is?

6. As a child, Mary is drawn to a teacher named Ms. Bolt, who has a very different take on womanhood than Mary is used to. What does Ms. Bolt teach Mary? Do you think Mary loses sight of these lessons as an adult?

7. Mary is a very sensual person, and she is powerfully attracted to her husband. Why does she resist him, even when he is desperate

for a physical connection with her? Why is she unable to ignore her own self-loathing?

8. Why do you think Jimmy chooses this moment — their twenty-fifth wedding anniversary — to leave Mary?

9. A theme of *The Wife's Tale* is the nourishment that novels can provide (especially compared with tabloids). How does Mary's reading relate to her eating? Did this theme resonate for you as you were reading *The Wife's Tale*? Are there things in your life that you find more nourishing than food?

10. Far away from home, Mary meets Big Avi, the driver for Miracle Limousine Service. What role does Big Avi play in the story? How would you explain his kindness?

11. In what ways do the themes of gain and loss surface in the book?

12. Mary keeps a terrible secret, which she later learns might not have been as secret as she thought. Have you ever kept something to yourself that you later found out you shouldn't have? What does *The Wife's Tale* have to say about keeping secrets from those we love?

13. How is Mary transformed in the course of the novel? Where do you think she will be five years after the novel ends?

14. Have you read either of Lori Lansens's other two novels? If so, what qualities or attributes do her books share, despite their very different plots and characters?